The Light Speakers

Guardians of the Deep, Volume 1

Wallace Berry

Published by Wallace Berry, 2025.

THE LIGHT SPEAKERS

First edition. October 29, 2025.

ISBN: 979-8999188458

Written by Wallace Berry.

Table of Contents

Chapter 1

The oscilloscope's green trace danced across the screen, its rhythmic pulse keeping time with the sunrise. Tod Blackstone leaned forward on his stool, one hand wrapped around a chipped "SHSU Alumni" mug, the other adjusting a dial with practiced precision. Outside the converted garage window, Copano Bay transformed from inky black to watercolor gray as the first light broke over the horizon.

"K5HUX, this is KG5ZRT. You copy?" The familiar voice crackled through the speaker, punctuated by static.

Tod's lips curved into a half-smile. Right on time. He set down his coffee and thumbed the transmit button.

"Morning, Barney. Reading you five-by. How's Port Lavaca treating you today?"

A chuckle came through the speaker. "Same as yesterday. Foggy and damp. Wife says I'm crazy for being up this early."

Tod glanced at his oscilloscope readings while reaching for a paper bag beside his equipment. He extracted a kolache, still warm from Mrs. Alvarez's bakery down the street. The sweet scent of peach filling mingled with the sharp tang of solder and electronics that permanently perfumed his shack.

"Your wife's known you were crazy for thirty years, Barn. Kind of late to complain about it now."

The radio hissed and popped. "True enough. Got my coffee and biscuits. You?"

Tod took a bite of his pastry, savoring the sweetness. "Kolache and dark roast. Looking at the bay right now. Water's calm today."

"Weather report says we might get some squalls later. Nothing serious."

Tod's eyes drifted to the water. From his elevated position, he could see the ghostly outlines of old pilings where Copano settlement once stood—history slowly reclaimed by the Gulf.

"Might head out fishing if it holds off. Need to test that new transducer anyway." Tod sipped his coffee, watching a blue heron glide silently across the water.

"Don't forget the tournament next month. Still planning to enter?"

The familiar rhythm of their morning conversation continued as sunlight strengthened, illuminating Tod's cluttered workspace—oscilloscope, spectrum analyzer, soldering station, and various radios in various states of repair or modification. Maps and charts pinned to walls. Coffee mug rings on technical manuals.

TOD REACHED FOR A SCREWDRIVER and tapped it against the edge of his workbench.

"Actually, wanted to show you something, Barn. Just finished a mod to the antenna system yesterday. You're my first test."

"What'd you do now?" Barney's voice carried equal parts curiosity and suspicion.

Tod swiveled on his stool to face the large window overlooking his backyard, where the skeletal frame of a 6-meter long-John Yagi antenna rose above his property. The antenna's aluminum elements glinted in the early light, its substantial 20-foot boom supported by a heavy-duty rotator.

"Added a solid state IC light sensor to the long-John. Interfaced it with the rotator control system."

"In English, college boy."

Tod grinned. "The antenna now tracks the sunrise automatically. Points itself east in the morning without me having to adjust it manually." He watched with satisfaction as the massive antenna began to move, the rotator motor humming softly as the Yagi pivoted eastward.

"So it's pointing at me right now?" Barney asked.

"That's right. Your signal's coming in clearer than usual, isn't it? The light sensor detects the brightest point on the horizon and aligns the antenna for optimal reception."

Barney's laugh boomed through the speaker. "Only you would build a robot to turn a knob, Blackstone. What happens when it's cloudy?"

"Secondary program kicks in with preset coordinates. I've mapped the seasonal sunrise variations."

"Lord have mercy." Barney sighed dramatically. "You spend three weekends building something that saves you five seconds of work. Typical engineer thinking."

The antenna stopped its rotation, now perfectly aligned with the brightening eastern horizon—and coincidentally, with Port Lavaca. Tod's signal meter jumped noticeably.

"Signal strength just improved by eight decibels," Tod noted, satisfaction warming his voice. "Not bad for something that saves me five seconds."

"Could've done the same by just standing up and turning the knob."

"Where's the fun in that?" Tod watched the bay waters turn from gray to blue as the sunlight intensified. The antenna remained fixed, tracking the light with electronic precision, while gulls wheeled against the morning sky. The oscilloscope's trace had stabilized into a strong, clean pattern.

"Some people fish. Some people hunt," Tod murmured. "I build things."

"And talk to old men on the radio at dawn," Barney added. "Don't forget that part of your fascinating life."

TOD ADJUSTED THE FINE-tuning knob on his transceiver and squinted at the oscilloscope display, where a peculiar anomaly had appeared among the familiar waveforms. A faint signal pulsed at regular intervals, barely distinguishable from the ambient noise.

"That's odd," he muttered, leaning closer to the screen.

"What's that?" Barney asked.

Tod didn't answer immediately. The signal didn't match any pattern he recognized—not sunspot activity, not atmospheric bounce, not any standard transmission protocol. It appeared for precisely two seconds, then disappeared, only to reappear ten to twelve seconds later.

"You seeing anything unusual on your receiver, Barn?" Tod asked, keeping his voice casual while his mind raced through possible explanations.

"Clear as a bell on my end. Why?"

Tod adjusted the frequency range, trying to isolate the anomaly. "I'm picking up something strange. Very faint signal, pulsing regularly. Comes in for exactly two seconds, disappears, then repeats about every ten seconds."

The oscilloscope trace showed another pulse, whispering above the noise floor before vanishing again. Tod checked his equipment connections, wondering if he'd introduced some feedback loop with his new antenna modification.

"What frequency?" Barney asked, his tone shifting from casual to curious.

"That's the thing—it's outside normal band allocations." Tod switched to a spectrum analyzer view, watching as the ghostly signal appeared again, precisely on schedule. "It's sitting in a weird spot, right between marine band and aircraft frequencies. Nobody should be broadcasting there."

"Equipment malfunction?"

Tod shook his head despite knowing Barney couldn't see him. "Don't think so. Signal's too regular, too... intentional." He watched another pulse appear and fade. "And it started right after sunrise, right when the antenna locked onto the horizon."

The regular cadence of the signal continued, soft but persistent, like a distant lighthouse beam sweeping across his instruments. Two seconds on, ten seconds off. Two seconds on, twelve seconds off.

"Barn, your signal's still clean?"

"Crystal clear. No anomalies."

Tod frowned. If Barney wasn't detecting it from Port Lavaca, that meant the source was likely local—or at least not between them.

"Well, something's out there," Tod murmured, watching the next pulse appear exactly when expected. "And whatever it is, it's broadcasting on a schedule."

TOD TAPPED HIS MULTIMETER probes along the connection points, methodically verifying each solder joint and crimped connector. Everything checked out—rock solid.

"Time to triangulate this thing," he muttered, disconnecting the automated tracking system and switching to manual control.

The worn plastic of the rotator control felt familiar in his palm as he slowly turned the dial. The massive Yagi antenna on his roof creaked obediently, pivoting away from the sunrise and sweeping across the morning sky. His eyes stayed locked on the oscilloscope display, watching for any change in the mysterious signal.

As the antenna rotated past southeast, the pulse flickered. When it reached due south—directly over Copano Bay—the signal strengthened noticeably.

"Well I'll be damned." Tod adjusted the gain, reducing amplification as the faint whisper transformed into a definite presence on his screen. Another pulse arrived, stronger than before.

He reached for his logbook and scribbled the time—6:47 AM—followed by signal characteristics, frequency observations, and bearing. The scientific part of his mind took over, methodically documenting what his instincts were screaming was impossible.

The next pulse arrived just as he finished noting the antenna position. Tod glanced at his watch.

"That wasn't ten seconds," he muttered. The interval had shortened to twelve seconds exactly. He circled the observation in his notebook.

Tod watched, transfixed, as the signal continued its metronomic appearance. His fingers traced the path of the coaxial cable running from his equipment to the rotator, following the electronics path in his mind. Everything was working correctly, but what he was seeing defied explanation.

"What the hell am I picking up?" He squinted toward the bay through his workshop window, seeing nothing but calm waters and distant shore.

Then reality hit him like a physical blow. The oscilloscope pattern, the timing, the direction...

"That's not RF," he whispered. Somehow, his modified antenna was picking up pulses of light, not radio frequency. But that was impossible—the Yagi wasn't designed to detect optical signals. His mind raced through the modifications he'd made. The new light sensor for the sunrise tracker shouldn't be interacting with the RF circuit at all.

Unless...

Tod frantically began rechecking his wiring diagram. Something was converting light pulses into electrical signals his equipment could detect, and whatever was sending those pulses was sitting somewhere out in Copano Bay.

THE MORNING SUN HAD fully crested the horizon now, bathing Tod's workshop in steady amber light. The signal, however, maintained its rhythmic pulsation, clearly independent of the sunlight that had first made him notice it.

"Barney, you still there?" Tod adjusted the oscilloscope's gain, bringing the waveform into sharper focus.

"Yeah, I'm here. You figure out what's causing that ghost signal yet?"

Tod leaned closer to the screen, fascinated by the signal's complexity. What had initially appeared as simple pulses now revealed intricate modulation patterns within each burst. The oscilloscope traced peaks and valleys that weren't random—they possessed structure, almost like...

"It's not just pulsing," Tod said slowly. "There's something else happening inside each signal. The pattern isn't mechanical."

He adjusted the time base, spreading the waveform across the screen to examine the internal structure of a single pulse. The signal expanded, revealing delicate fluctuations that rose and fell with subtle variation. Not the sharp, consistent edges of a digital transmission or the simple sine wave of most RF sources.

"This is weird, Barney. Real weird." Tod's voice dropped lower. "It's got this... organic quality. Like it's modulating itself."

The next pulse arrived, displaying the same complex internal pattern but with minute variations from the previous one. Tod stared at it, mesmerized by its rhythmic irregularity.

"Almost like it's breathing," he whispered.

Silence filled the radio channel for several seconds.

"Come again?" Barney finally replied. "Did you say breathing?"

Tod swallowed. "Yeah. It pulses at regular intervals, but inside each pulse, there's this... fluctuation. Not mechanical. More like a heartbeat or respiration pattern."

The signal continued its twelve-second cycle, each pulse arriving with perfect timing yet containing those subtle internal variations that seemed impossible for any standard transmission equipment to produce.

"Listen, Barney, I'm looking out at Copano Bay right now. Nothing unusual. No boats where this signal's coming from. But something out there is generating pulses of light that my equipment is somehow picking up."

Tod rubbed his eyes, calculating angles and distances in his head. "Whatever it is, it's definitely in the water. And I don't think it's any kind of equipment I've ever encountered."

THE RADIO CHANNEL REMAINED silent for several uncomfortable seconds.

"Tod? You still with me?" Barney's voice carried a note of concern. "You're not going all 'Close Encounters' on me, are you? Maybe you should take a break, get some coffee."

Tod ignored the suggestion, his attention locked on the pattern dancing across his oscilloscope. He reached for the antenna rotator control, deliberately turning the massive Yagi away from the sunrise in the east, sweeping it in a slow arc across the bay waters.

"I'm tracking it, Barney." His voice had taken on the flat, methodical tone he used when hunting elusive signals. "The source isn't from the east at all. It's definitely out there in the water."

As the antenna pointed toward a section of deeper water about half a mile offshore, the signal strength peaked dramatically. Tod marked the coordinates in his notebook with precise figures.

"Got you," he whispered.

The oscilloscope trace suddenly changed its rhythm. The twelve-second interval between pulses shortened to ten seconds, then eight.

"It's responding," Tod said, his voice barely audible.

"What's responding?" Barney asked. "Tod, you're starting to worry me."

Tod watched as the signal continued to accelerate its pulsation rate, now cycling every six seconds. The pattern remained complex but had become more energetic, almost agitated.

"Whatever's generating this signal just changed behavior when I pointed directly at it." Tod stood up and moved to the window, staring out at the calm morning waters of Copano Bay. Nothing visible marked the spot where his antenna was aimed. "It's like it knows we're watching."

"We? There is no 'we' here, buddy. This is starting to sound—"

"I need to check this out," Tod interrupted. He grabbed his keys from the workbench. "I'm taking the boat out."

"Whoa, hold on. That storm front is still moving in from the Gulf. Coast Guard already issued small craft advisories."

Tod glanced at the eastern horizon. Clear blue for now, but he knew the weather could change quickly on the Texas coast. It didn't matter.

"I'll be fine. Going to investigate and be back before anything hits. K5HUX clear."

"Tod, wait—"

Tod switched off the radio mid-protest. Within minutes, he had gathered his handheld transceiver, binoculars, and a waterproof pack. The mystery in Copano Bay was calling, and Tod Blackstone had never been able to resist a signal that shouldn't exist.

TOD SWITCHED OFF THE transceiver with a soft click, silencing Barney's distant protests. The workshop fell quiet except for the electric hum of equipment and the rhythmic tapping of his foot against the concrete floor. He returned to his workbench, eyes locked on the oscilloscope where the mysterious signal continued its dance across the screen.

"Six seconds," he muttered, watching the regular pulses. Then, as if responding to his voice, the signal's rhythm changed again. The interval between pulses shortened—now appearing every eight seconds. The acceleration troubled him more than the signal itself.

Tod slid into his chair and pulled a dusty external hard drive from a drawer beneath the workbench. He connected it to his laptop and launched a program he hadn't touched in years—a signal analysis suite he'd coded during his final year at Sam Houston State. The software was crude by current standards, but it offered visualization options commercial packages lacked.

The laptop screen filled with cascading spectral patterns as the program ingested data from the oscilloscope. Tod leaned forward, elbows on the desk, chin resting on his interlaced fingers. The frequency distribution appeared on screen, and he blinked in surprise.

"That can't be right."

The signal spread across an impossibly wide band—from near-infrared all the way to ultraviolet. No transmitter he'd ever encountered produced such a dispersed pattern. Man-made signals were efficient by design, concentrated into narrow frequency bands. This was diffuse, almost organic in its spread.

Tod ran a second analysis, this time focusing on the modulation pattern. The results only deepened the mystery. The signal showed characteristics of both amplitude and frequency modulation simultaneously, something that shouldn't occur naturally and would require impossibly complex equipment to produce artificially.

He tapped a sequence of commands, cross-referencing the signal against his light sensor data. The correlation was undeniable—the pulses weren't radio waves at all but light, captured by his modified sensor and translated into electrical signals his equipment could process.

"What are you?" Tod whispered to the screen.

Whatever lurked in Copano Bay was emitting pulses of light across the electromagnetic spectrum with a complexity beyond any technology Tod had encountered. As the signal accelerated again, now pulsing every seven seconds, Tod felt certain of one thing—he wasn't detecting equipment. He was detecting something alive.

TOD PUSHED BACK FROM his workbench, mind racing through possibilities. Something in Copano Bay was emitting complex light patterns—but how was his antenna's sensor detecting it? The Long-John Yagi towered six meters above his roof, designed for radio waves, not optical phenomena.

"Let's test this properly," he murmured.

He grabbed his handheld radio and stepped outside, squinting against the morning sunlight. The massive antenna jutted from his rooftop like a technological weathervane, its multiple elements gleaming in the sun. The photodiode sensor he'd installed for the sunrise tracker sat at the junction point, a small black eye facing eastward.

Tod keyed his radio. "Barney, you still there?"

"Yeah, been waiting. You going after that signal or what?"

"Quick test first. Keep an eye on your scope if you're still monitoring."

Tod climbed the access ladder mounted to the side of his workshop. At the top, he carefully made his way across to the antenna mount, balancing on the slightly pitched roof. The seven-second pulse rhythm continued, visible on the small handheld monitor he'd brought along.

He reached the sensor and carefully cupped his hand over the photodiode, completely blocking any light from reaching it.

The signal vanished instantly.

"Gotcha," Tod whispered. He uncovered the sensor, and the rhythmic pulses returned immediately.

"Barney, you seeing this? Signal drops when I cover the sensor, returns when exposed."

"Clear as day. What's it mean?"

Tod stared out across Copano Bay, the water glimmering under consistent sunlight. No clouds, no flashing lights, nothing visibly unusual. The sun hadn't changed—steady, uniform illumination across the entire landscape.

"Doesn't make sense," Tod said. "The sensor is only supposed to detect ambient light levels for the sunrise tracker. It's a basic photodiode—shouldn't be picking up modulated signals."

He turned slowly in place, scanning the horizon. The bay stretched before him, bordered by distant marshlands and scattered fishing piers. Nothing appeared out of the ordinary.

"Barney, I think we've got a paradox. The sensor is detecting light that isn't the sun. It's picking up some kind of optical signal from the bay, but there's no visible source."

"What light could it be detecting?"

Tod's eyes narrowed as he stared at the specific point in the bay where his antenna had been aimed.

"That's exactly the question. What light is out there that my eyes can't see, but my sensor can?"

TOD DESCENDED FROM the roof with the careful precision of someone who'd made the climb countless times before. Back inside his workshop, he moved to the bay window that offered the best vantage point of Copano Bay. He leaned against the frame, pressing his palms against the cool glass.

The water stretched out before him, a vast expanse of calm brilliance. Morning light transformed the surface into a rippling canvas of copper and gold, the gentle swells catching sunlight and breaking it into countless glimmering fragments. A few early fishing boats dotted the horizon, their distant silhouettes like paper cutouts against the brightening sky. Two gulls circled lazily over a shrimp trawler just visible at the farthest edge of his view.

Everything looked precisely as it had hundreds of mornings before. The familiar serenity of Copano Bay, unchanged for generations. Normal. Ordinary.

Yet the signal pulsed consistently every seven seconds on his equipment, synchronized with nothing visible to the naked eye.

"Barney, you still monitoring?" Tod asked, not taking his eyes off the water.

"Still here. Storm's building up west of you. Coast Guard's already issued advisories."

Tod barely registered the warning. His attention had narrowed to a single point about half a mile offshore, where his antenna had been aimed. The surface there appeared identical to the surrounding water—same coppery sheen, same gentle movement. No boats nearby, no unusual disturbance.

A realization clicked into place with the precision of tumblers in a lock.

"It's not on the water," Tod said, his voice dropping to almost a whisper. "It's under it. Something in the water is generating pulses of light."

He straightened suddenly, mind racing through possibilities. Bioluminescence was common in the Gulf—dinoflagellates that created blue sparkles in disturbed water at night. But this was morning, and those organisms didn't pulse with mechanical precision or emit complex modulated patterns.

"Whatever's out there," Tod continued, "it's beneath the surface, generating light pulses my modified sensor can detect, but in a spectrum I can't see with my eyes."

The water remained placid, innocent, revealing nothing of what might lie beneath its glimmering surface.

TOD STEPPED BACK FROM the window, mind racing. He moved to his workbench with the deliberate focus of someone trying to ground himself in familiar territory. His fingers traced the edge of his oscilloscope as the signal continued its steady pulse—seven seconds, precisely, like clockwork.

"My antenna," he murmured, half to himself and half to Barney still listening on the radio, "it's learned to listen to light."

The realization was both unsettling and thrilling. What had begun as a simple modification to track the sunrise had evolved into something far more profound—a bridge between electromagnetic domains never meant to communicate.

Tod reached for his coffee mug, now lukewarm, and took a long, contemplative drink. The bitter liquid slid down his throat, centering him. Around him, the workshop remained unchanged—screwdrivers precisely arranged by size, soldering station still warm from earlier work, technical manuals stacked according to frequency bands. Yet everything felt different now.

A smile crept across his face despite the gravity of the situation. His hands were steady as he set the mug down, leaving a ring on his signal propagation charts.

"My father used to tell me something when I'd take apart perfectly good appliances just to see how they worked," Tod said, adjusting the gain on his receiver. "He'd say, 'Tod, curiosity is both a gift and a curse. The trick is figuring out which one you're dealing with before it's too late.'"

The signal pulsed again on his screen, its complex internal patterns shifting subtly with each iteration. Something alive. Something hidden. Something communicating in patterns of light beneath Copano Bay's familiar waters.

Outside, the first clouds of the approaching storm system cast fleeting shadows across the workshop floor. The weather radio in the corner crackled with updated warnings, but Tod barely registered the words.

Which would this discovery prove to be—gift or curse? The answer lay half a mile offshore, hidden beneath the water's surface, pulsing steadily every seven seconds.

Tod began gathering equipment: his waterproof handheld transceiver, the modified light sensor detached from the roof mount, and his old diving watch. The decision had already been made in some quiet corner of his mind. Whatever waited beneath Copano Bay's surface, he would find it.

Chapter 2

The first hint of dawn had barely touched the horizon when Tod returned to his workshop. He'd managed three fitful hours of sleep, his dreams filled with undulating light patterns that matched the seven-second rhythm of the signal. Now, standing before his equipment with fresh coffee steaming in his Texas A&M mug, he reviewed the overnight data with narrowed eyes.

"Still there," he muttered, watching the oscilloscope trace its now-familiar pattern across the screen. If anything, the signal had intensified with the sunrise, its peaks sharper, valleys deeper. What had begun as an anomaly had evolved into something insistent—a summons.

Tod pulled up the NOAA weather interface on his computer, clicking through the radar maps with methodical precision. Clear skies now, visibility excellent. But the approaching front was organizing itself over the Gulf, the squall line predicted to hit Rockport by mid-afternoon. Three o'clock, maybe four if the system slowed.

"Six hours," he calculated aloud, tapping his finger against the screen. "More than enough time."

His mind cataloged equipment needs with the efficiency of a pre-flight checklist: boat fueled, battery charged, GPS calibrated. Water and protein bars in the dry bag. First aid kit. Spare batteries for the handheld. The modified light sensor, now repurposed and waterproofed in a makeshift housing of silicone sealant and acrylic.

Tod paused, coffee halfway to his lips, staring through the bay window toward where the signal originated. Nothing visible on the water's surface—just the familiar morning choreography of gulls and early fishing boats.

"This is probably nothing," he told himself, not for the first time. "Some piece of monitoring equipment that broke loose from a research vessel. Or some weird offshore oil platform electronics gone haywire."

But the rational explanation felt hollow against the evidence. The signal's organic patterns. The way it had responded when detected. The impossibility of what his equipment was receiving.

Tod drained the last of his coffee and set the mug down with finality. Whatever waited beneath Copano Bay's surface—equipment malfunction or something more profound—he would see it with his own eyes.

He grabbed his handheld radio and the modified sensor from the workbench, slipping them into his waterproof bag. The weight of the equipment felt reassuring against his side as he stepped out the workshop door, heading toward the wooden dock where his boat waited.

TOD'S BOOTS THUMPED rhythmically down the weathered dock planks, the familiar hollow sound marking each step toward his vessel. The center console boat hung suspended in the lift, its white hull gleaming in the early morning light. The name "K5HUX" adorned the transom in navy blue lettering – his ham radio callsign that had become his identity on water as much as over airwaves.

He pressed the down button on the lift control, watching as hydraulics lowered the twenty-two-footer into the calm waters of the bay. The hull kissed the surface with barely a ripple, settling into its element with practiced ease.

"Morning, girl," Tod murmured, running his hand along the gunwale as he stepped aboard.

His pre-departure ritual began without conscious thought – the product of years on Gulf waters where preparation meant survival. Fuel level checked and topped off. Battery connections inspected, terminals clean and tight. Life jackets stowed within reach beneath the forward seat. Anchor line free of tangles, ready to deploy.

He arranged his equipment with deliberate care: the waterproofed sensor secured in the forward compartment, binoculars hanging from the center console hook, handheld radio clipped to his belt. Water bottles and protein bars went into the cooler alongside ice packs. First aid kit – rarely needed but never forgotten – tucked beneath the helm.

Tod flipped on the VHF marine radio, its screen illuminating with channel 16 active. He adjusted volume, listening to the morning's crackle of distant communications.

"VHF check, check," he spoke into the handset, hearing his voice return clearly through the speaker.

The Yamaha outboard started with a turn of the key, settling into its reassuring purr. Tod let it idle, gauges registering normal readings across the board. Everything in order. Everything as it should be.

He paused, taking in the morning. The water lay flat and inviting, painted gold by the climbing sun. Gulls wheeled overhead, their cries carrying across the bay. Salt air filled his lungs – that distinctive coastal perfume of brine, marsh grass, and promise.

Any other day, this would be simply another fishing trip. Today, the familiar had acquired an edge of mystery that sharpened his senses, made ordinary beauty feel significant.

Tod released the dock lines, coiling them with practiced efficiency. With one smooth motion, he eased the throttle forward. The bow lifted slightly as the boat glided away from the dock, cutting a clean wake across the glassy surface of Copano Bay.

THE BOAT SLICED THROUGH the water, sending ripples across the glassy surface of Copano Bay. Tod consulted his GPS, adjusting course slightly to match the coordinates he'd recorded from his workshop. The morning sun warmed his face as he inhaled the salt air, savoring the solitude that came with being on the water at this hour.

He reached for the handheld HAM radio clipped to his belt, thumbing the transmit button twice before speaking.

"K5HUX to W5BAR, you up Barney?"

The radio crackled briefly before a familiar voice responded.

"W5BAR receiving. Morning, Tod. Figured you'd be calling. Got my coffee and already watching the weather radar."

Tod smiled. Barney was nothing if not reliable—always at his radio station before sunrise, monitoring frequencies and weather patterns with religious dedication.

"Heading out to check that signal. Should be back by noon." Tod adjusted the throttle, navigating around a crab pot marker. "Getting a stronger reading now that I'm on the water."

"Weather's going to turn. Don't stay out too long." Barney's voice carried the weight of experience. "Gulf storms have a way of accelerating faster than the forecasts show."

"Roger that. I'm keeping an eye on it."

"Still think you're chasing ghosts or malfunctioning oil rig equipment," Barney said, his skepticism evident even through the static. "But I'd be lying if I said I wasn't curious what you find."

"That makes two of us." Tod watched a mullet break the surface twenty yards off his port side. "I'll call in with updates. If it's just faulty equipment, I'll be back for lunch."

"And if it's not?"

Tod paused, considering the question. "Then I guess we'll have something interesting to talk about over beers tonight."

"Just watch yourself out there. That signal of yours started acting mighty peculiar yesterday."

"Will do. K5HUX clear."

Tod set the radio down in its holder, throttling up as he passed the last shallow-water marker. Ahead stretched the open bay, the coordinates drawing him toward a seemingly unremarkable patch of water. Nothing visible distinguished it from any other part of Copano, yet something beneath that surface was sending pulses of light with clockwork precision.

The engine's steady hum accompanied his thoughts as the shoreline receded behind him. Whatever waited at those coordinates, Tod would face it alone.

THE GPS DISPLAY BLINKED as Tod approached the coordinates, a half mile from shore in what appeared to be the most unremarkable section of Copano Bay. He throttled back, the Yamaha engine settling to a low rumble before he shifted to neutral. The boat drifted slightly with momentum, then settled into a gentle rise and fall with the morning swells.

Tod scanned the water around him. Nothing. Just the same murky, greenish-brown bay water he'd seen a thousand times before. No boats nearby, no unusual disturbance on the surface, not even a fish breaking the water.

"This is it?" he muttered to himself, glancing between the GPS and the empty water. "This is where you're hiding?"

He reached into his waterproof case and extracted the modified light sensor he'd reconfigured the night before. The device was simpler than his home setup—essentially a portable version of what his antenna had accidentally discovered. He powered it on, adjusted the sensitivity, and pointed it downward toward the water.

The readout immediately spiked, pulsing with the same seven-second rhythm he'd recorded from his workshop.

"Bingo."

The signal was strong—stronger than it had been from shore. Whatever was generating these pulses was directly beneath his boat. Tod leaned over the gunwale, staring hard into the water, but the murky depths revealed nothing.

He reached for the depth finder, studying the digital display. Eighteen feet to bottom. Sandy substrate. No structures, no unusual formations, no large fish. The sonar showed precisely what one would expect in this section of the bay—absolutely nothing of interest.

Tod grabbed his binoculars, methodically scanning the water's surface in all directions. Nothing but gentle swells catching the morning light, a few distant gulls, and the shoreline behind him.

"It's here. The signal is definitely here." His brow furrowed as he checked the readings again. "But there's nothing."

He ran through possibilities: buried equipment, something too small for the depth finder to register, or perhaps something that only activated periodically. None seemed satisfactory.

Tod checked his watch: 7:23 AM. The storm wasn't due for hours. He had time.

"Alright then," he said, reaching for the anchor. "Let's get a closer look."

The anchor chain rattled as it played out, disappearing into the depths. Tod secured the line and turned to his equipment case. If the mystery wouldn't reveal itself, he'd need more sensitive tools to uncover whatever lurked beneath the surface of Copano Bay.

THE ANCHOR HIT BOTTOM with a soft thud Tod felt through the line. He paid out additional scope, then tied off with a quick figure-eight around the cleat. The Yamaha idled in neutral as he ensured the anchor was set properly, feeling the satisfying resistance when he pulled against it. Satisfied, he throttled the engine down and switched it off.

Silence enveloped him. The abrupt transition from mechanical noise to natural sounds heightened his senses—water gently slapping against the hull, distant gulls crying, the subtle creaking of the boat as it settled into its anchored position. Morning sun warmed his shoulders as he moved purposefully around the deck.

"Let's see what you're hiding down there," Tod murmured, pulling his equipment from waterproof cases.

He transformed the console into an impromptu research station, arranging instruments with practiced efficiency. The fish finder came first, its transducer already mounted and calibrated. Next came the depth sounder with its more sensitive bottom-mapping capabilities. Finally, he positioned his modified light sensor, angling it to capture whatever might be emitting those mysterious pulses.

Tod powered up each device methodically, cross-checking initial readings. The depth sounder confirmed eighteen feet to bottom, but something about the return signal seemed off. Instead of the clean, solid line representing sandy substrate, the reading showed wavering, inconsistent patterns.

"That's not right," he frowned, adjusting settings and recalibrating. The pattern remained—neither solid bottom nor the distinct signatures of fish. Rather, it appeared as interference, like overlapping ripples in a pond.

The modified sensor practically screamed with activity, its display showing pulses stronger than any readings at his workshop. Seven seconds. Seven seconds. Seven seconds. Perfect rhythm, but now with complex harmonics within each pulse.

"This is incredible," Tod whispered, correlating data points between instruments. The light emissions seemed synchronized with the interference patterns on the depth sounder—impossible coincidence.

He leaned over the gunwale, squinting into the water. Nothing visible penetrated the murky green-brown barrier. Copano Bay jealously guarded its secrets below the surface, revealing nothing to the naked eye despite what his instruments insisted was there.

"What ARE you?" Tod asked the water, fascination overtaking caution.

He returned to his instruments, hunching over the console. Numbers, patterns, and correlations consumed his attention. The boat rocked gently, the distant storm forgotten, the passing time unnoticed. Something extraordinary lurked below, communicating in pulses of light, and Tod was determined to decipher its language.

THE OSCILLOSCOPE'S display captivated Tod completely, its rhythmic green pulses mesmerizing him as they danced across the screen. Each seven-second interval revealed new complexities—modulations within modulations, patterns suggesting something far beyond random natural phenomena. In twenty-eight years of life, he'd never encountered anything so utterly fascinating.

Above him, nature shifted its mood. Dark clouds gathered on the western horizon, their approach silent and swift. The wind, which had been a gentle caress, strengthened incrementally, pushing against the anchored vessel with growing insistence.

The boat rocked more pronouncedly, a motion that finally penetrated Tod's concentration when his coffee mug slid across the console, nearly toppling into his lap. He caught it reflexively, the movement breaking his trance.

"What the..." Tod looked up, and his stomach dropped.

A dark wall of clouds stretched across the horizon, much closer than it had any right to be. Below it, whitecaps advanced like an army across Copano Bay's surface, marking the wind line with stark precision. The forecast had called for deteriorating conditions by mid-afternoon, but this squall was bearing down with unmistakable urgency.

"Shit. That wasn't supposed to be here for hours."

Tod glanced at his watch—7:50 AM. The meteorologists had been catastrophically wrong, or perhaps the Gulf had simply decided to remind humans of their insignificance in predicting her moods.

Every instinct screamed at him to pull anchor immediately. He could outrun the squall if he left now, reach the protection of the harbor before conditions became dangerous. His hand moved toward the ignition key.

Then his eyes fell on the oscilloscope again. The signal had changed, growing stronger and more complex as if responding to the approaching storm. New harmonics appeared within the pulses, frequencies shifting in patterns that seemed almost... deliberate.

"Five more minutes," he muttered, hand dropping from the key. "Just five more minutes to document this."

The rational part of his brain protested loudly. The darkening sky, the whitecaps now visible within easy swimming distance, the boat's increasingly vigorous rocking—all warning signs no experienced boater should ignore.

But the mystery below pulled at him with irresistible force. Whatever generated these signals might disappear forever if he left now.

Tod turned back to his instruments, shoulders hunched protectively over the console. The squall line advanced, but his attention had already narrowed again to the green pulses on his screen, the outside world fading to insignificance.

THE SQUALL ARRIVED with the suddenness of a slap. One moment Tod was hunched over his instruments, the next, the wind hit with a howl that seemed to come from everywhere at once. The boat lurched violently beneath him as the first powerful gusts caught the hull.

Around him, Copano Bay transformed. The once-gentle surface erupted into angry chop, waves building with unnatural speed. White foam appeared on their crests as the wind tore at the water's surface. The anchored boat began to pitch and yaw, straining against its line.

Reality crashed into Tod's consciousness with the same force as the squall.

"I need to go. NOW."

His hands moved frantically, disconnecting cables and powering down equipment. The wind's howl intensified, drowning out the sound of gear sliding across the deck. Above him, dark clouds obliterated the morning sun, casting the bay in an eerie twilight. He managed to stow the oscilloscope in its waterproof case, latching it shut just as a wave slapped against the hull, sending spray across the deck.

The boat rocked significantly now, each wave lifting and dropping it with increasing violence. Tod stumbled to the console, bracing himself with one hand while entering final readings into his handheld device. Numbers mattered even in crisis—data that might explain the inexplicable pulses beneath the bay.

"Just a few more seconds," he muttered, eyes fixed on the small screen, fingers tapping rapidly.

He never saw the wave coming. A sudden gust drove a larger swell directly into the starboard side. The boat lurched violently, deck tilting at a sickening angle. Tod's feet slid across the wet surface as his free hand grasped at empty air.

His body twisted awkwardly as he fell. The gunwale rushed toward him, its hard edge catching him just above the right temple. The impact brought a blinding flash of white-hot pain, followed instantly by darkness.

Tod tumbled over the side, limp body striking the churning water with a splash lost in the storm's roar. His waterlogged clothes and equipment dragged him down immediately. Cold water enveloped him, stinging the fresh wound at his temple.

For one brief moment, a fragment of consciousness registered the cold, the pressure, the sensation of sinking into the murky depths of Copano Bay. Then even that disappeared, awareness extinguished as completely as a candle in a hurricane.

Tod Blackstone slipped beneath the waves, descending into the very mystery he had come to investigate.

DARKNESS. COMPLETE, all-consuming. Then—cold. A bone-deep chill that penetrated every fiber of his being.

Tod floated in a strange limbo between consciousness and oblivion. Pressure squeezed his chest, his limbs, his skull. Water filled his ears, muffling the world into silence broken only by his slowing heartbeat. Was he dying? His mind couldn't grasp the simple facts of his situation—only sensations remained.

Sinking.

Can't breathe.

Heavy.

His body dragged downward through the murky depths, equipment pulling him toward the bay floor. The darkness should have been absolute this deep, yet... something changed. The blackness wasn't complete anymore.

A faint blue-white glow appeared below, soft at first, then growing stronger. It spread outward, tendrils of light reaching toward him like ghostly fingers. The illumination pulsed—seven seconds, exactly seven seconds between pulses—the rhythm he'd tracked from shore.

Is this death? Tod wondered, his oxygen-starved brain offering the thought without emotion. The light looked like something from near-death accounts—the tunnel, the welcoming glow. But this light moved differently, with purpose, with awareness.

Something touched his arm. Not threatening—gentle. Another touch at his back, his leg, supporting him, slowing his descent. The blue-white radiance surrounded him completely now, bright enough to see through closed eyelids. Thousands of tiny points of illumination swirled around him in coordinated patterns.

The pressure in his lungs eased. Impossible, but... he drew breath. Water should have filled his lungs, but instead, somehow, oxygen reached his blood. The confusion overwhelmed his fading mind. Underwater but breathing? How?

The light pulsed faster now, surrounding him in a cocoon of gentle radiance. Whatever held him continued its careful examination—thousands of tiny contacts against his skin, coordinated, purposeful. Not creatures exactly, but parts of something larger, something collective.

Tod's remaining awareness flickered like a dying candle. The light grew more intense, more beautiful. His confusion faded into acceptance as consciousness slipped away again. His last sensation: being cradled within the luminous embrace as it carried him deeper into Copano Bay's mysteries.

TOD'S EYES FLUTTERED open, consciousness returning in waves. Water surrounded him—he was underwater, eighteen feet down on the bay bottom. His brain processed this fact with detached clarity before panic erupted. He tried to gasp, body convulsing with the instinctive need for air.

But the expected flood of water never came. Instead, oxygen filled his lungs. Somehow, impossibly, he was breathing underwater.

His vision cleared, revealing an otherworldly scene. Light—pure, ethereal light—surrounded him from all sides. Not the harsh beams of artificial illumination, but the soft, organic glow of living creatures. Hundreds—no, thousands—of translucent, basketball-sized organisms hovered around him in perfect formation. Each pulsed with bioluminescence, their bodies allowing glimpses of intricate internal structures unlike anything he'd ever seen.

They had formed a perfect dome around him, creating what appeared to be some kind of habitat. Was it an air pocket? Some kind of oxygen-rich bubble? Tod couldn't understand the mechanics, but the reality was undeniable—he was alive, conscious, breathing underwater.

The initial terror subsided, replaced by something Tod hadn't felt since childhood—pure, unfiltered wonder. The creatures moved in synchronized patterns, their lights blinking in sequence. The rhythm felt deliberate, coordinated.

Wait.

Those pulses.

His foggy mind began to recognize a pattern.

Dit-dit-dit... dah-dah-dah... dit-dit-dit...

SOS.

The international distress signal. Then another sequence followed:

K5HUX.

Tod froze. His amateur radio callsign. They knew who he was.

The creatures continued, their lights flashing:

FRIEND.

"You're... you're intelligent," Tod whispered, words emerging as bubbles that didn't disperse but somehow carried his voice. "You're TALKING to me."

The dome of creatures rippled in response, their collective movement creating a wave of light that circled him. They had saved him from drowning. They had created this impossible environment to keep him alive. They had been sending signals—the mysterious pulses he'd been tracking weren't equipment malfunctions or natural phenomena.

They were messages.

Everything Tod understood about life, intelligence, communication—it all transformed in this single, profound moment beneath Copano Bay.

TOD'S HEAD POUNDED with each heartbeat, a sharp throb radiating from where he'd struck the gunwale. The underwater habitat was miraculous, but a clear thought cut through his wonder—he needed to get back to his boat. Now.

He tried to move, limbs responding sluggishly. His waterlogged clothes dragged against his attempts, and waves of dizziness threatened to overwhelm him with each motion. Blood clouded the water near his temple.

The colony sensed his intention immediately. Their formation shifted, thousands of individual organisms moving with unified purpose. They clustered beneath him, their collective movement creating a gentle upward current. Tod felt their touch—cool, firm yet yielding—as they pressed against his back, legs, and arms.

"I need... to get to the surface," Tod mumbled through bubbles.

The creatures responded by intensifying their light, the dome opening above him like an iris. They began to lift him, not dragging or pushing, but supporting his weight with perfect distribution. Their movement was deliberate, careful, as if they understood his fragility.

Tod ascended through the murky bay water, the colony guiding his path. The journey seemed both eternal and instant—time distorted by injury and the impossibility of the situation. Light grew stronger above, not from his companions now but from daylight penetrating the water's surface.

He broke through into chaos. The squall had fully arrived, rain pelting the bay surface like buckshot while wind howled across the water. Tod gasped, real air filling his lungs—somehow both harsher and more welcome than whatever he'd been breathing below. The contrast shocked his system, sending him into a coughing fit as waves crashed around him.

Twenty feet away, his boat pitched violently against its anchor line, still miraculously in place. Tod began swimming, each stroke a monumental effort. His arms felt leaden, his legs barely responding. The head wound sapped his strength with each passing second.

Below him, the colony remained. Their light pulsed through the turbulent water as they pushed gently against his body, propelling him forward when his own strength faltered. With their help, Tod closed the distance to his boat, fingers finally grasping the aluminum boarding ladder that slapped against the hull.

The climb was agony. Every rung required total concentration, his vision narrowing to just the next handhold. Blood ran into his eyes, mixing with rain and seawater. With a final, desperate heave, Tod rolled over the gunwale, collapsing onto the deck. He lay there, chest heaving, as rain pounded his face.

After several minutes, Tod dragged himself to the edge, peering over the side. The colony hovered just below the surface, their lights visible despite the churning water. They pulsed in unison:

YOU SAFE

A profound gratitude washed over Tod. He trembled, partly from cold and shock, partly from emotion. He fumbled across the deck toward the console, hands shaking as he retrieved the waterproof spotlight from its mount.

Tod pointed the beam downward, clicking it on and off in deliberate sequence:

T-H-A-N-K Y-O-U

His Morse was clumsy, hands unsteady, but the meaning got through. The colony's response came immediately, thousands of individual lights coordinating perfectly to form a single message:

FRIEND

Tod slumped against the console, watching their lights shimmer beneath his boat as the storm raged around them. His world had irrevocably changed, yet in this moment of exhaustion and pain, one reality stood clear—he was not alone in Copano Bay.

REALITY CRASHED BACK into Tod's consciousness. The rhythmic pounding of rain against fiberglass. The deep throb of his head wound. The cold that had seeped into his core.

He needed to get home.

Tod dragged himself to his feet, swaying as the boat pitched. Blood trickled warm down his temple, contrasting with the icy rain. His vision swam, edges blurring then sharpening as he fought to focus. Functioning, but barely.

The anchor. He had to raise the anchor.

Tod stumbled to the bow, gripping the gunwale for support. The mechanical task of raising anchor—something he'd done thousands of times—now required his full concentration. Each pull sent daggers through his skull. His muscles trembled from cold and exertion, but the anchor finally broke surface, dripping and swinging wildly. He secured it with fumbling fingers.

At the console, Tod's training took over. Check gauges. Turn key. The Yamaha coughed once, then roared to life. He pointed the bow toward home and pushed the throttle forward, slower than usual. The boat responded sluggishly in the choppy water, or perhaps it was just his perception.

The squall was passing now, but steady rain still fell, obscuring visibility beyond fifty yards. Tod kept glancing behind him, searching the water's surface. Had they followed? The colony that saved his life—were they still there? The churning gray water revealed nothing.

The VHF radio crackled to life. "K5HUX, this is KG5ZRT. Tod, you copy? Saw that squall hit your position. You okay out there? Over."

Barney's voice seemed to come from another world. Tod stared at the handset but couldn't bring himself to reach for it. What would he say? That he'd drowned but was saved by intelligent, light-pulsing creatures living beneath Copano Bay? That he'd breathed underwater? The words wouldn't come.

He focused on navigation. Home. Dock. Safety. Those concepts alone filled his battered mind. His body moved on instinct—adjusting course, maintaining speed, scanning for hazards.

Twenty minutes stretched into an eternity. The normally familiar shoreline seemed alien through the rain and his concussed vision. Time fragmented, moments of clarity punctuated by gaps where his mind simply... drifted.

Finally, through sheets of rain, Tod spotted the silhouette of his dock. The simple wooden structure had never looked so beautiful. He eased back the throttle, approaching with exaggerated care. His sanctuary was within reach—a place to collapse, to think, to begin processing the impossible.

TOD SECURED HIS BOAT with mechanical precision, muscle memory taking over where conscious thought failed. The cleats, the bumpers, the stern line—his hands moved through the familiar pattern while his mind floated elsewhere. The rain had slackened to a drizzle as the squall moved inland, leaving him soaked and shivering.

He stumbled up the path from the dock, each step uncertain. Blood trickled into his left eye. He wiped it away with a waterlogged sleeve, smearing crimson across his face. The house beckoned—safety, warmth, normalcy.

Inside, Tod left a trail of puddles across the hardwood. Water dripped from his clothes, his hair, forming pools at his feet. The logical part of his brain registered tasks: treat head wound, call someone, change clothes. Instead, he lurched toward the couch and collapsed.

The ceiling spun above him, reality tilting on its axis. His temple throbbed in time with his heartbeat. He should call Barney. Should clean up. Should...

Tod closed his eyes. Just for a minute.

Darkness.

When Tod's eyes fluttered open, the house was pitch black. Night? How long had he been unconscious? Disoriented, he fumbled for his phone. The screen's harsh glow read 10:30 PM.

Thirteen hours. He'd been out for thirteen hours.

Tod pushed himself upright, wincing as his head protested the movement. The blood in his hair had dried to a crusty mass. He staggered to the bathroom and flipped on the light, blinking at his reflection. An ugly gash cut across his temple, surrounded by a purple bruise. Lucky. Could've been worse.

With trembling hands, he cleaned the wound, applied antiseptic, fumbled with butterfly bandages. Basic first aid, all he could manage.

But the wound wasn't what troubled him. The memories surfaced—breathing underwater, the glowing colony, the message: FRIEND. Was any of it real? Or just the hallucination of an oxygen-deprived, concussed brain?

Tod wandered to his workshop, drawn to the bay window overlooking the water. His dock was a dark silhouette against the black water. Calm. Empty. Normal.

He turned away, shoulders slumping in defeat.

Wait.

Something pulled him back to the window. There—at the end of his dock. A faint blue-white glow illuminated the water, pulsing with that same seven-second rhythm. Not above the surface, but beneath it.

They were there. They had followed him home. They were waiting.

Not a dream. Not a hallucination.

Real.

Tod grabbed a heavy-duty flashlight from his workbench, his hand trembling with exhaustion, pain, and something else—anticipation. He paused only to slip on a jacket before heading outside, drawn toward the dock and the pulsing light calling to him from the depths.

Chapter 3

Tod stepped from his back door into the night, the weight of the flashlight grounding him to reality. He hadn't turned it on—didn't need to. The moon cast enough silver light to trace his path, and ahead, that blue-white glow pulsed from the water's edge like a heartbeat.

Seven seconds. Pause. Seven seconds. Pause.

Each step felt deliberate, almost ceremonial. The gravel crunched beneath his boots. Wind rustled through the coastal grasses. In the distance, a night heron called once, then fell silent. The ordinary sounds of a Gulf Coast evening continued while something extraordinary waited for him.

"This is real," Tod whispered to himself. "They're real. What do I say?"

His temple throbbed with each pulse of his heart, but the pain seemed distant now, overwhelmed by the flood of adrenaline and wonder surging through his system. His hands trembled—from the lingering effects of the concussion? Fear? Anticipation? Tod couldn't tell anymore.

The wooden dock stretched before him, a pathway into the unknown. As his foot touched the first plank, it creaked beneath his weight. The sound carried across the water, and instantly, the blue-white glow intensified, brightening as if responding to his presence.

They knew he was coming.

Tod paused, swallowing hard. The bay water lapped gently against the pilings, a rhythmic shushing that matched his shallow breathing. Stars reflected on the surface where the bioluminescence didn't ripple and dance.

He advanced slowly along the dock, counting his steps to regulate his breathing. With each forward movement, the light beneath the water grew more defined—not just a general glow now, but distinct shapes moving in coordinated patterns, swirling and pulsing.

At the dock's end, Tod lowered himself to his knees, the boards rough beneath him. He set the still-unlit flashlight beside him and leaned forward, fingers gripping the edge of the weathered wood.

Below, the colony spread out like a living constellation—dozens, perhaps hundreds of the basketball-sized creatures. Their light painted the underside of the dock in ethereal blue, reflecting off Tod's awestruck face as he stared down into the impossible.

THE WATER BELOW WAS surprisingly clear in the moonlight, clearer than the murky depths of Copano Bay where he'd first encountered them. Here, close to the dock, Tod could see them with perfect clarity—dozens near the surface, their graceful forms suspended just beneath the gentle waves. How many more hovered in the deeper water beyond his sight? Hundreds? Thousands?

Each creature was roughly basketball-sized, with translucent bodies that reminded Tod of jellyfish, but with a more defined structure. Through their semi-transparent membranes, intricate arrangements of bioluminescent organs glowed like miniature constellations—points of blue-white light connected in patterns unique to each individual. They moved through gentle, rhythmic pulsations, propelling themselves with a fluid grace that no machine could ever replicate.

As Tod watched, they began to arrange themselves in formation beneath him—not random clustering but organized, purposeful movement. They formed concentric circles, the pattern shifting and realigning with perfect coordination. It struck Tod that he was witnessing something both beautiful and utterly alien, a complexity of behavior that defied his understanding of marine life.

"Hello," Tod whispered, barely louder than the water lapping against the pilings.

The response was immediate and unmistakable. The light pulses intensified, brightening until the dock beneath him was bathed in their glow. Then, with breathtaking synchronization, the creatures began to flash in unison—not the seven-second rhythm he'd tracked before, but something new. Shorter, more varied.

Tod's brain, trained by years of HAM radio operation, recognized the pattern instantly.

Dot-dot-dot. Dash-dash-dash. Dot-dot-dot.

SOS.

Then more complex sequences followed. The creatures flashed in perfect unison, their collective body forming letters through coordinated light:

F-R-I-E-N-D K-5-H-U-X F-R-I-E-N-D

Tod's amateur radio callsign. They knew him. They were speaking to him in Morse code, a human language they couldn't possibly have evolved to understand.

His scientific curiosity and emotional wonder collided as he realized what was happening. These weren't just strange animals. They were communicating—deliberately, intelligently—and they had been trying to reach him all along.

"You're incredible," Tod breathed, his fingers tightening on the dock's edge. "And you're ready to talk."

TOD'S HAND TREMBLED as he raised the flashlight, adrenaline and wonder coursing through his veins. He took a deep breath, steadying himself against the wooden planks of the dock. The cool night air filled his lungs as he exhaled slowly, calming his racing heart.

With deliberate movements, Tod pointed the beam toward the water and clicked it on and off in a pattern he'd used thousands of times over radio waves, but never like this:

W-H-O A-R-E Y-O-U

The light from his flashlight cut through the darkness, reflecting off the gentle ripples of the bay. Tod waited, heart pounding in his chest. One second. Two. Three. His breath caught in his throat.

The creatures beneath the water pulsed in perfect unison, their blue-white glow intensifying as they formed their response. Each letter appeared as a collective effort, the entire colony functioning as a single organism to communicate:

L-I-G-H-T S-P-E-A-K-E-R-S

Tod's mind reeled at the implication. They had a name for themselves—not just intelligence, but identity. Self-awareness. These beings weren't just responding to stimuli; they understood who they were.

He steadied the flashlight and signaled again:

W-H-E-R-E F-R-O-M

The creatures rearranged themselves, the pattern of their bodies shifting like a living constellation before they flashed their answer:

D-E-E-P W-A-T-E-R E-A-S-T

East. The Gulf of Mexico. Deeper water than Copano Bay's shallow mudflats. Tod's analytical mind began connecting dots, building a picture of what he was witnessing.

With growing confidence, he signaled:

W-H-Y H-E-R-E

Their response came with the same perfect synchronization:

S-T-O-R-M P-U-S-H-E-D L-O-S-T

The pieces clicked into place. The hurricane that had brushed the coast two weeks ago—not a direct hit, but enough to disrupt currents and push deep water species into the bays. These Light Speakers had been displaced from their home. Somehow they'd been carried into Copano Bay by storm surge, and now they couldn't find their way back to the deeper waters of the Gulf.

Tod lowered the flashlight for a moment, processing what he'd learned. An intelligent species—previously undiscovered by science—communicated through bioluminescence. They normally lived in the deep waters of the Gulf of Mexico. A storm had pushed them into the shallow bay, and now they were lost.

The enormity of the situation settled over him. These weren't just fascinating creatures; they were stranded beings in an environment not their own. Their attempts to communicate with him hadn't been random signals—they'd been calls for help.

He looked down at the gently pulsing light beneath the dock. The colony had fallen quiet, waiting for his next message. The Light Speakers had found the one person on this stretch of coastline who might understand their signals. Through some impossible stroke of luck or fate, Tod's modified antenna had picked up their bioluminescent pulses and translated them into something his equipment could detect.

They were far from home, in waters too shallow, too warm, and Tod realized he might be their only chance to return to where they belonged.

A QUESTION BURNED IN Tod's mind as he knelt on the dock, the colony of Light Speakers pulsing gently beneath him. Their intelligence was undeniable—they communicated in perfect Morse code and identified themselves with clarity. But something didn't add up.

Tod raised his flashlight, its beam cutting through the darkness:
H-O-W K-N-O-W M-Y C-A-L-L-S-I-G-N

The water below went still. The creatures ceased their rhythmic pulsing, their blue-white glow dimming to a soft ambient light. The silence stretched uncomfortably long. Tod wondered if they were conferring somehow, deciding what to tell him—or perhaps if they should answer at all.

Just as Tod began to worry they'd retreated, the colony flared to life again, arranging themselves into clear patterns:
W-E H-E-A-R Y-O-U R-A-D-I-O

Tod's jaw dropped. His hand gripped the flashlight tighter, knuckles whitening. They could detect electromagnetic waves? That seemed impossible for organic creatures—yet here they were, signaling him with perfect Morse code.
H-O-W

His question was simple but profound. The colony shifted, individuals moving in perfectly coordinated patterns before answering:
W-E A-R-E L-I-G-H-T W-E F-E-E-L L-I-G-H-T

Tod stared at the pulsing message, understanding dawning across his face. Of course. These weren't just bioluminescent creatures—they were beings whose entire existence centered around light. Their bodies had evolved to both generate and detect across the electromagnetic spectrum. Radio waves were simply light with a different wavelength than what human eyes could see.

They had been listening to his transmissions all along. His daily conversations with Barney, his signal testing—they had heard it all. Tod's hand trembled slightly as he signaled his next question:
H-O-W L-E-A-R-N M-O-R-S-E

The colony's response formed quickly:

S-H-I-P-S L-I-G-H-T-S L-O-N-G T-I-M-E

Tod nodded to himself, the pieces falling into place. For generations, these beings had observed human ships, watching the flashes of light from navigation signals and communication lamps. They'd recognized patterns, learned our language of dots and dashes. Their intellect had allowed them to decipher meaning from repetition, to translate human signals into understanding.

A new message formed in the water:

Y-O-U D-I-F-F-E-R-E-N-T

Tod's eyebrows raised. He signaled back:

H-O-W

The colony swirled, rearranging themselves before answering:

Y-O-U L-I-S-T-E-N T-O L-I-G-H-T

Tod sat back on his heels, the revelation washing over him. His modified photodiode sensor—the one he'd attached to his antenna to track the sunrise. The one that had started picking up their signals. That was how they'd found him. The cosmic irony struck him: he had discovered them precisely because he was looking in a way no one else was.

While others used radio antennas to detect radio waves, Tod had accidentally created a system that bridged the gap—translating light into radio signals. His equipment had heard them because he'd modified it to listen differently.

They hadn't randomly encountered him. They had chosen him specifically because he had shown the capacity to detect their communications. Among all the humans on the Gulf Coast, Tod Blackstone was the only one who had built equipment that could receive their signals. And they had recognized him by his callsign—K5HUX—the identifier he broadcast daily from his ham radio.

Tod looked down at the glowing creatures with new understanding. This wasn't just a chance meeting between species.

The Light Speakers had deliberately revealed themselves to the one human they knew could perceive them.

TOD'S MIND RACED WITH questions, but one took precedence. He raised his flashlight, signaling:

W-H-A-T D-O Y-O-U N-E-E-D

The colony's response came without hesitation, as if they'd been waiting for this precise opening:

H-O-M-E D-E-E-P W-A-T-E-R

Their formation shifted, continuing:

C-A-N-N-O-T F-I-N-D W-A-Y

W-A-T-E-R W-R-O-N-G H-E-R-E

Tod frowned, his face bathed in their urgent blue glow. They were lost—stranded in an environment that wasn't meant for them.

W-R-O-N-G H-O-W

The creatures pulsed their answer:

T-O-O W-A-R-M T-O-O B-R-I-G-H-T

Understanding dawned across Tod's face. The Light Speakers weren't coastal creatures—they were deep-water beings, evolved for the cold, dark pressures of the ocean depths. Copano Bay's warm, sun-drenched shallows must be unbearable for them. The salt concentration, temperature, light penetration—everything would be wrong.

Tod glanced across the bay, seeing it with new eyes. What had seemed like a peaceful home to countless marine species was a hostile environment to these creatures. Their magnificent light communication, so beautiful to him, was actually a desperate distress signal.

H-O-W L-O-N-G H-E-R-E

The colony rearranged itself:

F-O-U-R S-U-N-S

Four days. They'd been trapped in the bay for four days—likely since the last storm system had pushed through.

Tod's hands trembled slightly as he signaled his next question:

H-O-W L-O-N-G C-A-N S-T-A-Y

The colony went still, their lights dimming momentarily. When they responded, their pattern seemed less precise, the edges of their formation wavering:

T-W-O S-U-N-S M-A-Y-B-E T-H-R-E-E

Two days. Maybe three. Tod's stomach tightened.

They were dying.

He stared at the colony, the weight of realization settling across his shoulders. These weren't just fascinating creatures to study or communicate with. This wasn't a scientific discovery or a unique experience. This was a rescue mission.

The Light Speakers needed to return to deep water—needed the cold, dark pressure of their natural environment. And they had at most three days before Copano Bay killed them.

Tod sat back on his heels, running a hand through his salt-stiff hair. The head wound throbbed as the enormity of the situation became clear. Somehow, he had to find a way to transport an entire colony of deep-water organisms across miles of shallow bay, through passes and channels, and out into the Gulf of Mexico—deep enough that they could survive.

And he had less than three days to figure it out.

TOD GRIPPED THE EDGE of the dock, his mind racing through possibilities. These creatures needed deep water—Gulf water—not the warm, shallow confines of Copano Bay. But how could they get there? Miles of bay, channels, and passes stood between them and salvation.

Before he could formulate a plan, the colony shifted formation. Their lights pulsed with new urgency:

Y-O-U K-N-O-W W-A-T-E-R-S

Tod nodded slowly, understanding their meaning. He did know these waters—every channel, every sandbar, every hidden oyster reef.

Y-O-U H-A-V-E B-O-A-T

The colony continued, their message unmistakable. Tod glanced back at his center console, still tied to the dock after his earlier misadventure.

Y-O-U S-A-V-E-D U-S

Tod blinked, confused. His fingers moved almost reflexively as he flashed back:

I S-A-V-E-D Y-O-U

The colony's response came immediately:

Y-E-S Y-O-U C-A-M-E T-O F-I-N-D U-S

N-O O-N-E E-L-S-E L-O-O-K-E-D

Y-O-U S-A-W U-S

Tod's breath caught in his throat. They had reframed everything. His curiosity, his investigation of their signal—they hadn't seen it as intrusion but as recognition. By noticing them, by seeking them out, he had given them hope when no one else had even registered their existence.

And they had saved his life in return. The memory flooded back—sinking into the depths, the colony surrounding him, creating a space where he could breathe underwater. They had rescued him from certain drowning.

The colony shifted again, forming new patterns:

W-I-L-L Y-O-U H-E-L-P

L-E-A-D U-S H-O-M-E

The request hung in the air between them, illuminated by their pulsing blue light. Direct. Unmistakable. They needed him.

Tod felt his heart pounding against his ribs. These creatures—these intelligent, communicative beings—had saved him from death. Now they were asking him to return the favor, to lead them home through waters he knew like the back of his hand.

The weight of their request settled on his shoulders. This wasn't just about helping lost creatures. It was about honoring a debt, a connection formed in the depths of Copano Bay when they had chosen to save a stranger.

Their lights continued to pulse in that perfect seven-second rhythm, waiting. The question hung between them: Would he help? Would he lead them home?

Tod stared into the living constellation before him, knowing his answer even before he formed it.

TOD SAT BACK ON HIS heels, the enormity of what he was contemplating washing over him. Ten miles offshore, through winding channels and passes. He'd need to navigate around treacherous shallows and unpredictable boat traffic while keeping the colony together. The tides would have to be timed perfectly—they'd need an outgoing tide to help carry them through the passes.

He calculated risks with each breath. The danger of exposure—what would happen if others discovered these beings? Would they become specimens in some laboratory? Then there was his own safety—taking his small boat that far offshore alone carried its own perils.

And yet, the answer was obvious. Had been since the moment they'd surrounded him in the depths, creating that impossible bubble of life when he should have drowned.

Tod raised his flashlight, his hand steadier than it had been all night.

Y-E-S

He paused, then continued:

I W-I-L-L H-E-L-P

I W-I-L-L L-E-A-D Y-O-U H-O-M-E

The response was immediate. The colony's lights intensified to a brilliance that illuminated the dock and water around him. Their pulses quickened, no longer in the measured seven-second rhythm but rapid with what could only be joy.

T-H-A-N-K Y-O-U F-R-I-E-N-D

T-H-A-N-K Y-O-U K-5-H-U-X

Something warm slid down Tod's cheek. He reached up, surprised to find tears. Hadn't even realized he was crying.

The colony dimmed slightly, as if giving him space for his emotion. Then they flashed again:

W-H-E-N

Tod considered. He needed an outgoing tide, calm weather, and time to prepare properly. A journey like this couldn't be rushed—not with lives at stake.

N-E-X-T D-A-Y

D-A-W-N

The timing would be right. He could check weather reports, prepare his boat, gather supplies, and plan their route carefully. Every detail would matter.

The colony pulsed once, their lights forming a perfect circle beneath him:

W-E W-A-I-T

The simplicity of their response belied the profound trust they were placing in him. Tod nodded, knowing this was more than a promise—it was a sacred bond between species who had saved each other once, and would do so again.

TOD WATCHED THE COLONY'S synchronized lights, practical matters settled but his mind buzzing with questions. The scientist in him couldn't resist learning more about these extraordinary beings.

He raised his flashlight again:

W-H-A-T A-R-E Y-O-U

The colony's lights pulsed, rearranging as they considered his question. Their response came carefully:

W-E A-R-E L-I-G-H-T M-A-K-E-R-S

Tod waited, sensing there was more. After a moment, they added:

W-E A-R-E M-A-N-Y O-N-E

As they flashed this message, the entire colony moved in perfect unison, then separated into distinct patterns before reforming. Tod understood they were demonstrating their nature—individual beings that functioned as a collective.

H-O-W M-A-N-Y O-F Y-O-U

Tod asked, trying to gauge the colony's size. The water beneath his dock seemed filled with them, but he couldn't count their constantly moving forms.

M-A-N-Y M-A-N-Y

Their lights flickered in what Tod interpreted as the equivalent of a shrug. Either they couldn't express numbers in their limited vocabulary or there were too many to count.

D-O Y-O-U E-A-T

He was curious how they survived in the deep waters they called home.

W-E D-R-I-N-K L-I-G-H-T

This response surprised him. Were they photosynthetic? But that made little sense for deep-water organisms where sunlight barely penetrated.

A-L-S-O S-M-A-L-L T-H-I-N-G-S

A dual nutrition strategy, Tod realized. They absorbed energy from light but also consumed microorganisms—plankton perhaps. His mind cataloged these details automatically, the biology student in him awakening.

Yet as he continued this exchange, Tod felt something beyond scientific curiosity. When one of the Light Makers drifted closer to the surface, its internal constellation of organs clearly visible through its translucent body, Tod found himself reaching toward it. The creature gently touched his fingertips with its gelatinous form, a gesture that felt unmistakably like greeting.

These weren't specimens to be studied under microscopes. They were people—different in form and nature, but people nonetheless. People who had saved his life, who had called him friend, who needed his help.

As midnight approached, Tod realized he'd been kneeling on the dock for over an hour, flashlight in hand, engaged in the most extraordinary conversation of his life. The Light Makers' lights had settled into a gentler rhythm, almost like the breathing of a sleeping child.

TOD'S KNEES HAD GROWN stiff from kneeling on the dock, but his discomfort faded against the wonder of this encounter. Midnight approached, yet his curiosity remained insatiable.

W-H-E-R-E I-S Y-O-U-R H-O-M-E

The colony shifted, their lights softening momentarily before responding:

D-E-E-P C-O-L-D D-A-R-K

Tod nodded, understanding they needed conditions nothing like the shallow, warm bay.

H-O-W D-E-E-P

The Light Makers' formation wavered, their patterns fragmenting and reforming as if struggling with the concept. Numbers seemed difficult for them to express precisely.

M-A-N-Y M-A-N-Y F-E-E-T

Tod considered what this might mean in human terms. "A hundred feet? Deeper?" he whispered, not bothering with the flashlight. The colony pulsed affirmatively and continued flashing, suggesting even greater depths.

W-H-A-T I-S I-T L-I-K-E

Their response came without hesitation:

P-E-A-C-E-F-U-L

Then, after a brief pause:

W-E S-I-N-G

Tod's brow furrowed. "Sing? In light?"

The colony swirled in what seemed like excitement at his understanding:

L-I-G-H-T S-O-N-G-S

Tod sat back on his heels, mind racing. Not just communication, then, but expression—art, culture, transmitted through patterns of bioluminescence. These beings had developed their own forms of beauty, of meaning-making in the darkness.

D-O O-T-H-E-R-S L-I-K-E Y-O-U E-X-I-S-T

His heart pounded as he waited for their answer.

Y-E-S M-A-N-Y K-I-N-D-S

The words struck Tod like physical blows. Not just these Light Makers, but other intelligent species—plural—dwelling in the depths. His mind struggled to encompass the implications. When he prompted for details, their patterns became too complex, fragmenting into what seemed like conversations among themselves before simplifying again, apparently unable to translate the complexity of what they wished to share.

Tod gazed out past the colony, beyond his dock, toward the vast Gulf that stretched to the horizon. Beneath those dark waters existed entire civilizations, cultures, perhaps even societies that humans knew nothing about. Beings who communicated, who created art, who possessed awareness—all evolving and thriving beyond human detection.

All his life, Tod had thought he understood the coast where he'd grown up. But now he realized the hubris in that belief. Humans had mapped coastlines and charted shipping channels, but knew almost nothing of the ocean's true inhabitants.

"We've been so blind," Tod whispered, a profound humility washing over him. "All this time, right beneath us."

THE FIRST TENDRILS of exhaustion crept into Tod's consciousness as the dock's weathered clock showed 12:10 AM. Time to address the practical matters of their journey.

Tod raised his flashlight and began signaling:

T-H-R-O-U-G-H C-H-A-N-N-E-L-S T-O G-U-L-F

The colony pulsed in acknowledgment, their lights dimming and brightening in perfect rhythm.

T-E-N M-I-L-E-S, Tod continued. M-U-S-T F-O-L-L-O-W M-Y B-O-A-T

The Light Makers rearranged themselves in what Tod now recognized as their pattern for understanding. Their response came without hesitation:

W-E F-O-L-L-O-W

Tod nodded, his mind working through the coastal navigation challenges. He'd made the journey countless times, but never shepherding a colony of beings who couldn't survive in shallow waters.

T-I-D-E G-O-I-N-G O-U-T H-E-L-P-S, he flashed. C-A-R-R-I-E-S Y-O-U T-O D-E-E-P W-A-T-E-R

The colony swirled in what appeared to be approval. Tod understood their vulnerability—the outgoing tide would create a natural current, helping to push them offshore efficiently, reducing their exposure in hostile shallow waters.

D-A-W-N N-E-X-T D-A-Y

Tod paused, gauging their condition before adding:

S-T-A-Y H-E-R-E

His light swept toward the water beneath his dock.

I C-H-E-C-K O-N Y-O-U

The colony needed to conserve energy, minimize stress. Daily communication would allow Tod to monitor their condition until their journey began.

W-E S-T-A-Y, they responded, their formation settling into a peaceful arrangement beneath the dock's shadow.

After a moment's hesitation, they added:

W-E T-R-U-S-T Y-O-U

The words hit Tod like a physical blow. Trust. From beings he hadn't known existed two days ago. Trust earned not through grand gestures but through the simple act of noticing them when no one else had, through his willingness to help when they were lost.

The weight of their faith settled across his shoulders—crushing and beautiful simultaneously. These intelligent beings had placed their survival in his hands. Their lives now depended on his knowledge of coastal waters, his boat's reliability, his judgment about weather and tides.

Tod lowered the flashlight, his final message simple:

I W-I-L-L N-O-T F-A-I-L Y-O-U

As he stood to leave, the colony formed a perfect circle beneath the dock, their light pulsing in that now-familiar seven-second rhythm. A farewell for tonight, but also a promise. They would be waiting tomorrow, and Tod would return—the first human entrusted with guiding these remarkable beings home.

THE PRACTICAL DISCUSSIONS of navigation complete, Tod remained on his knees at the dock's edge. Silence enveloped the night, broken only by gentle lapping of water against wood pilings and the distant call of a night heron. The colony of Light Makers settled into a loose formation below, their pulsations slowing to a peaceful rhythm.

Tod set the flashlight aside. Words—even in Morse code—suddenly felt inadequate. He simply watched them, and they seemed to watch him in return, their collective attention focused upward through the water's surface.

Almost unconsciously, Tod extended his hand toward the water, palm down, hovering inches above the surface. He didn't break the plane, just held it there in a gesture that felt strangely natural despite its unusual circumstances.

One Light Maker detached from the group, rising slowly through the water. It approached the surface directly beneath Tod's outstretched hand, suspended maybe six inches below. Its luminescence brightened slightly, pulsing in a gentle rhythm unlike the structured Morse code they'd been using. This wasn't communication—at least not language. It was simply... presence.

A subtle warmth radiated upward against Tod's palm. The bioluminescent organs within the creature generated not just light but heat, creating a connection that bridged the barrier between their worlds without physical contact.

Something indescribable passed between them in that moment—an understanding that transcended language or symbols. Tod felt it with absolute certainty, the way you recognize being seen by another conscious mind.

The Light Maker pulsed clearly: "F-R-I-E-N-D"

"Friends," Tod whispered aloud, his voice barely audible.

The creature's light intensified briefly, then spelled out: "F-R-I-E-N-D-S"

Tod recognized the distinction immediately. Not just acknowledgment of his word, but a relationship. Plural. Mutual. They weren't specimen and researcher. Not human and alien. Not even rescuer and rescued. They were friends across an impossible gulf of evolution and environment.

The enormity of the moment washed over Tod. First contact with a non-human intelligence—something scientists had searched the stars to find—had happened in his backyard. And it wasn't about technology or power or even knowledge exchange.

It was friendship.

Tod's vision blurred with tears. The Light Maker held its position, its gentle pulsing a heartbeat-like rhythm that matched Tod's own. Two sentient beings from entirely different worlds, connected in the simplest, most profound way possible.

THE LIGHT MAKER'S GLOW pulsed three times in succession before dipping slightly back toward its colony. A new message flickered through the water:

"R-E-S-T N-O-W"

Then: "S-E-E Y-O-U T-O-M-O-R-R-O-W"

The colony began to sink deeper beneath the dock, their collective glow diminishing but not disappearing entirely. They weren't leaving—just settling for the night, finding shelter in the shadows beneath his dock. Protected. Close.

Tod stood slowly, his knees and back protesting after kneeling so long on hard wood. His body felt twice its age, every joint stiff and uncooperative. He picked up his flashlight, its beam now unnecessary and almost intrusive in the sacred quiet of the moment.

He walked back along the dock toward his house, footsteps hollow against weathered planks. At the shoreline, Tod turned and looked back. The faint blue-white glow remained visible beneath the water's surface—a living constellation temporarily at rest in the sanctuary of his dock.

Inside his workshop, Tod slumped onto his bench stool. The equipment that had detected those first mysterious signals sat dark and silent around him. The oscilloscope screen where he'd first seen those rhythmic pulses was now blank, yet the memory of those waveforms seemed permanently burned into his vision.

This morning, he'd been tracking an anomalous signal.

Tonight, he'd made first contact with an intelligent species.

Tomorrow, he would begin preparations to save them.

Eighteen hours had demolished and reconstructed his entire understanding of the world. The universe wasn't empty—it was teeming with consciousness in places humans never thought to look.

The wound at his temple throbbed, a persistent reminder of his near-death experience. His body craved sleep, but his mind raced with everything that needed doing tomorrow: studying navigation charts, planning the precise route through the channels, checking weather patterns, preparing his boat.

Could he really guide an entire colony of alien beings through miles of dangerous shallow water to the safety of the Gulf? What if he failed them?

The weight of their trust pressed down on him. "WE TRUST YOU," they had said. Not a request. A statement of complete faith.

He had to succeed. There was no alternative.

Tod's body finally betrayed his racing mind, pulling him toward the worn couch against the workshop wall. He collapsed onto it without bothering to turn off the lights or change his clothes.

Sleep took him instantly, as though he'd been drugged. In his dreams, patterns of light pulsed through dark water, calling him deeper, showing him things no human had ever seen.

Chapter 4

Tod woke with a violent start, his heart hammering against his ribs. Sunlight streamed through the workshop windows, casting geometric patterns across his cluttered workspace. He was still dressed in yesterday's clothes, his body stiff from a night on the too-small couch. The gash on his temple throbbed with a dull, persistent ache.

For a disorienting moment, fragments of strange dreams and memories collided in his mind—underwater breathing, pulsing lights, conversations through Morse code. Had it all been real? Or was it just the product of a concussion and an overactive imagination?

Tod pushed himself upright with a groan, wincing at the collection of aches that announced themselves from various parts of his body. He stumbled to the window, squinting against the morning glare across Copano Bay. The water lay flat and innocent in the morning light. His dock extended into the calm waters—empty, ordinary. No mysterious blue-white glow. No sign of anything unusual.

"Did that actually happen?" he whispered, pressing his palm against the cool glass.

His phone buzzed on the workbench where he'd left it charging. Tod shuffled over, noting the time—7:30 AM. The screen showed seven missed calls, three voicemails, and a dozen text messages. Most from Barney, growing increasingly concerned after Tod's radio silence yesterday.

Below the notifications sat three new email alerts from his charter website's booking system. Business continued, oblivious to his cosmic revelation. Tod reflexively opened his calendar app, the captain's habit of checking schedules too ingrained to ignore.

His stomach dropped. Two charters were scheduled this week—one tomorrow morning, another three days out. But worse, the day he'd promised the Light Speakers—just two days from now, dawn—already had two bookings. A corporate group from Austin, four executives paying premium rates for a team-building exercise. Six hundred dollars of income he'd been counting on.

Tod lowered himself onto his stool, suddenly feeling the weight of conflicting worlds. Charter Captain Tod Blackstone couldn't just cancel paying clients on a whim. But if last night was real—and he knew in his heart it was—those creatures needed him.

He stared at the digital calendar, the red dots marking his bookings seeming to pulse with the same seven-second rhythm that had changed his life. He couldn't have both. He had to choose.

TOD SHUFFLED DOWN TO the dock with a steaming mug of coffee clutched in one hand, moving stiffly as every muscle complained from yesterday's ordeal. The morning sun illuminated Copano Bay in perfect clarity, revealing nothing but normal, murky green-brown water lapping against the weathered pilings. No mysterious glow, no otherworldly presence—just the familiar Texas Gulf Coast waters he'd known his entire life.

A wave of disappointment washed over him. "They said they'd stay right here," he murmured, scanning the water's surface. The logical part of his brain began assembling alternative explanations: concussion-induced hallucinations, stress, an overactive imagination fed by years of science fiction.

Tod knelt at the dock's edge, wincing as his bruised knee pressed against the weathered boards. He peered into the murky water, searching for any sign of the colony that had saved his life and communicated through pulses of light. Nothing broke the ordinary surface—just floating bits of seagrass and the occasional small fish darting through the shallows.

"Maybe it really was just..." His words trailed off as doubt crept through his mind. The head injury could explain everything: underwater breathing, light conversations, intelligent creatures that no science had ever documented.

He was about to push himself back to his feet when something caught his eye—a faint shimmer beneath the surface, barely perceptible in the bright daylight. Tod froze, hardly daring to breathe as he leaned closer. There, several feet below, subtle movement disturbed the water in a coordinated pattern. Not random currents, but deliberate motion.

One of the shapes rose slightly, and Tod could just make out the dim pulse of bioluminescence—nearly washed out by sunlight but unmistakably forming a pattern: "F-R-I-E-N-D."

Relief flooded through Tod's body. They were real. Still here. Still waiting.

With trembling hands, he pulled his flashlight from his pocket, clicking it on and off in a pattern above the water: "G-O-O-D M-O-R-N-I-N-G." The beam seemed feeble against the morning light.

After a moment's hesitation, a dim, synchronized pulse responded: "G-O-O-D."

"S-E-E Y-O-U T-O-N-I-G-H-T," Tod signaled, understanding that their communication worked better in darkness.

"Y-E-S," came the barely visible response before the shapes sank deeper, disappearing from view—conserving their energy in the hostile daylight.

Tod remained kneeling, staring at the ordinary-looking water, now extraordinary in its secret. They were here. They were real. And they were waiting for him.

TOD SLUMPED INTO HIS desk chair, the computer screen's glow illuminating his troubled face. His booking calendar displayed the appointments that now stood between him and his promise to the Light Speakers. Two clients scheduled for dawn, two days from now—the exact time he needed to guide the colony to safety.

Mr. Peterson, vice president of a Houston energy firm, had booked a half-day trip at premium rates—$450 for four hours of guided fishing. The second booking, a father and son from Austin celebrating the boy's fourteenth birthday, was worth $600 for a full day. Together, they represented over a thousand dollars—mortgage money, boat maintenance funds, and groceries for the month.

"That's over a thousand dollars," Tod whispered to the empty room. "I need that money."

His cursor hovered over the entries as the reality of his situation sank in. The Light Speakers were weakening in Copano Bay's warm, bright waters. They had saved his life without hesitation, pulling him from certain drowning.

"But they'll die without help," he muttered.

Tod pulled up his calendar, scanning later dates. Could he push the rescue? Postpone until after these charters?

"No," he said firmly, remembering their message. Two, maybe three days maximum. The clock was ticking with each passing hour.

His fingers drummed against the desk. What excuse could possibly justify canceling on short notice? Equipment failure? Personal emergency? Whatever he chose would damage his reputation—charter captains lived and died by reliability.

Tod glanced toward the bay window, picturing the colony beneath his dock, waiting patiently, growing weaker by the hour. Their message echoed in his memory: "WE TRUST YOU."

Something crystallized inside him. Some choices transcended profit.

His fingers moved decisively across the keyboard, composing the first email to Mr. Peterson: "I deeply regret to inform you that I must cancel our scheduled charter due to unexpected equipment failure. Safety concerns prevent me from operating until repairs are complete. I sincerely apologize for this inconvenience and will process your full refund immediately. Please let me know if you would like to reschedule for a future date."

The second email to the father and son mirrored the first, with an added note of regret about missing the birthday celebration.

Tod's cursor hovered over "Send" for both messages. One click would erase a thousand dollars. One click would honor his commitment to beings who had placed their lives in his hands.

He took a deep breath and clicked.

Done.

The weight of lost income settled like a stone in his stomach even as something lighter—something right—lifted in his chest. Two contradictory feelings occupied the same moment: the practical anxiety of money gone and the deeper certainty of having made the only choice he could live with.

TOD HUNCHED OVER THE navigation charts spread across his workbench, pencil marking potential routes through Copano Bay. The morning sunlight streamed through the workshop windows as he measured distances between channels, noting depths and calculating tidal flows. His finger traced the safest path to the

Gulf—avoiding the shallowest stretches where the Light Speakers might be vulnerable.

"Five miles to the Intracoastal, then another five to Port Aransas Pass," he muttered, making notations on tide charts. "If we leave at dawn, we'll catch the outgoing tide."

A sharp knock interrupted his concentration.

"Tod? You in there?"

Barney's voice. Tod's heart jumped into his throat. Of all the times for a visit—he wasn't prepared to explain any of this. What could he possibly say?

Reluctantly, Tod crossed the workshop and pulled open the door. Barney stood on the threshold, concern etched into the lines around his eyes.

"You never called back yesterday. Lost radio contact, then nothing. You okay?"

Tod suddenly understood—Barney had been worried when radio communication dropped during the squall. The realization made him feel guilty for not checking in.

Barney's eyes narrowed, fixing on the angry red gash at Tod's temple. "Jesus, Tod. What happened?"

"Accident on the boat. Hit my head. I'm fine." Tod's hand automatically rose to cover the wound.

"You look like hell. And you're acting weird." Barney's gaze shifted past Tod to the workshop—the scattered charts, the hastily made notes.

"Just tired. Long day." Tod positioned himself to block the view.

Barney crossed his arms. "You sure? Because I'm getting worried about you. First that crazy signal you were chasing, then radio silence in the middle of a storm, now this." He gestured toward Tod's injury.

Tod felt his resolve crumbling. This was Barney—his friend for fifteen years. The weight of everything he'd experienced in the last twenty-four hours suddenly felt too heavy to bear alone.

A beat of silence hung between them.

"Come in," Tod said finally. "I need to tell you something."

Barney stepped inside, concern and curiosity mingling in his expression as he settled into the worn chair beside the workbench. His eyes took in the charts marked with unusual routes, the equipment modifications scattered across the desk, and Tod's exhausted face.

"I'm listening," he said quietly.

TOD PACED THE WORKSHOP, hands flexing as he struggled to find the right words. The magnitude of what he needed to explain felt impossible to convey.

"You're going to think I'm insane," he finally said, stopping to face Barney directly.

Barney leaned back in the chair, his expression carefully neutral. "Try me."

Tod took a deep breath and began. He described the strange signal detection, the modifications to his antenna, the ill-fated boat trip, and the accident during the squall. The story poured out in halting sentences, each detail sounding more implausible than the last.

Barney's face shifted from curiosity to alarm. "Wait—you fell overboard? During that storm? Tod, you almost drowned!"

"No. Listen." Tod held up his hand. "Something saved me."

He described waking up underwater, surrounded by basketball-sized glowing creatures. How he could somehow breathe eighteen feet beneath the surface. The dome of luminous bodies. Their intelligence. Their communication through light patterns.

Barney's expression transformed from concern to outright skepticism. His eyes kept returning to Tod's head wound.

"Tod... you hit your head pretty hard..." he said carefully.

Tod had anticipated this reaction. He nodded, resignation on his face. "I know how it sounds. But they're real, Barney. They communicate in Morse code. They call themselves the Light Speakers. They're intelligent—sentient—and they're stranded here. The hurricane pushed them into shallow water, and they're dying."

"Bioluminescent organisms? Sure, they exist. Intelligent? Tod..." Barney shook his head.

"They're at my dock right now. Come see."

Barney hesitated, clearly uncertain whether to humor a friend with possible brain damage or outright challenge his delusion.

"Tonight," Tod said firmly. "They communicate better in darkness. Meet me at 10 PM. You'll see for yourself."

After a long moment, Barney nodded. "Alright. Tonight." His tone betrayed his real thoughts—he was humoring Tod, probably planning to convince him to see a doctor after this dock visit revealed nothing unusual.

Tod recognized the look. He wasn't being believed, but he didn't need belief right now—he just needed Barney to show up. The Light Speakers would do the convincing themselves.

"Thank you," Tod said quietly. "Just... keep an open mind."

AFTER BARNEY LEFT, Tod unrolled his nautical charts across the workbench, weighing down the corners with fishing weights. He traced his finger along the blue expanse that represented their journey—from his dock in Copano Bay, through Aransas Bay, and finally to the deep waters of the Gulf of Mexico.

The route was straightforward but fraught with challenges. Tod uncapped a red marker and began plotting the course, muttering details to himself as he worked.

"We'll need to leave with the outgoing tide," he said, circling his dock and drawing a line through the deeper channels. His finger paused at the Copano Bay Causeway where Highway 35 bridged the water. "Under the causeway, then into Aransas Bay where we'll have more depth to work with."

Tod checked the tide charts pinned to his wall. Tomorrow's outgoing tide would begin around 5:15 AM—perfect timing for a dawn departure.

He jotted notes on a yellow legal pad:

The greatest unknowns were the Light Speakers themselves. Tod tapped his pen against the pad.

"How fast can they swim?" he wondered, adding another note:

Tod pulled up the weather forecast on his phone—clear conditions predicted to hold through tomorrow. Marine traffic reports showed typical patterns; early morning should have minimal boat traffic.

His eyes followed the red line he'd drawn from the harbor, past Harbor Island, through Aransas Pass and into open water. Ten miles offshore, the depth would finally reach over 100 feet—a sanctuary for the creatures accustomed to cold depths.

A sudden realization struck him. He hadn't tested whether the Light Speakers could keep pace with his boat. What if they tired halfway? What if the currents separated them?

Tod added a final note:

He stood back, surveying the marked charts and his growing list of preparations. This wasn't just a fishing trip; it was a rescue mission. Lives depended on his knowledge of these waters—lives of beings who had trusted him above all others.

The enormity of the responsibility settled on his shoulders as he reviewed the route once more, looking for any hazards he might have missed.

AT TWO O'CLOCK, TOD carried a clipboard with a handwritten checklist down to his dock. The familiar weight of his boat keys jingled in his pocket. He boarded K5HUX with practiced ease, setting the clipboard on the console.

"Alright, let's get you ready," he murmured to the boat as he always did before important charters.

Tod approached the preparation with methodical precision. First, he checked the fuel gauge—three-quarters full wouldn't be enough. He retrieved the fuel cans from his storage shed and carefully filled the tank to capacity, all sixty gallons. No room for error on this journey.

He moved to the engine compartment, lifting the hatch and inspecting the Yamaha outboard's vitals—oil level perfect, coolant full, belt tension just right. He ran his fingers along hose connections, ensuring everything was tight and secure.

"Safety gear," Tod muttered, checking items off his list. He verified each life jacket, tested the inflation mechanism on his throwable cushion, confirmed his flares hadn't expired, and made sure the fire extinguisher gauge showed full pressure. The first aid kit received additional supplies—extra bandages, antiseptic, and pain relievers.

At the console, Tod powered up the electronics one by one. The GPS blinked to life, displaying his position with satellite precision. His fish finder and depth sounder both functioned perfectly, though tomorrow they'd serve a different purpose than finding speckled trout.

"Navigation lights," he said, flipping switches to confirm the red and green running lights illuminated properly. He'd need them in the pre-dawn darkness.

Tod added redundancies for every critical system—handheld GPS with fresh batteries, backup VHF radio, three different flashlights. Into a waterproof bag went extra supplies: bottled water, energy bars, a thermal blanket, and an emergency beacon.

"Morning, Tod!" called Harry Thompson from the neighboring dock. "Getting ready for a charter?"

Tod looked up and waved. "Early morning trip tomorrow. Want to be prepared."

"You're always prepared, Tod. That's why folks book with you," Harry replied with a nod of approval.

"Appreciate that," Tod said, returning to his checklist while Harry continued his walk.

Tod's hands moved over his toolkit, verifying each tool was present. He checked his supply of spare parts—propeller, shear pins, fuses, spark plugs. Everything had its place, each item potentially crucial.

As the afternoon sun beat down on the deck, Tod felt a strange calm settle over him. This wasn't just another fishing trip—it was perhaps the most important journey of his life. Yet the familiar ritual of preparation centered him. He knew these waters. He knew this boat. Whatever lay ahead, he would be ready.

AT SIX IN THE EVENING, Tod returned to the dock as the sun began its descent toward the horizon. Golden light spread across Copano Bay, creating perfect conditions for communicating with the Light Speakers—bright enough to see but dim enough for their bioluminescence to be visible.

Tod carried his flashlight and a small waterproof notebook with questions written in neat block letters. He settled at the edge of the dock, legs dangling over the water, and waited.

The bay's surface remained still for several minutes. Then, almost imperceptibly at first, a blue-white glow emerged from the depths. The light intensified as dozens of translucent, basketball-sized beings rose toward the surface. Tod counted at least thirty visible specimens—more than last night, or perhaps they were simply more visible in the fading daylight.

Tod flashed his light in greeting: "G-O-O-D E-V-E-N-I-N-G"

The colony pulsed in unison, their light forming perfect Morse code: "F-R-I-E-N-D K-5-H-U-X"

Tod began working through his prepared questions. "H-O-W F-A-S-T C-A-N Y-O-U S-W-I-M"

The Light Speakers' response came quickly: "F-A-S-T A-S B-O-A-T"

Tod frowned, seeking clarification. "W-H-A-T S-P-E-E-D"

Their answer made him smile with understanding: "S-L-O-W B-O-A-T"

He nodded to himself. They could match a slow cruising speed, not his outboard at full throttle. His calculations of 2-6 mph would work perfectly.

"H-O-W L-O-N-G C-A-N Y-O-U S-W-I-M" Tod signaled next.

"M-A-N-Y H-O-U-R-S" came the reassuring response.

Tod hesitated before the next question, knowing its importance. "A-R-E Y-O-U W-E-A-K-E-R T-O-D-A-Y"

There was a pause, longer than their usual quick replies. Finally, the colony pulsed: "Y-E-S S-O-M-E"

The confirmation tightened something in Tod's chest. Their condition was deteriorating as expected. Two days remained at most.

"T-W-O D-A-Y-S D-A-W-N W-E G-O" Tod signaled with firm, crisp flashes.

"R-E-A-D-Y" the colony responded with steady, unwavering light.

Tod proceeded to explain the basics of their route—through the channel, into Aransas Bay, past the jetties, and into the Gulf. He wasn't sure how much they comprehended about human waterways, but they needed to understand the journey ahead.

"I W-I-L-L L-E-A-D Y-O-U S-A-F-E" Tod promised, the flashlight steady in his hand.

The Light Speakers formed a perfect circle beneath him, their collective response simple but profound: "W-E T-R-U-S-T"

In the gathering dusk, Tod watched their lights pulse in that now-familiar seven-second rhythm. The practical details were settled. Now they waited for dawn.

TOD LEANED AGAINST a piling, checking his watch for the third time in five minutes. The digital face read 9:58 PM. Barney would be punctual—he always was.

The night had settled completely over Copano Bay, stars sprinkled across the clear sky above. A perfect night for a revelation. Tod gripped his flashlight, rehearsing what to say when Barney arrived. The Light Speakers had retreated deeper after their conversation, conserving energy until they were needed.

Headlights swept across the yard as Barney's pickup pulled in. Tod took a deep breath.

"Hey there, Captain Concussion," Barney called, walking down to the dock. He carried a small first aid kit and what looked suspiciously like a thermos of coffee. "How's the head?"

"Better," Tod replied. "Thanks for coming."

Barney surveyed the empty dock, then the dark water. His expression mixed concern and indulgence. "So... where are these imaginary friends of yours?"

Tod didn't take the bait. "Just watch."

"Watch what, exactly?" Barney folded his arms.

Tod knelt at the dock's edge and flashed his light in a pattern: "C-O-M-E"

For a long moment, nothing happened. Tod felt sweat bead on his forehead despite the cool evening air.

Then it began—a faint blue-white glow from the depths, spreading outward like underwater dawn.

"What the..." Barney stepped back, then forward again, squinting.

The light intensified as dozens of translucent forms rose toward the surface. Their coordinated movement created ripples in the dark water as they arranged themselves in their now-familiar formation.

The first flash came, then another, then dozens in perfect synchronization.

"H-E-L-L-O B-A-R-N-E-Y"

Barney froze, mouth hanging open. The color drained from his face as he stared at the pulsing lights spelling his name.

"Holy shit. Tod. Holy SHIT."

"Told you," Tod said quietly.

"That's... they're... how do they—" Barney stumbled over his words, pointing at the water with a shaking hand.

Tod flashed his light again: "M-Y F-R-I-E-N-D B-A-R-N-E-Y"

The colony responded immediately: "F-R-I-E-N-D O-F K-5-H-U-X F-R-I-E-N-D O-F U-S"

Barney sat down hard on the dock, legs seemingly unable to support him. "I need a minute."

Tod nodded, remembering his own shock. He gave Barney space, watching his friend's expressions cycle through disbelief, wonder, and finally acceptance as the Light Speakers continued their synchronized display below.

After several minutes, Barney took a deep breath. "Okay. Okay." He turned to Tod with newfound resolve. "What do they need?"

Tod explained the rescue plan—the dawn departure, the channel route, the deep water destination.

Barney nodded slowly, processing. "And you're going to do this alone?"

"Was planning to."

"Not anymore." Barney's voice found its strength again. "How can I help?"

The Light Speakers pulsed beneath them, their circle widening to include both men in their glow.

TOD AND BARNEY RETREATED from the dock to the workshop, leaving the Light Speakers to rest beneath the water's surface. The fluorescent lights hummed overhead as Tod spread his nautical charts across the workbench.

Barney paced the small space, hands tucked into his pockets. He stopped suddenly, turning to Tod with wide eyes.

"Intelligent bioluminescent aliens. In Copano Bay." He shook his head in disbelief. "Right here. Under your dock."

Tod nodded, tracing the planned route with his finger. "I know. I'm still processing too."

"So you're taking your boat, leading them ten miles offshore. Alone." Barney's voice carried a note of concern that wasn't there before.

"That's the plan."

Barney frowned, crossing his arms. "What if something goes wrong? Engine trouble? Weather change? You get lost?"

Tod looked up from the chart, realizing he hadn't considered a backup plan. The safety of the Light Speakers had consumed his thoughts so completely that he'd overlooked his own.

"I'll track you," Barney said firmly. "We set up a radio schedule. Every fifteen minutes you check in."

"You don't have to—"

"Shut up." Barney cut him off. "You almost died two days ago. I'm not letting you go alone."

They spent the next twenty minutes establishing a communication protocol: VHF marine radio on Channel 72—rarely monitored by recreational boaters. Tod would check in every fifteen minutes with his position and status.

"If there's trouble, say 'equipment malfunction,'" Barney suggested. "I'll be at my house in Port Lavaca, monitoring. If you miss even one check-in, I'm calling the Coast Guard."

Tod nodded, grateful for his friend's thoroughness. The radio schedule gave structure to what had felt like an impossible task.

"And if someone else discovers them?" Barney asked, voicing the concern Tod had been avoiding.

Tod sighed, rubbing his temple where the wound still throbbed. "I don't know. Hope no one's out there at dawn."

"You're risking a lot."

Tod looked through the window toward the dock where the Light Speakers waited. "They saved my life. Worth the risk."

Barney studied Tod for a moment, then nodded. "Then let's make sure you succeed."

The simple statement carried the weight of true friendship. In the quiet workshop, with charts spread before them and plans carefully laid, Tod felt the first real sense of confidence since this strange journey began. Whatever happened tomorrow, he wouldn't face it alone.

TOD LAY IN BED STARING at the ceiling, sleep refusing to come despite his exhaustion. The digital clock on his nightstand blinked 11:30 PM in harsh red numerals. Dawn was less than six hours away.

He closed his eyes and ran through his mental checklist for the tenth time. The boat was ready—fueled, maintained, electronics triple-checked. His route was carefully planned and memorized, each channel and marker accounted for. Weather forecasts remained favorable—clear skies, light winds from the southeast at five to seven knots. The tide would turn at 5:15 AM, giving them a perfect window to ride the outgoing current through the channel. Barney was standing by, radio schedule confirmed. And beneath his dock, the Light Speakers waited, trusting him with their lives.

But what if something went wrong?

Engine failure. Tod had packed spare parts—fuel filter, spark plugs, fuses, even a small backup trolling motor. He'd cleaned the fuel lines yesterday.

Weather turning. He'd checked three different forecasts, all showing stable conditions until late afternoon.

The Light Speakers falling behind. They'd confirmed they could match his boat at slow speed for the required distance.

Discovery by others. Dawn on a weekday meant minimal traffic. Most fishing charters wouldn't launch until after sunrise.

Separation in open water. He'd keep his speed steady and stay within their visual range.

Getting lost in the channels. Tod almost smiled at this thought. He knew these waterways better than the streets of Rockport.

Coast Guard intervention. He was a licensed captain with all proper credentials. A routine fishing trip required no special explanation.

Tod exhaled slowly, realizing he'd addressed everything within his control. The rest was trust—in himself, in the Light Speakers, in the plan they'd created together.

His thoughts drifted to his parents in San Antonio. Should he call them? Tell them about the extraordinary beings he'd discovered? The words would sound insane over the phone.

After, he decided. If successful, he'd drive to San Antonio and tell them everything face-to-face. If not... they wouldn't need to know how their son had risked everything for creatures from another world.

Tod took a deep breath and felt the tension slowly release from his shoulders. He'd done everything possible to prepare. Sleep began to tug at the edges of his consciousness, his breathing deepened.

His final thought before drifting off was simple yet profound: "Tomorrow, I lead them home."

THE ALARM PIERCED THE darkness at 4:30 AM, earlier than even Tod's usual pre-charter wake-up. His hand silenced it before the second beep. No drowsiness, no desire to linger beneath the warm covers—just immediate, sharp alertness.

Tod dressed methodically, layering against the morning chill: moisture-wicking base layer, flannel shirt, light jacket. He pulled on his worn Ariat boots and grabbed his rain jacket from the hook by the door. Outside, the temperature would hover in the low sixties until the sun took full control of the day.

His phone screen glowed in the darkness. Weather update: clear skies, southeast winds at six knots, high tide at 5:07 AM. Perfect conditions. A text from Barney had arrived at 4:15: "Ready when you are." The man hadn't slept either.

In the kitchen, Tod filled his thermos with coffee, hot and black. He paused at the window overlooking the bay. Pre-dawn darkness shrouded everything, but he could make out a faint blue-white glow at his dock. They were waiting for him.

His heart thundered in his chest. This was it—the culmination of days that had altered his understanding of the world forever.

Tod gathered his equipment with practiced efficiency: VHF radio clipped to his belt, handheld HAM unit in his jacket pocket, waterproof flashlight, laminated chart, water bottles, energy bars. Everything had its place, every contingency covered.

The wooden dock creaked under his footsteps as he walked toward the water. Above him, stars still punctured the sky, though the eastern horizon had begun to soften with the barest suggestion of dawn. His center console boat sat ready on the lift, silhouetted against the water.

Below the surface, the Light Speakers had risen to meet him, their gentle blue-white radiance illuminating the dock pilings. Tod aimed his flashlight, flashing deliberately: "G-O-O-D M-O-R-N-I-N-G."

They responded immediately: "T-O-D-A-Y."

"Y-E-S T-O-D-A-Y," Tod confirmed.

"R-E-A-D-Y," they signaled.

"M-E T-O-O," he answered.

Tod boarded his vessel, settling into the familiar captain's position. The Yamaha outboard purred to life with a reassuring rumble. He lowered the boat lift slowly, checking his instruments as the hull settled into the water—fuel gauge full, GPS powered and tracking, VHF set to Channel 72, depth sounder painting a picture of the bottom.

"K5HUX to W5BAR, radio check," Tod spoke into the microphone.

Barney's voice came through clearly: "Loud and clear, Tod. Be safe out there."

"Will do. First check-in at 5:45."

The Light Speakers circled near the boat, their forms pulsing with anticipation beneath the surface. Tod looked eastward—the sky had begun its transformation, darkness yielding to a deep indigo that would soon give way to dawn's palette.

He drew a deep breath, filling his lungs with cool morning air.

"Okay, friends. Let's get you home."

Tod eased the throttle forward, the boat responding with gentle momentum. Behind him, the Light Speakers followed, their collective glow keeping perfect pace just below the surface.

As boat and beings moved away from the dock and into Copano Bay, the first true light of day touched the eastern horizon.

The journey had begun.

Chapter 5

Tod eased the throttle forward, maintaining a gentle idle speed of just under three knots. The boat sliced through the glassy surface of Copano Bay, leaving a perfect V-shaped wake that spread behind them like unfurling wings. Dawn approached with quiet determination, painting the eastern horizon in deepening shades of pink and orange that reflected on the water's mirrored surface.

Below the hull, a living cloud of blue-white light moved in perfect formation. The Light Speakers maintained their position without visible effort, hundreds of translucent bodies synchronized as though guided by a single mind. From above, they appeared as a ghostly reflection of the stars now fading with morning's approach.

Tod glanced back at his property growing smaller in the distance. His antenna tower stood in stark silhouette against the brightening sky, the Long-John Yagi that had first detected these beings now pointing uselessly toward the horizon. The dock, his workshop, his home—all the familiar landmarks of his life—receded with each passing moment.

This is it, he thought. No turning back now.

The weight of the responsibility settled on him as comfortably as his captain's responsibilities always did. His right hand rested steady on the throttle while his left traced their route on the laminated chart secured to the console. Ahead, the first red and green markers indicated the channel entrance that would guide them toward Aransas Bay.

Tod checked the depth sounder: 12 feet beneath the keel, sandy bottom clearly defined on the display. But between the bottom and his boat floated an unusual cloud of contacts—the Light Speakers registering as a diffuse, moving mass that the sonar couldn't properly interpret.

"5:32," Tod noted aloud, checking his watch. "Perfect timing."

The tide had begun its outward flow, invisible currents that would help carry them all to deeper water. His planning had been precise, the execution flawless so far. The Light Speakers kept perfect pace, neither struggling to catch up nor restlessly surging ahead.

Tod breathed deeply, filling his lungs with the salt-tinged morning air. The responsibility felt enormous yet somehow right—like something he'd been preparing for without knowing it.

"Here we go," he whispered, eyes fixed on the channel ahead as boat and beings moved together toward the first waypoint, leaving the safety of the familiar behind.

THE VHF RADIO CRACKLED to life at precisely 5:45 AM, breaking the morning stillness. Tod reached for the handset, his movements practiced and efficient.

"K5HUX to W5BAR, fifteen-minute check," he said, the formal call signs providing a comfortable structure in the strangeness of this mission.

Barney's voice came back instantly, clear and steady across the airwaves: "W5BAR receiving. Status?"

"Departed on schedule, 5:30. Currently heading toward Copano channel. Conditions excellent. They're keeping pace perfectly." Tod glanced down at the blue-white glow beneath his hull, the colony moving with an almost supernatural precision below the water's surface.

"Any other traffic?" Barney asked.

Tod swept his gaze across the bay, scanning the horizon in all directions. The world belonged exclusively to him and the Light Speakers at this hour—exactly as planned.

"Negative. We're alone out here."

"Weather holding?"

Tod took a moment to assess the conditions. The sky had lightened to a pale blue with streaks of gold where the sun approached. Only the thinnest wisps of clouds decorated the horizon. The water remained glassy with just enough breeze to create gentle ripples—nothing that would impede their journey.

"Affirmative. Looking good."

"Stay safe, buddy. Next check 6:00."

"Roger. K5HUX clear." Tod set the handset back in its cradle.

A quiet sense of reassurance settled over him. Despite the extraordinary circumstances—guiding an unknown species through treacherous waters—the familiar rhythm of radio protocols and Barney's steady presence on the other end grounded him. He wasn't physically alone, but neither was he truly alone.

Ahead, the channel markers came into view—red and green buoys marking the safe passage through shallower waters. The navigation would require precise attention now. Tod adjusted his course slightly, aligning the bow directly between the markers. The depth would decrease soon, funneling them through the narrowest part of their journey.

Below, the Light Speakers maintained their formation, their collective glow shifting subtly as they approached the channel. Tod wondered if they sensed the changing depth, the narrowing of their path. Their movements suggested awareness, anticipation.

He gripped the wheel more firmly, eyes focused on the channel markers. The real challenge began here—threading the needle through Copano's channels while keeping his unusual passengers safe and unseen. The morning light strengthened, making the Light

Speakers less visible beneath the surface, a small blessing as they entered more trafficked waters.

THE GREEN AND RED BUOYS emerged from the morning mist like sentries guarding the narrow channel. Tod steered his boat with practiced precision between them, following the age-old maritime rule: "red right returning" – keeping the red buoys to his right as they headed toward the open sea. The markers stood tall against the lightening sky, their reflective paint catching the first true rays of the rising sun.

"Green three," Tod murmured to himself, ticking off the waypoints. His eyes darted between the water ahead and the depth sounder display. The numbers fluctuated rapidly: 10 feet... 8 feet... back to 12 feet as they passed over the underwater contours of Copano Bay.

Tod eased back on the throttle, maintaining a careful three miles per hour. One wrong move here could ground them on hidden oyster reefs or sandbanks that flanked the channel. He'd navigated these waters hundreds of times, but never with such precious cargo following in his wake.

Below, the Light Speakers adjusted their formation with seamless coordination. As the channel narrowed, they compressed their ranks, staying perfectly centered in the deeper water. When the depth dropped suddenly to seven feet, the entire colony descended further, maintaining a safe distance from the treacherous shallows.

"Smart," Tod whispered, genuinely impressed. "You understand."

The colony's intelligence was evident in every movement – they weren't merely following; they were reading the underwater topography, adapting to it with a fluid grace no human swimmer could match.

Dawn had fully broken now. The sky blazed with spectacular oranges and pinks, light spilling across the water's surface in a dazzling display. With each passing minute, the Light Speakers' blue-white glow became less pronounced, the strengthening daylight diminishing their bioluminescence. They remained visible as a ghostly cloud beneath the surface, but the magical brilliance of their nighttime display had faded.

"Red four," Tod counted as they passed the next marker. "Green five."

This channel had been Tod's livelihood for years – guiding eager tourists and fishermen to the best spots, pointing out herons and pelicans, sharing the bay's secrets. Today, those familiar waters had transformed into something entirely different – a rescue route for beings unknown to science, intelligent creatures trusting him with their lives.

The irony wasn't lost on Tod. He knew these waters intimately, yet had never truly known what they contained.

Ahead, the concrete spans of the Copano Bay Causeway stretched across the water like a gray rainbow, Highway 35 crossing the bay. The bridge marked their first major milestone – the gateway from Copano into Aransas Bay beyond.

THE CONCRETE SPANS of the Copano Bay Causeway loomed ahead, Highway 35 stretching across the water like a massive gray serpent. Usually bustling with traffic and lined with fishermen casting their lines from above, at this early hour the bridge stood deserted, silhouetted against the dawn sky.

Tod eased back on the throttle, dropping their speed even further. He'd always approached bridges with extra caution—currents often changed unpredictably beneath these structures, and debris could collect around the pilings.

"Taking it slow through here," he murmured, though no one could hear.

Beneath the boat, the Light Speakers compressed their formation further, clustering tightly below the hull. Tod couldn't tell if they were nervous about the bridge or simply following his lead as the boat slowed. Their behavior seemed almost protective—staying close as if sensing potential danger.

The shadow of the causeway fell over them, momentarily plunging boat and beings into relative darkness. Tod glanced upward at the underbelly of the bridge—barnacle-encrusted concrete pilings, steel support structures, and the occasional abandoned fishing line dangling from above. The causeway wasn't high—maybe fifteen feet above the water's surface.

A sobering thought struck Tod. If anyone stood on that bridge right now and looked down, they'd see his boat—and beneath it, an unmistakable glowing cloud moving with purpose. The Light Speakers' bioluminescence was subdued in daylight, but still visible from above.

He scanned the railings. Empty. Not even a single early-rising fisherman had claimed a spot. Lucky.

They emerged from beneath the causeway, back into golden morning light. Aransas Bay opened before them—wider, deeper waters stretching toward the distant barrier islands. The water beneath the keel read sixteen feet now, giving the Light Speakers more room to maneuver.

The radio crackled to life: "K5HUX, you're late for check-in." Barney's voice carried a hint of concern.

Tod glanced at his watch with surprise: 6:03. He'd been so focused on navigating under the bridge that he'd forgotten the time.

"W5BAR, K5HUX. Sorry. Passing under causeway. All good."

"Copy. Next check 6:15," Barney responded, relief evident in his voice.

Tod placed the handset back in its cradle. They had passed a significant milestone—out of Copano Bay and into Aransas Bay now. They were halfway to the Gulf, making steady progress with no complications.

Below, the Light Speakers spread out in the deeper water, their formation relaxing as they left the confines of the channel behind. Tod watched their movements with growing respect. These beings understood navigation on an instinctive level, reading water in ways humans could only approximate with instruments.

Ahead lay open water and the promise of safety beyond.

THE WATERS OF ARANSAS Bay sprawled before Tod, vast and welcoming compared to the narrow channel they'd left behind. Here the water deepened to nearly thirty feet, allowing the Light Speakers to spread out beneath and around his boat. The colony no longer needed to compress into a tight formation, and Tod watched in wonder as they fanned out into what appeared to be their natural traveling pattern.

The morning sun had fully crested the horizon now, casting golden light across the bay's surface. Despite the brightness of day, Tod could see the Light Speakers clearly through the water—dozens, perhaps hundreds of translucent, basketball-sized forms moving with perfect coordination. Their blue-white glow pulsed in that familiar seven-second rhythm, creating an otherworldly escort beneath his hull.

Tod throttled up slightly, bringing their speed to around four knots. The outgoing tide added another knot or so, helping carry them toward the Gulf. The Light Speakers matched the increased pace effortlessly, adjusting their formation with fluid grace.

In the distance, several fishing boats headed out to their morning spots. White wakes cut across the glassy water as captains and their clients sought redfish and speckled trout. Tod adjusted his course slightly eastward, giving the other vessels a wide berth. The last thing he needed was another boat crossing his path and spotting what followed beneath his hull.

A squadron of pelicans glided overhead before one peeled away, tucking its wings and plunging into the water with a splash. It emerged moments later with a struggling fish in its pouch. The Light Speakers seemed to register the bird's impact, briefly pulsing brighter before resuming their steady rhythm.

Tod checked his GPS: they were already four miles from his dock, with only six miles remaining to reach the deep water of the Gulf. The depth sounder read 28 feet—comfortable conditions for the Light Speakers, who moved with noticeably more vigor than they had in the shallower waters.

For the first time since they'd departed, Tod allowed himself a dangerous thought: *We might actually make it.*

He immediately pushed the thought away. Hubris had no place on the water. Countless things could still go wrong before they reached the safe depths of the Gulf. But as he scanned the perfect morning—calm waters, light breeze, and the magnificent beings traveling faithfully beneath him—hope continued to build in his chest.

Tod remained focused on the course ahead, where the distant outline of Harbor Island marked their passage to the final stretch.

TOD MAINTAINED HIS heading, one hand steady on the wheel as the Light Speakers followed in perfect synchronization beneath his hull. The morning sun sparkled across Aransas Bay's surface, the conditions almost impossibly perfect for their journey.

His momentary optimism evaporated when he spotted a vessel ahead—a commercial shrimp boat anchored directly in their path, its outriggers extended like skeletal arms against the sky. The boat sat motionless on the water, crew visible on deck.

Tod's heartbeat quickened. The Light Speakers remained clearly visible beneath his boat, their blue-white glow discernible even in morning sunlight. He rapidly calculated options. Changing course would add precious time and distance, potentially exposing the weakening colony to shallow waters longer than necessary. But continuing straight meant passing within clear view of the other vessel.

After a moment's hesitation, he held his course. *Act normal. Just another boat passing by.*

Tod adjusted his throttle, keeping his speed steady as he angled for a path about two hundred yards from the shrimper. The distance seemed vast yet insufficient all at once. Through his binoculars, he counted three crew members working with nets or equipment on the deck. Their postures suggested routine maintenance, nothing unusual.

One of the men straightened, shading his eyes against the morning glare. He spotted Tod's approaching boat and raised his arm in the universal greeting of mariners passing on open water.

Tod forced himself to return the gesture casually, willing his face into a mask of ordinary morning pleasantry while acutely aware of the extraordinary procession beneath him.

As they drew parallel at about 150 yards, Tod gripped the wheel tighter. The Light Speakers continued pulsing their seven-second rhythm, their translucent bodies visible just below the surface. Tod stared straight ahead, fighting the urge to check if the other crew noticed.

Movement caught his peripheral vision. One of the crewmen was pointing toward the water in Tod's direction, saying something to his companions. Tod's stomach plummeted. *They see them.*

The men leaned over the railing, looking at the water. Then one laughed, gesturing dismissively. The others shrugged, returning to their tasks.

Tod kept moving, maintaining his heading and speed as they passed beyond the anchored vessel. Only when they were well past did he look back. The crew had resumed their work, showing no interest in pursuit or further observation.

A long breath escaped his lungs. They'd seen something—perhaps a strange reflection or what they assumed was a school of fish—but nothing warranting investigation.

The radio crackled. "K5HUX, this is KG5ZRT. Status check, over."

Barney's voice, right on schedule, grounded Tod back to the moment.

"KG5ZRT, this is K5HUX. All clear. Making good progress. Out."

TOD GUIDED HIS VESSEL toward the northern passage around Harbor Island, the uninhabited barrier island rising like a sentinel between them and the open Gulf. Tall dunes crowned with waving sea grass created a natural windbreak, though it offered less protection with each passing minute as they approached the mouth of the bay.

"Harbor Island, north passage," Tod noted into his voice recorder. "Six thirty-five, making good progress."

The channel narrowed here, its boundaries marked by occasional buoys, their lights now redundant in the strengthening morning sunlight. Depths ranged from fifteen to twenty feet – plenty of clearance, but a natural constriction that forced the Light Speakers to compress their formation beneath him.

Tod observed through polarized glasses how the colony adjusted, their movements reflecting an ancient intelligence that understood water passages far better than any human navigator. They pulsed in perfect synchronization, a living cloud flowing through the channel like mercury.

To the south, pelicans launched from their roosting sites, gliding low over the water in morning fishing formations. The island itself remained quiet, its northern end deliberately preserved from the development that crowded Aransas Pass on the southern side.

The first proper swell lifted Tod's boat, then dropped it with a gentle splash. Another followed, then another. Two-foot waves, nothing dangerous, but a clear signal they were approaching the boundary between protected bay and open ocean. The boat rocked more emphatically now, forcing Tod to widen his stance.

"Water conditions changing," he murmured. "Getting choppy."

The Light Speakers showed no distress. If anything, they seemed to brighten, their movements becoming more fluid and natural as they encountered deeper, more dynamic water. Tod realized this must feel like approaching home for them – the return of familiar conditions after days trapped in unnaturally warm shallows.

Tod checked his watch: 6:38 AM. They'd been on the water for over an hour already. His back ached from tension, but a glance at the GPS confirmed they were nearly there – just two miles to the hundred-foot depth line where the seafloor dropped away steeply.

The horizon opened ahead, the definitive line between sky and sea that marked the Gulf of Mexico. No more islands, no more channels, just open water stretching unbroken to the curve of the Earth.

Tod felt a surge of triumph mixed with unexpected melancholy. They were going to make it. The Light Speakers would survive. But soon they would descend into depths where he couldn't follow, returning to a world humans could barely imagine.

The vessel crested another swell, and Tod caught himself smiling despite his fatigue. The Gulf beckoned ahead, endless and blue, promising safety for his unusual friends and the conclusion of the strangest, most meaningful journey of his life.

THE GULF OF MEXICO opened before them as Tod's boat finally broke free from the protective bay system. The water itself transformed—the murky green of the bay giving way to a deeper, clearer blue-green that signaled their passage into the open Gulf. Three-foot swells rolled beneath the hull in rhythmic succession, lifting and dropping the vessel in a pattern as old as the sea itself.

Tod handled the changing conditions with practiced ease, adjusting his weight and stance automatically as the boat crested each wave. His hands rested lightly on the wheel, making minor corrections rather than fighting against the water's motion.

The depth sounder's numbers climbed steadily. Thirty feet. Forty. Fifty.

"They're going deeper," Tod noted, watching the Light Speakers' formation on the display. They maintained perfect position beneath his boat but had begun a gradual descent, spreading out and dropping down as the water deepened around them. Their movements became more fluid, more natural—creatures returning to their proper element.

"Just one more mile," Tod murmured, eyes fixed on the horizon. "One more mile."

The depth continued to increase. Sixty feet. Seventy. Eighty. Still not deep enough for the Light Speakers' needs. They required the cold, pressurized environment that only true depth could provide.

Tod glanced at his GPS: 9.5 miles from his dock. They'd come so far, yet still needed to push further.

His radio crackled. "K5HUX, this is KG5ZRT. Check-in time. You there, buddy?"

"Roger that, Barney. We're almost there. Depth at eighty feet and climbing."

"Copy that. Almost home."

Morning sunlight sparkled across the water's surface, transforming each wave crest into momentary diamonds. Despite his exhaustion, Tod couldn't help but appreciate the beauty surrounding him. In the distance, the silhouettes of oil platforms stood like industrial sentinels, marking the deeper waters of the Gulf. Tod adjusted course slightly, steering toward them.

The depth sounder's numbers continued their ascent. Ninety feet. Ninety-five. One hundred.

Tod's shoulders relaxed as he throttled back to idle, letting the boat settle into the gentle rhythm of the swells. The engine's rumble softened to a purr.

"We made it," he breathed, the simple statement carrying the weight of all they'd accomplished. Below, the Light Speakers pulsed with renewed vigor, their blue-white glow visible even as they began their descent into more comfortable depths.

THE BOAT ROCKED GENTLY in the Gulf swells, engine idling with a low rumble that vibrated through the hull. Tod stood at the console, gripping the edge as he leaned over to peer into the depths below. The Light Speakers were visible as a diffuse blue-white cloud, their glow dimmed by daylight but still detectable beneath the surface.

Something changed in their formation. Instead of continuing their descent into the welcoming depths, they began rising toward the surface again, their collective movement deliberate and graceful. They were coming to say goodbye.

Tod grabbed his flashlight, squinting against the morning sun. Communication would be difficult in the bright light, but he had to try. He aimed the beam into the water and tapped out the message carefully.

"Y-O-U A-R-E H-O-M-E"

The Light Speakers' response came fainter than before, their luminescence battling against the penetrating sunlight:

"H-O-M-E Y-E-S"

Tod's throat tightened. "A-R-E Y-O-U S-A-F-E H-E-R-E"

Their reply pulsed through the water: "Y-E-S C-O-L-D D-E-E-P G-O-O-D"

His chest constricted as reality settled over him. This was it—the end of their journey together. The creatures he'd risked everything to save would soon vanish into the depths beyond human reach. The thought left an unexpected hollow space inside him.

Tod flashed again: "W-I-L-L I S-E-E Y-O-U A-G-A-I-N"

A long pause followed, the Light Speakers seemingly conferring among themselves. Finally, they responded: "Y-E-S"

Relief washed through him. "H-O-W"

"W-E R-E-M-E-M-B-E-R Y-O-U"

"W-E C-O-M-E B-A-C-K"

Not gone forever, then. The knowledge loosened something in Tod's chest.

"W-H-E-N"

Their answer surprised him: "W-H-E-N Y-O-U C-A-L-L"

Tod blinked, understanding dawning. His modified sensor—the device that had detected them in the first place. He hadn't built a permanent version yet, but the Light Speakers knew he would. They trusted that he would find a way to call across the divide between their worlds.

Tod's eyes stung. From tears? Salt spray? Both, perhaps. He wiped at them with the back of his hand, the boat rising and falling beneath him as the Light Speakers hovered below, waiting for his response.

THE LIGHT SPEAKERS rose higher in the water, ascending to just beneath the surface—closer than they'd been since Tod's rescue. Their blue-white luminescence created a shifting constellation beneath his boat, pulsing with life and intelligence.

One of them broke away from the colony, approaching the hull until it hovered mere inches below the surface. Tod knelt at the gunwale, leaning over the edge as his boat gently rocked. He extended his hand toward the water, not quite touching the surface but close enough to feel the cool vapor rising from it.

The Light Speaker directly beneath his palm began to pulse, not in the structured patterns of Morse code but in something more primal—a rhythm like breathing or a heartbeat. The light ebbed and flowed, communicating something beyond words. Tod felt warmth radiating upward, carrying sensations of recognition and gratitude that transcended language.

"Thank you for saving my life," Tod whispered, his voice barely audible above the lapping waves and idling engine. The words felt inadequate yet necessary. "Thank you for letting me save yours."

His throat tightened as he added, "Go be safe. Be well."

The Light Speaker beneath his hand flared brilliantly, a final acknowledgment that needed no translation. Then it began to descend, sinking slowly into the darker water. The others followed in perfect formation, the entire colony withdrawing into the depths that were their true home.

Tod watched their descent, transfixed by the beauty of their departure. Twenty feet down, their glow remained strong. At forty feet, they became more diffuse, their edges softening. Sixty feet deep, and they transformed into a distant nebula of light. By eighty feet, they were fading ghosts, mere suggestions against the deep blue.

Then nothing. The water below his boat returned to its natural state—just waves and filtered sunlight penetrating the upper layers. They were gone.

Tod remained at the gunwale for several long moments, staring into the empty water. Only then did the magnitude of what had transpired truly hit him. He was alone on the Gulf now, his mission complete.

He stumbled back to the console seat and sat heavily, dropping his head into his hands. His shoulders began to shake as tears came—silent at first, then in hitching breaths that he couldn't control. Relief flooded through him that they were safe, alongside the sharp ache of loss. Pride in what he'd accomplished mingled with grief that it was over. Joy and sorrow intertwined into something too complex to name.

For several minutes, Tod sat alone on his boat, rocking gently on the Gulf waters, and let it all pour out of him—the fear, the wonder, the responsibility, and finally, the release.

TOD WIPED HIS EYES with the back of his hand and took several deep breaths, feeling the salt air fill his lungs. He straightened his shoulders and reached for the radio handset.

"K5HUX to W5BAR," he said, his voice still rough around the edges.

Barney's response came immediately, tension evident in his voice. "Tod? You're late for check-in. Status?"

"Mission accomplished." Tod swallowed hard, hearing the thickness in his own voice. "They're home. I'm heading back."

A brief pause. "You okay?"

Tod gazed out at the empty horizon where the sun now hung fully above the water. "Yeah. Yeah, I am. Just... it's done."

"You did good, brother. Real good," Barney said softly. "Come home safe."

"Will do. K5HUX clear." Tod replaced the handset and stood at the helm, surveying his surroundings.

The coastline stretched in a thin, distant line to the west. Between him and solid ground lay miles of open water, the entire bay system waiting to be traversed again. The journey back would be substantial, but different now. The weight of responsibility that had pressed down on him since he'd first detected those strange pulses was gone, evaporated into the morning air.

Tod turned the wheel and put the boat in gear, pointing the bow toward Rockport. Unlike the careful, measured journey outbound, he had no reason to proceed slowly now. The incoming tide would work with him rather than against him, helping to push the vessel homeward through the channels.

He throttled up, feeling the boat respond beneath him. At twenty-five miles per hour, the hull rose onto plane, cutting efficiently through the light chop. Wind whipped across his face, carrying away the last of his tears.

Physical exhaustion began seeping into his muscles as the adrenaline that had carried him through the night and morning faded. His body felt simultaneously heavy and hollow, drained of the nervous energy that had sustained him. Yet alongside the fatigue came a profound lightness—a sense of completion.

He had done what he promised. He had guided them safely to deep water. They were home, where they belonged.

For the first time in days, Tod felt like he could truly breathe. The mystery that had consumed his every waking moment was resolved, the mission complete. He was heading home alone, but the solitude no longer felt empty. It felt earned.

The boat sped across the water, carrying its single occupant back toward the shore, the rising sun warm on his back, the wind cool on his face, and the quiet satisfaction of having done something extraordinary filling the space in between.

TOD THROTTLED DOWN as he approached his property, the familiar outline of his workshop, house, and antenna tower coming into view. The fifty-minute return trip had passed in a blur of water and sunlight. Everything looked exactly as he'd left it hours earlier, yet somehow different—as though the buildings were the same but the eyes viewing them had changed.

He navigated carefully toward the dock, cutting the engine to idle and drifting the final distance. With practiced movements, Tod looped lines around the cleats, securing the boat. He raised it onto the lift, winching it clear of the water's surface where it hung, dripping quietly.

Standing on the dock, Tod looked back at the water. Empty now. No blue-white forms pulsed beneath the surface, no seven-second rhythm marked time in the depths. He realized with mild surprise how quickly he'd grown accustomed to their presence, how natural it had felt to have them waiting there.

Tod walked unsteadily up the dock toward the house, his legs shaky from exhaustion and the transition to solid ground. Inside his workshop, he set down his gear and sank onto the stool at his workbench, surrounded by the familiar chaos of equipment, tools, and parts that had defined his life before the Light Speakers.

The modified sensor—the innocent creation that had started everything—sat where he'd left it. Tod picked it up, turning it over in his hands.

"Thank you for working," he murmured, before setting it gently back on the workbench.

His phone buzzed in his pocket. A text from Barney: "Welcome home, hero."

Tod smiled, shaking his head slightly. He wasn't a hero, just someone who'd done what needed doing. His fingers tapped a response: "Just a guy with a boat. Thanks for being there."

He looked around the workshop. Normal life would resume now—charters to run, equipment to fix, bills to pay. Yet normal had shifted somehow. The world contained depths he'd only glimpsed, intelligences beyond human imagination living just miles offshore. He wasn't alone in the universe, and never had been.

Tod stood and moved to the window, gazing out toward where the Gulf of Mexico lay beyond the visible horizon. They were out there, in the cold, dark depths where they belonged.

"Until next time, friends," he whispered.

He turned back to his workshop, to the life that would continue tomorrow and the days after. The man who stood there was not the same one who had first detected an anomalous signal days ago. He was more—more aware, more connected, more capable than he'd ever realized.

And that was exactly right.

Chapter 6

Tod collapsed onto his bed shortly after nine, his body leaden with exhaustion. The sheets felt impossibly soft against his skin after the day's ordeal. His eyes closed immediately, mind already drifting toward what should have been instant, deep sleep.

But sleep didn't come.

Instead, an odd awareness crept through his consciousness. The walls around him seemed to hum with a subtle energy he'd never noticed before. Tod shifted uncomfortably, pulling the pillow over his head, but the sensation persisted—a faint electrical presence dancing at the edges of his perception.

He rolled over, trying to find a comfortable position. Across the room, his phone sat charging on the dresser. Strangely, Tod could sense it there—not see it in the darkness, but feel it somehow, the slow pulse of electricity flowing into its battery creating a distinct signature in the room. Next to it, his clock radio generated its own electrical pattern, different but equally distinct.

"Just overtired," he mumbled, pressing his palms against his eyes. "Stress and that knock on the head."

Tod focused on his breathing, trying to ignore the new awareness spreading through his body. The house wiring in the walls created pathways of energy that he could somehow track with his mind, following circuits through the ceiling and down into the workshop below. The refrigerator in the kitchen cycled on, and Tod felt the surge of power as clearly as if someone had flipped a light on in the bedroom.

Hours passed. Midnight came and went. Tod stared at the ceiling, increasingly frustrated as sleep remained elusive despite his bone-deep fatigue.

"Come on," he whispered to himself. "Just sleep."

Finally, around three in the morning, exhaustion won out. Tod's consciousness slipped away into dreams filled with pulsing blue-white lights and waves of energy flowing through water and air. In the dream, he could see radio waves, cell signals, and electricity moving around him like visible currents.

When morning light filtered through the blinds, Tod woke with a splitting headache centered precisely where his temple had struck the boat's gunwale. He groaned, pressing his fingers gingerly against the tender spot.

"Just the concussion," he told himself, pushing away memories of the strange sensations that had kept him awake. "Nothing some coffee and aspirin won't fix."

He swung his legs over the edge of the bed, unaware that the changes the Light Speakers had triggered were only beginning to manifest.

TWO MORNINGS LATER, Tod guided K5HUX across Copano Bay with a pair of retirees from Houston sitting comfortably at the bow. The familiar routine of a charter felt grounding after everything he'd experienced.

"Beautiful morning, Captain," called Walter, the older of the two men. "Your reputation wasn't exaggerated."

Tod nodded appreciatively. The booking had come through a referral, and he desperately needed both the income and the normalcy after cancelling his previous charters.

"We'll hit my usual spot first," Tod explained, throttling back as they approached a drop-off he'd fished successfully dozens of times. "Redfish should be active with this incoming tide."

As he prepared to anchor, something tugged at his awareness—a sensation beyond sight or sound. A presence. Three hundred yards east, something was happening in the water. Without fully understanding why, Tod steered away from his planned location.

"Change of plans, gentlemen. I'm feeling lucky about this direction."

Within minutes, Tod's sonar showed a massive school of redfish. The clients hadn't even cast their lines before the water erupted with feeding activity.

"My God, look at that!" Walter's companion exclaimed, hastily preparing his rod.

Walter's line went taut almost the moment it hit the water. "Got one!"

As the fish fought against the hook, something extraordinary happened. Tod felt a surge of panic that wasn't his own—a desperate, primal fear accompanied by exhaustion and pain. He gripped the console, overwhelmed by the sensations coursing through him.

"You okay there, Captain?" Walter called, fighting his catch.

Tod turned away. "Just checking our position," he managed, pretending to adjust equipment while gathering himself. The fish's distress pounded through him like it was his own pulse.

When Walter landed the redfish, Tod forced himself to approach with the landing net. The fish thrashed in desperate circles, and Tod felt each frantic heartbeat.

"Beauty!" Walter exclaimed. "Definitely a keeper."

Tod nodded mechanically, reaching for his knife. As he dispatched the fish with practiced efficiency, he felt the life force drain away—a hollow emptiness spreading where the frantic energy had been. Nausea surged through him.

The morning continued this way. The clients caught their limit quickly, whooping with excitement while Tod experienced the death of each fish as an intimate, visceral event. He maintained his professional demeanor through sheer will, cleaning their catch while his hands trembled slightly.

"Best charter we've ever had," Walter declared back at the dock, pressing an extra hundred-dollar bill into Tod's palm. "We'll be booking again!"

When they finally departed, Tod sat alone in his boat, staring at his hands. They looked the same—calloused, tanned, capable—but something fundamental had changed. He could still feel phantom echoes of each fish's death.

"What's happening to me?" he whispered to the empty boat.

No answer came, but somewhere deep in his mind, he knew exactly who had done this to him.

THE AFTERNOON SUN STREAMED through the windows of Tod's workshop as he hunched over his workbench, trying to repair a client's fish finder. The device lay disassembled, its circuit board exposed as Tod traced connections with a multimeter. He'd promised to have it fixed by tomorrow—a simple job that would normally take him less than an hour.

But today, nothing felt normal.

Without warning, a spike of pain shot through his temples. Tod dropped the soldering iron, barely missing his hand as it clattered against the bench. The pressure behind his eyes built rapidly, like someone was inflating a balloon inside his skull.

"Jesus," he gasped, pressing his palms against his forehead.

Every piece of electronic equipment in the workshop seemed to intensify, bombarding him with invisible signals. His oscilloscope, the ham radio transceiver, his laptop—each device screamed its electronic signature at him. The pain wasn't physical so much as informational—too much input flooding his consciousness.

Tod staggered back from the bench, eyes squeezed shut. Even with his eyes closed, he could feel where everything was. The powered-on oscilloscope pulsed differently than the laptop. The fish finder components emitted their own unique signature. His old tube-type radio hummed with a warm, analog flow unlike the sharp digital edges of his smartphone charging in the corner.

"This isn't possible," he whispered, eyes still closed.

He pointed around the room. "On... off... standby... charging... on but inactive." He opened his eyes to confirm. Every identification was correct.

Three seconds before his phone began ringing, Tod felt the incoming signal building, like pressure in a water pipe. He turned toward it just before the first tone sounded.

"Hey, Barney," he answered, voice strained.

"How'd you know it was me? You have caller ID on that ancient thing?"

Tod swallowed hard. "Just a guess."

"You sound weird. You okay?"

"Just tired," Tod lied, rubbing his temples. "Busy with charters."

"Still processing what happened out there?"

"Something like that. Look, I need to finish this repair. I'll call you tomorrow."

After hanging up, Tod killed the workshop lights and sat in the darkness. The electronic voices didn't diminish—they simply changed character, some equipment cycling into sleep modes, others maintaining their steady signatures.

He fumbled in the dark for the journal he kept for equipment modifications. Finding a blank page, he began writing, his hand trembling slightly.

"Day 4. Something is very wrong. I can sense electronic devices—not just hear or see them, but feel them somehow. Their signals, frequencies, power states. It started subtly but now it's overwhelming. This morning with the fish, now this." He paused, pen hovering over the paper. "What did the Light Speakers do to me?"

Outside, the sun continued its arc across the Texas sky, indifferent to the transformation unfolding beneath it.

TOD WHISTLED AS HE coiled rope on the dock, the late afternoon sun warming his shoulders. His charter tomorrow was a regular client—easy day, decent tip guaranteed. Blue skies stretched uninterrupted across Copano Bay, perfect conditions predicted through tomorrow.

The tingling started at the base of his skull.

Tod froze, rope dangling from his hand. The sensation spread across his skin like static electricity, making the hairs on his arms stand. Pressure built behind his eyes, not painful but insistent—an awareness of something vast gathering force.

"What the hell?" Tod turned in a slow circle.

Nothing but clear skies in every direction. No darkening clouds, no distant rumble of thunder. He checked his phone: weather app showed sunny conditions for the next twenty-four hours.

The sensation intensified, becoming distinctly directional. Tod found himself turning southeast, toward the Gulf of Mexico. Something was building out there, massive electrical potential accumulating like charge in a capacitor.

Inside his workshop, Tod pulled up the NOAA weather radar. The screen showed nothing unusual—clear conditions throughout the coastal region.

"I'm losing my damn mind," he muttered, rubbing his arms where the tingling continued.

Thirty minutes later, Tod refreshed the radar. A small cell had appeared exactly where he'd sensed it, still too small to trigger any warnings. He zoomed in, watching the storm building in real-time, feeding on warm Gulf waters.

By minute forty-five, the squall line had formed a defined front, visible as a dark smudge on the southeastern horizon. Tod rushed back to his boat, securing equipment and double-tying mooring lines as the first winds reached shore.

The storm hit with tropical ferocity. Lightning split the sky, and Tod collapsed onto the dock, crying out. Each electrical discharge felt like it was passing directly through his body. He could sense the massive electromagnetic pulses, the ionization of air, the building and release of charge in the atmosphere.

Tod dragged himself toward the workshop on hands and knees as rain lashed his back. Lightning struck a nearby power pole, and he convulsed, feeling the surge race through underground wires and into the grid.

Inside, he frantically shut down every electronic device, yanking plugs from walls. He crawled into the darkest corner, sunglasses jammed onto his face, hands pressed against his ears though they provided no protection from what he was feeling.

When the storm passed twenty minutes later, Tod lay exhausted on the floor, soaked and trembling.

"I felt the storm before it existed," he whispered into the empty room. "How is that possible?"

The question hung in the air, unanswered but undeniable.

TOD HADN'T SLEPT PROPERLY in days. Every electronic device hummed its signature into his brain, the house wiring pulsed like a living circulatory system, and twice he'd woken in the middle of the night, certain someone had turned on a radio three houses away.

"Enough," he muttered, dragging himself to the workshop. "If this is happening, I need to understand it."

Tod cleared his central workbench and began methodically arranging equipment. If his mind was playing tricks, he'd prove it. If not... he'd document exactly what had changed.

For Test One, he asked Barney over the phone to hide various electronic devices around the property while Tod waited in the bathroom with the door closed.

"Alright, I've hidden them," Barney called. "No way you could know where they are."

Tod emerged, eyes closed, and walked directly to the first device—his old weather radio tucked behind the living room curtains. Then to the second—a digital watch beneath the couch cushion. Then the third—a flashlight in the mailbox at the end of the driveway.

Barney's mouth fell open. "How did you—"

"I can feel them," Tod said. "Range is about fifty feet. Let's try something else."

Test Two: the electrical panel. Tod faced away, calling out which circuits activated as Barney flipped breakers in random order.

"Bedroom light. Kitchen outlets. Water heater. Workshop sub-panel."

Perfect accuracy. Every time.

Test Three required more precision. Tod modified his HAM radio to delay the transmission indicator light by half a second.

"Press the button whenever," Tod instructed Barney.

Ten times, Tod called "now" precisely as Barney's finger depressed the transmit button—half a second before the indicator light confirmed it.

In the yard, Tod walked blindfolded with a compass, stopping every few feet.

"North is..." he pointed. Each time, the compass confirmed his sense of magnetic orientation.

For hours, Tod documented everything—signal strength thresholds, accuracy percentages across distances, frequency sensitivities. His engineering background surfaced in detailed diagrams and measurements, each revealing the same conclusion.

As sunset approached, Tod performed his final test—unplugging the modified sensor completely and removing it from the property.

Nothing changed. He still felt every electronic pulse, every transmission, every electrical current.

"It's not the equipment," Tod whispered. "It's me."

He tried convincing himself these changes might fade, that his brain might return to normal once the concussion healed completely. But the data didn't lie—the accuracy was improving, not declining.

Tod's fingers trembled as he typed the final entry: "Conclusion: Contact with Light Speakers altered my brain. Changes appear permanent."

The scientific detachment he'd maintained crumbled. Tod pushed away from the workbench, hands shaking violently. The person who'd existed before encountering the colony was gone forever.

His life would never be normal again.

BARNEY'S TRUCK PULLED into Tod's driveway around four, the crunch of tires on gravel sending electromagnetic pulses through the vehicle's sensors that Tod felt before he heard anything. By the time Barney's boots hit the ground, Tod had already counted six active electronics in the truck and felt the precise battery level in Barney's phone.

"Hope you're hungry!" Barney called, hefting a brown paper bag that smelled of Salt Lick barbecue and a six-pack of Shiner. "Figured you might need some sustenance after everything."

Tod met him at the workshop door wearing sunglasses despite being indoors. "Hey. Didn't expect you."

"That's the point of a surprise visit." Barney stepped inside, eyes narrowing as he studied Tod's face. "You look like hell, buddy. What's going on?"

"Nothing. Just tired." Tod shifted, wincing as Barney's phone received a text message, the signal jabbing into his brain like a needle.

"Uh-huh." Barney set down the food, popping open two beers. "And the sunglasses indoors? New fashion statement?"

Tod accepted the beer, fighting the urge to look at the electrical junction box that had just switched compressor cycles. "Headache. Concussion stuff."

Barney watched Tod closely. "You keep looking at things that aren't there. And you're acting paranoid."

"Let's sit outside." Tod couldn't stand the enclosed space anymore, every device screaming its presence.

They settled at the end of the dock, feet dangling over the water. The natural environment provided some relief—fewer signals, more space between sources. Barney didn't push immediately, letting Tod take a long pull of his beer first.

"Talk to me," Barney finally said. "Something's wrong."

Tod wanted to tell him so badly. About feeling electrical currents through walls. About sensing storms before they formed. About knowing exactly how many electronic devices were active within fifty feet at all times. The loneliness of experiencing something so impossible was crushing him.

He opened his mouth, but the words caught. How could he explain? That he had what amounted to superpowers? That alien jellyfish had rewired his brain?

"Just adjusting after... everything. The rescue. Nearly drowning. It's a lot."

"That's not all of it." Barney's voice was gentle but firm. "I know you, Tod. Something else is going on."

The silence stretched between them, punctuated only by water lapping against pilings. Tod's jaw worked as he wrestled with his secret.

"I can't explain yet," he finally said. "But I'm okay. I promise. Just need time."

Barney studied him for a long moment, then nodded slowly. "I'm here when you're ready."

After Barney drove away, Tod stood alone on the dock, staring into the darkening waters of Copano Bay. The Light Speakers were miles away in the Gulf depths, but the changes they'd left behind remained. The isolation felt more crushing than ever—trapped between worlds, belonging fully to neither.

THE AFTERNOON CHARTER had started routinely enough. The Morgans—father, mother, and two children aged eight and ten—were delighted with the clear skies and gentle breeze. The kids bounced with excitement at the prospect of seeing dolphins, pelicans, and whatever else Aransas Bay might reveal.

"Will we see dolphins, Captain Tod?" Emma, the younger Morgan, asked for the third time.

"We might," Tod replied, guiding K5HUX across the bay's gentle chop. "No guarantees, but—"

The pain hit him mid-sentence—sharp, constricting, a desperate burning sensation around his torso and tail fin. Not his pain. Something else's. The sensation wasn't physical but emotional, a broadcast of distress so powerful it made him gasp.

"Captain?" Mr. Morgan leaned forward. "Everything okay?"

Tod gripped the wheel tighter, focusing on the direction of the sensation. Two hundred yards southeast, approximately. Whatever it was, it needed help immediately.

"I need to check something," Tod said, adjusting course sharply.

"But what about the fishing spot?" Mr. Morgan frowned.

"Trust me." Tod accelerated, following the distress signal like a beacon. With each yard closer, the sensations intensified—panic, exhaustion, the terrifying certainty of approaching death.

Then he saw it—a bottlenose dolphin thrashing weakly, abandoned fishing line cutting deep into its skin, a thin trail of blood in the water.

"Oh my God!" Mrs. Morgan covered her mouth.

"A dolphin!" shouted Tommy, the older child. Then, noticing the creature's condition: "It's hurt! We have to help it!"

Tod throttled down, approaching slowly. The dolphin's fear spiked as the boat drew near, and Tod felt every ounce of it. He breathed deeply, fighting to remain functional through the overwhelming empathic connection.

"I'll need to cut the line," Tod said, reaching for his knife. "Mr. Morgan, can you help steady the boat?"

Carefully, speaking in soft tones, Tod leaned over the gunwale. The dolphin's eye met his—intelligent, suffering, desperate.

"It's okay," Tod whispered, knowing somehow the creature could sense his intent. "I'm here to help."

Working methodically, Tod cut through the tangled mess of monofilament. Each touch brought fresh waves of the dolphin's pain crashing through him, but he continued, hands trembling. With the Morgans helping where they could, Tod finally severed the last strand.

The dolphin hesitated, then slipped away. As it swam free, a wave of something entirely unexpected washed over Tod—relief, gratitude, joy. Tears streamed down his face as he watched the creature disappear.

"That was incredible," Mr. Morgan said quietly. "How did you know it was there?"

Tod wiped his eyes. "Just... lucky, I guess. Right place, right time."

"You were crying," Mrs. Morgan said. "That was beautiful."

Tod couldn't explain that he had felt everything—every sensation, every emotion the dolphin experienced—as if it were happening to him.

Later, alone in his workshop, Tod added to his growing journal: "Marine life empathy confirmed. Range ~200 yards, extremely clear." He paused, then added: "It helped me save a life today."

Chapter 7

Tod needed supplies—electrical components, a new transducer, and various hardware items for his workshop. After thirteen days of avoiding crowds, he decided it was time to venture into Corpus Christi, forty-five minutes from his peaceful bayfront home.

The drive went smoothly enough. Highway 35 stretched before him, the coastal scrubland rolling past his window. But as Corpus Christi's skyline appeared on the horizon, a faint pressure began building at his temples.

He turned into the Walmart parking lot, navigating through rows of cars. The discomfort intensified with each passing second—a low-level headache throbbing behind his eyes.

"Just grab what you need and get out," Tod muttered, adjusting his sunglasses. He'd faced worse than a headache.

The automatic doors slid open. Tod stepped inside, and his world exploded.

Hundreds of electronic signatures assaulted him simultaneously—cell phones in pockets and purses, WiFi routers mounted on ceilings, security cameras tracking movement, fluorescent lights humming overhead, electronic price tags pulsing with updates. Each device screamed its unique electromagnetic signature directly into his brain.

Tod gasped, grabbing a shopping cart for support. The metal frame vibrated beneath his fingers, conducting the store's electronic symphony into his palms. The cacophony overwhelmed him, each signal fighting for dominance in his perception.

A woman asked if he was okay. Tod couldn't respond. Her voice came from underwater while her phone blasted its signature like a spotlight in his consciousness.

He pushed forward, squinting through pain as his vision narrowed to a tunnel. Twenty steps in. Thirty. The hardware section lay just ahead, but the pressure behind his eyes built to unbearable levels. His heartbeat pounded in his ears, synchronized with the pulsing agony.

Tod abandoned the cart mid-aisle. He turned, stumbling toward the exit, bumping shoulders with confused shoppers. Someone called after him, but their words dissolved into the electronic roar.

Outside, he collapsed into his truck's driver's seat, door barely closed behind him. With trembling hands, he covered his eyes, breathing in ragged gasps. Even here, surrounded by metal, the signals penetrated—weaker but persistent, hundreds of devices communicating, existing, screaming.

Forty minutes passed before the migraine subsided enough to drive. Tod pulled onto the highway, heading straight for home, for safety, for quiet.

The realization settled heavily in his chest: he couldn't function in high-density electronic environments anymore. Malls, airports, hospitals, conference centers—all now hostile territory. Another piece of his normal life chipped away, leaving him further isolated.

At home, Tod opened his laptop, wincing at its signature, and ordered the supplies online.

"One more way I'm not normal," he whispered to the empty room, fingers typing carefully as if the keyboard might shatter under his touch.

THE ROCKPORT MARINA bustled with morning activity as Tod backed his truck toward the loading area. Five charter boats already bobbed at their slips, captains readying for the day. The familiar scene should have been comforting, but something felt off.

Captain Reid nudged Captain Harry, both glancing toward Tod as he unloaded his cooler. Their thoughts weren't audible, but their body language spoke volumes—the sudden silence, the pointed looks.

Tod continued his preparations, pretending not to notice. He sensed the electronic signatures of their fish finders, depth sounders, and marine radios humming in a familiar chorus. Someone's phone buzzed with an incoming text near the bait shop.

"Morning, Blackstone." Captain Harry approached, coffee in hand, voice casual but eyes sharp. "Been meaning to ask—you using some new fish finder? Different sonar equipment on that boat of yours?"

Tod adjusted his cap, keeping his movements deliberate, unhurried. "No, same setup as always. Why?"

"Your success rate these past two weeks is... unusual." Harry sipped his coffee. "Clients all over town raving about it."

Behind Harry, Captain Mike approached, arms crossed. "Yeah, Blackstone. What's your secret? Every charter limited out, best spots every time."

The realization hit Tod with startling clarity. He'd been too good. His ability to sense fish beneath the surface—to feel their collective presence, their movements, their emotions—had made his success rate statistically impossible. In a profession where even the best had off days, Tod had become a machine of perfect efficiency.

"Just been lucky, I guess." Tod shrugged, checking his watch. "Right time of year. Fish are biting."

Mike snorted. "Lucky for two weeks straight? Every single charter? Come on."

The marina had gone quiet. Other captains pretended to work while straining to listen. The air thickened with professional jealousy turning rapidly to suspicion.

"Maybe I should start playing the lottery," Tod joked weakly, loading ice into his cooler. "Look, I'm just hitting the same spots everyone else is."

"With very different results," Harry observed.

Tod spotted his clients pulling into the parking lot—a family of four from Houston, right on time. "My charter's here. Gotta run. Good luck out there, guys."

Later, six miles out in Aransas Bay, Tod deliberately motored past a massive school of redfish he could feel pulsing beneath the surface. He headed instead to an empty stretch, pretended to study his depth finder, then circled back toward the school as if making an educated guess.

"Let's try here," he said, feigning uncertainty.

That evening, Tod wrote in his journal: "Have to hide abilities even when using them. Can never show full capacity. Not just equipment I need to adjust—my entire performance must be calibrated for believability."

He closed the journal, rubbing his temples. The pressure to be less than he was—to perform incompetence—felt like another prison forming around him.

TOD STARED AT HIS BEDROOM ceiling, the red numbers of his clock radio showing 11:52 PM. Sleep remained elusive, as it had for over two weeks. The house felt too quiet, too empty. His mind kept drifting to the depths of the Gulf where the Light Speakers now swam freely.

He threw back the covers and padded to his workshop. The modified sensor beacon sat on his workbench, completed three days ago but untested. Tod gathered the equipment and headed to the dock, the wooden planks creaking beneath his bare feet.

The night stretched dark and vast around him. Stars reflected on the bay's still surface as Tod connected the battery pack and aimed the beacon toward the distant Gulf. The signal would broadcast on the specific frequency the Light Speakers had responded to before—a frequency he could now feel resonating in his own altered brain.

"Probably won't even reach," Tod muttered, flipping the switch. The beacon hummed to life, invisible waves radiating outward.

Minutes ticked by. Ten. Twenty. Thirty.

Nothing.

Tod's shoulders slumped. He reached for the power switch, ready to call it a night, when a familiar tingling sensation sparked at the base of his skull. It spread across his scalp like gentle electricity—harmonic, resonant, unmistakable.

Their signature.

Tod gripped the dock's edge, heart pounding. He scanned the horizon and spotted it—a faint blue-white glow miles offshore, almost imperceptible but definitely there. The light pulsed rhythmically, and Tod instinctively translated the Morse code: "F-R-I-E-N-D."

His hands trembled as he grabbed his flashlight and signaled back: "Y-O-U R-E-M-E-M-B-E-R."

The distant glow pulsed: "A-L-W-A-Y-S."

"A-R-E Y-O-U W-E-L-L?" Tod asked.

"Y-E-S H-O-M-E G-O-O-D."

"Y-O-U W-E-L-L?"

Tod's thumb hesitated over the flashlight button. He could lie, pretend everything was normal, but something told him they would know. "D-I-F-F-E-R-E-N-T," he finally signaled.

A long pause followed. The distant glow remained steady before pulsing: "W-E K-N-O-W."

Tod's breath caught in his throat. They knew?

The light continued: "S-O-R-R-Y."

His throat tightened as understanding dawned. The Light Speakers had known this would happen when they saved him, when they touched him.

Tod signaled: "N-O-T Y-O-U-R F-A-U-L-T."

"Y-O-U W-I-L-L A-D-A-P-T."

"W-E H-E-L-P I-F N-E-E-D."

The blue-white glow flickered, then gradually faded—the distance too great to maintain the connection. Tod remained seated on the dock, legs dangling over the edge, a strange peace settling over him. He was not alone in this transformation. The Light Speakers were still watching, still connected to him across the miles of bay and Gulf waters.

They knew what had happened to him. They were sorry, but not surprised. And they would help if needed.

Tod gazed at the now-empty horizon, feeling the weight of isolation lift from his shoulders for the first time in eighteen days. Whatever came next, he wouldn't face it alone.

THE GRAVEL CRUNCHED under tires as a silver SUV pulled into Tod's driveway Saturday morning. Bill and Barbara Blackstone emerged, his father's tall frame stretching after the drive from Galveston while his mother immediately scanned the property with the practiced eye of someone who had raised him.

Tod stepped onto the porch, forcing a smile that didn't quite reach his eyes. Barbara rushed forward, enveloping him in a hug that smelled of familiar perfume and home.

She pulled back, hands on his shoulders. "You've lost weight. Honey, are you eating?"

"Course I am, Mom."

Bill clapped him on the shoulder. "And you look exhausted. Those charters running you ragged?"

"Just busy season," Tod deflected. "Come on in."

In the kitchen, Tod felt every appliance humming—the refrigerator's compressor cycling, the digital clock's faint pulse, the coffee maker warming. Each electronic signature demanded space in his awareness as he struggled to maintain conversation while preparing lunch.

Barbara watched him closely as he moved around the kitchen. When the microwave started, its electromagnetic field hit Tod like a slap. The fork in his hand clattered to the floor.

"Butterfingers," he joked weakly, retrieving it.

Barbara's eyes narrowed, that nurse's intuition kicking in. She knew something was wrong.

Later on the dock, Bill peppered Tod with questions about the charter business while Tod gave automatic responses, his attention split between his father's words and the rich tapestry of marine life surrounding them. A school of mullet moved in synchronized patterns seventy yards to the south. Further out, a pod of bottlenose dolphins played, their curious joy washing over Tod in waves.

"Son?" Bill waved a hand before Tod's face. "You keep zoning out. Where's your head at?"

"Sorry, Dad. Just thinking about tomorrow's weather."

During dinner, Barbara's gaze rarely left Tod's face, cataloging each distracted moment, each wince when the dishwasher cycled.

After Bill excused himself for an early night, she cornered Tod on the back porch.

"Sweetheart, I'm your mother. I can see something's wrong. Please talk to me."

The concern in her eyes nearly broke him. How desperately he wanted to share this burden, to tell someone who loved him unconditionally about the creatures who had saved him, changed him.

"What if..." he started, then stopped, throat tight. "What if you went through something that changed you? Permanently?"

Barbara leaned forward. "Changed how?"

"In ways you can't explain. That no one would believe."

She reached across the space between them, taking his hand. "I'd believe you. We'd figure it out together."

Tod felt the words crowding his throat—intelligent light beings, breathing underwater, sensing electrical currents and fish across miles of bay. The impossibility of it all choked him into silence.

"I'm okay, Mom. Really. Just... processing some things. I promise I'll tell you when I can."

Barbara squeezed his hand, reluctantly accepting his evasion.

Sunday morning arrived with farewell hugs. Barbara held him longer than usual, her embrace fierce and protective.

"Call me. Anytime," she whispered.

Tod watched their SUV disappear down the road, the distance between them feeling vaster than the miles. He loved them too much to burden them with truths that would only bring worry, disbelief, or worse—fear for his sanity. Some secrets were his alone to carry.

THE MORNING SUN GLINTED off Copano Bay as Tod guided his charter boat with the Peterson family aboard. Mr. Peterson, his wife, and their twelve-year-old son had booked a half-day trip, hoping for speckled trout.

Tod felt the school long before they approached—a cluster of thirty-seven trout hovering over an underwater ridge half a mile east. Their presence registered in his mind like a distant chorus.

"Let's try over by that channel marker," Tod suggested casually, deliberately steering slightly north of where he knew the fish were waiting. He made a show of scanning the water, checking depth, testing the current.

"Fish finder showing anything?" Mr. Peterson asked, eager.

"Not yet. Let's drift this area a bit." Tod knew exactly where the fish were, but revealing that knowledge would raise questions he couldn't answer.

After twenty minutes of "searching," Tod finally turned the boat toward the underwater ridge. "Water depth changes here. Good structure for trout. Let's try a few casts."

Young Tyler's first cast produced an immediate strike—a nineteen-inch speckled trout that fought brilliantly. Tod felt the fish's panic and pain as the hook set, but maintained his professional smile as he netted it.

"Perfect cast, buddy! Right where they're hiding."

Mrs. Peterson clapped excitedly while her husband prepared his own rod. As the family focused on their fishing, Tod's awareness shifted to a new presence approaching from the south—large, predatory, powerful. A bull shark, approximately seven feet long, moving purposefully toward their position, drawn by the struggling trout.

Tod calculated. The shark was still ninety yards away. No immediate danger, but that would change quickly.

"You know what? The tide's shifting. Let's move over to that point—might find some bigger ones there." Tod started the engine before anyone could protest.

"But we're catching fish here," Mr. Peterson frowned.

"Trust me. The bigger ones will be staging along that drop-off with the tide change." Tod steered away from the approaching predator, monitoring its movements as it investigated their previous location before moving on.

By day's end, the Petersons had caught seventeen trout—a good day, but not suspiciously excellent. As they unloaded at the dock, Mr. Peterson handed Tod his payment plus a generous tip.

"You're really good at this. Natural talent for finding fish."

Tod smiled. "Thanks. I just love being on the water."

Alone afterward, Tod secured his boat on the lift and sat on the dock, feet dangling. He'd successfully moderated his abilities today—used them enough to ensure a positive experience but concealed their full extent. The charter business could continue. His life could go on.

That evening, Tod spread his journal entries across the workshop table—twenty-four days of observations since his transformation. He created a summary document with clinical precision:

ELECTROMAGNETIC SENSITIVITY:

MARINE LIFE EMPATHY:

Tod continued through limitations and coping mechanisms before reaching his conclusion:

ASSESSMENT: These abilities are permanent. Fighting them won't work. Time to learn mastery.

He listed five goals, the last being "Maintain relationships," which made him pause, thinking of Barney and his parents.

Tod marked tomorrow on his calendar as a "mental health day"—no charters, just practice. He needed to learn control.

At sunset, Tod walked to the dock and sat cross-legged. He closed his eyes and focused on the electronic signals bombarding his awareness. Instead of fighting them, he imagined a radio dial, attempting to lower the volume. The input diminished slightly—not gone, but manageable.

Looking toward the Gulf, Tod detected a faint, familiar signature miles offshore—the Light Speakers, distant but present.

"I'm different now," he whispered. "That's okay. I can work with this."

For the first time in weeks, a genuine smile crossed his face. These abilities were both burden and gift—not chosen, but his nonetheless.

Back in his workshop, Tod began sketching designs for a permanent beacon to contact the Light Speakers. His new normal was taking shape.

In his journal, Tod wrote a final entry: "Day 25. I'm not the man I was. I'm learning to be the man I'm becoming."

TOD DRIFTED INTO SLEEP with unusual ease that night, the constant electromagnetic hum finally quieting as his consciousness slipped away. But this wasn't ordinary sleep.

He found himself suspended in deep water, the pressure comfortable against his skin despite being hundreds of feet below the surface. He breathed normally, no equipment needed. Around him, hundreds of Light Speakers formed a perfect sphere, their blue-white luminescence pulsating in harmony.

But something was different. Their lights didn't form Morse code. Instead, meaning flowed directly into his mind like water.

Welcome, friend-Tod. We speak truly now.

"I understand you," Tod marveled. "How is this possible?"

Your mind changed. Opens to our way. Easier in dream-space.

The Light Speakers swirled around him, and suddenly Tod was moving, carried through the water at impossible speed. They swept him over vast underwater canyons where strange bioluminescent communities clung to walls that dropped thousands of feet into darkness. Entire colonies—cities of light—pulsed with complex patterns that Tod somehow recognized as music, stories, history.

Many kinds exist, came the thought. *Many speak. Many sing.*

Tod watched in awe as other intelligences revealed themselves—gelatinous forms larger than whales communicating through rhythmic contractions, colonies of crystalline structures that manipulated water pressure to create sonic patterns, tiny cloud-like beings that moved as one organism through elaborate dances.

Network spans all waters. Gulf. Beyond. Always speaking. Humans never hear.

Images flashed through Tod's consciousness—currents of communication flowing through ocean waters like invisible highways, carrying thoughts and information between species humans had never classified, never even seen.

"Why show me this?" Tod asked.

You are bridge.

The Light Speakers formed a perfect ring around him, their meaning intensifying.

Between worlds. Between species. You translate.

Tod saw himself standing on his dock, modified equipment receiving signals from deep waters. He saw himself explaining to scientists, to government officials, to ordinary people—helping humans understand they weren't alone in their own oceans. He saw himself translating messages between species that had never communicated before.

The responsibility crushed him like deepwater pressure.

"Too much," Tod protested. "I'm just a charter captain. I fish for a living. I'm nobody."

The Light Speakers moved closer, surrounding him with gentle warmth. Their collective response carried patience and absolute certainty.

You are more. You will grow into this. Time.

Tod woke with a gasp, sunlight streaming through his bedroom window. His heart hammered against his ribs, the dream still vivid in his mind. But was it just a dream?

His electromagnetic sense tingled, detecting a fading signature unlike anything electronic—the residual presence of Light Speakers, retreating now that he was awake.

They had actually been here, in his mind.

Tod grabbed his journal from the nightstand, his hand trembling as he wrote: "Day 22. They can reach me in dreams. They have plans for me. I'm not ready."

He stared at the words, terror and wonder battling within him.

TOD KNELT ON HIS DOCK the following afternoon, replacing a worn cleat with a new stainless steel one. His muscles worked mechanically while his mind remained fixated on last night's dream-vision. The Light Speakers had shown him vast underwater civilizations, communication networks spanning oceans, and somehow appointed him as their ambassador to humanity.

"Bridge between worlds," he muttered, tightening a bolt. "As if I have any idea how to do that."

A vehicle crunched over the gravel driveway behind him. Tod's electromagnetic sense tingled as a car engine shut off, followed by the soft electronic beep of doors locking. Unfamiliar footsteps approached.

"Captain Blackstone?"

Tod turned to find a woman in her fifties with silver-streaked black hair pulled into a practical bun. She wore khaki field pants and a polo shirt with a university logo, clipboard in hand.

"I'm Dr. Sarah Chen, marine biologist from Texas A&M Corpus."

Tod's heart slammed against his ribs. He forced his face to remain neutral as he stood, wiping his hands on a rag.

"What can I do for you?"

She regarded him with sharp, analytical eyes. "I've been tracking unusual bioluminescent activity in the Gulf. Your name came up."

The breath caught in Tod's throat. "My name? How?"

"Coast Guard records show you were in the area during several unexplained light phenomena." She pulled a tablet from her shoulder bag. "Mind if we talk inside? The sun's rather intense."

Tod led her to his workshop, mind racing. Dr. Chen swept her gaze over his electronics equipment before turning the tablet toward him. The screen displayed satellite imagery with timestamps—diffuse blue-white glows in the Gulf, exactly matching the day he'd guided the Light Speakers home.

"This was taken the morning you filed your float plan," she said, watching his reaction carefully.

Tod shrugged. "I was fishing. Didn't notice anything unusual."

"Really? Because your route that morning matches the light pattern exactly." She swiped to another image showing his boat's path overlaid with the luminous trail.

A cold realization washed over Tod. Satellites had been watching. Their journey had created a data trail.

"Maybe bioluminescent algae?" he suggested. "Plankton bloom?"

"That's what I thought. But the pattern is too organized. Almost..." she paused, studying his face, "intentional."

Tod maintained his blank expression. "Sorry I can't help. Just fishing that day."

Dr. Chen lingered a moment longer before offering her card. "If you remember anything, call me. This could be a significant discovery."

After her car disappeared down the road, Tod paced his workshop, hands trembling. Scientists were looking. Satellites had recorded them. The secret wasn't as safe as he thought.

He grabbed his phone and dialed. "Barney? We have a problem."

TOD PACED HIS WORKSHOP floor, the HAM radio's frequency knob spinning beneath his fingers until he landed on an obscure channel.

"Barney, you reading me? Switch to the secondary frequency."

A brief static burst, then Barney's voice emerged through the speaker. "Got you. Using the scrambler pattern we set up."

Tod leaned against his workbench, eyes fixed on Dr. Chen's business card. "A marine biologist showed up at my door today. Texas A&M. She had satellite photos, Barney—our exact route from when we took the Light Speakers home."

"Jesus," Barney breathed. "How clear were the images?"

"Clear enough to match my boat's path perfectly. She saw the bioluminescence. Called it 'organized' and 'intentional.'"

The line went silent before Barney spoke again. "If scientists find them, what happens? Study? Capture? Dissection?"

Tod's stomach twisted. "I've been thinking about nothing else. Lab specimens. Research subjects."

"We have to assume the worst. How do we protect them?"

Tod rubbed his temples. "They're in deep water now. Hard to reach."

"But if researchers go looking specifically..." Barney left the thought hanging.

"We need options." Tod grabbed a notepad. "We could warn the Light Speakers, mislead the scientists somehow, monitor the research channels."

"All of the above," Barney said.

Tod's pen scratched across paper. "I need to tell them. They need to know humans are looking. I'll contact them tonight, warn them about surface observation."

"What if there are more researchers? More satellites watching?"

Tod stopped writing. "Then we've been careful for nothing. The secret's already compromised."

The weight of it settled between them—first contact might not stay secret much longer.

"What would public knowledge mean?" Barney asked quietly.

"For them? Danger." Tod's voice hardened. "For me? I'm the guy who hid intelligent aliens from science."

"You protected them."

"Did I do the right thing? Does humanity deserve to know? Or do Light Speakers deserve privacy?"

Static filled the pause. "No easy answers there."

Tod traced his finger along the satellite image. "Their safety comes first. Always."

"I'm with you," Barney said firmly. "Whatever you need."

Tod felt a surge of gratitude for his friend's unwavering support. "I'll contact them tonight. If they're being observed, they need to know. They deserve that warning at least."

"And then?"

Tod stared out his window toward the darkening Gulf. "Then we prepare for whatever comes next."

Chapter 8

The morning sun crept over the eastern horizon, painting Copano Bay in shades of amber and gold. Tod sat cross-legged on his dock, eyes closed, coffee mug cooling beside him. His morning ritual had evolved since the Light Speakers changed him—a systematic check of the electromagnetic landscape within his fifty-foot bubble of perception.

Three phones in sleep mode inside his house. The humming refrigerator compressor. His boat's electrical system on standby. The neighbor's security camera pivoting every forty seconds. Each signature distinct in Tod's mind, like different instruments in an orchestra he never asked to hear.

Barney's warning about Dr. Chen's satellite data lingered in his thoughts. Scientists were watching. Looking for patterns. For the Light Speakers. For something unexplainable in the Gulf waters.

Tod opened his eyes and sipped his coffee, grimacing at its lukewarm temperature. A movement caught his attention—a small rental boat about two hundred yards offshore, drifting sideways with the current. A woman stood at the stern, frantically paddling with what looked like a boat cushion. The vessel had no wake, no engine noise.

His electromagnetic sense confirmed it immediately: dead electronics, no electrical signature from the motor. Probably a sheared prop pin. Simple fix, but the current was pushing her toward Schuler's Reef—a treacherous oyster bed that could slice the fiberglass hull like paper.

Tod set his mug down harder than intended. Every instinct screamed for isolation, for safety, for maintaining the careful boundary he'd built around his changed life. Getting involved meant questions, conversation, proximity to another person who might notice his strange behaviors or reactions to their electronics.

But she was headed for trouble.

Tod stood, calculating. Ten minutes until she'd hit the oyster bed. Another five minutes for him to get his boat in the water.

"Damn it," he muttered, already moving toward his boat lift. The woman waved frantically when she spotted him, her relief visible even at this distance.

As Tod lowered his boat into the water, he prepared himself for the inevitable social interaction, the questions, the need to appear normal. One more complication he didn't need, but some responsibilities transcended his new condition.

Whatever the Light Speakers had changed in him, they hadn't altered that.

TOD WATCHED THE WOMAN'S increasingly desperate attempts to control her drifting boat. Her makeshift paddle—what appeared to be a seat cushion—slapped ineffectively at the water's surface. Each stroke moved the vessel mere inches against the persistent current.

He narrowed his eyes, mentally calculating trajectory and drift speed. The morning tide was pulling her southwest at roughly two knots. Schuler's Reef lay directly in her path—a menace of razor-sharp oyster shells waiting just beneath the surface. Fifteen minutes, maybe twenty if she managed to slow her drift, before inevitable collision.

A familiar tingling sensation spread across Tod's consciousness as his marine empathy reached out, unbidden. A school of speckled trout scattered beneath her boat, their collective alarm registering in Tod's mind like distant wind chimes. Their agitation only confirmed his calculation—the reef was close.

"Not my problem," Tod muttered, turning away. His fingers tightened around his coffee mug. The woman had rented a boat without proper knowledge or preparation. People made poor decisions on the water every day. That's why the Coast Guard existed.

He glanced back. She had stopped paddling, shoulders slumped in defeat. Even from this distance, her exhaustion was evident in the way she braced herself against the console, head bowed. Tod scanned the bay—not another boat in sight, no one coming to help.

Just him.

Something deep within Tod's consciousness stirred, a sense of obligation that had nothing to do with his new abilities. Before the Light Speakers, before the changes, he'd been someone who wouldn't let another person drift into danger. That part of him remained unchanged.

"Damn it," Tod sighed, setting his mug down on the dock with unnecessary force. The woman had spotted him now, was waving frantically, hope replacing resignation in her posture.

He headed toward his boat, recognizing that for all his desire for isolation, for all his fear of discovery, he couldn't simply watch someone crash into Schuler's Reef. Whatever the Light Speakers had transformed within his brain, they hadn't altered his fundamental nature.

Some things even alien contact couldn't change.

FIVE MINUTES LATER, Tod guided K5HUX alongside the stranded rental with practiced precision. The vessels bobbed in momentary synchronization before he cut the engine to idle, the distance between them narrowing to just a few feet.

The woman stood at the gunwale, auburn hair whipping across her face in the morning breeze. Despite her predicament, she didn't exhibit the wide-eyed panic typical of tourists in trouble. Instead, her expression balanced frustration with a certain calm acceptance of her situation. One hand clutched the boat's railing while the other protectively cradled an expensive camera with a telephoto lens.

Relief washed across her features at Tod's arrival, tinged with the pink flush of embarrassment.

"I'm going to guess you're not out here for the view," Tod called over, tossing her a line to secure the boats together.

She caught it with surprising deftness, quickly wrapping it around a cleat with proper technique. "The view is great. The boat, not so much." Her laugh carried across the water, genuine despite her circumstances. "I was photographing the sunrise when the engine just... died. Complete silence, then drifting."

Tod stepped carefully from his vessel to hers, feeling the subtle shift in electromagnetic fields as he crossed the threshold between boats. The rental's electrical system was completely dead—no current flowing anywhere.

"I'm Claire," she offered, extending her hand. "Claire Westbrook. Thanks for the rescue."

"Tod Blackstone."

As their hands met, Tod felt something unexpected—not electromagnetic or empathic—something entirely human yet profound. Claire's eyes met his, hazel shifting to green in the morning light, and in that moment of connection, a mutual recognition passed between them. Her gaze held none of the casual dismissiveness that characterized most brief encounters. Instead, she studied him with an artist's perception, taking in details others would miss.

Those observant eyes made Tod feel oddly exposed, as if she might somehow see the changes within him that others couldn't detect. Yet strangely, the sensation didn't trigger his usual defensiveness.

Claire tilted her head slightly, a small crease forming between her brows as she regarded him with undisguised curiosity. "You're not what I expected out here."

Tod found himself returning her gaze with equal intensity, recognizing something in her he couldn't quite name—a quality of separateness, of viewing the world from a different angle.

"Funny," he replied. "I was thinking the same about you."

"LET ME TAKE A LOOK at your engine," Tod said, moving toward the stern with practiced efficiency.

Claire followed, keeping a respectful distance as Tod removed the engine cowling. His hands moved with mechanical precision, fingers tracing connections and components without hesitation. Within moments, he identified the issue.

"Sheared prop pin," he announced. "Happens with these rentals when they hit something underwater. Probably a submerged branch or debris."

Claire nodded, her photographer's eye catching the way the morning light played across Tod's face as he worked. Something about his movements seemed almost preternatural—too efficient, too aware of each component without having to search or fumble.

"I can tow you back to the marina," Tod offered, replacing the cowling. "Shouldn't take more than forty minutes."

"I'd appreciate that," Claire said, adjusting the camera strap around her neck. "I was starting to calculate how long it would take to paddle back with that piece of driftwood."

"Longer than you'd want," Tod replied with the ghost of a smile. "Especially with the current."

As they moved to secure the tow line, Claire introduced herself more fully. "I moved to Rockport about eight months ago. I'm a photographer—nature, wildlife, coastal scenes."

Tod's hands worked the line into a proper bridle configuration, his movements automatic while his attention seemed divided between the task and studying her. "Fishing charters. Been here my whole life, more or less."

When he handed her the line to secure to her boat's bow cleat, their fingers brushed. Their eyes met again, and something electric passed between them that had nothing to do with Tod's enhanced senses. Claire felt it too—a momentary connection, unexpected and compelling.

"I've seen your property from the water," Claire said, breaking the charged silence. "That antenna tower is quite the landmark. The morning light on it is spectacular."

Tod's expression shifted subtly, a wariness returning to his eyes. The mention of his tower—his connection to the Light Speakers—triggered his protective instincts.

"I'd love to photograph the docks sometime," Claire continued, oblivious to his internal shift. "The way the pilings create those patterns in the water is fascinating."

"Maybe," Tod replied, his tone cooling slightly as he returned to his boat. "We'll get you back first."

As he started his engine and took up the slack in the tow line, Tod glanced back at Claire, who stood watching him with those perceptive eyes. Something about her both drew him in and set off warning signals. She saw too much.

TOD THROTTLED DOWN to a careful towing speed, the rental boat trailing behind his own like an obedient puppy. The morning had fully bloomed now, transforming Copano Bay into a canvas of dancing light and shadow. He glanced back occasionally, watching as Claire balanced easily at the bow of her rented vessel, seemingly unconcerned by their slow pace.

She raised her camera, framing shots of the water's surface where sunlight fractured into a thousand glittering points. Then she turned the lens toward his boat, capturing the wake as it spread behind K5HUX. Tod felt the strange sensation of being observed—not just seen, but truly noticed—in a way that was different from the suspicious glances of other captains or the clinical interest of Dr. Chen.

"You're a photographer?" he called back over the low rumble of the engine.

Claire lowered her camera, smiling. "Trying to be. Nature stuff mostly. Coastal birds, seascapes, that kind of thing." She gestured to the bay around them. "Moved from Austin about eight months ago. Couldn't resist this light."

"What brought you to Rockport specifically?" Tod found himself asking, surprising himself with his curiosity.

"The whooping cranes, initially," she replied, adjusting her stance as the boat gently rocked. "Then I fell in love with the whole coast. Something about the edges of places—where land meets water, where light meets shadow."

Tod nodded, understanding exactly what she meant though he'd never articulated it that way himself. His electromagnetic sense registered the standard signatures from her camera, phone, and watch—nothing unusual there. Yet something about her presence felt different. Not threatening, just... alert. Aware.

"You must know these waters pretty well," Claire observed, capturing another image. "Been running charters long?"

"Most of my life," Tod answered, automatically checking their heading. "Grew up on the water."

They fell into a comfortable silence then, the kind Tod usually only experienced alone or with Barney. It felt strange to share quiet with someone new without the awkwardness he'd come to expect. Claire seemed content to photograph, and Tod to navigate, neither feeling pressured to fill the air with unnecessary words.

The silence itself felt like a conversation—one conducted in the language of light on water, in the rhythm of small waves against fiberglass, in the occasional calls of laughing gulls overhead. Tod found himself stealing glances back at Claire, wondering what her camera saw that others might miss.

TOD GUIDED BOTH VESSELS into the channel leading to the Rockport Marina, slowing as they approached the rental dock. The morning had fully developed around them, with other boats now dotting the bay and the marina bustling with early activity. He felt Claire watching him from behind as he executed a perfect approach, the culmination of thousands of similar maneuvers.

Mike Sanderson, the marina attendant, looked up from his clipboard as they neared. Recognition flashed across his weathered face when he spotted Claire in the trailing boat.

"What happened out there, Miss Westbrook?" Mike called, grabbing the bow line Tod tossed to him.

Claire stepped carefully onto the dock. "Engine died about a mile out. Luckily, Mr. Blackstone was kind enough to rescue me before I drifted onto Schuler's Reef."

Tod secured his own vessel before examining the rental boat's propeller. "Sheared pin," he announced, pointing to the damage. "Pretty clean break. Probably hit something small in the water."

Mike knelt to inspect it himself, then stood with a sigh. "Third one this month. I keep telling the boss we need better pins." He turned to Claire. "No charge for today's rental, of course. Sorry about the trouble."

"Not your fault," Claire replied, slinging her camera bag over her shoulder.

Mike glanced between them with sudden interest. "Didn't know you two knew each other."

"We don't," Tod said quickly. "Just saw her drifting from my dock."

"Right place, right time," Claire added with a small smile.

Mike's face settled into a knowing look that made Tod uncomfortable. "Well, lucky coincidence then."

Claire turned to Tod. "Let me buy you coffee at Dockside as thanks. Least I can do."

Tod felt a pull toward her that unsettled him—a connection he hadn't anticipated. Part of him wanted to accept, to hear more about her photography, her perspective on the coast they both loved. But another part remembered Dr. Chen's visit, the satellite photos, the danger of letting anyone too close.

"I don't drink much coffee," he lied, avoiding her eyes.

"Oh." Claire nodded, disappointment briefly crossing her face before she recovered. "No problem. Thanks again for the rescue."

"Anyone would have done the same," Tod mumbled, already retreating toward his boat.

"Not everyone would," Claire replied softly, her gaze holding his for a moment longer than was comfortable before she turned away.

Tod watched her walk toward the marina office, her auburn hair catching the morning light. He felt the weight of his isolation more acutely than he had in weeks.

TOD BUSIED HIMSELF with untying K5HUX from the dock, his movements deliberate and practiced. He sensed rather than saw Claire lingering at the edge of the marina office, her gaze resting on him with unspoken questions. Around them, the morning unfolded with the usual marina symphony—boats creaking against their moorings, seagulls arguing overhead, fishermen calling to one another as they prepared for the day.

Claire took a few steps back toward the dock, her camera hanging at her side. Something about this man called to her professional eye—the way he moved with such precision, how the light caught his profile against the water.

"The light's really special from your property," she called out, her voice carrying over the distance between them. "The way it hits Copano Bay at sunrise."

Tod's hands paused on the line. He turned slightly, regarding her with a guarded expression that seemed to soften almost imperceptibly.

"Yeah. It is," he admitted, and for a moment, they shared an appreciation that transcended words—two people who understood what it meant to truly see the world around them.

"Would you ever let someone photograph from there?" The question escaped her lips before she could reconsider. Claire watched his expression shift, knowing she was asking something personal, perhaps too forward for their brief acquaintance.

Tod should have said no. Every instinct screamed to protect his sanctuary, to keep his altered life isolated from curious eyes. But her genuine appreciation for something he treasured daily made him hesitate.

"Maybe," he found himself saying. "I'd have to think about it."

Claire smiled, and the expression transformed her face entirely—hazel eyes crinkling at the corners, freckles dancing across the bridge of her nose. She reached into her pocket and pulled out a simple white business card.

"If you change your mind about coffee. Or photography. Or anything," she said, extending it toward him.

Tod took the card, and their fingers brushed briefly. An unexpected jolt passed between them—something electric yet entirely human. Claire's eyes widened slightly, and Tod felt a rush of warmth that had nothing to do with his altered senses.

For a suspended moment, neither moved. Then Tod carefully tucked the card into his pocket.

"Thanks for the tow," Claire said softly.

"Thanks for needing one," Tod replied, then winced at his own awkwardness.

But Claire just laughed—a genuine sound that seemed to linger in the air even as she turned and walked away, leaving Tod with a card in his pocket and an unfamiliar sensation in his chest.

TOD EASED K5HUX INTO its slip, cutting the engine and securing the vessel with practiced motions that required little thought. The water lapped gently against the hull, a familiar rhythm that normally brought him peace. Today, however, his mind buzzed with something altogether different.

Back on solid ground, Tod reached into his pocket and extracted Claire's business card. He examined it in the mid-morning light—cream-colored stock with minimalist design, "Claire

Westbrook Photography" in elegant serif font. Below her name, small text listed her specialties: "Natural Light • Wildlife • Coastal Landscapes." The card's edge bore a subtle embossed pattern that resembled waves.

"Just throw it away," Tod muttered to himself, his thumb tracing the raised texture. "Last thing you need is someone with a camera poking around."

He walked into his workshop, setting the card down on his cluttered desk rather than the trash can. It sat there like a beacon among the wiring diagrams and electronic components, demanding attention.

Tod busied himself hanging his life vest and checking his gear, but found his mind wandering back to their conversation at the marina, the way her eyes had sparkled when she talked about the light on Copano Bay. The way she'd noticed something that mattered to him.

"Stop it," he commanded the empty room, rubbing his temples where a dull ache persisted.

Despite his better judgment, Tod picked up his phone. He hesitated only briefly before typing "Claire Westbrook photography" into the search bar. Her Instagram appeared first, and his thumb hovered for a second before tapping.

The screen filled with stunning images—a great blue heron silhouetted against a fiery sunset, waves breaking over jetty rocks in perfect golden hour light, a weathered shrimp boat framed against gathering storm clouds. Tod scrolled, absorbed by her eye for composition, the way she captured light and shadow.

A caption beneath a photo of Copano Bay at dawn caught his attention: "Grandmother always said light tells truth if we learn to listen. Still trying to understand what she meant."

Tod closed the app abruptly, setting his phone down with more force than necessary. He was getting too interested, too quickly. This photographer with her perceptive gaze and quiet confidence represented complications he couldn't afford—not with what he'd become, not with what he protected.

Yet even as he turned away, Tod knew the card would remain on his desk, a possibility he wasn't quite ready to discard.

THE WORKSHOP DARKENED as evening settled across Copano Bay. Tod sat at his workbench, tinkering with circuit boards for his new beacon design. Seagulls called in the distance as they settled for the night, their cries mingling with the gentle lapping of water against the pilings beneath his dock.

The HAM radio crackled to life, its electronic signature pulsing in Tod's mind before the sound even reached his ears.

"K5YWB calling K5HUX, you reading me, Tod?"

Tod reached for the microphone, the familiar weight of it in his hand a small comfort in his increasingly unfamiliar life. "K5HUX receiving. Evening, Barney. How's Port Lavaca treating you?"

"Can't complain. Dinner was decent, weather's fair." Barney's voice carried through the speaker with the slight distortion Tod had grown accustomed to over the years. "Heard you played hero this morning."

Tod continued soldering a connection. "Nothing heroic about it. Just helped someone with a broken rental."

"That so?" Barney's tone shifted, amusement coloring his words. "Harry down at the marina said it was a pretty girl. Photographer type."

Tod's hand slipped, nearly burning his finger. He set the soldering iron down with more force than necessary.

"I didn't notice," he replied curtly.

"Uh-huh." The radio fell silent for a moment. "What was her name?"

Tod glanced at the business card still sitting on his desk, the embossed wave pattern catching the workshop's dim light. He didn't answer.

"Tod? You still there?" Barney's voice softened. "Would it be so bad? To let someone in?"

Outside, the first stars appeared over the bay. Tod watched their reflection waver on the water's surface.

"It's complicated," he finally said.

"It's always complicated with you." Barney's laugh came through warm and genuine. "Doesn't mean it's not worth it."

Tod's fingers brushed against the card. Claire Westbrook Photography. The memory of her smile as she'd taken his photo from the bow of her rented boat surfaced unbidden.

"I've got responsibilities now," Tod said. "Things I can't explain."

"Maybe you don't have to explain everything right away." Barney paused. "Just something to think about. Over and out."

The radio fell silent, leaving Tod alone with his thoughts and the distant, comforting pulse of the Light Speakers somewhere out in the Gulf.

THE MOON ROSE ABOVE Copano Bay, casting silver ribbons across the dark water. Tod sat cross-legged at the end of his dock, the new beacon prototype resting beside him. His nightly check-in with the Light Speakers had become ritual—a moment of connection that grounded him in this new reality.

He activated the beacon at precisely 10:00 PM, its soft electronic hum joining the chorus of night insects. Within minutes, the familiar blue-white glow appeared beneath the surface, pulsing with that seven-second rhythm that had become as familiar to Tod as his own heartbeat.

"HELLO FRIEND K5HUX," they signaled.

Tod smiled and flashed his response with the handheld light: "HELLO FRIENDS. ARE YOU WELL?"

"YES. DEEP WATER GOOD. HOME SOON." Their patterns shifted, forming complex harmonics. "YOU WELL TOO."

It wasn't a question but an observation. Tod considered their perception, how they sensed his state beyond what he communicated.

"QUESTION," Tod signaled after a moment's hesitation. "IF SOMEONE SAW YOU WOULD THEY UNDERSTAND."

The colony pulsed in unison before responding: "SOME SEE - SOME FEEL - RARE."

Tod leaned closer to the water's edge. "HOW KNOW WHO."

"THEY SEE MORE - LIKE YOU - NOTICE LIGHT."

Tod's thoughts immediately turned to Claire Westbrook. He remembered scrolling through her Instagram, lingering on a particular caption beneath a sunrise photo: "The light speaks if we learn to listen." At the time, he'd dismissed it as artistic sentiment. Now, he wondered.

The Light Speakers' patterns shifted, growing more complex as if sensing his thoughts. "YOU NOT ALONE ANYMORE - GOOD."

Tod blinked, surprised by their perception. "WHAT DO YOU MEAN."

"YOU LESS HEAVY - WE FEEL IT - GOOD CHANGE."

A warmth spread across Tod's face that had nothing to do with temperature. Even these beings from the deep ocean depths could perceive the subtle shift in him—the lightening he'd felt since his encounter with Claire that morning.

"I NEED TO GO NOW," Tod signaled, suddenly self-conscious.

The colony pulsed gently, their light gradually dimming. "REST WELL FRIEND K5HUX."

As they faded back into the depths, Tod remained sitting on the dock, the business card between his fingers, the memory of Claire's smile competing with the afterimage of bioluminescent patterns still dancing behind his eyelids.

THE SCREEN CAST A BLUE glow over Claire's face as she swiped through the morning's photos. Her small bungalow was quiet save for the ceiling fan's lazy circles and distant waves brushing the shore. Outside her window, Rockport had settled into evening stillness.

Claire paused on a particular image—Tod Blackstone's silhouette against the morning light, one hand on the wheel, the other adjusting the throttle. The composition was accidental but perfect: man and machine as one entity, completely in his element.

"There's something here," she murmured, zooming in.

She'd taken dozens of shots during the tow back to the marina. The rental boat's engine failure had been frustrating, but her photographer's instinct recognized the gift—uninterrupted access to Tod's property from the water, the morning light on his dock, and most intriguingly, the man himself.

Claire opened another image—a profile shot captured when Tod wasn't looking. His features were sharp against the water, eyes scanning the horizon with practiced intensity. There was confidence in his posture, the ease of someone born to navigate these waters. But something else lingered beneath—a solitude that felt deliberate, a heaviness behind his eyes.

She minimized the photos and opened a new document, fingers hovering over the keyboard before typing:

T. Blackstone - charter captain, lives on bay, early 30s?, alone. Helped without asking anything. Watches water like listening to it. Same way I watch light. Guarded. Lonely? Want to photograph him. Worth pursuing? (Yes.)

Claire stared at the last word, surprised by her certainty. "Why do I care?" she asked the empty room.

Her eyes drifted to the framed watercolor on her desk—her grandmother Maggie painting the coast years ago. Beside it, a photograph of Maggie herself, paintbrush in hand, eyes crinkling with joy.

"What do you think, Grandma?" Claire touched the frame gently. "You always said the best subjects are the ones that haunt you after you've put the camera down."

The photograph offered no answer, but Claire didn't need one. Something about Tod Blackstone called to her artistic instinct—the way he moved through the world as if tuned to frequencies others couldn't hear. Like her, he seemed to see beyond surfaces.

Claire returned to the photos, lingering on the shot of his property with its curious antenna tower reaching skyward.

"What are you listening for out there, Tod Blackstone?" she whispered.

THE WORKSHOP CLOCK read 1:07 AM, its digital readout sending faint electrical pulses that Tod could feel without looking. Sleep had abandoned him hours ago, leaving him alone with thoughts that refused to settle. He'd tried reading technical manuals, tinkering with circuit boards, even counting the electrical signatures of devices around the house.

Nothing worked.

Tod's eyes drifted to his desk where Claire's business card lay. In the darkness, it seemed to emit its own subtle glow—not physically luminescent but somehow commanding attention in the electromagnetic landscape of his workshop. He picked it up, running his thumb across the raised lettering. His altered senses could feel the subtle texture differences between ink and paper.

"Claire Elizabeth Westbrook - Visual Artist & Photographer."

Barney's words echoed: "Would it be so bad to let someone in? Just a little?"

Then the Light Speakers: "You less heavy now."

Tod remembered how Claire had looked at the water—not as a blank surface or mere background, but with reverence. The way she framed shots through her viewfinder reminded him of how he sensed the bay through his modified equipment. Both seeking patterns others missed.

Before he could talk himself out of it, Tod grabbed his phone. The screen's electrical signature made his fingertips tingle as he typed:

"This is Tod Blackstone. You can photograph from my dock if you want. Sunrise usually best. Let me know when."

His thumb hovered over the send button. Three breaths. Then he pressed it.

The phone went silent. One minute. Two. Three.

Tod set it down, heart pounding harder than when he'd sensed the approaching storm. Just as he turned away, the device buzzed. Three dots appeared, disappeared, then reappeared.

"Thank you. How's tomorrow morning? I'll bring coffee even if you don't drink it. 6:15?"

Tod stared at the message, feeling the rush of blood in his temples, the electric current of nervous anticipation.

He typed back: "Okay. 6:15."

Setting the phone down, Tod whispered to the empty workshop, "What are you doing?"

But the corners of his mouth turned upward slightly.

Outside, moonlight washed over his empty dock where tomorrow two different worlds might meet. Across town, Claire's light clicked off as she set her alarm for 5:30 AM. Both lay awake in their separate beds, unable to sleep, minds fixed on the morning and the stranger who somehow didn't feel like a stranger at all.

Chapter 9

The eastern sky turned molten gold as Claire's battered Subaru rolled to a stop beside Tod's workshop at 6:10 AM. He'd been standing at his kitchen window for twenty minutes, sensing her approach before her headlights appeared on the road. When her car door opened, Tod stepped outside, pretending he'd only just emerged rather than having rehearsed this moment since dawn.

Claire balanced two coffees and a white paper bag in her hands, her camera bag slung across her body. Morning light caught in her auburn hair, which she'd hastily pulled into a messy bun. Tod stood awkwardly at the edge of his property, hands shoved into the pockets of his worn fishing shorts.

"You're early," he said, then winced at his own stiffness.

"Light waits for no one," Claire replied, extending one of the coffees. "You said you don't drink coffee."

Tod took the cup, fingers carefully avoiding hers in the exchange. "I lied."

Claire's laugh—spontaneous and unguarded—broke something loose in the air between them. Her shoulders relaxed, and Tod felt his own tension ebb like an outgoing tide.

"Kolaches," she said, lifting the bag slightly. "From Mrs. Alvarez. The peach ones are still warm."

Tod nodded, surprised she'd remembered his local bakery.

Claire set down her coffee on a wooden post and began unpacking her gear with practiced efficiency. Her movements were economical, almost like a dance she'd performed thousands of times. Three different lenses, filters, and a tripod emerged from her

143

weatherproof bag. Tod held her coffee when she needed both hands, watching as Claire transformed from nervous visitor to focused artist within moments.

The light spread across the bay—that special coastal light that seemed to come from everywhere and nowhere. Claire began shooting, moving with deliberate steps across his dock. She captured the water's surface, the texture of sky, his boat's reflection, the weathered grain of dock boards.

"F-stop four... maybe three-five," she murmured, mostly to herself. "God, look at that light catcher... need to bracket this..."

Tod watched her work—completely absorbed in her element, forgetting he was there. He recognized that focus, that connection to something beyond oneself. He'd felt it when building electronics, when tracking signals. Claire was listening to light the way he listened to electromagnetic fields, speaking its language with her camera.

She smiled at something only she could see through her viewfinder, and Tod found himself smiling too.

CLAIRE MOVED AROUND the dock with the precision of a dancer, each step purposeful as she sought perfect compositions in the morning light. She pivoted from the weathered pilings to the horizon, her camera an extension of herself. Tod leaned against his workshop door, trying to stay clear of her work, observing her quiet intensity.

"Do you mind?" she asked, gesturing with her camera toward him.

Tod stiffened. "I'm not much for pictures."

"Just keep coiling that rope," Claire said, already framing the shot.

Tod looked down, realizing he'd unconsciously picked up a length of nylon line and had been working it through his hands. He continued the familiar motion, aware of her lens capturing him but trying to ignore it.

"Most people pose when they see a camera," Claire said, adjusting her settings without looking up. "They perform some version of themselves. You don't."

She circled around, capturing his silhouette against the sunrise, the way his hands worked the rope with practiced precision. The shutter clicked in rhythmic bursts.

"That's enough," Tod said finally, setting the coiled rope on a cleat.

Claire lowered her camera. "Sorry. Occupational hazard. When I see good light on something real, I can't help myself."

She walked over and turned her camera to show him the display. Tod expected to see awkward images of himself but instead found striking compositions—his weathered hands working the rope with the bay as backdrop, his profile in golden light, details of his boat and dock that somehow told a story.

"You make everything look intentional," he said quietly.

Claire studied him with those observant hazel eyes. "You are intentional. Most people aren't."

The words hung between them, carrying more weight than their simplicity suggested. Tod recognized something in her then—a similar quality of attention, of really seeing the world rather than merely looking at it. Claire understood patterns and details in light the way he understood electromagnetic fields and signals.

"You listen," he said.

Claire tilted her head slightly. "To what?"

"To whatever speaks to you. Most people don't bother."

A smile touched the corner of her mouth, genuine understanding passing between them. Two observers who'd spent their lives paying attention to things others missed, speaking different languages but recognizing the same underlying truth.

"Yes," she said simply. "I do."

CLAIRE STOOD AT THE edge of the dock, camera raised to capture a formation of brown pelicans gliding inches above the water's surface. The morning light caught their wings at perfect angles, transforming ordinary birds into creatures of myth. Tod watched her work, appreciating her singular focus and the way she anticipated their movements before they happened.

Suddenly, a familiar tingling sensation crawled across Tod's scalp. His skin prickled as electromagnetic patterns shifted in the atmosphere around him. He closed his eyes momentarily, sensing the building electrical charge miles away—a storm forming over the Gulf, moving faster than it should.

"We should head inside. Weather's changing," Tod said, his voice cutting through the peaceful morning.

Claire lowered her camera and looked at the clear blue sky overhead. "What? It's perfect out here." She pulled out her phone, checking the forecast. "Says clear all morning. Not a cloud for miles."

"Forecast is wrong. Twenty minutes, maybe less."

Claire studied his face, noting the certainty in his expression. His eyes scanned the horizon where nothing yet appeared. She hesitated, then started collapsing her tripod.

"How do you know?" she asked, carefully placing her camera in its padded case.

Tod looked away, already regretting the slip. "I just... feel it. Pressure changes."

Ten minutes later, as Claire packed her last lens, the wind shifted direction. The pleasant morning breeze turned cooler, carrying the unmistakable scent of rain. On the southeastern horizon, dark clouds gathered, moving with unnatural speed toward the shoreline.

Claire stared at Tod, then back at the approaching storm front. "That's impossible. The forecast just updated five minutes ago still showing clear skies."

Tod shrugged, already gathering her equipment bags. "But it's happening."

The first fat raindrop hit the dock between them as distant thunder rolled across the water. Claire's eyes widened, fixed on Tod's face with newfound curiosity. Whatever calculations she was running behind those hazel eyes, Tod could see her perspective shifting, recategorizing him from interesting stranger to something else entirely.

"Let's get inside," he said, gesturing toward his workshop.

As they hurried across the lawn, rain beginning to patter around them, Claire cast another glance at Tod. He pretended not to notice, but he felt the weight of her attention—her photographer's eye now seeing details it had missed before. The comfortable connection between them had shifted into something more complicated.

By the time they reached the workshop door, the sky had darkened completely, and the storm Tod had felt building in his nerves poured down around them.

RAIN HAMMERED AGAINST the metal roof of the workshop, creating a rhythmic percussion that filled the small space. Inside, the room felt unexpectedly cozy—a shelter from the sudden squall, with the scent of coffee and kolaches warming the air. Claire peeled off her damp outer shirt and draped it over a nearby stool while Tod poured coffee into mismatched mugs.

Claire's eyes wandered across the workshop, taking in the organized chaos. Her gaze lingered on the HAM radio setup in the corner, the half-assembled electronic components on the workbench, and the detailed maritime charts pinned to the wall with handwritten notations.

"You built all this?" she asked, gesturing toward a complex array of circuits connected to what looked like a modified antenna control system.

Tod handed her a steaming mug. "Most of it. I modify commercial equipment when it doesn't do exactly what I need."

Claire moved closer to examine the intricate soldering work. "This is incredible craftsmanship. My dad tried to teach me basic electronics when I was a kid, but I never had the patience." She pointed to the HAM radio. "That's how you communicate with other operators? K5HUX, right?"

Tod's eyebrows lifted. "You know HAM radio?"

"I recognize a callsign when I see one." She smiled, tapping the label on his equipment. "I did a photo series on emergency responders after Hurricane Harvey. Some of the only communication getting through was from operators like you."

As the rain continued its steady rhythm overhead, their conversation flowed naturally. Claire told him about leaving Austin, her grandmother Maggie's watercolors that inspired her photography, and how capturing nature made her feel connected to something larger than herself.

Tod found himself relaxing, sharing more than he had with anyone except Barney. He explained his antenna system and the modifications he'd made to improve reception across unusual frequency bands.

"So you're listening for something specific?" Claire asked.

Tod hesitated only briefly. "Just... exploring what's out there."

The rain stopped as suddenly as it had begun, sunlight breaking through the workshop windows. Claire checked her watch and sighed.

"I should go. I've got an editing deadline for Texas Highways." She gathered her equipment, then paused at the door. "Would it be okay if I came back? Maybe for an evening shoot? The light on the bay at sunset is supposed to be incredible."

Tod felt the familiar urge to protect his solitude wrestling with something new—a desire for her company.

"Yeah," he said, surprising himself with how quickly the answer came. "Evenings are good."

THE AFTERNOON SUN BEAT down on Tod's back as he leaned over K5HUX's engine compartment. Sweat dripped from his forehead while he methodically replaced the raw water impeller. The methodical work helped quiet his mind after Claire's morning visit—a welcome distraction from thoughts that kept circling back to her smile and the way she saw the world.

The crunch of tires on gravel cut through his concentration. Tod straightened, instinctively scanning the electromagnetic landscape before spotting the white Toyota SUV with the Texas A&M Marine Biology Department logo emblazoned on its door. Dr. Chen had returned.

Tod wiped his hands on a rag and watched her approach, her stride purposeful across his property.

"Mr. Blackstone," she called. "I'm sorry to drop in unannounced again."

"Seems to be happening a lot lately," Tod replied, keeping his voice neutral despite the tension climbing his spine.

Dr. Chen offered an apologetic smile that didn't reach her eyes. "I wouldn't keep bothering you if it wasn't important." She pulled a tablet from her messenger bag. "We've enhanced the satellite imagery I showed you before."

She turned the screen toward him. The bioluminescent pattern Tod had created with the Light Speakers was unmistakably clearer—organized in perfect concentric circles, repeating in seven-second intervals. A cold weight settled in Tod's stomach.

"Mr. Blackstone, I need to know what you saw that day."

Tod crossed his arms. "I told you. Fishing."

"You're lying." Dr. Chen's tone hardened. "And I think you're protecting something."

They stood in tense silence, the only sound the distant call of gulls and the gentle lap of water against the dock. Tod felt the weight of the Light Speakers' trust heavy on his shoulders. Dr. Chen studied his face, searching for answers he refused to give.

Then she shifted strategy. "I'm hiring a photographer to document Gulf phenomena. Aerial and surface shoots." She watched Tod's reaction carefully. "Maybe they'll see what you won't tell me."

Tod's stomach dropped. "Who?"

"Haven't decided yet. Local preferably." She slid the tablet back into her bag. "Someone who knows these waters."

Claire's face flashed through Tod's mind—her camera pointed toward the bay at sunrise, her talk of capturing what speaks to her. If Dr. Chen hired her, would Claire unwittingly expose the Light Speakers? Or worse, would Claire feel betrayed when she discovered Tod's connection to whatever she might photograph?

The threat was no longer abstract. It had a timeline now, and potential faces attached to it.

THE WHITE SUV DISAPPEARED down the road, leaving Tod alone with a torrent of uncomfortable possibilities. He paced the length of his workshop, the floorboards creaking beneath his agitated strides. The digital clock on his workbench read 2:30 PM. Only hours had passed since Claire had stood on his dock, her camera capturing the morning light—the same light that illuminated the beings swimming miles offshore.

"Dammit," Tod muttered, running a hand through his hair. If Dr. Chen approached Claire with a photography job, what then? Claire already had access to his dock, already took photos of the bay at sunrise—the very time when the Light Speakers were most active. It wouldn't take much for her to capture something unusual, something unexplainable.

Tod grabbed his phone and pulled up Claire's number, his thumb hovering over the message field. What could he possibly say? *Hey, if a marine biologist offers you work, please say no*? He couldn't forbid her from taking a job. From what she'd mentioned, freelance photographers lived gig-to-gig. She needed the money.

He tossed the phone onto the workbench and gripped the edge until his knuckles whitened. Telling Claire about the Light Speakers wasn't an option. He barely knew her. And yet something about her—the way she talked about listening to the light, how she found meaning in the overlooked—made him think she might understand.

But if Dr. Chen showed Claire those satellite images...if she connected what she saw on Tod's dock with the organized patterns in the Gulf...

"She'd see it," Tod whispered to the empty room. "She'd see what no one else has."

His phone screen glowed as he snatched it back up, scrolling past Claire's contact to Barney's. This wasn't a decision he could make alone.

Barney answered on the third ring. "What's up, bud? Thought you had your photographer friend over this morning."

"Chen was just here. She's hiring a photographer to document 'Gulf phenomena.' She knows, Barney. Those satellite images—they show exactly what we did."

"Slow down. What photographer?"

"She didn't say, but—" Tod glanced at Claire's business card sitting on his desk. "What if it's Claire? What if she already approached her?"

The silence on the other end stretched uncomfortably long before Barney spoke. "Maybe it's time to trust someone else with what you know."

"SO LET ME GET THIS straight," Barney's voice crackled through the phone. "You're worried the scientist will hire the girl you like to photograph the aliens you're protecting?"

Tod paced the length of his workshop. "I don't like her. And yes."

A long silence stretched across the connection before Barney sighed. "Tod, you're going to have to trust someone eventually. Maybe Claire's that person."

"I just met her." Tod stopped at the window, looking out at the bay where, miles beyond his view, the Light Speakers lived their secret lives.

"You just met the Light Speakers too. Worked out okay."

Tod rubbed the back of his neck, frustration building inside him. He wanted to argue, but Barney had a point. He'd entrusted his life to strange, bioluminescent beings without hesitation. Yet the thought of confiding in Claire—a human—twisted his stomach into knots.

"What if she takes the job?" Tod asked quietly.

"Then you tell her the truth before Chen does." Barney's voice had that calm assurance Tod both appreciated and resented. "At least then you control the story."

Tod leaned against his workbench, feeling the weight of responsibility press down on him. "What if she doesn't believe me? Or worse, what if she does believe me and then tells everyone?"

"You gonna play the what-if game all day? Because we could be here awhile."

The water outside shimmered in the afternoon sun, waves catching and reflecting light in patterns that only Tod could fully appreciate now. His new abilities had changed everything—his perception, his isolation, his purpose. But they hadn't changed his need for human connection.

"You can't protect them alone, Tod. Not forever."

"I know," Tod admitted, the words sticking in his throat. "I just didn't think I'd have to make this decision so soon."

"Yeah, well, life's funny that way. Throws curveballs when you're looking for fastballs."

Tod closed his eyes, feeling the hum of electronics around him, the distant presence of marine life, and somewhere beyond his reach, the Light Speakers.

"I'm already in too deep, aren't I?"

Barney chuckled. "Brother, you were in deep the moment you decided to follow that signal. The only question now is whether you're gonna swim alone."

CLAIRE LEANED CLOSER to her laptop screen, squinting at the image from her morning shoot. The golden light captured on Tod's dock was exactly what she'd hoped for—perfect reflections on still water, the weathered wood catching the sunrise. But something else caught her eye.

"What is that?" she murmured, zooming in on a faint bluish glow beneath the water's surface near the dock pilings.

The luminescence wasn't random. It had structure—concentric circles with what looked like purposeful organization. Claire scrolled through her other photos, finding the same phenomenon in three different shots, always near Tod's dock, always with the same distinctive pattern.

"Not lens flare." Claire clicked through filters, adjusting exposure and contrast. The patterns became more pronounced rather than disappearing. "Not a reflection either."

She sat back, running her fingers through her messy bun as she considered the implications. The patterns were too organized, too consistent. Whatever generated that light was in the water, not on her lens or in the sky.

Claire's training in environmental science kicked in, complementing her artist's eye. She opened her browser and typed: "bioluminescence Copano Bay."

Several scholarly articles appeared, most authored by Dr. Sarah Chen from Texas A&M Marine Biology Department. Claire clicked the most recent publication, scanning through technical language about "organized bioluminescent phenomena" and "non-random light emission patterns detected via satellite."

The images in Chen's paper showed patterns similar to what Claire had captured—but on a much larger scale. Claire checked the dates of the satellite data.

"Last Tuesday," she whispered, eyes widening. The exact day Tod had towed her boat back to the marina.

She clicked through more articles, piecing together the mystery. Dr. Chen had documented unusual light patterns following specific routes from Copano Bay out to the Gulf. Routes that would require intimate knowledge of local channels and tides.

Claire pulled up the map included in Chen's paper, tracing the path with her finger, remembering Tod's confident navigation through those same waters.

She opened a new browser tab and searched for Tod's name along with "fishing charter" and "Rockport." His website appeared, showing the same boat that had rescued her. Tod Blackstone, licensed captain, local guide.

Claire closed her laptop and stared out her window toward Copano Bay, where Tod's property sat on the distant shoreline.

"He knows something," she said to the empty room, certainty settling in her chest. "And I'm going to find out what it is."

THE SUN HUNG LOW OVER Copano Bay, painting the water in shades of amber and gold as Claire parked her Subaru beside Tod's workshop. She gathered her camera bag and a brown paper sack from Rosita's Taqueria, the savory scent of carne asada filling the car. Her fingers tapped anxiously on the steering wheel before she finally stepped out.

Tod emerged from his workshop at the sound of her car door, his posture rigid despite his casual wave. His eyes darted from Claire to the water and back again, a tension in his shoulders that hadn't been there that morning.

"Figured you might be hungry," Claire called, holding up the bag. "Tacos seemed like fair payment for dock access."

Tod's smile didn't quite reach his eyes. "You didn't have to do that."

They sat on the edge of the dock, legs dangling above the water that was now turning to liquid fire with the setting sun. Claire distributed foil-wrapped tacos and bottled waters, watching Tod from the corner of her eye.

A business card lay on his desk—Dr. Sarah Chen, Texas A&M Marine Biology. The same researcher whose papers Claire had been reading hours earlier. Questions burned on her tongue, fighting to escape.

Tod chewed mechanically, gaze fixed on the horizon, then sweeping across the water's surface. Searching for something. His free hand tapped a rhythm against the weathered wood—one-two-three-four-five-six-seven. Repeat.

Claire opened her mouth to ask about the storm that morning, how he'd known it was coming when no forecaster had predicted it. She wanted to ask about the glowing patterns in her photographs, about Dr. Chen's research, about why he kept looking at the water like something might emerge from it at any moment.

But something in Tod's expression stopped her. Behind his forced calm was a man struggling, wrestling with some burden he wasn't ready to share. Whatever secrets lay beneath that water, he carried them alone.

"The light's incredible right now," Claire said instead, reaching for her camera.

Tod's shoulders relaxed slightly, tension ebbing. "Yeah. This is the best time."

Claire raised her camera, focusing on the golden light dancing across the bay. Through her viewfinder, she captured the moment—the fiery sunset, Tod's silhouette against the burning sky, and the water that seemed to hold secrets beneath its glassy surface.

Behind her, Tod watched the water nervously, counting seconds under his breath.

THE SKY DEEPENED FROM orange to indigo as Claire methodically packed her gear. She wiped her lenses with a microfiber cloth, replaced lens caps, and nestled each piece into its padded compartment with practiced precision. Tod leaned against a piling, arms crossed, eyes darting between Claire, the water, and his watch.

Nine forty-five. Fifteen minutes until the Light Speakers usually arrived.

"Getting late," Tod observed, his casual tone slightly forced. "You probably want to get home before it's completely dark."

Claire caught the dismissal but didn't challenge it. Something in Tod's restlessness spoke of anticipation rather than impatience. He wasn't tired of her company—he was waiting for something else.

"Yeah, I should go." Claire zipped her camera bag closed with finality. "Thank you for today. Both sessions. The light was exactly what I hoped for."

Their eyes met, and genuine warmth passed between them despite Tod's obvious distraction. Something had shifted since morning—a connection neither fully understood but both felt.

"Anytime," Tod said, then caught himself. "Well, not anytime. But... you know."

Claire smiled. "I know."

Tod helped her carry equipment to the Subaru. Their hands brushed as they loaded the trunk, and both pretended not to notice the electricity in that fleeting contact. Claire climbed into the driver's seat and rolled down her window.

"Good night, Tod Blackstone."

"Night, Claire."

Tod stood in his driveway watching her taillights disappear down the coastal road. He waited a full ten minutes, checking and rechecking that she was truly gone. The water whispered against the dock pilings, almost impatient.

Tod retrieved a small device from his workshop—his modified beacon—and walked purposefully toward the dock, unaware of Claire's Subaru parked on the roadside a quarter mile away, tucked beneath the shadow of a gnarled live oak.

He never saw Claire making her way back through the brush, carrying only her telephoto lens and a portable tripod. Her feet moved silently through the coastal vegetation, guided by the pale moonlight and the conviction that whatever Tod was hiding would reveal itself tonight.

As Tod settled at the edge of the dock with his beacon, Claire found her vantage point, adjusted her tripod, and attached her lens. Tonight, she would see what no one else had documented. Tonight, she would understand what pulled at Tod like a tide.

THE CYPRESS TREES CAST crooked shadows as Claire crouched at the property line, guilt and exhilaration battling within her chest. She steadied her hands on the Canon's telephoto lens, the weight of her decision pressing against her sternum. Professional photographers respected boundaries—they didn't hide in the dark photographing people without permission. Yet something extraordinary pulled her forward, a magnetic certainty that transcended ordinary ethics.

Through the viewfinder, Tod appeared closer, his profile etched against the bay. His hands moved with purpose over a peculiar electronic contraption—circuit boards connected to what looked like a modified antenna with copper wiring. The moonlight caught his furrowed brow, revealing concentration and vulnerability in equal measure.

"What are you up to?" Claire whispered to herself, adjusting her aperture for the low light.

Tod's gaze swept across the water, expectant yet apprehensive. There was something tender in his vigilance, a man both burdened and lifted by a secret. Claire had photographed enough faces to recognize the complexity in his expression—worry shadowed by hope, isolation pierced by connection.

At exactly 10:00 PM, Tod activated the device. A soft glow emanated from its components as he pointed it toward the darkened water. He waited, perfectly still, watching.

The water remained black for long seconds.

Then—a flicker. A pulse. A glow.

Claire's finger froze on the shutter as blue-white light bloomed beneath the surface, spreading outward like liquid stars. Her breath caught, lungs forgetting their function. The luminescence coalesced into distinct shapes—dozens of basketball-sized, translucent organisms rising in perfect formation around the dock.

"Oh my God," she breathed.

Tod reached for his flashlight, clicking it in deliberate patterns—three short, three long, three short. The classic distress signal: SOS.

The creatures responded, their collective bioluminescence flashing in synchronized patterns. Not random. Deliberate. Communication.

Claire's hands trembled as she captured frame after frame, her photographer's discipline barely containing her shock. This was impossible. This was magnificent. This was real.

The beings arranged themselves in a perfect circle beneath Tod, pulsing with a rhythm that seemed to match his movements. He was speaking to them, and they were answering in a language of light.

"What are you, Tod Blackstone?" Claire whispered, unable to tear her eyes away from the viewfinder. "And what have you found?"

THE LIGHT SPEAKERS' glow rippled beneath the dock in hypnotic patterns as Tod's flashlight moved in precise bursts. Their communication, now comfortable after weeks of practice, flowed between them—a language of light bridging two worlds.

"ALL WELL?" Tod signaled.

"YES SAFE DEEP WATERS GOOD," came their collective reply, each creature pulsing in perfect synchronization. "NEW QUESTION."

Tod tilted his head. "GO AHEAD."

"THE WOMAN WHO SEES - WHO?"

Tod's shoulders tensed. "You mean Claire? The woman from today?"

"YES - SHE HAS GIFT - NOTICES LIGHT - LIKE YOU."

Tod scanned the shoreline, seeing only darkness and cypress shadows. "She doesn't know about you yet," he signaled back, trying to convince himself as much as them.

"SHE WILL - SHE ALREADY SEES."

A chill ran through Tod that had nothing to do with the night air. He squinted toward the tree line but saw no movement, no reflection from a camera lens. Just paranoia, he told himself, remembering Dr. Chen's questions and his own worries about Claire working with her.

"Goodnight, friends," he signaled finally. "Stay safe."

The Light Speakers flashed once more—"SLEEP WELL K5HUX"—before descending into deeper water, their glow diminishing until the bay returned to darkness.

Tod gathered his equipment and walked back to his workshop, muscles relaxing with each step. Despite his concerns, today with Claire had felt like opening a window in a stuffy room—uncomfortable initially, but ultimately bringing something necessary.

Two hundred yards away, Claire's hands trembled as she scrolled through the images on her camera's display. Crystal clear shots of Tod, the device, and most incredibly, the organized colony of luminous beings that had risen from the water at his signal.

"Holy shit," she whispered, enlarging an image that showed their translucent bodies, internal structures glowing like private constellations. She could see their deliberate formation, the obvious intelligence in their arrangement, the unmistakable conversation occurring through light.

Claire's finger hovered over her phone. Who would she even call? Her parents? Dr. Chen, whose card she'd spotted on Tod's desk? The images on her screen were worth a fortune, a career, international recognition—first contact documented by Claire Westbrook.

She looked back toward Tod's house, now dark and still against the night sky. He'd invited her into his space today. Shared coffee, conversation, his dock, his view. And she'd repaid him by hiding in the shadows, photographing his most carefully guarded secret.

"What do I do now?" she whispered, torn between journalistic duty and personal ethics.

Claire started her car but didn't pull away, sitting motionless on the roadside. Her face glowed in the blue light of the camera screen, the Light Speakers' image illuminating her features as questions without answers tumbled through her mind.

Chapter 10

Claire sat cross-legged on her rumpled bed at 2:30 AM, the blue glow of her laptop screen illuminating her exhausted face. She'd been cycling through the photos for hours—hundreds of shots documenting what should have been impossible. The luminous organisms beneath Tod's dock. Their coordinated movements. The conversation of light between them and Tod.

Each image was more extraordinary than the last. Perfect exposure. Tack-sharp focus. Undeniable evidence of intelligent non-human life communicating with a human being. The sort of discovery that would upend scientific understanding, make international headlines, launch her career into the stratosphere.

And she'd captured it all by hiding in the shadows, betraying a man who'd invited her into his space.

"Pulitzer or pariah," she whispered, rubbing her burning eyes. She glanced at the watercolor on her wall—her grandmother Maggie painting on a beach, brush capturing the light off Gulf waters. The old photograph was Claire's compass, her north star.

"What would you do, Grandma?" Claire asked the silent room. "These photos could change everything—science, religion, our place in the universe."

But she already knew Maggie's answer. The same words her grandmother had repeated whenever Claire faced ethical dilemmas: The truth isn't just what you capture, but how you capture it.

Claire grabbed her phone, fingers hovering over the screen. She typed: "Can we talk this morning? Important." Stared at it. Deleted it.

She tried again: "I need to tell you something." Too ominous. Delete.

Finally: "Coming by early if that's okay." Simple. Noncommittal. She pressed send before she could reconsider.

No response. Of course not—normal people were asleep at this hour.

Claire closed her laptop and set it aside, but sleep remained elusive. Her ceiling became a projection screen for imagined scenarios: Tod's face when she confessed. His anger. The possibility he might demand she delete everything. The greater possibility that something magnificent would be lost forever if she did.

Outside her window, the sky gradually lightened from black to deep blue. Claire watched the stars disappear one by one, the weight of her confession hanging over her like a storm cloud about to break.

DAWN PAINTED THE HORIZON in watercolor strokes of pink and gold as Claire's Subaru crunched over the gravel of Tod's driveway. She gripped her camera bag tightly, clutching it like a shield though she had no real plan for what would happen next. The weight of the memory cards inside—filled with evidence of something extraordinary—felt impossibly heavy.

Tod was already standing on the dock, silhouette dark against the brightening sky, coffee mug steaming in hand. He turned at the sound of her approach, surprise evident in the slight tilt of his head.

"Got your text," he called as she approached. "Everything okay?"

All of Claire's carefully rehearsed confessions evaporated like morning mist. The words she'd practiced during her sleepless night dissolved on her tongue.

"I... wanted to catch different morning light," she said, the lie tumbling out reflexively. "Is that weird?"

Tod studied her face, his eyes lingering a moment too long. Something in his expression suggested he'd cataloged the shadows beneath her eyes, the tension in her shoulders.

"You seem tense," he observed quietly.

"Just tired. Couldn't sleep." Claire shifted her weight, aware of how her voice pitched slightly higher than normal.

"Me either."

A silence stretched between them, delicate and charged. Two people standing mere feet apart, both guarding secrets. Both aware something remained unspoken.

"Want coffee?" Tod finally asked, lifting his mug slightly.

Claire nodded, grateful for the reprieve. "God, yes."

They walked toward the house side by side, not touching, not speaking. Claire's gaze drifted toward the far end of the dock—the exact spot where she'd hidden last night, lens trained on Tod and the luminous beings beneath the water. Her stomach twisted with guilt.

The morning breeze carried the scent of salt and fish, the same as yesterday, yet everything felt fundamentally different. Behind them, the water of Copano Bay lapped gently against the pilings, oblivious to the silent drama unfolding on its shores or the miraculous secret it harbored in its depths.

INSIDE TOD'S WORKSHOP, morning light streamed through the windows, catching dust motes that danced between them. Claire sat perched on a stool, her fingers wrapped tightly around a coffee mug, while Tod leaned against his workbench. The silence between them had a weight, pressing against them both.

"So, the light this morning is—" Claire began, then stopped abruptly.

Tod watched her carefully, noting how her eyes flitted between him and the window facing the bay.

"I was thinking that maybe I could—" She tried again, trailing off as she stared into her coffee.

Each attempt at conversation fell flat, leaving remnants of unfinished thoughts hanging in the air. Tod's gaze never left her face, studying her with the same intensity he might examine one of his circuit boards.

"Claire, what's going on?" he finally asked, his voice low and steady.

She looked up, meeting his eyes briefly. "Nothing, I just—"

Her phone buzzed loudly on the workbench between them, screen illuminating with an incoming call. DR. SARAH CHEN flashed across the display in bold letters.

Claire's face drained of color. Her hand froze halfway to the device.

"You know her?" Tod asked sharply, his posture instantly stiffening.

"I... no. Maybe? I don't know why she'd—" Claire stammered, her eyes wide with genuine confusion.

The phone continued its insistent buzzing, the name glowing accusingly between them.

Tod's jaw tightened, muscles working beneath the skin. "You should answer that." It wasn't a suggestion.

Claire hesitated, her fingers hovering over the phone as if it might burn her. Finally, she picked it up and swiped to accept.

"Hello?" Her voice cracked slightly.

Tod gestured toward the speaker button, his expression leaving no room for refusal. Claire complied, placing the phone between them on the workbench.

"Ms. Westbrook? Dr. Sarah Chen, Texas A&M Marine Biology." The voice emerged clear and professional, yet warmly confident. "I hope this isn't too early."

The space between Claire and Tod seemed to contract, tension coiling like a spring. Claire's eyes locked with Tod's, her expression a mixture of bewilderment and fear, while his had hardened into something unreadable, all traces of the morning's earlier warmth completely gone.

"ACTUALLY, I'VE BEEN following your work for some time," Dr. Chen continued through the speaker. "That Texas Highways feature you shot last year was extraordinary—your eye for light on water is exactly what we're looking for."

Claire's fingers tightened around her coffee mug as she watched Tod's face harden further with each word. His shoulders had gone rigid, his breathing shallow.

"I'm putting together a research team," Dr. Chen explained. "We need a professional photographer to document certain Gulf phenomena we've been tracking. Specifically bioluminescent phenomena. Unusual patterns we've detected via satellite."

Claire's eyes met Tod's across the workshop. He stood perfectly still, like a deer caught in headlights, every muscle tensed as he listened.

"I... what kind of phenomena?" Claire asked, her voice barely audible.

"Organized light patterns beneath the surface," Chen replied enthusiastically. "Unlike anything in the scientific literature. They appear to move with purpose, not random like typical bioluminescent blooms. We've tracked significant activity in the Copano Bay area."

Tod's knuckles whitened as he gripped the edge of his workbench. A muscle twitched in his jaw.

"Your knowledge of local waters would be invaluable," Chen continued. "The pay is fifteen thousand for three weeks of work."

Claire inhaled sharply. Fifteen thousand dollars. Three months of rent and expenses. New camera equipment she desperately needed. Financial security she hadn't felt in years.

But across from her stood Tod, watching her face with an intensity that made her skin prickle. Whatever lay beneath the water was his secret, one he guarded fiercely. One she had already violated by hiding on his property last night.

"I need to think about it," Claire said finally.

"Of course. I'll email the details today," Chen replied. "But please don't take too long. This could be career-making, Ms. Westbrook. Publications, gallery exhibitions—this would open doors."

"I understand. Thank you for the opportunity."

The call ended, leaving the workshop in suffocating silence. Claire set her phone down carefully, as if it might detonate. Tod hadn't moved, his eyes never leaving her face, waiting for what would come next.

The truth hung between them, unspoken but impossible to ignore. Tod's secret lived in her camera, while Claire's decision now balanced precariously between opportunity and betrayal.

THE SILENCE STRETCHED between them like a live wire, dangerous and electric. Tod's face had gone completely still, a mask hiding whatever storm raged beneath.

"I'm not taking it," Claire said finally, the words rushing out. "You don't know what she's talking about, right? The bioluminescence?"

Her eyes darted away from his, unable to hold his penetrating gaze. "Tod, I—"

Her phone chimed with an incoming email. Chen's name appeared on the notification with several image attachments. Claire's fingers moved before she could stop herself, opening the message. The satellite images loaded slowly—grainy at first, then sharpening into familiar patterns. Blue-white formations moving in coordinated sequences through water.

The exact patterns she had photographed last night.

Tod watched her face as recognition dawned, his expression hardening further. "You do know." Not a question. A realization.

Claire's eyes filled with tears. "I need to tell you something." The confession she'd rehearsed all night rose in her throat. "Last night I—"

Tod's attention suddenly shifted. His eyes widened, focusing on something beyond the workshop window. His entire body tensed.

"No. No no no." He pushed past Claire, knocking her coffee mug to the floor where it shattered, forgotten. "They never surface during the day."

Claire turned to see what had captured his attention. Through the window, out in Copano Bay, a faint blue-white glow pulsed beneath the surface—visible even in morning sunlight. Impossible.

Tod was already moving, rushing through the door and toward the dock with unexpected urgency. Claire grabbed her camera instinctively and followed, stumbling over the workshop threshold.

"Tod, wait!" she called after him.

He didn't slow, his strides eating up the distance to the water's edge. His body language had transformed completely—no longer defensive or angry, but flooded with something that looked like fear. Whatever those lights were, something was terribly wrong.

Claire's confession hung unfinished in the workshop behind them as she ran after Tod, her camera clutched against her chest and guilt momentarily forgotten. Whatever crisis was unfolding, it had instantly superseded their fragile human drama.

Out in the bay, the blue-white glow intensified, pulsing erratically in a way Claire somehow knew was not normal. Not natural. Not right.

THE MORNING SUN ILLUMINATED the water's surface as Tod reached the dock, his feet pounding against the weathered wood. Claire followed several paces behind, her camera forgotten in her hands as she witnessed the impossible.

Dozens of translucent, basketball-sized creatures had risen to the surface, their bodies clearly visible beneath the gentle morning waves. Their internal organs pulsed with blue-white light, creating patterns too deliberate to be anything but communication. The Light Speakers moved with obvious agitation, their normal seven-second rhythm replaced by rapid, erratic flashes.

Claire gasped, stopping abruptly. "Oh my god," she whispered, her photographer's eye registering every detail of their graceful, fluid movements—the constellation-like arrangement of light organs, the coordinated way they circled each other. These weren't animals. They were something else entirely.

Tod dropped to his knees at the dock's edge, reaching for the beacon he kept hidden beneath a loose board. His fingers worked quickly, adjusting settings as he pointed it toward the colony.

"WHAT WRONG - WHY HERE - DANGER," he signaled with flashing light.

The colony responded immediately, their synchronized flashes forming clear Morse code that reflected against the dock pilings: "HUNTERS COMING - WOMAN WITH MACHINES - DANGER TO US."

Tod's stomach dropped. He turned to look at Claire, his face pale. "They mean Chen."

The creatures continued their message: "WE FEEL HER SEARCHING - METAL BIRDS IN SKY - LISTENING DEVICES."

"She has drones," Tod translated, his voice tight with urgency. "Probably submersibles. She's actively hunting them."

Claire stared at the Light Speakers, then back at her camera—the instrument that could have helped expose these beings to precisely the kind of danger they now faced. The magnitude of what she'd almost done crashed over her. She'd been mere hours away from potentially calling Chen, from accepting money to help document these creatures for science. For fame. For her career.

"They're intelligent," she whispered, watching as the beings continued their frantic communication. "They understand what's happening. They're afraid."

"Yes," Tod said simply, turning back to signal something else to the colony. The desperation in his movements, the protective stance of his body between the dock and the Light Speakers told Claire everything she needed to know about where Tod stood.

Where she needed to stand too.

THE MORNING LIGHT CAUGHT the ripples of water as the colony suddenly shifted. Like a single organism, the Light Speakers redirected their attention—away from Tod and toward Claire. They moved in perfect unison, gliding through the water to surround her side of the dock, their blue-white organs pulsing in synchronized rhythm directly at her.

Tod stiffened. "They sense something about you."

Claire stood frozen at the edge of the dock, her camera hanging limply at her side as dozens of translucent beings studied her with their luminous organs. The silence stretched between heartbeats until the water beneath her erupted in organized patterns of light.

"THIS ONE - SHE SEES US - SHE ALREADY KNOWS."

Tod translated the message automatically, then the words sank in. He turned to Claire slowly, the color draining from his face. His eyes, which had begun to trust her, now searched her expression with dawning comprehension.

"What do they mean 'already knows'?" His voice was barely audible over the gentle lapping of water against the pilings.

Claire's throat tightened as the weight of her deception crashed down upon her. "Tod, I'm sorry. I didn't mean to—"

"When?" The word came out flat, hollow.

"Last night." She swallowed hard. "I was still here when you... when they came. I photographed everything."

Tod took a step backward, his body physically recoiling from her words. The betrayal washed across his features in waves—shock, hurt, anger, and finally, a cold remoteness as his walls slammed back into place. All the careful trust he'd begun building with her collapsed in an instant.

Below them, the Light Speakers continued their communication, their message stark in its simplicity: "FRIEND OR DANGER - YOU DECIDE."

Tod's jaw tightened as he looked from Claire to her camera, then to the colony waiting beneath them.

"You hid on my property and took photographs of them?" His voice trembled slightly. "After I invited you here? After I trusted you?"

The Light Speakers pulsed more rapidly now, their patterns reflecting against Claire's face as she stood at the precipice of a decision that would forever change multiple worlds.

"SHOW ME." TOD'S VOICE was cold as winter water.

Claire retrieved her camera from her bag with shaking hands, her fingers fumbling with the dials. She scrolled through the images—hundreds of shots capturing the impossible. Light Speakers arranged in perfect formations. Tod signaling with his flashlight. Their responses in synchronized pulses. Morse code exchanges translated on-screen through long exposure. The images revealed undeniable intelligence and communication between species.

The photographs were extraordinary—professional quality with perfect focus even in low light, the blue-white glow captured with striking clarity against the black water. They were beautiful, compelling, and absolutely damning.

Tod stared at the screen, his face illuminated by the soft glow. "These could destroy them. You understand that, right? Chen would pay a fortune for these." His jaw clenched. "That's why she called you."

"I wasn't going to—" Claire began.

"How do I know that?" Tod cut her off, his voice rising. "You spied on me. You photographed them without permission. What exactly were you planning to do with these?"

Claire felt tears welling up, hot and sudden. "I don't know. I was confused. Curious." A tear slid down her cheek. "But I wasn't going to give them to her. I swear."

"You're a photographer. This is career-making material." Tod gestured at the screen, where a particularly striking image showed a Light Speaker rising toward his outstretched hand, their connection unmistakable. "National Geographic. Time. BBC. Name your price." His eyes hardened. "Why should I believe you?"

Below them, the Light Speakers pulsed anxiously, their rhythm accelerating as they sensed the conflict above. Their collective consciousness registered the threat—images of themselves captured and stored, the secret of their existence held in electronic memory, ready to be shared with the world that would never understand them.

"DECIDE," they flashed from beneath the water's surface. "FRIEND OR DANGER."

Claire looked from Tod to the colony and back again, the weight of their fate resting in her trembling hands.

THE LIGHT SPEAKERS pulsed beneath the dock, their blue-white glow reflecting the emotional turmoil transpiring above. They moved in agitated patterns, internal organs flickering with anxiety as they sensed the human conflict that could determine their fate.

Claire looked down at the colony, then at her camera, then at Tod's face—hard with betrayal but also fear for beings he'd sworn to protect. She drew a deep breath and opened the camera's menu, navigating through the options with practiced fingers.

"What are you doing?" Tod asked, suspicion edging his voice.

"Proving it." Claire selected the folder containing all photos from the previous night, hundreds of images that could launch her career, provide financial security, and make her name legendary in wildlife photography. Two hundred and forty-seven irreplaceable photographs of first contact with an unknown intelligent species.

Her thumb hovered over DELETE ALL.

"Claire, wait—" Tod reached toward the camera, conflict crossing his features.

She met his eyes. "Some things matter more than career. More than money. More than the biggest story of my life." Her voice broke, but her resolve didn't. She pressed delete.

The confirmation dialog appeared. Claire didn't hesitate. The screen flashed briefly: 247 FILES DELETED.

Gone. All gone. Evidence erased, their secret protected, her potential glory sacrificed.

She turned the camera toward the Light Speakers, showing them the empty screen. "I choose you. Both of you."

The colony responded immediately, surging closer to the surface in a coordinated wave. Their pattern changed, becoming more ordered, more deliberate as they flashed in perfect unison: "SHE DELETES TRUTH TO PROTECT US - THIS IS FRIEND."

Tod stared at Claire, his expression softening with something between disbelief and dawning trust.

"I'm sorry I violated your trust," Claire said, setting the camera down between them. "But I'm not sorry I know." She glanced at the Light Speakers, their glow reflecting in her hazel eyes. "And I want to help protect them."

The colony pulsed beneath them—steady, rhythmic, accepting—as the first full rays of morning sunlight stretched across Copano Bay, illuminating three different worlds beginning to align.

TOD CLOSED THE WORKSHOP door behind them, the sounds of the bay muffled through the walls. Claire sat quietly on a stool near his workbench, watching him pace the room before finally coming to rest against the edge of his desk. The morning light filtered through the blinds, casting alternating shadows and warmth across his troubled face.

"I found them by accident," Tod began, his voice low. "Or maybe they found me. A signal my equipment shouldn't have been able to detect."

The words tumbled out then—a dam breaking after months of careful containment. The mysterious pulses. The storm. His near-drowning. Being rescued by creatures who created an air pocket eighteen feet underwater. The journey guiding them home through the channel. Their gratitude. Their intelligence.

"And then they changed me," Tod said, pushing away from the desk and spreading his hands. "I can sense electromagnetic fields now. Feel storms before they form. Connect with marine life." He tapped his temple. "My brain's different. Rewired."

Claire listened, tears welling in her eyes, not from disbelief but from understanding. The pieces clicking together—his isolation, his unnatural weather predictions, his perfect fishing instincts.

"You've been carrying this alone," she whispered.

Tod's shoulders slumped slightly. "Barney knows. My parents. That's it. Until now."

"And Dr. Chen? The scientist who called me? She suspects something."

"She wants to study them." Tod's voice hardened. "Dissect them, you mean. Put them in tanks. They're people, Claire. Not specimens."

Claire nodded, wiping away a tear. "I know. I saw that last night. The way they communicated with you. That's friendship. Love, even."

Something in Tod's expression softened slightly. "They saved my life. I can't let anyone hurt them."

"Then we don't let anyone hurt them." Claire's voice was steady now, resolved.

Tod looked up, studying her face. "We?"

The word hung between them—the first indication of inclusion, of alliance, of trust beginning to rebuild.

Claire held his gaze. "Yes. We."

Outside, the bay sparkled under the morning sun, concealing beneath its surface both extraordinary danger and extraordinary possibility.

THE WORKSHOP CLOCK read 7:30 AM as sunlight strengthened outside, warming the room where Tod and Claire sat contemplating their predicament. The air between them had shifted—no longer charged with suspicion but with shared purpose.

"Chen isn't going to stop searching," Claire said, fingers drumming against the edge of her camera case. "That job offer wasn't random. It was reconnaissance. She suspects I know something."

Tod leaned forward, elbows on his knees. "Why would she think that?"

"She probably saw my car here multiple times. At the marina too. The way Mike greeted me that day you towed me in." Claire shook her head. "I've been obvious."

"I've been obvious too," Tod admitted. "My boat route that day I guided them home. The way I've dodged her questions. She's smart—scary smart. Marine biologists don't typically track bioluminescent phenomena with military-grade satellite imaging."

Claire looked up suddenly, her eyes widening with an idea. "What if I take the job?"

"What?"

"I take it. Feed her false information. Lead her away from your dock, away from where the Light Speakers actually are."

Tod stood, pacing the length of the workshop. "That's risky. She'll expect results. Photos. Evidence."

"I'll give her results," Claire said, confidence building in her voice. "Just not the truth. I can photograph regular bioluminescence. Algae blooms. Maybe even stage some shots farther up the coast."

Tod stopped pacing, considering the proposition. Outside, unseen by either human, several translucent forms had risen to the edge of the dock, sensing the vibrations of their conversation through the wooden pilings, listening in their own way.

Tod moved to the window, noticing them. He stepped onto the deck, Claire following close behind. Using his flashlight, he signaled a summary of their discussion.

The water churned with blue-white light as the colony responded: "TRUST HER - SHE CHOSE US - NOW WE CHOOSE HER."

Tod turned to Claire, the morning light illuminating her face. "They approve. Which means I do too." He extended his hand. "Welcome to the secret."

Claire took his hand, feeling the warmth of his palm against hers. In that moment, something shifted between them—a partnership forged in shared responsibility for something extraordinary. Whatever came next, they would face it together.

THE MORNING SUN CLIMBED higher as Tod and Claire stood on the dock, its golden light dancing across the water's surface. Below them, the Light Speakers pulsed with increasing agitation, their translucent bodies more vulnerable in the strengthening daylight.

Claire knelt at the dock's edge, extending her hand over the water. A single Light Speaker detached from the group and rose toward her, stopping just below her palm—mirroring the same connection Tod had formed during their rescue journey. Warmth radiated upward, an impossible heat that shouldn't travel through air yet somehow did.

Tears welled in Claire's eyes, spilling down her cheeks. "They're beautiful," she whispered.

Tod watched her face, seeing the wonder he'd felt himself. "They're family."

Below them, the colony flashed in unison: "THREE PROTECT TOGETHER - YOU - YOU - WE."

Tod crouched beside Claire, his voice low and serious. "Are you sure? This isn't photography. This is your life changing."

Claire didn't look away from the pulsing light below her hand. "It already changed. The moment I saw them, I changed." She turned to meet his eyes. "The moment I met you, actually."

The admission hung between them, the first acknowledgment of something deeper than coincidence in their meeting. Tod met her gaze, the protective walls he'd built finally lowering. "Some things matter more than money," he echoed her earlier words. "Like you."

The Light Speakers began descending as the sun's rays penetrated deeper into the bay. Claire set her camera bag aside—present in the moment rather than documenting it. "Now what?" she asked.

"Now we protect them together." Tod's hand found Claire's. Their first intentional touch, fingers intertwining with purpose.

As they turned to leave the dock, Tod suddenly stiffened. His enhanced senses flared, head turning southeast. "Wait." He felt it—the distinctive electronic pulse of a drone's guidance system.

"What is it?"

"She's already searching." Tod pointed toward the horizon where a small aerial drone moved methodically across the bay's surface. "She's coming."

"Then we prepare." Claire squeezed his hand, a united front formed in shared purpose.

Walking back toward the workshop, Claire stopped him with a gentle tug on his hand. "Why didn't you turn me away? After what I did?"

Tod studied her face in the morning light. "Because you chose right when it mattered. That's who you are."

"How do you know?"

"Same way you knew I was different. We see each other."

The space between them narrowed, their faces drawing closer in an almost-kiss. Too soon, too much happening—but the promise remained, suspended in the salt-tinged air between them.

"Help me understand your world?" Claire whispered.

Tod smiled, the first genuine smile she'd seen from him. "Our world now."

Claire's answering smile held both determination and tenderness. "Our world."

Chapter 11

The digital clock glowed 2:30 AM in Claire's darkened bungalow, its pale blue light the only illumination besides her laptop screen. Sleep remained a distant possibility as Claire scrolled through photo after photo, each more extraordinary than the last. The images cast an ethereal blue-white glow across her face, illuminating eyes wide with wonder and conflict.

Frame 47: Tod kneeling at the dock's edge, flashlight in hand, signaling into the water.

Frame 48: The first response—hundreds of translucent forms rising in perfect unison.

Frame 103: A single Light Speaker approaching Tod's outstretched hand.

Frame 172: An intricate pattern of light pulses that Claire now recognized as Morse code.

Each image represented both the pinnacle of her career and a profound betrayal of trust. Any one of these photos could land on the cover of National Geographic. All of them together could rewrite humanity's understanding of intelligence and consciousness. She'd captured irrefutable evidence of non-human sentience communicating with a human being.

"I'm sitting on a Pulitzer," she whispered to the empty room, her voice hollow.

Claire's eyes drifted to the watercolor hanging beside her bed—a coastal scene painted by her grandmother Maggie. The old woman's eyes seemed to watch her from the small photograph tucked into the frame.

"What would you do, Grandma?" Claire asked the silent photograph.

The answer came immediately, as if Maggie had whispered directly into her ear: Tell the truth. Always tell the truth, even when it hurts.

Claire reached for her phone, fingers hovering over the keyboard. She typed: "Can we talk this morning? Important." Then deleted it—too ominous.

She tried again: "I need to tell you something." Deleted that too—melodramatic.

Finally: "Coming by early if that's okay."

Claire hit send before she could reconsider, then waited, holding her breath. No response came. Of course not—Tod was surely asleep like any reasonable person at this hour.

Setting her phone aside, Claire closed her laptop but couldn't close her mind. She stared at the ceiling, watching shadows shift as occasional cars passed outside, imagining Tod's face when she confessed. Would he demand she delete everything? Would he ever trust her again?

Dawn began to seep through her curtains, finding Claire still awake, still wrestling with the weight of truth and consequences.

THE MORNING MIST CLUNG to the surface of Copano Bay as Claire's Subaru rolled to a stop beside Tod's workshop. Her camera bag sat heavy on the passenger seat, filled with equipment, memory cards, and the weight of what she'd witnessed. She'd rehearsed her confession a dozen times on the drive over, but each version sounded worse than the last.

Tod stood on the dock already, silhouette sharp against the pastel dawn, a mug of steaming coffee in hand. He turned at the sound of her car door closing, surprise registering on his face.

"Morning," he called, walking toward her. "Got your text. Everything okay?"

The words she'd practiced evaporated from Claire's mind. His direct gaze made her palms sweat as she clutched her camera bag tighter.

"I... wanted to catch different morning light. Is that weird?" The lie tasted bitter on her tongue.

Tod studied her face longer than comfortable, his eyes narrowing slightly. "You seem tense."

"Just tired. Couldn't sleep." At least that part was true.

"Me either."

A charged silence fell between them, each guarding secrets that hung invisible in the salt-tinged air. The water lapped against the pilings, a patient timekeeper marking the moments neither spoke.

"Want coffee?" Tod finally asked, gesturing toward the house with his mug.

Claire nodded, grateful for the reprieve. "That would be great."

As they walked away from the water, Claire's eyes drifted back to the spot where she'd hidden the night before, crouched in shadows with her camera aimed at Tod and the luminous beings beneath his dock. Her stomach knotted tighter with each step.

Tod moved ahead of her toward the workshop door, his shoulders stiff with an anxiety that mirrored her own. Behind them, Copano Bay continued its eternal rhythm against the shore, concealing its miraculous secret beneath unremarkable waves.

Claire took a deep breath as Tod held the door for her. She'd come here to confess, to show him the photos, to explain herself. Instead, she was following him inside, the truth still locked behind her lips, getting heavier by the second.

COFFEE STEAMED IN MISMATCHED mugs on Tod's workbench as morning light streamed through the windows. Claire perched awkwardly on a stool, fingers drumming against ceramic, while Tod leaned against the counter, watching her with unreadable eyes.

"So," Claire began, then stopped. She glanced at her camera bag, resting by her feet. "I was thinking about those sunrise shots from yesterday..."

Tod said nothing, just sipped his coffee.

"The light was really something," she continued. "The way it caught the—" She trailed off again, unable to maintain the pretense of casual conversation.

The silence between them stretched, punctuated only by the distant call of gulls and the gentle ticking of a wall clock.

"Claire," Tod finally said, his voice even but firm. "What's going on?"

She looked up, meeting his eyes. "Nothing, I just—"

Her phone rang suddenly, vibrating against the wooden bench. Claire glanced down, and her face drained of color as she read the screen: DR. SARAH CHEN.

Tod noticed her reaction immediately. "You know her?" he asked, his tone sharpening.

"I... no. Maybe? I don't know why she'd—" Claire stammered, staring at the phone as if it might bite her.

The ringing continued, insistent and accusing in the small space.

Tod's jaw tightened, the muscles working beneath his skin. "You should answer that," he said, no longer bothering to hide the suspicion in his voice.

Claire's hand hovered over the phone, her eyes darting between it and Tod's hardening expression. With reluctant fingers, she accepted the call. "Hello?"

Tod gestured firmly toward the speaker button. Claire hesitated, then pressed it, placing the phone between them on the workbench.

"Ms. Westbrook?" The voice was crisp, professional, yet warm. "Dr. Sarah Chen, Texas A&M Marine Biology. I hope this isn't too early."

Tod's eyes never left Claire's face, his hands gripping his coffee mug with whitened knuckles. Claire looked back at him with a mixture of bewilderment and fear, her earlier planned confession forgotten in the face of this unexpected complication.

"No, it's... I'm already up," Claire managed, her voice unnaturally high as the tension in the workshop thickened around them.

THE RESEARCH VESSEL cut through the glassy morning waters of Copano Bay, its wake spreading behind it like unfurling ribbons. Claire balanced her camera equipment on her lap, watching the horizon blush with first light. Dr. Chen stood at the bow, her silhouette sharp against the dawn sky, while Marcus adjusted controls at the small navigation station.

"We're approaching the first coordinates, Dr. Chen," Marcus called out, his voice carrying the eager enthusiasm of a graduate student still thrilled by fieldwork. He tapped the drone case beside him. "Ready to launch whenever you are."

Chen nodded, turning to face them. "Ms. Westbrook, are you prepared? This first location showed moderate activity three nights ago."

"All set," Claire replied, patting her equipment with a confidence she didn't feel. Her thoughts drifted to Tod, alone at his workshop, trusting her to protect the Light Speakers.

Marcus released the drone with practiced efficiency. It rose above them, a mechanical hummingbird against the lavender sky. "You've got control of the camera now, Claire," he said, handing her the tablet.

Claire nodded, focusing the lens on the water below. The screen revealed ordinary bioluminescent algae, beautiful but nothing like the organized intelligence she'd photographed at Tod's dock.

"Hmm," Chen muttered, studying the monitors. "Move to the second coordinates. Perhaps the morning current shifted the concentration."

The second location yielded similar results—random patterns of blue-white organisms, lacking any sign of collective behavior.

Chen's disappointment was palpable. "These are just standard dinoflagellate blooms," she said, frustration edging her voice. "Let's try the third location."

Claire's heart quickened as Marcus guided the boat toward waters dangerously close to Tod's property. The tablet trembled slightly in her hands as the drone hovered over the exact area where she knew the Light Speakers sometimes gathered.

When the camera feed revealed faint, suspicious movement, Claire deliberately tilted the angle and adjusted the aperture, overexposing the image. "Sorry," she mumbled, "sun glare is really tough there." The resulting footage showed blurry, indistinct patches of light that could be anything.

Chen leaned closer, squinting at the screen. "There's definitely something there, but these images are nearly unusable." She straightened, a determined set to her jaw. "We'll try again at sunset. Different light conditions might give us better results."

Claire's stomach dropped as she realized this deception would need to continue. "Right," she managed. "Sunset."

As they turned back toward the marina, Claire stared at the water's deep blue surface, wondering what intelligent eyes might be watching them from below.

CLAIRE'S KNUCKLES WHITENED around her phone as she typed the message from the bow of the research vessel. She glanced over her shoulder to ensure Dr. Chen and Marcus remained focused on their equipment before hitting send.

"She wants second pass at sunset. Same location. Need LS moved NOW."

Twenty miles away, Tod felt his phone vibrate in his pocket. He stood at the helm of K5HUX, pointing out a school of redfish to the Morrison brothers who had booked his charter for the day. The men whooped with excitement as their lines cut through the water.

Tod checked his message, and his blood ran cold. His clients' excited voices faded to background noise as he calculated the timing. Sunset. Chen would find them. There was no other option.

"Gentlemen, I hate to say this, but we've got a problem." Tod throttled down, his face a mask of regret. "I'm hearing something in the engine I don't like. Could be the fuel pump. We need to head back."

"Are you serious?" Jeff Morrison scowled, reeling in his line. "We paid for a full day."

"I understand, and I'll refund half your fee," Tod said, already turning the boat. "But I'm responsible for your safety, and I don't want us stranded miles from shore."

The brothers exchanged irritated glances but grudgingly packed up their gear. Tod pushed the throttle forward, navigating K5HUX back toward the marina faster than was strictly necessary for a fuel pump concern.

After dropping off his disgruntled clients with promises of discounts and refunds, Tod raced home, his boat skipping over the water at dangerous speeds. The Light Speakers weren't due at his dock until evening. If Chen returned at sunset, they'd be trapped.

In his workshop, Tod fumbled with the modified beacon, his fingers slick with sweat as he adjusted the frequency to the emergency pattern they had established. The device hummed to life, sending out pulses in a rapid, irregular rhythm—danger signal.

Tod paced on the dock, his eyes scanning the depths. Minutes stretched into an hour. Nothing.

"Come on," he whispered. "Please."

At 1:42 PM, the water beneath his dock began to shimmer. Blue-white lights appeared, rising cautiously toward the surface. In broad daylight—they never came in daylight.

Tod grabbed his flashlight, signaling rapidly: "DANGER - HUNTERS COMING TODAY - MUST MOVE NOW."

The colony's response was immediate: "WHERE GO."

Tod had already calculated this, marking coordinates in the deeper channels of Aransas Bay to the north. A place with more cover, where research vessels rarely ventured.

"GO NORTH ARANSAS BAY," he signaled, providing exact coordinates. "DEEPER WATER. LESS BOATS. GO NOW - I FOLLOW - MAKE SURE SAFE."

The Light Speakers' collective consciousness processed this, their formation tightening and then dispersing in a smooth, coordinated movement. They began to descend, their lights dimming as they moved north beneath the surface.

Tod didn't wait. He raced back to his boat, grabbing emergency gear and his navigation equipment. His hand reached for his phone, sending Claire a quick text: "Moving them north. Will follow. Tell me when Chen leaves."

As he guided K5HUX away from the dock, Tod's heart hammered against his ribs. For the first time, he was moving the Light Speakers in daylight. The risk was enormous, but the alternative—capture by Chen's team—was unthinkable.

He throttled forward, skimming across Copano Bay, watching for any sign of the blue-white glow beneath the surface. They had saved his life once. Now it was his turn to save theirs, no matter the cost.

THE AFTERNOON SUN BEAT down mercilessly as Tod guided K5HUX through the narrow channels of Aransas Bay. His eyes constantly scanned the water's surface while his other senses—the ones the Light Speakers had awakened in him—reached deeper.

Beneath the hull, the colony moved in tight formation, their blue-white glow dimmed to near invisibility in the daylight. Tod felt their distress like a physical sensation in his chest—sharp, anxious pulses of fear radiating upward through the water. They were nocturnal beings, evolved for darkness and depth. Here in the shallow bay, exposed to sunlight, they were horribly vulnerable.

"Just a little farther," Tod murmured, though they couldn't hear his voice. His empathic connection told him they were tiring, struggling against the current and the unnatural conditions.

His electromagnetic sense stretched outward, scanning for threats. Two fishing boats three-quarters of a mile east. A pleasure cruiser heading south toward Rockport. Nothing overhead—no drones, no surveillance. Yet.

Tod guided the boat around a bend, where a small, uninhabited spoil island rose from the water—remnants of a dredging operation years ago. Beyond it lay a deeper channel, sheltered by the island's curve and shaded by its sparse vegetation.

"Here," Tod whispered, throttling down. The depth finder showed thirty-two feet—not deep by Gulf standards, but significantly better than the eighteen feet at his dock. The water here ran darker, cooled by underwater springs and protected from the worst of the sun's glare.

Tod watched as the Light Speakers spread cautiously through their new territory, their formation loosening as they explored the contours of the channel bottom. Their distress signals gradually shifted, the sharp pulses softening into something steadier.

After several minutes, they gathered beneath his boat, their lights brightening momentarily to signal: "GOOD PLACE - WE STAY - THANK YOU."

Tod grabbed his flashlight: "SORRY TO RUSH - NECESSARY."

Their response came immediately: "YOU PROTECT - WE TRUST."

The simple message hit Tod with unexpected force. He sat heavily on the center console, suddenly aware of how tightly wound his body had been. The Light Speakers dispersed, settling into the deeper pocket of water, and Tod felt their collective relief wash through his empathic connection—cool waves replacing the earlier sharp pulses.

He checked his watch: 2:18 PM. Chen's sunset shoot with Claire wouldn't begin for another five hours. This location, hidden behind the spoil island in deeper, cooler water, should be safe from detection.

Should be.

Tod scanned the horizon again, his enhanced senses stretched to their limits, searching for any hint of threat. For now, at least, they had bought some time.

GOLDEN HOUR LIGHT SPILLED across Copano Bay, turning the water into a shimmering canvas of amber and crimson. Claire stood at the stern of Dr. Chen's research vessel, her camera capturing the stunning sunset while her thoughts remained with Tod and the Light Speakers.

"Launching the drone for coordinate three," Marcus announced, his fingers dancing across the tablet controls. The small black device ascended with a mechanical whine, hovering momentarily before speeding toward the area where the Light Speakers had previously gathered.

Dr. Chen hunched over her monitoring equipment, eyes fixed on the thermal and light-spectrum displays. "We should be seeing something... anything... by now."

Claire continued photographing, her expensive camera lens capturing perfect golden hour images. Each frame showed exactly what it should—empty water, stunning light, nothing extraordinary. Just as planned.

"I'm getting some bioluminescent readings," Marcus called out, adjusting settings on his tablet. "But it's just plankton, standard algal bloom patterns. Nothing organized."

Chen's jaw tightened. She paced the deck, reviewing the satellite images on her tablet once more. "I was so sure..." she muttered, tapping the screen with increasing frustration. "The patterns were right here. Organized. Moving with purpose."

"Maybe the satellite data was corrupted?" Marcus suggested, lowering the drone to just above the water's surface. "Happens sometimes."

"No," Chen snapped. "It was here. Something was here."

Claire lowered her camera, her heart pounding against her ribs as Chen's eyes found hers. The researcher's gaze was penetrating, suspicious.

"Claire," Chen said, her voice deceptively casual, "you've been photographing in this area frequently. Did you see anything unusual? Patterns in the water? Lights where they shouldn't be?"

Claire's fingers tightened around her camera. The lie came easily, practiced during the hours she'd waited for this moment. "Just the usual. Fish, birds, boats. Beautiful light." She gestured toward the sunset. "That's what drew me here—the way the light plays on the water."

Chen held her gaze a moment too long. "Hmm."

Claire turned back to her camera, pretending to adjust settings while her stomach knotted. In her peripheral vision, she saw Chen continuing to study her, head slightly tilted as if reassessing everything she knew about the photographer.

"We should head back," Marcus called out. "Losing light fast now."

"One more sweep," Chen insisted, eyes still on Claire. "I know what I saw in those images. And I intend to find it."

THE RESEARCH VESSEL glided into the marina slip as darkness settled over Copano Bay. The last traces of sunset faded from the sky, replaced by the first pinpricks of starlight. Claire helped Marcus unload equipment while Dr. Chen meticulously logged data from their unsuccessful expedition.

"Well, that was a bust," Marcus sighed, hefting a heavy case of monitoring equipment onto the dock.

Claire nodded, relief hidden beneath her disappointed expression. "Sometimes nature doesn't cooperate with our schedules."

Dr. Chen secured her tablet in a waterproof case, her movements deliberate and unhurried. "Claire, I've been meaning to ask you something." Her tone was conversational, almost friendly. "You've been photographing around Tod Blackstone's property quite a bit, right? The marina staff mentioned you're there often."

Claire felt her pulse quicken but kept her face neutral as she lifted her camera bag. "Yes, the light's exceptional from his dock. He's let me shoot from there a few times."

"Interesting." Chen stepped onto the dock, turning to face Claire directly. "He was in the exact area where we first detected the organized patterns. I tried to interview him about it. Very evasive man."

"He's private," Claire replied, carefully choosing her words. "Lots of locals are suspicious of outsiders asking questions. It's just how things work in small coastal towns."

Chen studied Claire's face with the same intensity she'd earlier applied to her monitoring equipment. "Maybe. Or maybe he knows something." She paused, letting the implication hang in the salt-tinged air. "You two seem close. Has he mentioned anything unusual? Strange sightings, unexplained phenomena?"

Claire felt the weight of Chen's scrutiny pressing down on her. "No. Just fishing talk. Tides, weather patterns, where the redfish are biting."

Chen smiled, but the expression remained confined to her mouth, never reaching her calculating eyes. "Let me know if that changes. My card has my cell number. Any time, day or night."

Claire nodded, suddenly aware of how thoroughly she'd underestimated the scientist's intelligence and intuition. This wasn't just scientific curiosity—it was targeted investigation, and Tod was firmly in the crosshairs.

"Of course," Claire said, returning the smile with equal insincerity.

As Chen walked away toward her car, Claire realized with absolute certainty: she wasn't just taking photographs for Chen anymore—she was being tested.

THE EVENING SETTLED over Copano Bay, transforming its surface into a dark mirror that reflected the emerging stars. Tod stood at the edge of his dock, watching for any signs of surveillance, his enhanced senses scanning for electronic signatures nearby. The soft crunch of tires on gravel announced Claire's arrival.

She approached with hurried steps, her face tight with worry in the dim light spilling from Tod's workshop.

"She knows something," Claire said without preamble, her voice quiet but urgent. "Chen asked about you specifically. Said you were evasive, mentioned how often I'm here. She suspects something. Maybe not what, but she knows I'm connected to you."

Tod nodded, unsurprised. "She's smart. We knew this was risky."

"What if she's watching me? Following me?" Claire glanced over her shoulder toward the road. "What if she followed me here tonight?"

Tod considered this, looking past Claire to the darkness beyond his property. "Then we're careful. No more communication here. I'll meet the Light Speakers at the new location only."

Claire wrapped her arms around herself, not from cold but from the weight of their situation. "I hate lying to her, Tod. She's not evil. She's just curious. Passionate about her work."

"I know." Tod's voice softened. "But passion doesn't make her safe. She'd still publish, bring others, turn them into research subjects. The Light Speakers would never know peace again."

The water lapped gently against the pilings beneath them. Both stood in silence, watching the dark surface that concealed so many secrets.

"What if there was a way to let her know without risking them?" Claire finally asked. "Some controlled revelation that satisfies her curiosity without endangering the Light Speakers?"

Tod shook his head, his expression hardening. "There isn't. We've been over this."

The moral complexity of their situation hung between them like the humid Gulf air—thick, inescapable. No matter which path they chose, someone's trust would be broken, someone's hopes disappointed. In protecting one truth, they were forced to bury another.

"I just wish..." Claire began, but let the thought fade unfinished.

Tod reached for her hand in the darkness, understanding her unspoken sentiment perfectly.

UNDER THE BLANKET OF night, Tod anchored his boat in the deeper waters near the uninhabited spoil island. The stars above were pinpricks of distant light, but beneath his hull, a more immediate constellation gathered. The Light Speakers rose from the depths, their blue-white glow diffusing through the dark water like living stars.

Tod activated his beacon, the familiar rhythm connecting them across species barriers. Their response was immediate—a synchronized pulse that confirmed their presence.

"HOW ARE YOU?" Tod signaled, his flashlight cutting through the darkness.

The Light Speakers arranged themselves in intricate patterns, their collective answer emerging through coordinated flashes: "WE FIND FOOD - WATER COLD ENOUGH - SAFE HERE."

Tod nodded, relieved. The colony had adapted to their new territory, exploring the deeper channel he'd found for them. Yet as he observed their movements, something felt different—less fluid, more constrained. Their usual graceful dance seemed muted, cautious.

"HUNTER WOMAN - SHE FEELS CLOSE - SHE SEARCHES HARD," the Light Speakers signaled, their pulses quickening with anxiety.

Tod's grip tightened on his flashlight. "YES - SHE WON'T STOP - WE KEEP MOVING YOU IF NEEDED."

The response came slowly, deliberate, as if they'd been discussing this among themselves: "RUNNING NOT LIVING - WE CANNOT HIDE FOREVER."

Tod stared into the water, struck by the profound simplicity of their statement. "WHAT DO YOU MEAN?"

The colony shifted, forming a perfect circle beneath his boat. Their light dimmed then brightened in unison: "HOME IS WHERE WE SPEAK - WHERE WE CONNECT - CANNOT CONNECT IF HIDING."

The weight of their words settled in Tod's chest. He had been so focused on their physical safety that he'd overlooked what made their existence meaningful. They weren't just surviving—they were beings with social needs, with culture, with connections that transcended mere proximity.

"I'M SORRY - TRYING TO PROTECT YOU," he signaled, a lump forming in his throat.

"WE KNOW - WE GRATEFUL - BUT THIS NOT LIFE WE WANT."

Tod looked across the bay toward the lights of Rockport in the distance. In his efforts to shield them from human curiosity, he had confined them to a life of secrecy and fear. Protection had become imprisonment. The irony wasn't lost on him—he understood isolation all too well since his transformation.

The Light Speakers pulsed again, gentler now, as if sensing his realization. Their message was clear: safety without freedom was its own kind of death.

THE DIGITAL CLOCK ON Claire's kitchen counter flipped to 11:30 PM as knuckles rapped gently against her front door. She rose from her editing desk where dozens of sunset photos from Dr. Chen's expedition glowed on the screen, none revealing the secrets she was protecting.

"Tod," she whispered, surprised, opening the door to find him standing there, looking haggard and uncertain in the porch light. His eyes held the weight of the ocean itself.

"Sorry. I know it's late." He shifted his weight. "I couldn't sleep."

"Neither could I." Claire stepped aside, inviting him into her small bungalow. Family photographs and framed prints lined the walls, while stacks of photography books created makeshift end tables. "What's wrong?"

Tod sank into her worn couch, running a hand through his hair. "I talked to them tonight. The Light Speakers. They told me something I can't shake."

Claire sat beside him, tucking one leg beneath her. "What did they say?"

"That running isn't living. That they can't hide forever." Tod's voice cracked slightly. "They said connection is essential to them—that home is where they can speak, where they connect. And they can't do that if they're hiding."

Claire processed this, the photographer in her immediately understanding. "So we're protecting them but also isolating them. From their purpose."

"Exactly." Tod slumped deeper into the cushions. "I don't know what I'm doing. Maybe this whole thing is wrong. Maybe I should just tell Chen everything, let the chips fall."

Claire leaned forward, her eyes intense. "No. You're doing the right thing. We just need a better solution."

"What solution? There isn't one." Tod's frustration seeped through his words. "Either they're studied and captured or they hide forever. What middle ground exists?"

Claire reached for his hand, her fingers warm against his. "We find one. Together. We're smart, they're smart. There's an answer we haven't thought of yet."

Tod looked at her, studying the certainty in her expression. "How are you so sure?"

"Because the alternative is unacceptable." Claire squeezed his hand, her determination flowing between them. "We didn't come this far, they didn't find you across impossible barriers, just to end up either imprisoned or in hiding."

A moment of silence stretched between them, filled with the sound of waves through Claire's open window and the weight of worlds in collision.

TOD HUNCHED OVER HIS weather station at 6:00 AM, his electromagnetic sense prickling like static electricity across his skin. For two days, the sensation had been building—a pressure behind his eyes and a tingling along his spine that preceded significant weather events. This wasn't his imagination. This was real.

The NOAA website confirmed what his altered nervous system already knew. A squall line was developing in the Gulf, rapidly organizing into something dangerous. Not a hurricane, but nothing to dismiss—sustained winds of 40 mph with stronger gusts, heavy rain, and seas building to eight feet or higher. The system would hit the coast in approximately 36 hours.

Tod's fingers moved across the keyboard as he checked additional forecasts, all confirming what he already sensed. He picked up his phone and texted Claire:

"Bad storm coming. NOAA tracking squall line. Will hit coast Thursday night."

He rubbed his temples, trying to ease the pressure there, when his eyes caught something on the marine traffic report. Dr. Sarah Chen's research vessel was scheduled for an overnight data collection mission tonight, twelve miles offshore—directly in the developing storm's path.

"Damn it," Tod muttered, his stomach dropping.

He pulled up the coordinates and cross-referenced them with the projected storm track. The timing couldn't be worse. Chen would be in open water when the worst of it hit. Tod stared at the screen, his jaw clenched.

He picked up his phone again, thumbs hovering over the screen before typing another message to Claire:

"Chen going out tonight. Storm coming. She doesn't know how bad."

The response came back almost immediately: "Should we warn her?"

Tod placed the phone on his desk, turning to stare out the window at the deceptively calm morning water. Chen was hunting the Light Speakers—was determined to find them, study them, expose them. Her absence would give them breathing room, time to figure out a better plan.

And if nature intervened... well, that wouldn't be on his conscience, would it?

Tod's thumb hovered over his phone's keyboard as conflicting thoughts battled in his mind. He could let the storm handle Chen. One less problem to worry about.

The Light Speakers' message echoed in his head: "RUNNING NOT LIVING."

What kind of guardian would he be if he used the same tactics as those he feared? What kind of man?

Finally, he typed: "Yes. Tell her."

He pressed send, a weight lifting from his shoulders even as a new responsibility settled in its place.

At his workshop window, Tod studied the distant horizon where clouds were beginning to build to the southeast. His altered senses detected the increasing electrical activity, a distant drumbeat growing steadily louder. The Light Speakers were safe for now in their new location, and Claire had positioned herself as the perfect double agent. Meanwhile, Chen continued her obsessive hunt, unwittingly sailing into a dangerous confluence of forces—natural and otherwise.

Too many pieces in motion. Too many ways it could all fall apart.

On the deck of the research vessel "Horizon," Dr. Sarah Chen supervised as Marcus loaded the last of their equipment. Specialized cameras, sonar arrays, and collection nets—all designed to document and potentially capture whatever was causing the organized bioluminescent patterns.

"Weather report just updated," Marcus said, checking his phone. "Storm's tracking north. Might get rough out there."

Chen barely glanced up from her clipboard. "Forecast says it'll pass south of us. We'll be fine."

She moved to the navigation table, studying their planned route one more time. The X marked where satellite imagery had captured the most consistent patterns. Where Tod Blackstone had been observed multiple times. Where Claire Westbrook seemed to focus her photography.

"Something's out there," she whispered, tapping the mark on the chart. "I can feel it. Tonight we find it."

Chen had no way of knowing she was sailing directly into a danger that would transform everything she thought she knew—about the Gulf, about intelligence, and about herself.

The storm was coming. In more ways than one.

Chapter 12

The sun hung low in the western sky as Claire stood on the marina dock, arms crossed against the strengthening breeze. The research vessel "Horizon" bobbed at the end of the pier while Marcus secured equipment to the deck. Dr. Chen moved with practiced efficiency, checking items off her clipboard as the afternoon shadows lengthened.

Claire approached, feeling the wind shift direction—another sign of the approaching weather system Tod had warned her about. "Dr. Chen, the forecast's changing. Local fishermen are saying this squall's going to be worse than predicted."

Chen barely glanced up from her clipboard. "Weather service says we're fine. And locals always exaggerate."

Marcus paused, a crate of monitoring equipment in his arms, his eyes darting between the darkening southeastern horizon and his employer. A flicker of uncertainty crossed his face before he continued loading.

"At least take someone experienced," Claire pressed, stepping closer. "Tod Blackstone knows these waters—"

"I don't need a charter captain," Chen cut her off with a dismissive wave. "We have GPS, radar, full safety equipment." She paused, studying Claire with sudden intensity. "You're very concerned. Any particular reason?"

Claire felt her pulse quicken under Chen's scrutiny. "Just... be careful."

"We're scientists, Ms. Westbrook. Caution is part of our methodology." Chen's tone softened slightly. "I appreciate your concern, but it's unnecessary."

Claire remained on the dock as Marcus untied the moorings and Chen started the engines. The vessel backed away, turning toward the Gulf with mechanical precision. Chen stood at the helm, her silhouette rigid against the darkening sky, determination evident in every line of her body. Marcus moved about the deck, his movements betraying the nervousness he wouldn't voice aloud.

The "Horizon" grew smaller against the expanse of Copano Bay, heading toward the narrow channel that would eventually lead to open water. Claire watched until the vessel was merely a speck, then pulled out her phone.

"She went. Wouldn't listen," she texted Tod.

Claire stared at the horizon where clouds were gathering, feeling a hollowness in her stomach. Scientists, fishermen, photographers—they all claimed to observe and interpret the world around them. But Chen's scientific certainty had blinded her to what any experienced local could feel: the air pressure dropping, the wind shifting, the peculiar stillness that preceded violence.

She turned toward her Subaru, unable to shake the feeling that she'd just watched someone sail directly into danger with a smile and a clipboard.

TOD STALKED THE LENGTH of his dock, one hand pressed against his temple where a dull throb pulsed in sync with the approaching storm. Six o'clock, and already the sky had taken on that sickly greenish hue that spelled trouble on the Texas coast. His electromagnetic sense hummed with warning—not just the usual background noise of electronics and radio waves, but the distinctive signature of atmospheric electricity building to dangerous levels.

"Damn it," he muttered, checking the NOAA radar on his phone again. The squall line was accelerating, intensifying as it moved across the Gulf. The red-and-yellow mass on his screen told a story the weather service hadn't caught up with yet. This storm would hit the coast by 10 PM, not midnight as forecasted. And Chen's research vessel would be directly in its path.

Tod glanced toward his boat, then back at the darkening horizon. The barometer was dropping faster than he'd seen in months. His fingers trembled slightly as he dialed the Coast Guard station.

"This is Tod Blackstone, local captain," he said when they answered. "I'm watching this system approach—it's moving much faster than forecast. Going to be dangerous out there."

"We're aware, Mr. Blackstone. Small craft advisories are being issued. All vessels should seek shelter immediately."

Tod hesitated, gripping the phone tighter. "Any vessels we should specifically warn?"

Mentioning Chen would connect him to her investigation. Make him part of whatever happened next. But she was out there, heading straight into danger, utterly convinced of her own assessment.

"Research vessel out of Rockport marina," he said finally. "Dr. Sarah Chen. She's about twelve miles out by now."

"We'll attempt radio contact. Thanks for the report."

Tod ended the call and stared at his boat. The Coast Guard might not reach her in time. He could go after her himself. Find her before the worst hit. But that was insane—putting himself directly in harm's way for someone who was actively investigating the Light Speakers. Someone who could destroy everything he was protecting.

Thunder rumbled in the distance. The rational choice was clear. Stay put. Let the professionals handle it.

But if something happened to Chen out there, could he live with himself?

TOD SECURED THE WATERPROOF container of emergency flares in K5HUX's storage compartment just as the sound of tires on gravel cut through the rumble of distant thunder. He glanced up to see Claire's Subaru skidding to a stop, her door flying open before the engine had fully quieted.

"What are you doing?" Claire demanded, taking in the scene—emergency gear piled on the dock, Tod's determined expression, the boat already untied from its moorings.

"Going after her." Tod tossed another waterproof bag into the boat.

Claire stepped onto the dock, wind whipping her hair across her face. "In this? Tod, the storm—"

"Will hit her harder than it'll hit me." He paused, meeting her eyes. "I know these waters. I can sense the weather. She can't."

Lightning flashed across the darkening sky, briefly illuminating the churning waters of Copano Bay. Claire's eyes narrowed.

"You hate her. She's trying to find them."

Tod's hands stilled on the rope he was coiling. The weight of her words hung between them as another gust of wind rocked the boat against the dock.

"Yeah," he finally said. "And I'm still going. Because that's what we do. We save people. Even the ones hunting us."

Claire stared at him, understanding dawning on her face. "The Light Speakers saved you."

"Exactly." Tod turned back to his preparations, voice quieter but firm. "They showed me what it means to be better than your survival instinct."

He reached for the ignition switch, and the engine rumbled to life, almost drowning out the thunder. Claire didn't hesitate. She stepped from the dock into the boat in one fluid motion.

"Then I'm coming."

"No—" Tod started.

"Not arguing." Claire grabbed a life vest from the bench. "You need another set of hands. I'm coming."

Their eyes met over the noise of the engine and the building storm. In Claire's gaze, Tod saw not just determination but something deeper—a reflection of his own choice to put what was right above what was safe. He gave her a single nod, accepting her decision and what it meant for both of them.

Together, they cast off from the dock, K5HUX's bow cutting through the first choppy waves as they headed into the darkening evening, united in purpose as the sky continued to darken above them.

THE CENTER CONSOLE boat slammed against the swells, saltwater spraying over the gunwale with each impact. Tod gripped the wheel with white knuckles, his jaw clenched as he navigated by the dim glow of instrument panels and the crackling energy he sensed in the atmosphere around them.

"You feel it, don't you?" Claire shouted over the wind, her knuckles white as she clung to the console. Her eyes never stopped scanning the horizon, searching for any sign of the research vessel.

Tod nodded grimly. The electrical fields in the approaching storm system washed over his consciousness like waves of pressure—massive cells of energy building, swirling, gathering strength. His modified brain interpreted the data with absolute clarity: this wasn't just a squall.

"It's going to be bad," he called back. "Worse than forecast. The front's accelerating."

A curtain of rain swept across them, stinging their faces. Claire wiped water from her eyes, her camera equipment safely stowed in waterproof cases beneath the console. Lightning branched across the sky behind them, followed by a boom that vibrated through the hull.

The VHF radio crackled to life with the measured cadence of the Coast Guard: "Attention all vessels, attention all vessels. This is U.S. Coast Guard Sector Corpus Christi. Urgent weather warning issued for Aransas Bay, Copano Bay, and adjacent Gulf waters. Severe thunderstorm with wind gusts exceeding sixty knots approaching rapidly. All vessels return to port immediately. Repeat, all vessels—"

Tod snatched the handset. "Research vessel, research vessel, this is K5HUX. Dr. Chen, you need to turn back now." He repeated the call twice before slamming the handset down. "Nothing but static."

"They might have their radio off while using sensitive equipment," Claire suggested, her face pale in the fading light.

The boat crested a particularly large wave, momentarily airborne before crashing down with a spine-jarring impact. Claire's finger suddenly shot forward, pointing.

"There!"

Two miles ahead, barely visible through sheets of rain, navigation lights bobbed on the swells—red and green pinpricks cutting through the gathering darkness.

"That's them." Tod pushed the throttle forward, engine roaring in response. "They're still heading offshore."

K5HUX surged forward, the bow lifting as they raced against the rapidly deteriorating conditions. Tod felt the electrical charge building in the atmosphere, like pressure against his skin, his skull.

Behind them, toward shore and safety, lightning continued to illuminate the churning sky. Ahead lay only darkness, broken only by the distant lights of Chen's vessel.

"Come on, come on..." Tod murmured, willing his boat faster as the distance between them and Chen's vessel gradually decreased.

THE HORIZON PITCHED violently as Tod maneuvered K5HUX alongside, his bow barely missing their stern as a wave pushed them together then apart. On the research vessel's deck, Dr. Chen and Marcus worked frantically with equipment—a submersible drone dangled half-deployed over the side while Marcus struggled with a tangle of cables.

"Dr. Chen!" Tod bellowed over the howling wind. "Storm's accelerating! You need to pull gear and run for port now!"

Chen's head snapped up, shock registering on her face at seeing Tod and Claire on the neighboring vessel. Her hair whipped wildly around her face as she shouted back, "We're fine! We have sophisticated weather tracking equipment on board! This system isn't supposed to—"

A brilliant flash of lightning split the sky, momentarily illuminating the massive wall of black clouds bearing down on them from the northwest. The thunder that followed was immediate and deafening.

"Jesus Christ," Marcus whispered, abandoning his cables. "Dr. Chen, maybe we should listen to them. That doesn't look like what was in the forecast."

Chen gripped the rail, her knuckles white. "We're getting readings! Something's down there! I can feel it!" Her eyes blazed with a fervor that transcended the danger surrounding them. "Twenty more minutes! That's all I need!"

"You're going to die out here for readings!" Tod yelled, fighting to keep his boat steady as another wave crashed over the bow. Claire clung to a handhold, her face rigid with determination as saltwater streamed down her cheeks.

"Why do you care?" Chen shouted back, genuine confusion in her voice. "You've been actively trying to prevent my research!"

"Because I'm not an asshole!" Tod roared. "Now pull your gear!"

Marcus was already moving, disconnecting equipment and securing loose items. The young researcher's panicked efficiency spoke volumes about his assessment of their situation.

Chen turned to look northwest, where another flash revealed the storm's true magnitude—a churning black mass consuming the horizon. Whatever confidence had sustained her scientific certainty evaporated in that moment of clarity.

"Marcus, secure everything! We're leaving!" She turned to help, but immediately saw the problem—the submersible's cable had tangled in the winch mechanism. "Dammit!"

Both researchers struggled with the equipment, precious minutes ticking away as the storm front approached with terrifying speed. Tod felt every hair on his body stand on end, his enhanced senses screaming warnings of the electrical maelstrom bearing down on them.

In the western sky, cloud-to-cloud lightning danced in continuous, silent flashes, like a giant approaching with a lantern. The electrical signature was unlike anything Tod had ever sensed—a wall of pure energy moving toward them across the water.

THE STORM HIT LIKE a physical wall. One moment they were in rough seas; the next, they were engulfed in a howling maelstrom. Wind that had been gusting at twenty knots suddenly screamed past forty-five, transforming the surface of the Gulf into a churning cauldron of white-capped waves that grew from three to six feet in seconds.

"Hold on!" Tod shouted, but his words vanished into the roar.

On the Horizon, equipment broke loose as the vessel pitched violently. A storage container slid across the deck and smashed against the gunwale. Dr. Chen scrambled toward the cabin where Marcus was trying to secure the navigation system.

Without warning, the boom swung free, whipping across the deck with deadly force. It struck Marcus squarely across the shoulders, sending him crashing to the deck. He lay motionless as water washed over him.

"Tod! Stay close to them!" Claire screamed, her knuckles white on the grab rail of K5HUX. Her hair plastered against her face, eyes wide with terror and determination.

Tod wrestled with the wheel, his enhanced senses a jumble of information. Electromagnetic pulses surged through his awareness as lightning formed above. He jerked the boat starboard, narrowly avoiding where a bolt would strike seconds later.

On the Horizon, Chen abandoned the controls, crawling toward Marcus's unconscious form. Her fingers slipped on the wet deck as she fought to maintain her balance. Just as she reached him, a massive wave struck the research vessel broadside.

The Horizon lurched like a wounded animal. Chen, caught in the open with nothing to hold, was thrown against the rail. It gave way with a crack of splintering fiberglass.

Her scream lasted only a second before the wind swallowed it whole. Tod's head snapped up, his marine empathy flaring with sudden, horrifying intensity. He felt her terror as she hit the water—the cold shock, the disorientation, the primal fear as waves closed over her head.

"MAN OVERBOARD!" Tod bellowed, already spinning the wheel.

Claire whipped around, scanning the churning seas. "WHERE?"

"There! Twenty yards off their port side!" Tod pointed into the darkness, where only his enhanced perception could detect Chen's desperate struggle.

Visibility had collapsed to mere feet in the driving rain. Waves obscured everything beyond their bow. Claire strained her eyes but saw nothing except angry whitecaps. Dr. Chen was already disappearing, a lone human in an uncaring ocean, her panicked thrashing growing weaker with each passing second.

On the Horizon, Marcus remained motionless on the deck, unaware his colleague was fighting for her life in the murderous sea.

TOD SCANNED THE CHURNING water, his enhanced senses straining against the electromagnetic chaos of the storm. Lightning fractured the sky, casting bizarre shadows across the waves. In one of those flashes, he caught a glimpse of Chen's arm breaking the surface before disappearing again.

"There!" He grabbed the life ring from its mount and hurled it toward Chen's position with all his strength. The wind caught it mid-arc, sending it careening in the wrong direction, the line snaking uselessly across the water.

"Damn it!"

Claire fumbled for the radio. "We need the Coast Guard! Now!"

Tod shook his head, already kicking off his boots. "No time! She'll drown!" He grabbed a spare tether line, securing one end to a cleat.

"Tod, no—" Claire's protest died as he dove over the side.

The cold water hit like concrete. For a disorienting moment, everything went silent beneath the surface before he broke back into the cacophony of wind and thunder. A wave crashed over his head, salt water burning his eyes, filling his nose.

His electromagnetic sense—usually so precise—went haywire in the electrical storm. Lightning strikes scattered across the water's surface created a blinding static in his awareness. But his marine empathy, that connection the Light Speakers had given him, remained. Through the turbulent darkness, he felt her—a desperate, fading human presence about thirty feet away. Struggling. Failing.

Tod swam hard, arms cutting through the water, the tether line trailing behind him. Each stroke pushed him closer to that fluttering awareness that was growing weaker by the second. Another wave lifted him up and slammed him back down, but he kept going, pushed by something more powerful than fear.

His hand struck something solid—an arm. Chen was floating face-down, barely conscious. Tod grabbed her, turning her over. Her eyes fluttered, unseeing, water streaming from her mouth in a weak cough. She'd swallowed too much already.

He wrapped the line around his arm and gave three sharp tugs—the signal to Claire.

On K5HUX, Claire felt the line go taut. She braced her feet against the gunwale and hauled with everything she had. The nylon bit into her palms as she pulled hand over hand, muscles screaming. The boat pitched wildly, threatening to throw her overboard with each wave. But she held firm, her determination matching the storm's fury.

"Come on, come on," she muttered, teeth clenched against the effort and the fear.

First Chen appeared, limp and pale, at the side of the boat. Claire hooked her arms under Chen's shoulders and heaved her aboard with a strength she didn't know she possessed. The scientist collapsed on the deck, coughing seawater, her body trembling violently with hypothermia and terror.

Tod came next, hauling himself over the side with the last of his strength before collapsing beside Chen. They lay there as the boat bucked beneath them, rain pelting their faces, both gasping for breath.

Claire scrambled to cover Chen with the emergency blanket from under the console. Chen's eyes found Tod's face, recognition and confusion battling in her expression.

"You..." she managed between chattering teeth, "...came for me."

Tod pushed himself to his knees, water streaming from his sodden clothes. "Got you. You're okay." He met her gaze, steady despite his exhaustion. "You're okay now."

The storm raged on around them, but for a moment, something shifted between them—rescuer and rescued, protector and threat—their roles suddenly, irrevocably changed.

THE STORM ROARED AROUND them with renewed fury, as if angered by their defiance. Tod steadied himself against the console while Claire tended to Dr. Chen, wrapping the emergency blanket tightly around her shivering form.

A crackle burst from the radio, cutting through the howling wind. A panicked voice—Marcus—broke through the static.

"MAYDAY, MAYDAY! This is research vessel Horizon! Crew member overboard, repeat, crew member overboard!" His voice cracked with desperation. "Position approximately twelve miles west of Rockport Marina. We need immediate assistance!"

Tod grabbed the radio handset. "Marcus, this is Tod Blackstone on K5HUX. We have Dr. Chen. She's alive."

A moment of stunned silence followed.

"Tod? You—you have Sarah? She's okay?" The relief in Marcus's voice was palpable even through the distortion.

"Recovering, but yes," Tod confirmed as another flash of lightning illuminated the Horizon about fifty yards away, pitching dangerously in the waves.

The Coast Guard broke in. "Research vessel Horizon, this is Coast Guard Station Port Aransas. We've dispatched a response vessel to your coordinates."

Tod pressed the transmit button again. "Coast Guard, this is K5HUX. We recovered the crew member. Repeat, crew member recovered and aboard our vessel."

"Copy K5HUX," the operator's voice came back, professional but with clear relief. "Good work. Can you assist the disabled vessel until our units arrive?"

Tod looked toward the Horizon. Through the rain-streaked darkness, he could see Marcus moving frantically around the deck. The vessel was sitting low in the water, taking on more with each passing wave.

"My engine's flooded," Marcus's voice broke through again. "Taking on water through the aft hatch. I—I don't think—" His transmission cut off as a wave crashed over the Horizon's bow.

Tod turned to Claire. "We have to tow them."

Claire's eyes widened. "In this?" She gestured to the violence surrounding them, the waves now cresting at seven feet, threatening to capsize them with each pass.

Tod was already moving, pulling a heavy tow line from the storage compartment. "If we don't, that boat's going down."

Dr. Chen pushed herself up on one elbow, still pale but alert. "Let me help," she said, her voice weak but determined.

"Stay down," Tod ordered, not unkindly. He maneuvered K5HUX closer to the Horizon, fighting the current with every adjustment of the throttle.

When they came alongside, Marcus appeared at the rail, face a mask of terror. Tod heaved the tow line across the gap.

"Secure it to your bow cleat!" he shouted over the storm. "Double wrap it! We'll get you home!"

Marcus fumbled with the line, his hands shaking violently. After what seemed an eternity, he gave a thumbs-up.

"Coast Guard, this is K5HUX," Tod radioed. "We're towing the Horizon to port. ETA approximately one hour if we can maintain heading."

"Copy that, K5HUX. Our vessel is twenty minutes from your position. We'll intercept and assist."

Claire took the wheel while Tod checked the tow line's tension. "Keep us at four knots," he instructed. "Any faster and the line might snap."

For the next hour, they fought through what felt like the longest miles of their lives. When the Coast Guard cutter finally appeared through the sheets of rain, its powerful searchlight cutting through the darkness, a collective breath of relief filled K5HUX's cabin.

The three vessels formed a fragile convoy—K5HUX leading, the Horizon being towed behind, and the Coast Guard cutter providing stability alongside—all battling their way through the storm's fury toward the distant safety of port.

Dr. Chen watched Tod as he worked, her scientific mind cataloging each decisive action, each moment of skill in the face of nature's wrath. The man she had viewed as an obstacle had just risked everything to save her life. The implications of this would require careful examination—later, when they weren't fighting for survival.

"Almost there," Tod called over his shoulder as the faint lights of Rockport Marina appeared in the distance. "Almost home."

THE ROCKPORT MARINA emerged from the storm's darkness like a beacon of salvation. Emergency vehicles waited on the dock, their red and blue lights pulsing against the curtain of rain. Harbor master Frank Miller and his assistant rushed to secure lines as Tod guided K5HUX into its slip, the Coast Guard cutter following with the Horizon in tow.

"Get the woman first!" someone shouted as EMTs rushed forward with a stretcher.

Dr. Chen sat huddled beneath the emergency blanket, her body still convulsing with shivers. The EMTs lifted her gently from Tod's boat, checking vitals as they moved.

"Moderate hypothermia, possible shock, lacerations to left shoulder," one called out as they wrapped thermal blankets around her. "Core temperature 94.3 – we need to get her warmed up now."

Marina workers helped a dazed Marcus from the Horizon. His eyes found Tod's across the dock, and he nodded once – a silent acknowledgment that transcended words.

As they prepared to load Dr. Chen into the waiting ambulance, she reached out with a trembling hand, grabbing Tod's wrist with surprising strength.

"You saved my life," she said, her voice barely audible above the rain drumming on the dock.

Tod shifted uncomfortably. "Just... what anyone would do."

"No." Her eyes, though clouded with exhaustion, held his firmly. "You came after me. Into that storm. After how I've treated you."

Tod's shoulders rose and fell in a half-shrug. "Yeah, well. Seemed like the right thing."

The EMTs began loading her into the ambulance, but Chen maintained her grip on Tod's hand, pulling him closer.

"Why?" The question seemed to contain a lifetime of scientific inquiry. "Why did you save me?"

Tod met her gaze steadily. "Because all life is sacred. Even when it's complicated."

Something shifted in Chen's expression – confusion, wonder, perhaps the first trembling recognition of a truth beyond her scientific parameters. Before she could respond, the EMTs pulled the stretcher fully into the ambulance and closed the doors.

The emergency vehicle pulled away, its siren cutting through the storm's diminishing fury, leaving Tod and Claire standing on the dock, water streaming from their clothes.

"You were amazing out there," Claire said, her voice soft with admiration as she tucked a strand of wet hair behind her ear.

Tod turned to her, his face softening. "We were amazing. Couldn't have done it without you."

They stood together in the rain, both understanding that something fundamental had changed – not just for Dr. Chen, whose worldview had just been upended, but between them as well. Some bonds could only be forged in fire and storm, in moments when life and death hung in the balance.

TOD AND CLAIRE SAT in his workshop, towels around their shoulders, steam rising from mugs of black coffee clutched in their hands. The storm had receded to a gentle patter against the roof, the violence of earlier now just an echo in their memories. Their clothes hung from makeshift lines across the room, still dripping onto the concrete floor.

"I can't believe we made it," Claire said, her voice rough with exhaustion. She tucked her legs beneath her on the couch, the oversized T-shirt Tod had lent her falling past her knees.

Tod checked his phone, scrolling through messages. "Coast Guard wants a formal statement tomorrow. Marcus sent thanks—looks like the Horizon will need major repairs." He paused on another notification. "Hospital says Chen is stable. Mild hypothermia, some cuts, but she'll recover."

Claire studied him over the rim of her mug. "Think she'll back off now?"

"Maybe." Tod's gaze drifted toward the window. "Near-death experience changes people. Makes them reconsider what matters."

Suddenly Tod stiffened, his mug freezing halfway to his lips. The familiar tingling sensation crawled across his skin—electromagnetic energy pulsing from outside. His enhanced perception registered a familiar signature.

"Wait." He rushed to the workshop window facing Copano Bay. The water glowed with unmistakable blue-white light. "No. They shouldn't be here. Too exposed."

He bolted for the door, Claire following close behind. At the dock, the scene stopped them both in their tracks. Dozens of Light Speakers had surfaced, their translucent bodies forming a luminous constellation on the dark water. Their pulsing seemed agitated, more rapid than normal.

Tod grabbed his flashlight, signaling in Morse code: "WHY HERE - DANGEROUS."

The colony responded in perfect unison: "WE WERE THERE." Tod frowned, confused. "WHERE?"

Their answer made his breath catch: "WITH WOMAN - IN STORM - WE HELPED."

Claire gasped beside him.

Tod's hands trembled as he signaled back: "YOU SAVED HER TOO?"

The Light Speakers' response illuminated the water like silent lightning: "YOU SAVED - WE HELPED - ALL LIFE SACRED."

Tod sank to his knees on the dock. All this time he'd been protecting them from Chen, yet they had chosen to help save her life.

They had witnessed his choice in the storm and had made their own parallel decision, following the same moral compass that had guided Tod himself.

Claire knelt beside him, her hand finding his. Together they watched the beings who had just redefined everything about this conflict with a single act of compassion.

TOD'S FINGERS TREMBLED slightly as he signaled with the flashlight: "HOW DID YOU HELP."

The colony's response came in coordinated pulses of blue-white light, their collective intelligence forming words that rippled across the water's surface: "FELT YOUR FEAR - YOUR NEED - WOMAN SINKING."

Claire edged closer to Tod, her shoulder brushing his as they knelt on the dock. The Light Speakers continued their explanation, each flash illuminating the night with purpose and meaning.

"FOLLOWED YOU - WHEN YOU JUMPED - COULD NOT LET EITHER DIE."

Tod and Claire exchanged glances. The colony hadn't just been passive observers—they had taken action.

"MADE LIGHT PATH - ONLY YOU COULD SEE - PUSHED HER UP - WHEN SHE SANK - GAVE BREATH."

Tod's eyes widened as understanding dawned. "I found her so fast. In complete darkness. You were lighting the way."

"YES," flashed the Light Speakers in unison, a single brilliant pulse that reflected off the underside of the dock.

"But she hunts you," Tod signaled, his movements sharp with confusion. "She wants to study you. Why save her?"

The water seemed to pause before their answer formed: "SAME REASON YOU DID - RIGHT THING - SHE DID NOT CHOOSE DEATH - WE DO NOT CHOOSE HER DEATH."

Claire's breath caught. Tears welled in her eyes, spilling down her cheeks in silvery tracks. "They're better than us," she whispered, voice barely audible above the gentle lapping of water against the pilings.

Something profound shifted in Tod as he absorbed their words. These beings he'd been trying to protect had revealed a moral clarity that humbled him. They hadn't calculated risk versus reward or weighed their own safety against Chen's life. They had simply done what was right.

Tod's flashlight moved slowly, deliberately: "THANK YOU - FOR HELPING - FOR BEING WHO YOU ARE."

The Light Speakers pulsed gently in response, forming one final message that lingered on the water's surface: "NOW SHE OWES LIFE - MAYBE SHE UNDERSTANDS."

The three species—human, human, and Light Speaker—remained in silent communion beneath the clearing sky, stars beginning to emerge as the storm clouds retreated. What had begun as a rescue mission had transformed into something far more profound: a lesson in compassion that transcended species, language, and the divide between worlds.

DR. SARAH CHEN STARED at the acoustic ceiling tiles of her hospital room, counting the tiny perforations to distract herself from the memories that wouldn't fade. The clock on the wall read 2:07 AM, its minute hand ticking with a rhythm that seemed unnaturally loud in the quiet room.

She closed her eyes, but immediately the sensations returned—the crushing pressure of the waves, the burn of saltwater in her lungs, and then... something else. Something impossible.

Blue-white lights surrounding her in the darkness. A strange feeling of being... held? Carried? And most disturbing of all, a distinct memory of drawing breath underwater.

"Hallucinations from oxygen deprivation," she whispered to the empty room, the scientific explanation providing momentary comfort. Yet the memories refused to dissolve like dreams should. They remained crisp, precise, insistent.

Chen pushed herself upright, wincing at the pull of stitches in her shoulder. The hospital gown felt rough against her skin as she swung her legs over the side of the bed. Every sensation seemed heightened—the cool linoleum beneath her feet, the antiseptic smell hanging in the air, the distant murmur of nurses at their station.

She made her way to the small bathroom, flipping on the light switch only to immediately recoil. The fluorescent bulb buzzed like a swarm of angry insects, the light piercing her retinas like needles.

"Too bright," she gasped, quickly dimming it to the lowest setting.

In the mirror, her reflection appeared normal—pale, certainly, with dark circles under her eyes, but physically intact. The wound on her shoulder had been neatly stitched and bandaged. Yet something felt profoundly different.

A strange tingling sensation crawled across her scalp, down her spine, through her fingertips. The medical equipment in her room—the heart monitor, the IV pump, even the electric clock—hummed with energy she could somehow perceive. Each device radiated a signature as distinct as a voice or a fingerprint.

Chen returned to bed, her scientific mind racing through possibilities—post-traumatic stress, neurological impact from hypothermia, medication side effects. But none felt right.

She reached toward the heart monitor, not quite touching it. The tingling in her fingertips intensified. Suddenly, she knew—knew with absolute certainty—that the machine would alarm in exactly two seconds.

One.

Two.

The monitor emitted a high-pitched beep, flashing a warning about lead displacement.

Rapid footsteps approached, and the door swung open as a nurse rushed in.

"What happened?" the young woman asked, scanning Chen and the equipment.

Chen stared at her own hands as if they belonged to someone else. "I don't know," she lied.

But she did know. Something fundamental had changed in that water. Something had touched her, altered her, rewired her perception of the world in ways that defied scientific explanation.

And Tod Blackstone had answers.

Chen waited until the nurse left before reaching for her phone on the nightstand. Her fingers hovered over the screen, poised to call him. Not yet. First, she needed to understand what was happening to her, catalog the changes, establish patterns. Then she would find him, and he would tell her everything.

Or she would make him.

On the dock behind Tod's home, Claire's camera lay forgotten in its bag as she and Tod stood watching the Light Speakers descend into the depths of Copano Bay, their blue-white glow fading as they sought safety in deeper water.

Tod's arm encircled Claire's waist, drawing her close against the night's chill. "Everything just got more complicated," he murmured.

Claire rested her head against his shoulder. "Or simpler. She owes them her life. Maybe that matters."

"Maybe."

Beneath the surface, the Light Speakers communicated in patterns too complex for human translation, their thoughts rippling through the colony like currents:

THE HUNTER IS SAVED. NOW SHE CARRIES OUR GIFT. SHE WILL UNDERSTAND. OR SHE WILL NOT. WE WAIT.

In her darkened hospital room, Chen lay alone, staring at her hands. She had dimmed the lights to their lowest setting—still too bright, still too painful. The electrical systems throughout the building sang to her: pulse, hum, flow. The cardiac monitor three rooms down. The elevator motors. The refrigeration units in the pharmacy.

She reached for her phone again, Tod's number displayed on the screen. Her finger hovered over the call button.

Not yet.

Chen set the phone down, closed her eyes, and focused on the new awareness flowing through her veins like an alien current. Whatever had happened in those waters, whatever had saved her and changed her, she would unravel it methodically, scientifically.

And when she understood, she would confront Tod Blackstone. The hunter had become something else entirely—not quite prey, but a seeker of a different kind of truth. And she would have it, no matter what it took.

Chapter 13

The fluorescent lights in Rockport Regional Hospital hummed with a frequency that made Dr. Sarah Chen's teeth ache. She lay in bed staring at the acoustic ceiling tiles, counting perforations to distract herself from the impossible memories that wouldn't fade. The bedside clock read 2:07 AM, its digital display painfully bright in the darkened room.

Three days since the storm. Three days since she'd drowned.

Except she hadn't drowned. That was the problem.

Chen closed her eyes, but immediately the sensations returned—the crushing pressure of the waves, the burn of saltwater in her lungs, the certain knowledge that she was dying. And then... light. Blue-white brilliance surrounding her in the darkness. A strange feeling of being held, carried, guided upward through impossible depths.

And breathing. She remembered *breathing* underwater.

"Hypoxia-induced hallucination," she whispered to the empty room, her voice hoarse from disuse. "Oxygen deprivation causes vivid sensory experiences. Well-documented in near-drowning cases."

But even as she spoke the words, she knew they were a lie. Her scientific training demanded rational explanations, yet the memory possessed a clarity that hallucinations never achieved. The lights had been real. The sensation of breathing had been real.

Something had saved her in that water. Something intelligent.

Chen shifted in the hospital bed, and the movement sent a fresh wave of discomfort through her body. Not pain exactly—more like heightened awareness. Every texture felt amplified: the rough cotton of the hospital gown, the synthetic weave of the blanket, the adhesive edges of the IV tape on her inner arm.

The fluorescent lights buzzed louder, their electrical hum seeming to bore directly into her skull. She reached for the call button to ask the nurse to dim them, but stopped as her fingers touched the plastic device.

A tingle. Not static electricity—something else. A faint awareness of current flowing through the wiring, of electrons moving through circuits. She jerked her hand back, staring at her fingertips in the dim light.

"Neurological side effects from hypothermia," she told herself firmly. "Temporary nerve damage. Will resolve with time."

But her pulse quickened as she recognized the symptoms from somewhere else. From someone else.

Tod Blackstone.

The charter captain who had saved her life. The man who had sailed directly into a killer storm to pull her from the water. The same man she'd been investigating, whose behavior she'd catalogued as aberrant.

He always seemed to know when his electronics were active before looking at them. Touched equipment with unusual hesitation. Kept lights dim in his workshop. Claimed to "sense" weather changes before instruments detected them.

Chen sat up slowly, ignoring the spike of dizziness. Her scientific mind assembled the pieces with terrible clarity.

If Tod Blackstone had similar symptoms...

If he'd been experiencing electromagnetic sensitivity...

If something in these waters had affected him the same way...

"No," she breathed. "That's not possible. That's not—"

A nurse appeared in the doorway, backlit by the harsh hallway fluorescents. The light stabbed into Chen's eyes like needles, forcing her to shield her face.

"Dr. Chen? Are you alright? Your heart rate spiked."

"The lights," Chen managed through gritted teeth. "Please. Dimmer."

The nurse moved to the controls, lowering the overhead fluorescents to their minimum setting. The relief was immediate and profound.

"Better?" the nurse asked with concern.

Chen nodded, not trusting her voice. Better. But not normal. Nothing about this was normal.

After the nurse left, Chen lay back against the pillows, her mind racing. Tomorrow she would demand her discharge. Tomorrow she would find Tod Blackstone. Tomorrow she would get answers.

Because the alternative—that she was experiencing something science couldn't explain, that her entire worldview needed to be rewritten—was simply impossible to accept.

The lights hummed their electronic song, and somewhere deep in Chen's rewiring neural pathways, something hummed back.

THE MORNING SUN STREAMING through Chen's hospital window felt like molten metal on her skin. She'd pulled the blinds closed twice, only to have nurses open them cheerfully, insisting that "sunshine helps healing."

They didn't understand. Couldn't understand.

Chen sat cross-legged on the bed, hospital gown replaced by her own clothes salvaged from her apartment. Her laptop balanced on her knees, screen brightness reduced to its lowest setting. Even that felt too intense, the pixels seeming to pulse with their own light source.

She'd spent the past hour researching her symptoms with growing dread:

Electromagnetic hypersensitivity Synesthesia Traumatic brain injury side effects Decompression sickness neurological complications

None of it fit. The symptoms were too specific, too acute, too familiar.

Chen opened a new document and began typing:

PERSONAL OBSERVATION LOG - DAY 3 POST-INCIDENT

0630 hours: Woke to sensation of "buzzing" from electronics. Can identify active devices without visual confirmation. Phone charging = distinct vibration in awareness (not physical). Laptop on standby = different frequency. IV pump = steady pulse I can feel across room.

0715 hours: Breakfast attempt. Food tastes different. Not bad, but... enhanced? Can distinguish metal traces in water. Salt content in eggs feels like information rather than flavor.

0803 hours: Dr. Morrison visited for discharge paperwork. Standing near him triggered strange sensation—like knowing his phone was about to ring before it did. It rang 3 seconds later.

Notable: This is not hallucination or delusion. These perceptions are consistent and repeatable. I am measuring phenomena outside normal human sensory range.

Hypothesis requiring investigation: Similar symptoms observed in Tod Blackstone. Correlation? Causation? What variable connects us?

Chen stopped typing, her fingers hovering over the keys. The answer was obvious, terrifying, and scientifically impossible.

The water. Something in the water during the storm.

She remembered Tod's behavior during the rescue—his uncanny ability to locate her in zero visibility, his navigation through the electrical chaos of the storm, the way he'd known exactly where she was beneath the waves. Not luck. Not skill.

Enhancement.

"Jesus Christ," Chen whispered, closing the laptop carefully. Her hands trembled.

A knock at the door made her jump. Dr. Morrison entered, clipboard in hand, his kind face creased with professional concern.

"Good morning, Dr. Chen. How are you feeling?"

"I need to be discharged," she said flatly. "Today."

Morrison frowned, consulting his notes. "Your vitals are stable, but given the severity of the incident—"

"I'm a scientist, Doctor. I understand the risks. I'm experiencing no respiratory difficulties, core temperature is normal, cognitive function is intact." She met his eyes steadily. "I need to continue my research."

It was a lie. Her research seemed laughably trivial now compared to what was happening inside her own body.

Morrison studied her for a long moment. "The neurologist wants to run a few more tests. Your brain activity showed some... unusual patterns."

Chen's heart rate spiked. She forced herself to breathe slowly, evenly. "What kind of patterns?"

"Enhanced activity in the sensory processing regions. Nothing alarming, but atypical for someone post-trauma." He glanced at his clipboard. "Have you been experiencing any sensory disturbances? Heightened awareness? Synesthesia?"

The world seemed to narrow to a pinpoint. They'd measured it. Her changes were detectable.

"Nothing significant," Chen lied smoothly. "Perhaps just residual stress response."

Morrison didn't look convinced, but he nodded. "I'll approve your discharge if you agree to follow-up appointments. Weekly for the first month."

"Of course."

After he left, Chen sat motionless, processing the implications. If her neurological changes were measurable, they were real. If they were real, they needed an explanation. And if Tod Blackstone had similar changes...

She reached for her phone, then stopped. Calling Tod would show her hand too early. She needed to observe him first, confirm her hypothesis, understand what was happening before confronting him directly.

But there was someone else. Someone who spent time with Tod, who might have noticed his symptoms.

Chen found Claire Westbrook's number in her contacts and typed out a message:

"Claire, this is Dr. Chen. I'm being discharged today. Would you be available to meet? I'd like to discuss the photography project and... other matters. - SC"

She stared at the message, her thumb hovering over send. This was it—the moment she chose between scientific inquiry and plausible deniability. Once she started asking questions, there was no going back.

Chen pressed send.

Outside her window, seagulls wheeled and cried. And for the first time in her life, Dr. Sarah Chen could *feel* them—not just see them. Their presence registered as ripples in some invisible field she'd never known existed, never believed was possible.

The world had become a different place. Or perhaps she had.

FOUR DAYS AFTER THE storm, Chen sat in her car outside Claire Westbrook's bungalow, hands gripping the steering wheel, trying to gather the courage to knock on the door.

The drive from Corpus Christi had been an ordeal. Every traffic light sent pulses through her awareness. Power lines overhead created a constant low-frequency hum she couldn't ignore. Her own car's electrical system buzzed against her skin like a living thing.

And the water. God, the water.

Crossing the Copano Bay Causeway, Chen had nearly pulled over as a wave of sensation overwhelmed her. It wasn't sight or sound—it was *awareness*. The bay teemed with life she could somehow sense: fish moving in schools, shrimp scattered across the bottom, even the subtle disturbances of boat propellers cutting through distant water.

It was impossible. It was happening. And she was terrified.

Claire's text response had been cautious but agreeable: *"I can meet tomorrow afternoon. 2pm? My place? Hope you're recovering well."*

Chen checked her watch: 1:57. Time to face this.

She climbed out of the car, immediately aware of the electrical signatures of the houses around her. WiFi routers, smart thermostats, phone chargers—a symphony of electromagnetic noise she'd never known existed. She pressed her palm against her temple, trying to will it away.

The front door opened before she could knock. Claire stood in the doorway, concern evident in her expression.

"Dr. Chen. You look..." Claire paused, clearly searching for diplomatic words.

"Terrible?" Chen supplied. "That's accurate." She attempted a smile that felt more like a grimace. "May I come in?"

Claire stepped aside, gesturing her inside. The bungalow was small but charming, walls covered with Claire's photographs. Normally Chen would have admired the composition, the technical skill. Now she could barely focus on the images themselves—her attention kept dragging toward the electronic devices scattered throughout the space.

"Can I get you something? Water? Coffee?"

"Water, please. And... could you turn off your wifi router?"

Claire paused mid-step. "My... wifi?"

"I know it sounds strange." Chen rubbed her temples again. "I've been having some sensitivity issues since the accident. Electronics are... bothering me."

She watched Claire's face carefully, looking for recognition, for understanding. Instead, she saw only polite confusion.

"I think it's in the closet," Claire said slowly. "I can turn it off if you need."

"Please."

While Claire disappeared down the hallway, Chen sank onto the couch, closing her eyes. The moment the router powered down, the relief was tangible—one source of noise eliminated from the overwhelming cacophony.

Claire returned with a glass of water, settling into the chair across from Chen with visible concern. "Are you sure you should be out of the hospital?"

"I'm fine. Mostly." Chen took a careful sip, distinctly aware of the mineral content in the water, the trace metals, the chlorine. She set the glass down. "Claire, I need to ask you something, and I need you to be honest with me."

Claire's posture shifted subtly. More guarded. "Okay."

"Tod Blackstone. You spend a lot of time with him. Have you noticed anything... unusual about his behavior?"

The guardedness increased. "Unusual how?"

Chen leaned forward. "Does he react strangely to electronics? Seem sensitive to lights? Avoid certain equipment? Know things before he should be able to know them?"

The silence stretched between them. Claire's fingers tightened on her water glass.

"Why are you asking?"

"Because," Chen said carefully, "I think something happened to me in that water. Something I can't explain. And I think it happened to Tod too."

Claire stood abruptly, moving to the window. "I don't know what you're talking about."

But her voice betrayed her. Chen heard the lie, saw the protective stance, recognized the fear beneath the deflection.

"Claire." Chen's voice softened. "I'm not here as a researcher. I'm here because I'm *scared*. Something is changing inside me and I don't understand it, and I think Tod Blackstone is the only person who might."

Claire turned from the window, arms crossed. "Have you asked him?"

"I'm asking you first. Because I need to know—is this temporary? Does it get worse? Better? Can I trust him?"

The photographer studied Chen for a long moment, some internal calculation happening behind her hazel eyes.

"He saved your life," Claire finally said. "Risked his own to pull you out of that water. If you can't trust that, I don't know what to tell you."

"That's not an answer."

"It's the only one I'm giving you." Claire moved toward the door. "You want to know what's happening to you? Go ask Tod yourself. But Dr. Chen?" She paused, hand on the doorknob. "Maybe consider that some things aren't meant to be studied. Maybe some things are meant to be *lived with*."

Chen stood on the front porch moments later, Claire's door clicking shut behind her. The photographer knew. She knew, and she was protecting Tod, and that meant everything Chen suspected was true.

She walked to her car, pulling out her phone to look up Tod's address. She already knew it—had it memorized from her investigation. But now she wasn't going as a researcher hunting an anomaly.

She was going as someone looking for answers about what she'd become.

CHEN'S CAR ROLLED TO a stop in front of Tod Blackstone's property just after sunset. The sky burned orange and purple over Copano Bay, the water reflecting the colors in shimmering bands. Normally she would have appreciated the natural beauty. Now all she could feel was the *presence* of the water—its mass, its movement, the life within it calling to something new inside her.

Tod's workshop lights were on, casting a warm glow through the windows. His boat bobbed at the dock, and from somewhere nearby she heard the distinctive crackling of a radio transmission.

Chen sat in the car for several minutes, rehearsing what to say. *I think you know what's happening to me. I think something in that water changed us both. I need help understanding.*

No. Too direct. Too demanding.

Thank you for saving my life. I've been experiencing some unusual symptoms. I wondered if we could talk.

Better. Less confrontational. Leave room for him to—

A wave of sensation crashed over her. Something in the water. No—somethings. Plural. Organized. Moving with purpose.

Chen's hands tightened on the steering wheel as she *felt* them approaching—dozens of individual presences, their collective movement creating patterns in her awareness like music she could see. The same organized light patterns she'd been chasing for months.

They were here. At Tod's property. Right now.

She grabbed her flashlight from the glove box and stumbled out of the car, her scientific instincts overriding everything else. This was it—proof, validation, everything she'd been seeking.

Chen half-ran toward the dock, flashlight gripped in one hand, her other hand pressed against her temple as the sensations intensified. So many of them. So close. The electromagnetic signatures of their bioluminescence singing across the water like—

"Dr. Chen."

She spun around. Tod Blackstone stood twenty feet away, perfectly silhouetted against his workshop lights. His posture was calm but alert, hands loose at his sides.

"Tod. I—" She gestured toward the water. "I can feel them. In the water. Can you feel them too?"

Something shifted in Tod's expression. Not quite surprise. More like resignation.

"You should go home, Dr. Chen."

"No." She shook her head, taking a step closer. "No, I'm not leaving. Not until you tell me what's happening to me. The lights, the sensitivity, the way I can feel electronics and water and—" Her voice cracked. "What did they do to me, Tod?"

"They saved your life."

"And *changed* me." Chen's hand trembled as she pointed toward the bay. "I can feel them out there right now. The same ones you've been protecting. The ones I was hunting." A bitter laugh escaped her. "The ones that apparently decided to give me whatever you have."

Tod remained still, his eyes reflecting the last light of sunset. "Come down to the dock."

"What?"

"If you want answers, come down to the dock. But Dr. Chen?" His voice carried a weight she'd never heard before. "Once you see them—really see them—everything changes. Your career, your research, your understanding of what's possible. Are you ready for that?"

Chen thought of her university position, her publications, her reputation. Everything she'd built on the foundation of rigorous science and empirical evidence. Then she thought of the buzzing in her skull, the strange awareness of the water, the knowledge that her body was changing in ways she couldn't explain.

"I don't have a choice," she said quietly. "Do I?"

"Everyone has a choice." Tod walked past her toward the dock. "But yeah, I know what you mean."

Chen followed him down the wooden planks, her flashlight beam shaking slightly. The water below was dark now, the sunset colors fading to gray twilight. But she could *feel* them down there, waiting, their presence as real as the dock beneath her feet.

Tod knelt at the edge, pulling out his own flashlight. "They communicate through light. Morse code." He glanced up at her. "You were right about them being organized. You were right about a lot of things."

"What are they?"

"I call them Light Speakers. They're... intelligent. Refugees. Got displaced by a hurricane." Tod's flashlight moved in quick patterns. "I've been trying to protect them. Keep them hidden."

"From people like me," Chen supplied.

"Yeah."

The water began to glow. Not the random sparkle of dinoflagellates—deliberate, patterned light forming words in a code Chen had learned decades ago in Girl Scouts.

"W-E S-A-V-E-D Y-O-U"

Chen's legs gave out. She sat down hard on the dock, flashlight clattering beside her. "Oh my God."

"They gave you the gift," Tod said quietly. "Same thing that happened to me after they saved me from drowning. The electromagnetic sensitivity, the marine empathy—it's permanent. You're one of us now."

"One of *us*?" Chen looked at him sharply. "How many?"

"So far? Two. You and me." Tod turned back to the water. "They don't give this to everyone. You have to earn it somehow. Nearly dying isn't enough. You have to..." He struggled for words. "You have to be worth saving."

The lights in the water pulsed again: "S-H-E E-A-R-N-E-D I-T - W-E G-A-V-E G-I-F-T - S-H-E M-U-S-T U-N-D-E-R-S-T-A-N-D"

Chen stared at the luminescent words, her entire scientific worldview crumbling. "I was hunting them."

"They know."

"I wanted to capture them. Study them. Make my career out of them." Her voice broke. "And they saved me anyway."

Tod was quiet for a moment. "They're better than us. That's what Claire said when she found out. I think she's right."

Chen watched the lights pulse in their seven-second rhythm, feeling their collective presence in the water like a song she'd never known she could hear. All her research, all her ambition, all her certainty about the world—it meant nothing now.

"What do I do?" she whispered.

"That depends." Tod looked at her directly. "You can walk away. Try to ignore the changes, pretend this never happened. Or you can stay. Help protect them. Learn from them." He paused. "But if you stay, your career is done. Your research has to stop. Everything you were working toward—it all ends here."

Chen thought of her lab, her students, her pursuit of tenure. Everything she'd sacrificed for science. And then she thought of the beings in the water below—creatures that had shown her more mercy than she'd ever shown them.

"I can't betray them," she heard herself say. "Can I?"

"No," Tod said simply. "You really can't."

The workshop door opened, and Claire emerged, moving down the dock with careful steps. She settled beside Tod, her presence clearly a comfort to him.

"You told her," Claire said. It wasn't a question.

"She could already feel them. Seemed like the moment for truth."

Claire looked at Chen with those observant artist's eyes. "So what now, Dr. Chen? Are you going to study them? Expose them? Make them famous?"

Chen shook her head slowly. "I'm going to..." She stopped, really considering the question for the first time. "I don't know. I need to think."

"While you're thinking," Tod said, his voice hardening slightly, "they're vulnerable. Every minute you delay deciding is a minute they're at risk. So yeah, think. But think fast."

"I—" Chen looked at the three of them: Tod, Claire, and the glowing beings below. A strange alliance. A secret impossible to keep. "I quit."

"What?"

"I'll quit. Tomorrow. I'll destroy my research data, burn my notes, tell the university I'm having a mental health crisis." Chen laughed, slightly unhinged. "Which might actually be true."

Tod exchanged a glance with Claire. "You're sure?"

"No." Chen pulled her knees to her chest, wrapping her arms around them. "I'm not sure about anything anymore. But I know what I owe them. They saved my life when they could have let me drown. When maybe they *should* have let me drown." She met Tod's eyes. "You did the same thing. You came after me in that storm even though I'd been hunting your secret. So no, I'm not going to be the person who destroys them. I'm going to be the person who protects them."

The Light Speakers pulsed a new message: "W-E A-C-C-E-P-T"

Claire reached across Tod to touch Chen's arm gently. "Welcome to the most complicated secret on the Texas coast."

Chen nodded, unable to speak past the lump in her throat. Three days ago she'd been a scientist on the verge of the discovery of a lifetime. Now she was something else entirely—transformed, humbled, and irrevocably changed by beings she'd never imagined could exist.

The night settled around them, four consciousnesses sharing the dock: two humans, one photographer, and a colony of light.

And somewhere in Chen's rewiring mind, the question whispered: *What have I become?*

But she already knew the answer. She'd become someone who understood that mercy was worth more than fame, that wonder trumped ambition, and that sometimes the most important discoveries were the ones you agreed to keep secret.

Tod stood, offering her his hand. "Come on. We need to talk about what happens next. The abilities get stronger. You need to learn how to manage them."

Chen accepted his help, rising on unsteady legs. "You'll teach me?"

"I'm only a few weeks ahead of you. But yeah, I'll tell you what I know."

As they walked back toward the workshop, Chen glanced over her shoulder at the glowing water. The Light Speakers had settled into a peaceful formation, their collective rhythm steady and calm.

For the first time in three days, the buzzing in Chen's head didn't feel like a curse.

It felt like a connection.

Chapter 14

T he sun hadn't yet cleared the eastern horizon when Chen arrived at Tod's property, her hands trembling on the steering wheel. Not from nervousness—from the overwhelming sensory input that had awakened her at 4 AM and refused to let her rest.

She could feel the fish.

Not see them, not hear them. *Feel* them. Every redfish cruising the shallows, every mullet school moving in synchronized patterns, every crab scuttling across the bottom. The entire bay registered in her awareness like a living map, constantly updating, impossible to ignore.

Tod was already waiting on the dock, two mugs of coffee steaming in the cool morning air. He raised one in greeting as Chen approached, her exhaustion evident in every step.

"Couldn't sleep?" he asked.

"Couldn't *stop* sensing." Chen accepted the coffee gratefully, wrapping both hands around the mug. "Tod, it's getting worse. Or stronger. I don't know which. Every living thing in the water—I can feel them all at once. It's like trying to listen to a hundred radio stations simultaneously."

Tod nodded, his expression sympathetic but not surprised. "Sit down. Let's work on filtering."

They settled at the dock's edge, legs dangling above the water. The sky brightened gradually from black to deep blue to purple, the first rays of sun painting the clouds in shades of orange and gold. Normally Chen would have appreciated the beauty. Now she could barely focus past the cacophony of marine life registering in her consciousness.

"When it first happened to me," Tod said quietly, "I thought I was losing my mind. The electromagnetic noise was constant—every device, every power line, every radio wave. I couldn't function."

"How did you manage it?"

"Barney helped. Made me think of it like tuning a radio." Tod set his coffee aside, his posture relaxing into teaching mode. "You're not trying to eliminate the signals. You're learning to adjust the volume, to focus on what matters and let the rest become background noise."

Chen closed her eyes, immediately assaulted by the sensory input. A school of speckled trout two hundred yards away. Shrimp scattered across the muddy bottom. A stingray gliding along the channel edge. Dozens of blue crabs. The Light Speakers resting in deeper water, their presence distinct and somehow musical compared to the others.

"I can feel them all," she whispered. "Every single one."

"Pick just one creature. The closest one."

Chen focused, trying to isolate individual signals from the overwhelming chorus. "There's... a redfish. Maybe twenty feet away. Moving along the pilings."

"Good. Now describe everything you sense about it."

She concentrated, surprised by the depth of information available. "It's big. Maybe thirty inches. Hungry—actively hunting. I can feel its... attention? Like it's scanning for prey." She paused, processing. "This is insane. I'm describing fish behavior I shouldn't be able to detect."

"Now expand. Add one more creature."

Chen's awareness stretched to include a second signal. "Another redfish. Smaller. Following the first one. They're... communicating? No, that's not right. Coordinating. Pack hunting."

"You're doing it." Tod's voice carried approval. "You're filtering. Choosing what to focus on."

"But it takes so much concentration. How do you function normally when—" Chen stopped as a massive presence suddenly registered in her awareness. Something large moving through deeper water, its electromagnetic signature different from anything else she'd sensed.

"Tod." Her eyes snapped open. "What is that?"

He followed her gaze toward the bay's deeper channel. "Tarpon, probably. Big one, maybe six feet. They migrate through here."

Chen stared at the water, feeling the creature's power, its ancient vitality, the way it moved through the bay like it owned the place. "I can sense its heartbeat. The electrical activity in its muscles. This is..." She trailed off, unable to find words.

"Overwhelming. Beautiful. Terrifying." Tod finished for her. "Yeah. I know."

They sat in companionable silence as the sun finally broke free of the horizon, flooding the bay with golden light. Chen practiced her filtering technique, selecting individual creatures and studying their signatures, then gradually expanding her awareness to encompass multiple signals without losing control.

"Your marine empathy is stronger than mine," Tod observed after a while. "Way stronger. You're sensing things I can't."

"Really?" Chen looked at him with surprise. "But you've had this longer."

"Doesn't matter. We're different." He gestured to the workshop behind them. "My electromagnetic sense is more acute—I can feel radio waves, power lines, electronics at greater distances. But you?" He nodded toward the water. "You've got a direct line to everything alive in there. The Light Speakers gave us similar gifts, but they manifested differently."

Chen processed this, her scientific mind cataloging the implications. "Different exposure during transformation? Different neural chemistry? Genetic factors?"

"All of the above, probably." Tod stood, stretching. "But right now, you need to learn control. Because if you can't filter this, you won't be able to function. And we need you functional."

"Why?" The question came out sharper than Chen intended. "I quit my career. Destroyed my research. What use am I now?"

Tod looked at her steadily. "You know things. About marine biology, geology, oceanography. You understand this environment in ways Claire and I never will. Your scientific knowledge doesn't disappear just because you're not publishing papers anymore."

Chen wanted to argue, but a new presence interrupted—Claire's car pulling into the driveway. The photographer emerged carrying a bag from the local bakery, her smile bright despite the early hour.

"Figured you two might need breakfast," Claire called, making her way down to the dock. She paused, studying Chen's face. "How's the training going?"

"She's picking it up fast," Tod said. "Faster than I did."

Claire settled beside them, distributing kolaches and fresh coffee from a thermos. For several minutes they ate in comfortable silence, watching the bay come alive with morning activity. Boats appeared in the distance—shrimpers heading out, a few early recreational fishermen.

"I've been thinking," Chen said finally, wiping crumbs from her fingers. "About protection strategies. Long-term sustainability. We can't keep hiding them in the bay forever—it's too shallow, too accessible, too many boats passing through daily."

"We know," Tod said quietly. "Been keeping me up at night."

"What if I told you I might know a place? A real sanctuary where they could hide indefinitely?"

Tod and Claire exchanged glances. "We're listening," Claire said.

Chen pulled out her phone, opening a file she'd been reviewing since yesterday. "When I was working on my dissertation, I researched submerged karst formations along the Texas coast. Most people don't realize that during the last Ice Age, sea levels were much lower. The coastline extended miles farther out than it does now."

She swiped through images—sonar scans, geological surveys, depth charts. "Limestone caves that formed on dry land got flooded when the ice melted and sea levels rose. They're still out there, sixty to a hundred feet underwater, largely unexplored because they're difficult to access and there's been no commercial reason to map them extensively."

Tod leaned closer, studying the images with growing interest. "You're saying there are underwater caves offshore from here?"

"I'm saying I have sonar evidence of a significant cave system approximately eighteen miles offshore from Copano Bay. Deep enough to be protected from storms and surface activity. Remote enough that recreational divers won't stumble across it." Chen zoomed in on a particularly detailed scan. "I never got funding to explore it fully, but the preliminary data suggests extensive chambers, stable conditions, and freshwater seepage from underground aquifer connections mixing with the saltwater."

"Which means the Light Speakers could adapt to it," Claire said, understanding dawning. "Brackish water—not pure saltwater or pure freshwater."

"Exactly." Chen's exhaustion momentarily forgotten, animated by the scientific problem. "It's the perfect refuge. Protected, hidden, and large enough for the entire colony. Maybe multiple colonies if others exist."

Tod studied the sonar images, his expression shifting from skepticism to cautious hope. "How do we verify it's suitable? We can't just relocate them without confirming."

"Reconnaissance dive. You and me." Chen met his eyes. "I know the coordinates, I have the dive experience, and with your connection to the Light Speakers, you can assess if they'll accept it. We go tomorrow, verify the location, and if it checks out, we move them within forty-eight hours."

"I don't dive," Tod admitted. "I mean, I can swim, but cave diving is—"

"I'll teach you what you need to know. It's not a technical cave dive—the entrance is accessible, the chambers are large. We'll use full safety protocols, backup equipment, redundant air supplies." She saw his hesitation. "Tod, I've logged over three hundred dives. I won't let anything happen to you."

Claire set down her coffee carefully. "What about me?"

Both Tod and Chen turned to her. "You'll coordinate from the surface," Chen said. "Radio communications, emergency protocols, tracking our position. You're essential to safety."

But Claire's expression suggested she'd heard something else entirely. *You don't have abilities, so you stay in the boat.*

Tod caught it too. He reached for Claire's hand. "You okay?"

"Fine." Claire's smile was too bright, too quick. "Makes sense. I'll hold down the fort."

An uncomfortable silence settled over the dock. Chen recognized the dynamic she'd inadvertently triggered—the division between those who'd been transformed and those who hadn't. She'd been so focused on the practical problem that she'd missed the emotional one.

"Claire," Chen said carefully. "You're the reason Tod trusted me. The reason I'm sitting here instead of back in my lab trying to capture the Light Speakers. Your judgment matters. If you think this cave idea is wrong, we don't do it."

Claire looked at Chen with surprise, then at Tod, who nodded agreement.

"We're a team," Tod added quietly. "All three of us. Different roles, but nobody's expendable."

The tension eased slightly. Claire squeezed Tod's hand. "Then let's go find this cave."

THREE DAYS LATER, CHEN stood in her Corpus Christi apartment staring at her laptop screen, her finger hovering over the delete button. Nine years of research data. Seventeen published papers. Hundreds of field observations. Her entire academic career compressed into digital files that she was about to permanently destroy.

Her phone buzzed for the fourteenth time that morning. Another call from Dr. Morrison, the department head. She'd been ignoring him for days, but the messages were becoming increasingly urgent. The last voicemail had mentioned "psychiatric evaluation" and "emergency leave."

Chen opened her email, finding three new messages:

From: Dr. Richard Morrison *Subject: URGENT - Meeting Required Sarah, your continued absence and refusal to communicate is deeply concerning. The dean has asked me to formally request your presence at a departmental review meeting Friday at 2 PM. This is not optional. We need to understand what happened during your research expedition and why you've suddenly resigned. - Richard*

From: Marcus Chen (no relation) *Subject: Dr. Chen - Are you okay? Dr. Chen, I've been trying to reach you. The department is asking questions about the bioluminescent research. They want to know if I have copies of your data. I told them no, but Dr. Morrison seems to think you might have had a breakdown after the storm incident. Please call me. I'm worried about you. - Marcus*

From: Dr. Jennifer Hartley, NOAA *Subject: Collaboration Opportunity Dr. Chen, I read your preliminary report on organized bioluminescent patterns with great interest. I'd like to discuss a potential collaboration. NOAA has funding available for unusual marine phenomena research. Your satellite imagery analysis was particularly intriguing. Please contact me at your earliest convenience.*

Chen closed her laptop and walked to the window, looking out over Corpus Christi Bay. From here, the water looked peaceful, ordinary. She couldn't sense the marine life from this distance, though she'd learned to extend her awareness nearly a quarter mile when she concentrated.

A knock at the door made her jump. She froze, considering not answering, but the knock came again, more insistent.

"Dr. Chen? It's Marcus. I know you're in there—your car's in the parking lot."

Chen cursed under her breath. She'd been avoiding this conversation, but Marcus was persistent. And kind. He deserved better than being ghosted by his advisor.

She opened the door. Marcus stood in the hallway, backpack slung over one shoulder, concern evident on his young face. At twenty-four, he still had that eager graduate student energy that Chen remembered from her own early career. Before cynicism and ambition had hardened her.

"Marcus. This isn't a good time."

"When is a good time? You haven't returned anyone's calls in days." He gestured to the apartment. "Can I come in? Just for a minute?"

Chen stepped aside reluctantly. Marcus entered, immediately noticing the packed boxes, the bare walls where her academic awards had hung, the general air of abandonment.

"You're really leaving," he said quietly.

"I quit. Remember?"

"But why?" Marcus set his backpack down, genuine confusion in his voice. "Dr. Chen, you were so close. The bioluminescent patterns, the satellite data—you had something incredible. Why throw it all away?"

Chen moved to the window, unable to meet his eyes. "I was wrong. The patterns weren't what I thought."

"That's not what the data showed."

"The data was flawed." The lie came easier than it should have. "Satellite artifacts, seasonal algae blooms, nothing more."

"I don't believe you." Marcus pulled out his own laptop. "I've been reviewing your field notes from the night of the storm. You found something out there, Dr. Chen. Just before the storm hit, you noted 'organized movement confirmed' and 'collective behavior observed.' What did you see?"

Chen's hands clenched. She could feel the electromagnetic signature of Marcus's laptop, his phone in his pocket, the wifi router in the apartment below. Since the transformation, electronics had become a constant presence in her awareness—like a persistent ringing she could never quite ignore.

"Nothing that matters."

"But—"

"Marcus." Chen turned to face him, forcing steel into her voice. "Drop it. Destroy any copies of my research you have. Tell the department I had a breakdown if that's easier. But this line of investigation is closed. Permanently."

Marcus stared at her, hurt and confusion warring on his face. "You're protecting something."

The accusation hung in the air. Chen said nothing.

"There's something out there," Marcus continued, his voice dropping. "Something you found. And for some reason, you've decided it's more important to keep it secret than to advance human knowledge." He shook his head. "I thought you were better than that. I thought science mattered to you."

"It did," Chen said quietly. "It does. But some things matter more."

Marcus grabbed his backpack, heading for the door. He paused at the threshold, looking back. "The old Dr. Chen would have called that weakness. Giving up because the truth was inconvenient."

After he left, Chen stood motionless for several minutes, his words echoing in her mind. He was right, of course. A week ago, she would have said exactly the same thing. Science demanded truth, demanded publication, demanded sharing knowledge with the world regardless of consequences.

But that was before she'd drowned. Before beings of light had saved her life. Before she'd felt the consciousness of every living thing in the bay. Before mercy had transformed her understanding of what mattered.

Chen returned to her laptop, opened the file directory containing her research, and highlighted everything. Nine years of work. Her finger pressed delete.

Are you sure you want to permanently delete these items?

"Yes," she whispered, and pressed confirm.

The files vanished. Years of her life erased in seconds.

Chen felt lighter. And terrified. And somehow, inexplicably, more certain of her choices than she'd been in years.

Her phone buzzed again. This time, it was Tod: *Weather window tomorrow perfect for dive. 6 AM departure. You ready?*

Chen typed back: *Ready. See you at dawn.*

She had destroyed her old life. Time to build a new one.

CLAIRE SAT IN TOD'S workshop, surrounded by photographs she'd taken over the past two weeks. The Light Speakers glowing beneath the dock. Tod teaching Chen to filter her marine empathy. The three of them planning around charts and sonar images. She'd documented everything, building a visual record of the impossible.

But lately, she'd felt increasingly like an observer rather than a participant. The person behind the camera instead of in the frame.

The workshop door opened, and Tod entered carrying takeout from the local taqueria. "Figured you'd still be here," he said, setting down the bag. "You've been editing for six hours."

"Lost track of time." Claire accepted a taco gratefully. "How's the dive prep going?"

"Chen's thorough. We've gone through every scenario, backup plan, emergency protocol. She's treating this like a NASA mission." Tod settled beside her, studying the photographs on the monitor. "These are incredible, Claire."

"Thanks."

Something in her tone made him pause. "What's wrong?"

"Nothing."

"Claire."

She set down her taco, not meeting his eyes. "Do you ever wish I had it too? The abilities?"

Tod was quiet for a moment. "No."

"Really?" Claire turned to face him. "It doesn't bother you that Chen can sense what you sense, understand what you're experiencing, while I'm just... normal?"

"You're not normal." Tod's hand found hers. "You're extraordinary. You saw me when I was trying to be invisible. You chose to help protect the Light Speakers before you knew what they were. You risked everything to become Chen's mole. You're brave and brilliant and—"

"Not transformed." Claire pulled away gently. "Tod, I see it. The way you and Chen look at the water now. The way you communicate without words. There's a connection between you that I can't share."

Tod was silent, and Claire knew she'd struck truth.

"I'm not jealous," she clarified. "Not exactly. It's more like... I'm afraid. That you'll eventually realize you need someone who can truly understand what you've become. Someone who can stand beside you in both worlds—the human one and the other one the Light Speakers showed you."

Tod pulled her close, his arms wrapping around her firmly. "Listen to me. What we have—it's not about abilities. It's about trust. About choosing each other every day, even when it's complicated and scary and we don't have all the answers." He tilted her chin up, forcing her to meet his eyes. "You ground me, Claire. Without you, I'd lose myself in the sensory noise, in the isolation, in the weight of keeping this secret. You remind me how to be human."

"But—"

"No buts. You're essential. Not despite being unchanged, but because of it. You're our bridge to the normal world. Our reminder of what we're protecting and why." Tod's thumb brushed her cheek. "Chen and I may share abilities, but you and I? We share something more important. We share a life."

Claire felt tears threatening. "Promise me something?"

"Anything."

"If you ever start to drift away—to get lost in whatever you're becoming—you'll let me pull you back."

"I promise." Tod kissed her forehead. "And Claire? The Light Speakers could have transformed you during the storm rescue. They didn't. That was a choice. Maybe they knew we needed someone unchanged. Someone to keep us tethered."

Claire considered this, finding comfort in the idea. "You think they planned that?"

"I think they're smarter than we give them credit for." Tod returned to the photographs on the monitor. "These matter, Claire. Years from now, when we're trying to remember how this all started, these images will tell the story. That's your role. The witness. The chronicler. The one who makes sure this chapter of history isn't forgotten."

Claire leaned against him, feeling the steadiness of his presence, the warmth of his certainty. Maybe he was right. Maybe being unchanged wasn't a deficit but a strength.

"I love you," she said quietly.

"I love you too." Tod's arm tightened around her shoulders. "Now eat your taco before it gets cold. We've got a big day tomorrow."

They sat together in the workshop's warm light, surrounded by images of wonder and impossibility, two people choosing each other despite the strangeness that had entered their lives.

DAWN BROKE CLEAR AND calm as Tod's boat cut through glassy water, heading toward open Gulf. Claire sat at the console monitoring their position while Tod and Chen organized dive equipment in the stern. The Light Speakers followed beneath the hull, their presence a comforting constant in Tod's awareness.

Eighteen miles offshore. Water depth increasing steadily as they left the shallow bay system behind. Tod felt his marine empathy stretching, the range expanding as they entered deeper water with more diverse life. Grouper lurking near bottom structure. Schools of mackerel passing through. The distant presence of something large—possibly a bull shark—prowling the deeper channel.

"Coordinates coming up," Claire called. "Half a mile."

Chen checked her dive computer, then Tod's, verifying both were synchronized. "Remember the protocol. Stay within visual contact. If anything feels wrong, we surface immediately. Three tugs on the line means emergency ascent."

Tod nodded, his stomach tight with nervous anticipation. He'd done shallow recreational dives before, but nothing like this. Seventy-five feet deep, searching for a cave entrance Chen had only seen via sonar. If they couldn't find it, the whole plan collapsed.

"Dropping anchor," Claire announced, cutting the engine. The boat drifted to a stop, gentle swells rocking the hull. "This is it. Right over the coordinates."

Tod and Chen donned their equipment with practiced efficiency—BCDs, regulators, fins, masks. Chen had insisted on redundant everything: two air supplies each, backup lights, dive computers, emergency surface markers. She wasn't taking chances.

"You've got this," Claire said, checking Tod's equipment one final time. "Trust Chen. Trust yourself."

Tod kissed her quickly. "Back in an hour."

He and Chen rolled backward off the gunwale, hitting the water with simultaneous splashes. The Gulf swallowed them immediately, warm surface water giving way to cooler temperatures as they descended.

Tod's marine empathy exploded with input. Life everywhere—baitfish schooling in massive clouds, bottom dwellers stirring from their hiding places, larger predators circling at the edge of his awareness. It was overwhelming and magnificent.

Chen led the way down, her dive light cutting through the blue-green water. Tod followed, equalizing pressure in his ears, watching the depth gauge tick upward. Thirty feet. Forty. Fifty.

The bottom came into view—a landscape of limestone and sand, scattered with small formations. Chen consulted her dive computer, then adjusted their heading, swimming parallel to the bottom, searching.

Tod felt the Light Speakers approaching, their curiosity evident even without words. They'd followed them down, obviously interested in what the humans were seeking. Their bioluminescence provided additional light, painting the underwater landscape in blues and whites.

Chen stopped abruptly, pointing. Tod swam closer and saw it—a dark opening in the limestone, partially hidden by sediment and small growth. The entrance was narrow, maybe four feet across, but it clearly led somewhere deeper.

Chen turned to Tod, making the "okay?" sign. He returned it, and they approached the entrance together.

The Light Speakers went first, their collective glow illuminating the passage. Tod and Chen followed, swimming single file through the opening. The passage widened after about fifteen feet, opening into...

Tod's breath caught. Even through the regulator, he couldn't suppress his awe.

A massive chamber stretched before them, easily a hundred feet across and thirty feet high. Limestone formations hung from the ceiling like frozen waterfalls. The floor was covered in fine sand, undisturbed for probably centuries. And everywhere—absolutely everywhere—freshwater springs seeped from cracks in the stone, mixing with the saltwater in visible currents.

The Light Speakers spread out through the chamber, exploring with obvious excitement. Their bioluminescence filled the space with dancing light, revealing details: small fish that had adapted to cave life, crustaceans unlike anything Tod had seen, minerals deposited in beautiful patterns across the walls.

Chen swam to Tod, gave him an emphatic thumbs up. This was it. The perfect sanctuary.

They spent forty minutes exploring, finding multiple chambers connected by passages, each one protected and pristine. The cave system was even larger than Chen's sonar had suggested—a labyrinth of limestone carved over millennia, now filled with brackish water and teeming with unique life.

When they finally surfaced beside the boat, both were grinning behind their masks.

"Well?" Claire called down anxiously.

Tod pulled out his regulator. "It's perfect. Better than perfect. The Light Speakers love it."

Chen hauled herself aboard, pulling off her mask. "I've explored caves all over the world, and this is... it's extraordinary. Stable, protected, enormous. We could relocate them today if conditions hold."

Claire helped Tod aboard, relief evident in her expression. "So we're really doing this?"

"We're doing this." Tod looked toward the water where the Light Speakers' glow was still visible below. "Tomorrow night. Low light conditions, minimal boat traffic. We lead them out here and they stay. No more hiding in the bay, no more risking discovery. They'll be safe."

The three of them stood together on the boat, the Gulf stretching endlessly around them, a secret refuge found, a plan taking shape. For the first time since the storm, Tod felt something like hope.

Maybe they could actually protect the Light Speakers. Maybe this could work.

THAT EVENING, TOD'S workshop television played local news while the three of them reviewed the relocation plan. Tod was marking the route on a chart when Claire suddenly grabbed the remote and turned up the volume.

"—unusual marine phenomena in the Gulf," the reporter was saying. She stood on a dock in Rockport, interviewing an elderly man in a captain's cap. The graphic identified him as Captain Wayne Mitchell, Retired.

"Been fishing these waters fifty years," Captain Mitchell said, his weathered face serious. "Never seen anything like it. Organized lights moving under the surface, all in formation. Not natural. Not normal."

The reporter turned to the camera. "Captain Mitchell says he witnessed the phenomenon three nights ago approximately eight miles offshore from Copano Bay. He's not the only one. At least four other local fishermen have reported similar sightings over the past two weeks."

Tod felt his blood run cold.

The report continued: "Coast Guard records also reference 'unusual circumstances' in the rescue of marine biologist Dr. Sarah Chen during last week's severe squall. While officials won't comment on specifics, anonymous sources suggest the rescue involved atypical elements that are still under review."

Chen leaned forward, her face pale. "They're connecting the dots."

The reporter concluded: "The Texas Parks and Wildlife Department has announced they'll be sending a research team to investigate these reports. Marine biologists from multiple universities have also expressed interest. Whatever is happening in the Gulf, it seems we'll be getting answers soon."

The news segment ended, cutting to a commercial. Tod muted the television, and the three of them sat in heavy silence.

"How long do we have?" Claire asked quietly.

"Days," Chen said. "Maybe a week before researchers start systematic searches. Captain Mitchell gave them a general area—they'll focus there first. But eventually..." She didn't need to finish.

Tod stood, pacing. "Then we move them tomorrow night as planned. Get them to the cave before anyone else finds them. Once they're in the cave system, they're invisible. No satellite can see through seventy-five feet of water into a limestone formation."

"What about us?" Claire gestured to the television. "The Coast Guard mentioned unusual circumstances in your rescue, Chen. They're going to investigate. What if they figure out there's a connection between Tod and the sightings? Between you and the organized light patterns you were researching?"

"Then we lie," Chen said flatly. "We say I had a breakdown after nearly drowning. That I destroyed my research in a moment of trauma. That Tod's just a local captain who happened to be in the right place at the right time." She met their eyes. "And we make damn sure the Light Speakers are hidden before anyone can prove otherwise."

Tod moved to the window, looking out at the dark bay. Somewhere out there, the Light Speakers rested, unaware that the net was closing around them. That human curiosity and scientific ambition were about to descend on their temporary home.

"We've always known this day would come," he said quietly. "That keeping them secret forever was impossible. We just need to buy them time. Get them safe. After that..." He turned back to Claire and Chen. "After that, we figure out what comes next."

Claire joined him at the window, slipping her hand into his. "Together."

"Together," Chen echoed, standing to join them.

The three guardians stood side by side, watching the water, preparing for the most critical mission yet. Tomorrow they would move the Light Speakers to safety. And after that, they would face whatever came next.

The secret was slipping away, revelation closing in. But they weren't done fighting yet.

Not by a long shot.

Chapter 15

D
r. Sarah Chen stared at her laptop screen in the pre-dawn darkness of her apartment, willing the data to be wrong. She'd run the analysis three times, checked against two separate datasets, even called a colleague at NOAA to verify the oceanographic models.

The numbers didn't change.

A massive low-oxygen event—hypoxia—was moving toward Copano Bay. The stalled eddy system that had been sitting offshore for a week had finally started moving, and it was pushing a dead zone ahead of it like a slow-motion tsunami.

Chen's fingers trembled as she pulled up the latest satellite imagery. The water temperature gradients told the story: warm surface water trapping cooler, oxygen-depleted water beneath. The combination of agricultural runoff from the Mission and Aransas Rivers, unusually warm temperatures, and now this pressure system had created the perfect conditions for disaster.

She checked the clock: 4:47 AM. The oxygen readings from the bay's monitoring stations showed normal levels for now, but the projection models were clear. In approximately forty-eight hours, dissolved oxygen would drop to levels incompatible with complex marine life.

The Light Speakers would suffocate.

Chen grabbed her phone, her marine empathy already registering the bay's subtle changes before the instruments could. The fish were restless, moving toward deeper water, sensing something wrong in ways human technology was only beginning to understand.

She called Tod. He answered on the second ring, voice thick with sleep.

"Chen? What's wrong?"

"Get to my place. Now. Bring Claire." Her voice was steady despite the panic clawing at her chest. "We have a problem."

FORTY MINUTES LATER, the three guardians sat around Chen's small dining table, coffee cooling in forgotten mugs as they studied the laptop screen. Outside, the sun was just beginning to lighten the eastern sky, painting Corpus Christi Bay in shades of gray and pink.

"Explain it again," Tod said, his jaw tight. "In terms I can understand."

Chen pulled up a diagram showing the bay's cross-section. "Hypoxia. Dead zone. The warm surface layer acts like a lid, trapping oxygen-poor water underneath. As organisms die and decompose, they consume more oxygen, making it worse. It's a cascade effect."

"How bad?" Claire asked quietly.

"Fish will start dying in forty-eight hours. Anything that can't escape the bay will suffocate." Chen met their eyes. "Including the Light Speakers."

Tod stood abruptly, pacing to the window. His marine empathy had been registering subtle distress signals from the bay since he'd woken, but he'd attributed it to his own anxiety. Now he realized the water itself was changing, becoming hostile.

"The cave," Claire said. "We move them early. Today."

"Tonight," Chen corrected. "New moon. Darkest conditions we'll get. But we have to move fast—if we wait for the oxygen levels to drop, they'll be too weak to make the journey."

Tod turned from the window. "Eighteen miles. Through busy waters. In one night."

"It's the only option." Chen's scientific calm was fracturing at the edges. "Tod, if we don't move them, they die. All of them."

The silence stretched between them, heavy with the weight of impossible decisions.

"Then we move them," Tod said finally. "But we do it right. Full plan, backup protocols, everything we can think of to keep them hidden." He looked at Chen. "You have the sonar data for the route?"

"Already plotted. I'll mark the deepest channels, avoiding all the shallow areas and major traffic lanes."

"Claire, we'll need your LED decoys. Whatever you've been working on—now's the time."

Claire nodded, already pulling out her phone to make notes. "I can rig up something for tonight. Enough to create multiple false signatures if anyone's watching."

"And Marcus," Chen added quietly. "We need him."

Tod's head snapped toward her. "Your grad student? The one who's been asking questions?"

"He showed up yesterday. He knows something's happening." Chen met Tod's skeptical gaze. "But I think... I think he'll help. If we ask."

"That's a hell of a risk."

"Everything about this is a hell of a risk." Chen's voice hardened. "But Marcus understands data. He can spoof boat traffic information, create digital false trails. Without him, every marine traffic monitoring system will see us making a straight line from the bay to that cave."

Tod wanted to argue, but the logic was sound. They needed all the help they could get.

"Fine. But if he betrays us—"

"He won't," Chen said with more certainty than she felt.

THE REST OF THE MORNING was a blur of preparation. Tod returned to Rockport, checking and rechecking his boat's systems, loading extra fuel, testing backup equipment. Every system had to be redundant, every failure point addressed. They wouldn't get a second chance at this.

Claire spread LED strips across her bungalow's floor, programming sequences that would mimic bioluminescent patterns. She'd mount them on small flotation devices and deploy them at strategic points along the coast. Anyone monitoring for unusual lights would have multiple targets to chase, all of them leading away from the real convoy.

Chen made the call she'd been dreading.

Marcus answered on the third ring. "Dr. Chen? I wasn't expecting—"

"I need your help," she said without preamble. "And I need you to not ask questions until after you've said yes or no."

A pause. "That's not very scientific."

"This isn't about science. It's about doing the right thing when the right thing is illegal, unethical by conventional standards, and absolutely necessary." Chen took a breath. "Will you help me protect something that shouldn't be protected according to every professional standard we were taught?"

Another pause, longer this time. Chen could hear him thinking, weighing his career against his conscience.

"The bioluminescent phenomenon," Marcus said finally. "You didn't have a breakdown. You found something. Something intelligent."

Chen closed her eyes. "Yes."

"And now it's in danger."

"Yes."

"What do you need?"

Relief flooded through her. "Can you access the Coast Guard's Automatic Identification System database? Marine traffic monitoring?"

"That's... that's actually illegal without authorization."

"I know."

Marcus was quiet for a long moment. "I'll need two hours and a really good VPN. What am I looking for?"

"I need you to create false boat traffic. Make it look like there are multiple vessels operating in areas they're not. Enough confusion that one real convoy gets lost in the noise."

"You're moving them."

"Tonight. New moon. We have one chance."

"Send me the coordinates you want masked. I'll create enough digital chaos that no one will know what's real and what's not." Marcus hesitated. "Dr. Chen? Whatever they are... they're worth this, right?"

Chen thought of the Light Speakers surrounding her in the storm, saving her when they could have let her drown. Of their message tapped on Tod's dock: "SHE EARNED IT."

"They're worth everything," she said quietly.

BY EARLY AFTERNOON, Tod's dock had become a staging area. Both boats were fueled and equipped—Tod's charter boat and Chen's smaller research vessel, the damaged Horizon having been replaced with a borrowed craft from a colleague who didn't ask questions.

Claire arrived with a bag full of LED strips, batteries, and waterproof timers. "I can deploy six decoy systems," she said, spreading her equipment across the dock. "Program them to activate in sequence, starting two hours before we launch. They'll draw attention north and south of our actual route."

Tod studied the modified fishing floats she'd prepared, each one housing a sophisticated LED array. "These are good. Really good."

"I've been photographing light for years. I know how to fake it." Claire's smile was tight. "Never thought I'd use the skill for this."

Chen joined them, her laptop open to a navigation chart covered in colored lines. "Marcus came through. He's creating phantom AIS signals for twelve vessels operating in a pattern that will make maritime traffic control think there's a regatta happening twenty miles north of us. Anyone looking at the screens will be watching that, not a couple of boats heading offshore."

"How long until they figure out it's fake?" Tod asked.

"Marcus says four to six hours. Long enough for us to complete the mission and get back."

Tod checked his watch: 2:17 PM. Sunset at 7:34. Full darkness by 8:15. They'd launch at 9:00, giving them the darkest possible conditions for the crossing.

"We need to talk to them," he said. "Make sure they understand what's happening."

The three of them moved to the end of the dock, where the bay stretched out in afternoon sunlight. Tod pulled out his flashlight, unnecessary in the bright day but the Light Speakers would see it regardless of ambient light.

He tapped out the pattern they'd established: two-seven-two. Two flashes, pause, seven flashes, pause, two flashes. *Tod calling. Emergency.*

The water remained still for several heartbeats. Then, from the deeper channel, a faint blue-white glow began to rise. Even in daylight, even at risk of exposure, they came.

The colony assembled beneath the dock, their presence registering in Tod's awareness like a familiar song. Chen gasped softly—her marine empathy must be picking them up clearly now, the collective consciousness of hundreds of beings moving as one.

Tod began signing with the flashlight, keeping the beam angled down to minimize visibility from shore:

"DANGER IN WATER - OXYGEN DYING - MUST MOVE YOU TONIGHT"

The Light Speakers pulsed in their seven-second rhythm, processing. Then:

"WHERE"

"CAVE - EIGHTEEN MILES - SAFE FOREVER"

A longer pause. Tod could feel their uncertainty through his connection, the collective weighing risk against survival.

"DARK JOURNEY?" they asked.

"YES - NEW MOON - YOU FOLLOW BOATS - WE PROTECT"

"TRUST YOU"

Those two words hit Tod harder than he expected. They'd nearly died trusting him once before, during their first journey. Now they were being asked to trust again, to follow humans into the darkness toward a sanctuary they'd never seen.

"WE WILL NOT FAIL YOU," Tod signaled.

The colony swirled beneath the dock, their light patterns shifting in ways Tod was learning to read. Agreement. Acceptance. And underneath it all, something that felt like gratitude.

"WHEN?" they asked.

"NINE TONIGHT - STAY DEEP UNTIL THEN - SAVE STRENGTH"

"WE READY"

The Light Speakers descended, their glow fading back into the bay's depths. Tod lowered the flashlight, his hand trembling slightly.

"They're scared," Chen said quietly. She was gripping the dock railing, her knuckles white. "I can feel it. They're terrified but they're going to do it anyway."

Claire moved closer to Tod, slipping her hand into his. "Then we make sure they have nothing to be scared of. We get them there safe."

Tod nodded, looking out across the bay that had been home to the Light Speakers for weeks, that was now slowly turning toxic. By tomorrow night, fish would be floating dead on the surface. By the following morning, the bay would be a graveyard.

"Six hours," he said. "Let's make sure we're ready."

AS EVENING APPROACHED, the three guardians made their final preparations. Claire deployed her LED decoys along the coast, each one programmed to activate on schedule. The fake lights would create a breadcrumb trail of false sightings, drawing any curious observers away from the real convoy.

Marcus called Chen at 7:15. "Phantom vessels are active. Maritime traffic control is already getting confused reports. I've got twelve boats showing on AIS that don't actually exist, all running a coordinated pattern that looks like a night fishing tournament. They'll be chasing ghosts all night."

"How'd you create the signals?" Chen asked, genuinely curious despite the tension.

"Raspberry Pi units with GPS spoofers and AIS transmitters. Not exactly legal, but they'll work. I've got them positioned on buoys and floating debris all along the coast. By the time anyone figures out what's happening, you'll be done."

"Marcus... thank you."

"Don't thank me yet. Just get them safe." He paused. "And Dr. Chen? I'm deleting the code that created this after tonight. No evidence, no trail. We were never on this call."

"Smart."

"That's why you recruited me."

Chen smiled despite everything. "That's why I recruited you."

AT 8:45 PM, TOD STOOD on his dock watching the last light fade from the western sky. The new moon meant there would be no lunar illumination, just stars and the distant glow of Rockport's lights. Perfect conditions for moving something that glowed in the dark.

Claire and Chen waited in their respective boats, engines idling quietly. All systems were checked, all equipment secured. The bay was nearly empty—most recreational boaters had headed in hours ago, and the commercial fleet wouldn't launch until early morning.

Tod activated his radio. "K5HUX to support vessels. Final comm check."

"Support One ready," Chen's voice came back.

"Support Two ready," Claire confirmed.

"Launching in ten minutes. Stay on channel seven-two. Radio silence unless emergency." Tod glanced at the water. "Let's bring them home."

He climbed aboard his boat, feeling the gentle rock of the hull, the familiar weight of the wheel under his hands. This boat had carried him through thousands of charters, through storms and calms, through the ordinary work of a coastal captain's life.

Tonight it would carry him through something extraordinary.

At exactly 9:00 PM, Tod tapped out the signal: two-seven-two.

The response was immediate. From the deep channel, blue-white light began to rise, spreading across the bottom like dawn breaking underwater. The Light Speakers assembled in their familiar formation, hundreds of individuals moving as a unified whole.

Tod's marine empathy registered their readiness, their trust, and underneath it all, their fear. They knew the water was dying. They knew this journey was survival.

"Okay," Tod whispered, engaging the throttle. "Let's go."

His boat began to move, cutting through the dark water. Behind him, Chen and Claire fell into formation. And beneath all three vessels, the Light Speakers followed, a constellation of living light heading toward an uncertain future.

The convoy had launched. The crossing had begun.

And somewhere in the darkness ahead, eighteen miles of open water waited, filled with obstacles they couldn't predict and dangers they could only prepare for.

Tod checked his GPS, confirmed his heading, and pushed the throttle forward another notch. The Light Speakers matched his speed instantly, their formation adapting to the faster pace.

"Four knots," Tod murmured, watching the speed indicator. "Holding steady."

Chen's voice crackled over the radio. "Support One confirms. Colony maintaining formation. Looking good."

"Support Two confirms," Claire added. "LED decoys are active. Social media's already lighting up with 'mystery lights' reports from the decoy sites."

Tod allowed himself a tight smile. The plan was working. For now.

They passed under the Highway 35 causeway, the massive concrete structure looming overhead in the darkness. Cars hummed across above them, ordinary people heading to ordinary destinations, completely unaware of the impossible convoy passing beneath.

The channel opened up beyond the causeway, water depth increasing to twenty-five feet. The Light Speakers spread out slightly, their formation loosening in the more comfortable depth.

"Five miles down," Tod reported. "Thirteen to go."

The night stretched ahead, dark and full of unknowns. But they were moving, the Light Speakers were following, and for now, that was enough.

Tod tightened his grip on the wheel and focused on the heading. Eighteen miles. They could do this.

They had to.

Chapter 16

The convoy moved through the darkness like a ghost fleet, three boats running with minimal lights, following a course that existed only on GPS screens and in Tod's intimate knowledge of these waters. Behind them, Copano Bay receded into the night. Ahead, the open Gulf waited with its promise of sanctuary.

Tod kept his eyes on the depth sounder and the radar screen, monitoring both the bottom contours and the surface traffic. So far, the route was clear—the combination of new moon darkness, late hour, and Marcus's phantom vessel distractions had created a window of opportunity.

But windows closed.

"Support One to Lead," Chen's voice crackled over the radio. "How are they doing?"

Tod glanced at the water, his marine empathy reading the colony's status like a vital signs monitor. "Strong. Holding formation. They're actually... excited? The deeper water feels better to them."

It was true. As they'd moved from the bay's shallow warmth into the cooler, deeper waters of Aransas Bay, the Light Speakers had brightened, their movements becoming more fluid and confident. This was closer to their natural environment—the cold depths they'd come from before the hurricane had displaced them.

"Ten miles from cave entrance," Claire reported from Support Two. "LED decoy three just activated. Twitter's going crazy about lights near Port Aransas."

Tod smiled grimly. Every fake sighting pulled attention away from them, bought them precious minutes of invisibility. Marcus's digital ghosts were doing their job too—when Tod checked the marine traffic overlay on his GPS, he could see a dozen phantom vessels clustered twenty miles north, creating exactly the kind of mysterious activity that would obsess anyone monitoring the area.

The Aransas Pass jetties appeared ahead, two long fingers of rock extending into the Gulf, marking the transition from bay to open ocean. Tod had navigated this passage hundreds of times, but never at night with such precious cargo.

"Approaching the jetties," he radioed. "Stay tight. Current picks up here."

The boats throttled back slightly as they entered the pass. The water compressed between the jetties, creating eddies and turbulence that could be treacherous. Tod felt the current grab his hull, trying to push him off course. His hands moved automatically, adjusting the wheel, compensating with practiced precision.

Below, the Light Speakers compressed their formation, staying in the deepest part of the channel. A large bull shark registered in Tod's awareness—the apex predator drawn by the unusual activity. The shark approached the colony, curious, then suddenly veered away as if hitting an invisible wall.

They can defend themselves, Tod realized. The collective consciousness of hundreds of beings was apparently intimidating even to a creature that feared nothing else in these waters.

The jetties fell behind. The boats emerged into open Gulf water, and immediately the character of the sea changed. Swells rolled under the hulls—not dangerous, but substantial, the long fetch of open ocean making itself felt. The depth gauge climbed: forty feet, fifty, sixty.

The Light Speakers spread out, their formation blooming like a flower opening to the sun. Tod could feel their relief, their joy at being back in water that felt like home.

"We're in the Gulf," Tod radioed. "Colony is responding well. Looking good."

"Support One confirms," Chen said. "Nine miles to destination. Holding course three-three-five."

Nine miles. Less than two hours at their current speed. They were going to make it.

Tod had barely finished the thought when his electromagnetic sense screamed a warning.

THE ELECTRICAL SIGNATURE was faint at first, just a tickle at the edge of Tod's awareness. But it was growing, intensifying, coming from the south. He grabbed his weather radar display, zooming out to see beyond the immediate area.

His stomach dropped.

A line of thunderstorms—small cells, nothing catastrophic, but electrically active—was developing along a convergence zone about fifteen miles south. The weather models hadn't predicted this. The atmosphere was unstable in ways the computers hadn't caught.

"We've got weather developing," Tod radioed, keeping his voice calm. "Electrical storms to the south. Still small, but building."

"How long until they reach us?" Chen asked.

Tod studied the radar, cross-referencing with what his enhanced senses were telling him. The electrical activity was growing exponentially, the atmosphere crackling with potential energy.

"Hour. Maybe less." He adjusted course slightly north. "Picking up speed. We need to get them to the cave before those cells mature."

The boats accelerated to six knots, the Light Speakers matching pace easily. But Tod could feel the change in the air, the buildup of charge that preceded major electrical activity. His skin prickled, the hair on his arms standing up despite the humid night air.

Lightning flickered on the southern horizon—cloud to cloud, still distant, but powerful. The electromagnetic pulse registered in Tod's awareness like someone striking a gong next to his head. He gritted his teeth, forcing himself to focus past the sensory noise.

"Light activity increasing," Claire reported, her voice tight. "Social media's picking it up. Multiple posts about lightning over the Gulf."

Of course they were. In the age of smartphones, nothing went unnoticed. Someone would have posted video already, and if those videos showed anything unusual in the water...

"Stay focused on the mission," Tod said. "Seven miles out. We're close."

The swells were building now, the approaching storm system disturbing the sea's rhythm. Three-foot waves became four-foot waves, the boats pitching more noticeably. Tod adjusted his stance, his body automatically compensating for the motion.

Below, the Light Speakers maintained formation, but Tod could sense their nervousness. Electrical storms were dangerous for beings that generated their own bioluminescence—the charged atmosphere could interfere with their light-producing organs, cause painful disruptions.

"Hang on," Tod whispered to the water. "Almost there."

Another lightning strike, closer now. The boom of thunder rolled across the Gulf three seconds later. Tod's electromagnetic sense flared, the atmospheric charge building to dangerous levels. The storm was accelerating, growing faster than the models predicted.

"Six miles," Chen reported. "But Tod, I'm picking up something else on radar. Surface contact, bearing zero-eight-five, range three miles."

Tod's eyes snapped to his radar screen. There—a solid return, moving slowly, heading northwest. Big enough to be a commercial vessel or...

"Coast Guard," he said quietly. "Running patrol."

The situation had just become exponentially more complicated.

THE COAST GUARD RIB—RESPONSE Boat—was running a standard patrol pattern, its twin engines producing a distinctive signature that Tod could feel through the charged air. It was heading on an intercept course, not deliberately, but geometry and timing were bringing them together.

"Options?" Claire asked over the radio, her voice steady despite the tension.

Tod ran calculations in his head. They could turn back, but that would put them directly into the approaching storm. They could try to outrun the patrol boat, but that would look suspicious and they weren't fast enough anyway. Or they could hold course and pray the RIB passed them without stopping.

"We hold course," Tod decided. "Act normal. We're just night fishing, got caught out by weather developing. Nothing unusual."

"Except for the glowing aliens following us," Claire muttered.

"They'll dive deep," Tod said, watching the Light Speakers already beginning to descend in response to his unspoken concern. "They know danger when they sense it."

The colony dropped to seventy feet, their light dimming to barely perceptible glows. On radar, they would appear as a diffuse scatter—fish school, thermocline effect, nothing that would trigger suspicion.

The RIB's searchlight swept across the water, the beam cutting through darkness like a sword. Tod kept his hands steady on the wheel, maintaining course and speed, everything normal. Just a charter captain and two friends, out for some night fishing.

The searchlight found them, pinning Tod's boat in harsh white light. A loudhailer crackled to life.

"VESSEL K5HUX, THIS IS UNITED STATES COAST GUARD. STATE YOUR INTENTIONS."

Tod reached for his radio mic, switching to Channel 16—the emergency and hailing frequency. "Coast Guard, this is K5HUX. We're conducting night fishing operations. Got three boats, heading back to harbor due to weather developing to the south."

A pause. The searchlight swept across Chen's boat, then Claire's. Tod could see the RIB more clearly now—twenty-five footer, two crew visible, one at the helm and one manning the searchlight.

"K5HUX, you're operating in an area that's been flagged for unusual activity. We need to conduct a safety inspection."

Tod's mind raced. A safety inspection would take twenty minutes, maybe more. The storm was fifteen minutes out, maximum. And if they got close enough to see what was following the boats...

"Coast Guard, we're happy to comply, but we've got electrical storm cells approaching fast. Can we do this back in harbor?"

Another pause. The searchlight held steady on Tod's boat. Lightning flashed to the south, the thunder following six seconds later. Closer.

"K5HUX, we need to verify—"

The radio transmission cut off as a massive lightning strike hit the water two miles south. The electromagnetic pulse was so powerful that every radio on the Gulf briefly squelched, filled with static. Tod's entire nervous system lit up, the charge racing through his enhanced pathways like fire.

He gasped, gripping the console to stay upright. Through blurred vision, he saw the RIB's crew also reacting, their electronics flickering, the searchlight momentarily dimming.

When the radios cleared, a different voice came through—the coxswain, making the decision. "All vessels, this is Coast Guard unit seven-three. Weather is deteriorating rapidly. All vessels make for nearest safe harbor immediately. K5HUX, inspection postponed. Get to safety."

"Coast Guard, K5HUX copies. Making for harbor. Thank you."

The searchlight went dark. The RIB turned south, heading to assist other vessels caught out by the unexpected storm. Tod watched them go, his heart pounding, sweat running down his face despite the cool night air.

"Support One to Lead," Chen's voice was shaky. "That was close."

"Too close." Tod checked his GPS. "Five miles. Let's move."

The convoy accelerated, racing the storm toward the cave entrance. Lightning was striking every thirty seconds now, the electrical activity building toward something massive. Tod's enhanced senses were screaming, every nerve ending on fire with the atmospheric charge.

Below, the Light Speakers had risen back to forty feet, their formation tight and purposeful. They could sense the danger, understood the urgency. They moved with Tod's boats like synchronized swimmers, every adjustment matched instantly.

Four miles. Three.

The storm caught them at two and a half miles from the cave.

THE FIRST STRIKE HIT the water half a mile behind them, a massive bolt that turned night into day for a split second. The boom was instant—no delay between flash and sound. The electromagnetic pulse hit Tod like a physical blow, driving him to his knees on the deck.

"Tod!" Claire's voice screamed over the radio.

He couldn't respond. Every sense he possessed was overloading, the electrical activity so intense it was like being inside a Tesla coil. He felt Chen's boat nearby, felt Claire's, felt the Light Speakers below—but it was all wrapped in a cocoon of electrical fire that made coherent thought nearly impossible.

Rain began to fall, not gradually but all at once, like someone had opened a valve in the sky. Visibility dropped to nothing. The GPS was the only reference point, the only thing keeping them on course.

Another strike, closer. Tod felt it coming a microsecond before it hit—his electromagnetic sense giving him just enough warning to brace. The bolt connected with the water three hundred yards to starboard, the explosion of superheated steam visible even through the rain.

The Light Speakers scattered in panic. Tod felt their terror through his marine empathy, the collective consciousness fragmenting under the assault of electrical energy. Young ones were breaking from the formation, swimming blindly, lost in the chaos.

"NO!" Tod tried to stand, couldn't. The sensory overload was too much. He was going to pass out, and if he did, the boats would lose their way, the Light Speakers would scatter, everything would fail.

I have to stay conscious. I have to hold on.

Another strike, and another. The storm was directly overhead now, the electrical activity so intense that the air itself seemed to glow. Tod's vision was graying at the edges, consciousness slipping despite his desperate grip on it.

Through the haze, he heard Chen's voice on the radio, distorted but determined. "I've got them! I can feel the young ones. I'm guiding them back!"

Chen's marine empathy—stronger than Tod's, more focused. She was using her abilities to herd the scattered Light Speakers, her consciousness reaching out to theirs, creating a beacon they could follow back to the group.

"Claire!" Chen's voice again. "Take Tod's wheel! He's down!"

Tod felt Claire's boat bump alongside his, felt her scrambling aboard. Her hands found the wheel, steadying the boat as it began to drift off course. She checked the GPS, corrected their heading, kept them moving toward the cave.

Another lightning strike, the closest yet. Tod's entire body convulsed, every muscle contracting simultaneously. He tasted copper in his mouth, felt something inside him break—not physically, but energetically. A connection severing, a sense dying.

His storm-sense—the ability to feel weather patterns, to predict electrical activity—was burning out. Like a fuse overloaded, like a wire melting under too much current. He could feel it going, fragmenting, the intricate neural pathways that had been rewired by the Light Speakers' gift now being destroyed by the very phenomenon they'd been designed to detect.

Let it go, some part of him realized. *Use it. Channel it.*

Tod stopped fighting. Instead, he opened himself fully to the electrical storm, became a conduit for it. He pressed his hands flat against the deck, grounding himself to the boat's hull, and let the charge flow through him instead of battering against him.

The effect was immediate. The scattered electrical energy found a path through Tod's enhanced nervous system, earthing itself through the boat and into the water. He became a human lightning rod, channeling the storm's fury safely away from the vulnerable colony below.

The Light Speakers felt it. Tod sensed their awareness, their understanding of what he was doing. They began to calm, to reform their pattern, using Tod's sacrifice as an anchor point. Chen kept guiding the young ones, Claire kept the boats on course, and Tod held his position as conductor, letting the storm burn through him.

One more massive strike, this one connecting with the water directly beneath Tod's boat. The entire hull lit up with electrical discharge, every metal fitting glowing blue-white. The charge raced through Tod's body, every cell screaming, and then...

Silence.

Not physical silence—the storm still raged, rain still hammered down, thunder still rolled across the Gulf. But in Tod's head, the electromagnetic noise simply... stopped.

His storm-sense was gone. Burned away. The neural pathways that had given him weather-sight were now just scar tissue, dead ends, biological fuses that had blown to protect the rest of his system.

But he was conscious. And more importantly—

"Cave entrance!" Chen's voice, triumphant. "Dead ahead! One hundred yards!"

Tod lifted his head, saw the GPS marker that indicated the limestone outcropping they'd found two weeks ago. Through the rain and darkness, he could just make out Chen's dive light, already in the water, illuminating the cave mouth.

The Light Speakers surged forward, their terror transforming to relief. They poured into the cave entrance, a river of blue-white light disappearing into the stone, flowing into safety like water finding its level.

Claire guided Tod's boat alongside Chen's, killed the engine. The storm raged around them, but here, in the lee of the limestone formation, the water was slightly calmer. Protected.

"Tod?" Claire was at his side, her hands on his face. "Tod, can you hear me?"

He nodded weakly. "I'm okay. Just... burned out."

"You were glowing," she said, her voice shaking. "When that last strike hit, you were glowing blue-white, just like them."

"Storm-sense is gone," Tod said, the words coming with difficulty. "Channeled too much. It's... it's gone."

Chen surfaced beside the boat, pulling off her mask. Rain streamed down her face, mixing with tears. "They're in. All of them. Every single Light Speaker is in the cave. They're safe."

Safe. The word hung in the air, heavy with meaning. Tod let his head fall back against the gunwale, rain washing over his face, electricity still crackling across his skin in fading aftershocks.

They'd done it. Against impossible odds, through a Coast Guard encounter and an electrical storm that should have scattered the colony forever, they'd done it.

The Light Speakers were home.

THE STORM MOVED NORTH, its fury spent, leaving behind heavy rain and confused seas. The three guardians waited, boats lashed together, too exhausted to attempt the return journey immediately. They would wait for the weather to clear, for some semblance of calm to return.

Tod sat in his cabin, wrapped in a blanket, Claire beside him. He kept testing his senses, feeling the boundaries of what remained. His electromagnetic sensitivity was still there—he could feel the boats' electronics, the storm's fading charge. His marine empathy remained intact—he could sense the Light Speakers in the cave, their collective relief and joy at finding sanctuary.

But the storm-sense—the ability that had saved them countless times, that had let him predict weather with uncanny accuracy—was simply gone. Dead as a burned-out light bulb.

"How do you feel?" Claire asked softly.

Tod considered the question. "Lighter," he said finally. "That sense was... heavy. Like carrying a battery that was always charging, always warning. Now it's just... quiet."

"Do you regret it?"

"No." The answer came without hesitation. "They needed it. I gave it. That's what guardians do."

Chen appeared in the cabin doorway, still in her wetsuit, her hair plastered to her head. "They want to talk to you. They're at the cave entrance."

Tod hauled himself up, accepting Claire's steadying hand. Together, the three of them moved to the bow, where Tod's waterproof flashlight waited. He aimed it at the cave entrance, barely visible in the darkness and rain.

He tapped out the code: two-seven-two.

The response was immediate. Light bloomed from the cave mouth, spilling out into the Gulf like dawn breaking underwater. The entire colony had come to the entrance, hundreds of beings pulsing in perfect synchronization.

Their message formed slowly, each word deliberate:

"F-R-I-E-N-D"

Pause.

"G-U-A-R-D-I-A-N"

Pause.

"T-H-A-N-K-Y-O-U"

Then something Tod had never seen before. The Light Speakers broke their usual pattern, creating a new one—a complex, swirling display of light that seemed to have no specific meaning, no message. It was pure expression, pure beauty. Art.

"They're celebrating," Chen whispered, her voice filled with wonder. "They're showing us joy."

The display continued for several minutes, the Light Speakers pouring their relief and gratitude into light, turning the cave entrance into a living aurora. And then, slowly, they descended back into the depths, back into their new home.

The last message came from a single speaker, probably the eldest:

"S-L-E-E-P-N-O-W-G-U-A-R-D-I-A-N-W-E-S-A-F-E"

The light faded. The cave went dark. The Light Speakers were home, and they were telling Tod to rest, that he'd done enough.

Tod lowered the flashlight, his hand trembling. Claire wrapped her arms around him from behind, her chin on his shoulder.

"You did it," she murmured. "You got them home."

"We did it," Tod corrected. "All of us."

Chen moved to the rail, looking toward the cave. "I'll file the navigation hazard report tomorrow. Get this area designated as protected benthic habitat. No trawling, no anchoring, minimal boat traffic. The Gulf Conservancy paperwork is already prepared."

"And the AIS spoofing?" Claire asked.

"Marcus is deleting all evidence as we speak. By morning, it'll be like tonight never happened. Just another stormy night on the Gulf."

Tod felt the boat rock beneath him, felt the rain on his face, felt the absence where his storm-sense used to be. He also felt Claire's arms around him, Chen's presence beside them, and far below, the Light Speakers settling into their limestone sanctuary.

He'd lost something tonight. But he'd gained something more important: the knowledge that the beings he'd sworn to protect were finally, truly safe.

"Let's go home," Tod said quietly.

Claire started the engine. Chen returned to her boat. And as the first light of dawn began to gray the eastern horizon, the three guardian vessels turned toward Rockport, leaving behind an empty stretch of Gulf that hid the most important secret on the Texas coast.

The crossing was complete. The Light Speakers were home. And Tod Blackstone, diminished but not defeated, headed toward whatever came next.

Chapter 17

Six weeks later, Tod stood on his dock in the pre-dawn chill, a kolache from Rosita's still warm in his hand, watching his sunrise tracker slowly rotate toward the east. The familiar ritual felt different now—simpler, quieter. The electromagnetic hum that had once accompanied every sunrise was gone, that particular sense burned away in the storm.

He didn't miss it as much as he'd expected.

The bay stretched before him, calm and clear in the October morning. The hypoxic event had passed, the dead zone dispersing as weather patterns shifted and fresh water flushed the system. Fish had returned in abundance—redfish, trout, flounder—the bay recovering with the resilience that had sustained it for millennia.

No one would ever know how close it had come to becoming a graveyard for something far more precious than fish.

Tod's phone buzzed. A text from Barney: *Coffee at 0700? Got a new antenna design to show you.*

He smiled, typing back: *See you then.*

Life had returned to something resembling normal. Charters were booked through November. His workshop projects were piling up in the satisfying way they always did. The Rockport community had absorbed him back into its rhythms without comment—just another captain doing the work, living the life.

But nothing was truly the same.

Tod finished his kolache, brushed crumbs from his hands, and checked the tracker one more time. The Yagi antenna pointed due east now, ready for whatever signals the morning might bring. He'd repaired it last week, more from habit than necessity. Without his storm-sense, the weather alerts it provided were just data now, not confirmation of what his body already knew.

But some habits were worth keeping.

A pelican landed on the dock piling, regarding Tod with one ancient eye. He nodded to the bird, a silent acknowledgment between two creatures who made their living from these waters.

"Morning," he said quietly.

The pelican didn't respond, but that was okay. Not everything needed to communicate to be understood.

DR. SARAH CHEN STOOD before a classroom of seventh-graders at Rockport-Fulton Middle School, her laptop connected to the projector, displaying satellite imagery of the Gulf. Twenty-eight faces looked back at her with varying degrees of interest—some engaged, some bored, a few actively trying to appear invisible.

"What you're seeing here," Chen explained, pointing to a swirl of color on the screen, "is a phytoplankton bloom. These microscopic organisms are the foundation of the entire Gulf ecosystem. Everything—and I mean everything—depends on them."

A hand shot up. Chen nodded to a girl in the front row.

"Ms. Chen, is it true you used to work at a university?"

"Dr. Chen," she corrected gently. "And yes, I did. Texas A&M."

"Why'd you quit?"

Chen paused, considering how to answer. The truth was too complicated, too strange. The official story was easier.

"I realized I cared more about protecting what we study than publishing papers about it. The Gulf Conservancy lets me do that work."

It wasn't entirely a lie. The Gulf Conservancy—which Chen had founded six weeks ago with a hastily assembled board and surprisingly generous anonymous donations—gave her the perfect cover for what she actually did: protect a limestone cave system eighteen miles offshore that harbored the most important secret in marine biology.

"Now," Chen continued, advancing the slide, "who can tell me what happens when oxygen levels in water drop too low?"

Several hands went up. Chen called on a boy in a Corpus Christi Hooks baseball cap.

"Fish die?"

"Exactly. And two months ago, we had a hypoxic event right here in Copano Bay. The oxygen dropped dangerously low. But the bay recovered, partly because of natural water circulation, partly because—" she emphasized this next part, "—we have protected areas where marine life can shelter during environmental stress."

She advanced to the next slide, showing a map of the Gulf with several shaded areas. One of them, if anyone bothered to check the coordinates carefully, was directly over the limestone cave system.

"These are benthic reserves. No trawling, no anchoring, minimal human interference. They act as refuges, safe zones where ecosystems can rebuild after damage."

"That's boring," a voice muttered from the back. "Can we talk about sharks?"

Chen smiled. "Sharks depend on these boring protected zones to survive. Everything's connected. That's the point."

After class, as students filed out, the girl from the front row lingered.

"Dr. Chen? Did you really have a mental breakdown?"

Chen blinked. "Excuse me?"

"My mom works at the university. She said you quit suddenly and destroyed all your research because you had a breakdown after almost drowning."

Of course the rumors had spread. Chen had encouraged them, actually—better to be thought unstable than to have people asking the right questions.

"Your mom's partly right," Chen said carefully. "I did almost drown. It made me rethink what matters. Research papers or the actual ocean? I chose the ocean."

The girl nodded slowly. "That makes sense, I guess."

After she left, Chen packed up her laptop, checking her phone. Three emails from former colleagues, all asking variations of the same question: *Are you okay? We're worried about you.*

She drafted the same response she always did: *I'm better than I've been in years. Thank you for asking.*

It was true. Her career was over, her reputation in academic circles permanently damaged. She taught middle school science part-time and ran a conservation non-profit that barely paid her salary.

And she'd never been happier.

Chen locked the classroom, heading for her car. She had a meeting this afternoon with the Coast Guard to discuss navigation safety protocols near the benthic reserve. The paperwork was tedious, but necessary. Every regulation she put in place, every restriction on boat traffic, was another layer of protection for the beings in the cave.

Her phone buzzed with a text from Marcus: *Monthly data review at 3? Coffee on me.*

Chen smiled. Marcus had become her unofficial deputy at the conservancy, handling the technical work while maintaining his graduate studies. He'd managed to explain his involvement in the

"AIS spoofing incident" as a research project gone wrong, accepting a minor academic censure and moving on.

More importantly, he'd become a friend. One of the few people who knew the truth.

She texted back: *See you at 3. And you're buying donuts too.*

CLAIRE'S GALLERY OPENING had drawn a surprising crowd. The small space in downtown Rockport was packed with locals, tourists, and a few actual critics from Houston and Austin who'd made the drive based on buzz they'd seen online.

The exhibition was titled simply: *Listening to Light.*

Claire stood in the corner, uncomfortable being the center of attention, watching people move through the space. The photographs covered the walls—images of water, boats, horizons, the interplay of natural and artificial light. Abstract enough to be beautiful, specific enough to hint at something more.

There were no Light Speakers in any of the images. Claire had been careful about that, selecting only shots that showed the *feeling* of contact without proof of it. Dawn breaking over Copano Bay. Moonlight on rippling water. The play of bioluminescence through long exposures that could be plankton, could be something else, deliberately ambiguous.

One photograph had generated the most attention: a long exposure shot taken the night of the convoy, showing multiple streaks of light moving through dark water. It looked like abstract art, like someone had painted with light underwater. Only three people in the world knew those streaks were the Light Speakers in formation.

A woman in her sixties, wearing turquoise jewelry and an artist's critical eye, studied the image closely. "Remarkable. The movement has such intentionality. Almost like choreography."

Claire moved to stand beside her. "Thank you. That one's special to me."

"I can see why. There's something..." the woman paused, searching for words. "It feels like communication. Like you captured a conversation between light and water."

"That's exactly what it was," Claire said quietly.

The woman looked at her sharply, as if sensing a deeper truth, but Claire had already moved on, greeting other guests.

A critic from *Houston Arts Magazine* cornered her near the refreshment table. "Ms. Westbrook, your artist statement mentions 'bearing witness to the incomprehensible.' Can you elaborate?"

Claire sipped her wine, choosing words carefully. "We spend so much time trying to explain everything, to categorize and define. Sometimes the most important moments are the ones we can't fully articulate. My job is to document them anyway, to say 'this happened, I saw it, it mattered,' even if I can't tell you exactly what 'it' was."

The critic scribbled notes. "And the light in your photographs—there's recurring themes of bioluminescence, of living light. Is that metaphorical?"

"No," Claire said simply. "It's literal. The Gulf is full of creatures that make their own light. I just pay attention."

"But surely some of these images—particularly the convoy piece—are digitally enhanced?"

"Every photograph is exactly as captured. No compositing, no artificial elements. What you see is what was there."

The critic looked skeptical but intrigued. "Well, it's certainly provocative work. I'll be interested to see where you go from here."

After he left, Tod appeared at Claire's elbow, two wine glasses in hand. "You survived the interrogation."

"Barely." She accepted the glass gratefully. "How are you holding up?"

"I hate crowds." Tod glanced around the packed gallery. "But I'm proud of you. These are incredible."

Claire leaned against him, drawing comfort from his solid presence. Tod had been her rock through the preparation for this show, helping her select images, building frames, running a hundred small errands while she obsessed over presentation.

He'd also been the one to talk her down when she'd nearly included a too-clear image of the Light Speakers, the one to remind her that protection meant discretion, that some truths were meant to be felt rather than proven.

"One sold," Claire said, nodding toward a red dot beside a print of sunrise over the bay. "The money's going to Chen's conservancy."

"She'll appreciate that."

They stood together, watching the crowd move through the space, watching people connect with images that held secrets they'd never fully understand. Claire had found her voice, the way to tell the truth without betraying it.

An older man approached, his weathered face and calloused hands marking him as a waterman. He studied the convoy photograph for a long moment before speaking.

"I've seen that," he said quietly. "Forty years fishing these waters. Seen lights moving with intention, with purpose. Always wondered what they were."

Claire met his eyes, recognizing a kindred spirit. Someone who'd witnessed the impossible and kept it to himself.

"Maybe some mysteries are meant to stay mysterious," she said.

The old fisherman smiled. "Maybe so. But it's good to know someone else saw it too. Makes you feel less crazy."

After he left, Tod squeezed Claire's hand. "You did good. You found the line."

"The line?"

"Between witness and betrayal. Between truth and discretion." Tod gestured to the photographs. "These honor them without exposing them. That's the balance."

Claire nodded, feeling the weight of responsibility settle more comfortably on her shoulders. This was her role—the chronicler, the artist, the one who bore witness in ways that protected rather than exploited.

The gallery lights seemed to pulse slightly, though that was probably just her imagination. Or maybe it was the memory of other lights, the ones that had changed everything.

THREE DAYS LATER, THE three guardians sat in Tod's workshop, laptops open, reviewing the month's monitoring data. It had become their ritual—a monthly check-in to assess any threats, coordinate their protective efforts, and maintain the secret that bound them together.

Marcus had joined them via video call, his face pixelated on Chen's laptop screen.

"Coast Guard patrol patterns are holding steady," Marcus reported. "No unusual interest in the benthic reserve area. The navigation hazard designation is working—boats are giving it a wide berth."

"Marine traffic?" Tod asked.

"Down forty percent in the protected zone since we implemented the restrictions. Mostly just research vessels with permits, all legitimate." Marcus pulled up a chart. "The cover story is holding. Everyone thinks it's about protecting seagrass beds and juvenile fish habitat."

"Which it is," Chen interjected. "Those things matter too. We're not lying, just... prioritizing."

Claire looked up from her own laptop. "Social media monitoring shows declining interest in the 'Gulf lights mystery.' The LED decoy campaign worked—people got bored when sightings became random and infrequent. We're down to one or two posts per week, mostly old stories rehashed."

"What about the university?" Tod asked Chen.

"They've stopped calling. Official diagnosis: stress-induced career change following near-death experience. Some colleagues still think I'm crazy, but most have moved on." Chen shrugged. "My reputation took a hit, but that was the price."

"Any regrets?"

"None." The answer came without hesitation. "I teach kids about protecting the ocean. I run a conservancy that actually conserves something important. And once a month, I check on the most significant discovery in marine biology and make sure it stays protected." She smiled. "I'm exactly where I'm supposed to be."

Marcus leaned closer to his camera. "Dr. Chen, I got accepted to the PhD program at UCSD. Scripps Oceanography."

Chen's face lit up. "Marcus! That's incredible!"

"I'll be moving in January. But before I go..." He paused. "I need to know they're okay. That what we did mattered."

Tod, Chen, and Claire exchanged glances. They'd kept Marcus at arm's length since the convoy, protecting him from deeper involvement. But he'd earned the right to know.

"They're thriving," Tod said simply. "The cave system is perfect for them. Deep enough, protected, plenty of space. They're not just surviving—they're flourishing."

"How do you know?"

"Because I visit them," Tod admitted. "Once a week. Just to check in, let them know we're still here."

Marcus was quiet for a moment. "Can I... I mean, would it be possible to see them? Before I leave? Just once?"

The guardians looked at each other. It was Claire who finally answered.

"That's up to Tod. He's their primary contact."

Tod considered. Marcus had proven his trustworthiness, his discretion. He'd sacrificed his own reputation to help protect the Light Speakers, and he'd kept the secret perfectly.

"Let me ask them," Tod said. "It has to be their choice."

After the video call ended, the three sat in comfortable silence for a while. Outside, the October afternoon was cooling toward evening, the light taking on that golden quality that photographers loved.

"How are you really doing?" Chen asked Tod. "With the abilities you lost?"

Tod flexed his fingers, still able to feel the phantom echoes of his storm-sense sometimes, like a limb that was no longer there. "Honestly? It's a relief. That sense was heavy—always on, always warning. I sleep better now."

"But you can still sense electronics? Marine life?"

"Yeah. Those are weaker than they were, but still functional. I can feel boats approaching, sense fish in the water, pick up strong EM fields." Tod smiled slightly. "Enough to do the job. Just not enough to drive me crazy."

"And the Light Speakers?" Claire asked. "Can you still communicate?"

"Better than ever, actually. Losing the storm-sense made room for the other connections to strengthen. My marine empathy is clearer now, more focused." Tod looked toward the bay. "It's like turning down one radio so you can hear another one better."

Chen nodded slowly, processing. "Your neural plasticity might have—" She stopped herself, shaking her head. "Sorry. Scientist brain. You don't need the technical explanation."

"Actually, I'm curious," Tod said. "What's your theory?"

"The transformation we underwent rewired specific neural pathways. When your storm-sense burned out, your brain had extra capacity. Neural plasticity—the brain's ability to reorganize itself—probably redirected those resources to strengthen the pathways that remained." Chen leaned forward, animated by the puzzle. "You didn't lose the gift. You redistributed it."

"Huh." Tod considered that. "So I'm not diminished. Just... rebalanced."

"Exactly."

Claire stood, stretching. "I need to get going. Gallery wants me to do another show in the spring, and I need to start shooting new work."

"Nothing with glowing subjects," Tod reminded her.

"Nothing provable," Claire corrected with a grin. "There's a difference."

After she left, Chen and Tod remained in the workshop, the comfortable silence of people who'd been through something extraordinary together.

"Thank you," Chen said finally.

"For what?"

"For trusting me. For giving me a chance to be better than I was." She looked down at her hands. "Six weeks ago, I would have dissected them, published papers, made my career. You and Claire showed me there was another way."

"You showed yourself," Tod said. "We just gave you the option."

Chen smiled. "Either way, I'm grateful." She packed up her laptop. "Same time next month?"

"Same time."

After she left, Tod sat alone in his workshop, surrounded by his equipment and projects, the familiar space that had been his refuge for years. He thought about the journey that had brought him here—from isolation to connection, from secret-keeper to guardian, from someone defined by what he'd lost to someone shaped by what he'd chosen.

The sun was setting, painting the workshop windows in shades of orange and gold. Tod stood, grabbing his flashlight, and walked down to the dock.

It was time for his weekly check-in.

THE WATER WAS DARK now, the sun fully set, stars beginning to appear in the clear October sky. Tod knelt at the end of his dock, flashlight in hand, and tapped out the code he'd established six weeks ago.

Two-seven-two. Two flashes, pause, seven flashes, pause, two flashes.

Tod calling. Checking in.

He waited, watching the water. Nothing at first, just the gentle lap of waves against the pilings. Then, from deep in the channel, a faint glow began to rise.

A single Light Speaker—not the whole colony, just one messenger—ascended to within sight of the surface. Their light pulsed in the familiar seven-second rhythm, and then they responded:

"H-E-L-L-O-F-R-I-E-N-D"

Tod smiled, warmth spreading through his chest. "HELLO. ARE YOU WELL?"

"Y-E-S - C-A-V-E-G-O-O-D - A-L-L-S-A-F-E"

"GOOD. THANK YOU FOR TRUSTING US."

A pause. Then the Light Speaker pulsed a new message, one Tod had never seen before:

"Y-O-U-P-A-I-D-P-R-I-C-E   -   W-E-S-E-E   - W-E-R-E-M-E-M-B-E-R"

Tod's throat tightened. They knew. They understood what he'd sacrificed to get them to safety.

"PRICE WAS FAIR," he signaled back. "YOU ARE WORTH IT."

"W-E-A-G-R-E-E - Y-O-U-W-O-R-T-H-I-T-T-O-O"

The simple statement hit Tod harder than he'd expected. These beings, so different from anything human, saw him as an equal. Not a curiosity, not an inferior species to be studied, but a companion worth protecting in return.

"YOUNG ONE ASKS TO MEET MARCUS," the Light Speaker continued. "THE HELPER. MAY HE COME?"

So they'd been listening somehow, aware of the conversation earlier. Or maybe Tod's marine empathy had carried the discussion to them unconsciously. Either way, they knew about Marcus's request.

"YOU CHOOSE," Tod signaled. "HE IS GOOD. HE HELPED SAVE YOU. BUT ONLY IF YOU WANT."

"W-E-W-A-N-T - B-R-I-N-G-H-I-M"

Tod felt something settle in his chest, a rightness. Marcus deserved to see what he'd helped protect.

"I WILL BRING HIM NEXT WEEK."

"G-O-O-D" The Light Speaker began to descend, then paused, sending one final message:

"S-L-E-E-P-W-E-L-L-G-U-A-R-D-I-A-N"

The light faded, disappearing back into the depths. Tod sat on the dock for a long time afterward, flashlight resting on his knee, watching the dark water.

Guardian. That's what he was now. Not just a charter captain, not just a man with strange abilities, but something more important: a bridge between species, a keeper of secrets, a protector of wonders.

The weight of it felt less heavy than it once had. Shared with Claire and Chen, distributed across three people instead of borne by one, the responsibility had become bearable. More than bearable—purposeful.

Tod stood, stretching muscles that had grown stiff from kneeling. He walked back to his workshop, the familiar path worn smooth by years of footsteps. Inside, his equipment waited, his projects beckoned, the ordinary work of an ordinary life ready to resume.

But nothing about his life was ordinary anymore. And that, Tod realized, was exactly how it should be.

He pulled out his phone, texting Marcus: *They said yes. Next Saturday, midnight. Bring a wetsuit if you want to dive to the cave entrance.*

The reply came almost instantly: *I'll be there. Thank you.*

Tod smiled, pocketing his phone. Seven more days until Marcus got to see what he'd helped save. Seven more days of normal life before sharing the extraordinary.

He could manage that.

THE FOLLOWING SATURDAY, four people stood on Tod's dock at 11:45 PM—Tod, Claire, Chen, and Marcus, who looked simultaneously terrified and excited. The night was clear and calm, perfect conditions for the eighteen-mile journey.

"You sure about this?" Claire asked Tod quietly while Marcus and Chen loaded dive gear.

"They invited him," Tod said. "That makes it their decision, not ours."

"But one more person knowing—"

"We trusted Chen. We trusted Barney. We trusted you." Tod turned to face her. "Sometimes trust has to expand, not contract. Marcus earned this."

Claire nodded, accepting his judgment. Tod was the primary guardian, the one with the deepest connection to the Light Speakers. If he said it was safe, it was safe.

The four of them boarded Tod's boat, the engine rumbling to life. As they pulled away from the dock, Marcus stood at the rail, staring back at Rockport's lights.

"I'm about to see something impossible," he said quietly. "Aren't I?"

"You're about to see something important," Chen corrected. "That's different."

The journey took two hours, the boat cutting through calm Gulf waters under a waning moon. Marcus peppered them with questions at first, then gradually fell silent as the magnitude of what was happening settled over him.

When they reached the coordinates, Tod cut the engine. The GPS showed them directly above the cave entrance, seventy-five feet down in water so clear the stars seemed to extend beneath the surface.

"They're here," Tod said, his marine empathy picking up the familiar presence. "Waiting."

Chen handed Marcus a dive light. "If you want to see them up close, we dive. But only to the entrance. We don't go into the cave—that's their space, their sanctuary."

Marcus nodded, pulling on his wetsuit with shaking hands. "I understand."

Tod and Chen went in first, Marcus following between them. They descended through the darkness, lights cutting cones of illumination through the water. At sixty feet, the limestone outcropping came into view. At seventy feet, they reached the cave entrance.

And there, waiting just inside, was the entire colony.

Hundreds of Light Speakers hovered in formation, their collective bioluminescence turning the cave mouth into a gateway of blue-white light. Marcus stopped swimming, hanging suspended in the water, his dive light falling from nerveless fingers.

Through his regulator, Tod could hear Marcus's sharp intake of breath.

The Light Speakers moved forward in perfect synchronization, forming words with their light:

"W-E-L-C-O-M-E-M-A-R-C-U-S"

"H-E-L-P-E-R"

"F-R-I-E-N-D"

Marcus's shoulders shook. He was crying behind his mask, tears mixing with seawater. He raised his hand in a slow wave, the universal gesture of greeting.

The Light Speakers responded by creating a spiral of light around the three divers, a welcoming display that filled the water with living radiance. It lasted perhaps thirty seconds, and then they retreated back into the cave, their light fading to a gentle glow.

One speaker remained, floating near Marcus. This one pulsed a final message:

"T-H-A-N-K-Y-O-U"

Then it too descended into the cave, leaving the humans in the ordinary darkness of the Gulf.

They surfaced slowly, following proper ascent protocols. When they finally broke the surface beside the boat, Marcus tore off his mask and just floated there, looking up at the stars.

"They're real," he whispered. "They're actually real."

"Yeah," Tod said. "They are."

"And intelligent. And kind. And—" Marcus struggled for words. "We have to protect them. Forever. No matter what."

"That's the job," Chen said, hauling herself into the boat. "Welcome to the team."

TWO WEEKS LATER, ON a November morning sharp with the first real cold front of the season, Tod stood on his dock with his sunrise tracker rotating toward the east, a steaming cup of coffee in one hand and the last of Rosita's kolaches in the other.

The bay was empty, the water calm, the sky lightening from black to gray to the faintest suggestion of pink. Somewhere out there, eighteen miles offshore, the Light Speakers were waking in their limestone sanctuary, safe and protected, the secret holding firm.

Tod had lost his storm-sense, sacrificed it for their safety. But what he'd gained was immeasurable—purpose, partnership, a mission that made the strange gifts he'd been given meaningful.

His phone buzzed. A text from Claire: *Morning, love. Coffee at my place when you're done with your sunrise ritual?*

He smiled, typing back: *See you in 20.*

Another text came through, this one from Chen: *Monthly meeting Tuesday? Marcus wants to join via video before he heads to California.*

Tuesday works, Tod replied. *Bring donuts.*

The sun broke free of the horizon, flooding the bay with golden light. Tod's sunrise tracker locked onto the signal, the familiar clicks and whirs confirming function. Without his storm-sense, he couldn't feel the weather patterns the way he once had. But he could see the clear sky, feel the cold wind, know in ordinary human ways that it was going to be a beautiful day.

And that was enough.

Tod knelt at the dock's edge, pulling out his flashlight even though the morning sun made it almost unnecessary. He tapped out the code one more time: two-seven-two.

He waited.

From the deep channel, so faint he almost missed it, a single pulse of light answered. Seven seconds of glow, too brief for anyone but him to notice, too subtle for any camera to capture.

The covenant held. The bond remained. The Light Speakers were out there, alive and safe, and they remembered.

Tod stood, pocketing the flashlight, and headed toward his workshop. He had charters booked this afternoon, equipment to maintain, the ordinary work of an ordinary life waiting.

But he walked lighter now, knowing that some conversations—the most important ones—happened in the spaces between words, in flashes of light across dark water, in the shared silence of beings who'd chosen to trust each other.

"Some conversations," Tod said to the morning air, "are worth keeping quiet."

The bay whispered its agreement, and somewhere far below, in a limestone cave that would never appear on any tourist map, living light pulsed in a seven-second rhythm that meant home, and safety, and peace.

Chapter 18

Three months later — Late January

The winter morning was cold enough that Tod could see his breath, a rarity on the Texas coast. He stood on his dock wrapped in a heavy flannel jacket, the kolache from Rosita's gone cold in his hand, watching his sunrise tracker complete its slow rotation toward the eastern horizon.

The bay stretched before him, still and gray in the pre-dawn light. A great blue heron stood motionless on the nearest piling, a statue carved from patience and hunger. Somewhere in the distance, a boat engine rumbled to life—another captain heading out for the day's work.

Three months since the Light Speakers had found sanctuary. Three months of ordinary days stacked on top of each other, the rhythm of coastal life reasserting itself with the inexorable patience of tides.

Tod took a sip of coffee that had gone lukewarm, grimacing but drinking it anyway. Some mornings he still reached for his storm-sense, expecting to feel weather patterns in his bones. The absence was like checking for a phone that wasn't in his pocket—a habitual reach for something no longer there.

But the other senses remained. He could feel the marina's electrical systems beginning to wake up, generators kicking on, the electromagnetic signature of the town stirring to life. And his marine empathy registered the bay's inhabitants: mullet schools moving in the shallows, a stingray gliding along the bottom, gulls overhead with their simple, fierce awareness of breakfast and survival.

Different than it was. Not worse. Just different.

His phone buzzed. A text from Claire: *Morning. Want company?*

He smiled, typing back: *Always.*

Five minutes later, she appeared on the dock, two fresh cups of coffee in hand, her camera bag slung over one shoulder. She'd been staying at his place more often than not these days, her bungalow becoming a studio and storage space while his house became home.

"Thought you might need a warm-up," she said, handing him a steaming cup.

"You're a saint."

They stood together, shoulders touching, watching the slow transformation of night to day. The heron finally struck, its beak spearing down into the water and coming up with a small fish that disappeared in a few efficient gulps.

"Chen called last night," Claire said. "They're doing water quality testing near the reserve next week. She wanted to make sure we knew, in case the Light Speakers sense the activity."

"I'll let them know." Tod checked his watch. "Weekly check-in's tonight anyway."

The ritual had become so normal—tapping out two-seven-two into the water, waiting for the answering pulse from eighteen miles offshore. Sometimes Tod wondered what would happen if he missed a week, if the connection would fray from neglect. But he never found out, because he never missed a week.

Some promises were too important to test.

"How's the new show coming?" Tod asked.

Claire made a face. "Slowly. I'm trying to capture something about patience, about waiting for things you can't control. But I think I might be too close to the subject."

"You'll figure it out. You always do."

The sun finally broke free of the horizon, light spilling across the water in shades of gold and amber. Tod's sunrise tracker locked onto the signal, the familiar clicks confirming function. Behind them, Rockport was waking—doors opening, cars starting, the small sounds of a community beginning its day.

"I've been thinking," Claire said carefully. "About the long term. About how long we can keep this secret."

Tod had been thinking about that too. "Chen says the reserve protections should hold for at least five years. After that, there'll be pressure to reassess, maybe open it up for more research."

"And then?"

"Then we deal with it. Maybe by then there will be more guardians. Maybe the Light Speakers will be ready to be known." Tod shrugged. "Or maybe we'll find another cave, another sanctuary, and the secret continues."

"You're okay with that? The uncertainty?"

Tod considered the question, watching light play across the water. "I used to need to know what was coming. The storm-sense made me feel in control, like I could predict everything. Now?" He shook his head. "I've learned to live with not knowing. Maybe that's the real gift they gave me."

Claire leaned against him, and they stood in comfortable silence as the morning brightened around them. After a while, she raised her camera, framing a shot of the sunrise through the pilings, the light creating geometric patterns against dark wood.

"Some things don't need explaining," she said, clicking the shutter. "They just need to be seen."

DR. SARAH CHEN SAT in her small office at the Gulf Conservancy headquarters—really just a converted garage space behind a marine supply shop—reviewing grant applications on her laptop. The heater rattled in the corner, fighting a losing battle against the January cold seeping through the walls.

Her phone showed three missed calls from a former colleague at Texas A&M. She'd stopped returning those calls two months ago. There was nothing left to say. Her academic career was finished, her research destroyed, her reputation as a scientist permanently compromised.

And she'd never felt more useful.

A knock at the door interrupted her concentration. "Come in."

Barney Whitmore entered, his weathered face creasing with a smile. "Dr. Chen. Got those water samples you wanted from the bay."

"Thank you, Barney." Chen accepted the sample containers, labeled with dates and GPS coordinates. "Any changes in the oxygen levels?"

"Holding steady. Whatever that hypoxic event was, it's long gone." Barney settled into the rickety chair across from her desk. "You know, I've been fishing these waters forty years. Never seen the bay recover so fast from something that bad."

"Resilient ecosystem," Chen said, not meeting his eyes.

"Sure. Resilient." Barney's tone suggested he knew there was more to the story. "Tod says you're doing good work here. Says the conservancy might actually make a difference."

Chen looked up sharply. Barney was one of the few people who knew the full truth, though they'd never discussed it directly. He'd been Tod's friend long before Chen had entered the picture, had helped protect the secret in those early, chaotic days.

"We're trying," she said carefully.

"Well, keep trying. Some things are worth protecting, even if nobody else knows you're doing it." Barney stood, tipping an imaginary hat. "Let me know if you need more samples."

After he left, Chen returned to her grant applications, but her mind wandered. In two weeks, she'd start teaching a new semester of middle school science. In three weeks, the Coast Guard would conduct their quarterly review of the benthic reserve. In a month, the conservancy's board—all carefully selected allies—would meet to discuss expansion of protected areas.

The work was endless, tedious, and absolutely critical. Every regulation she implemented, every restriction she justified, every bureaucratic battle she won was another layer of protection for beings that most people would never know existed.

Her old colleagues thought she'd given up science for activism. They didn't understand that this *was* science—the applied kind, the kind that protected what it studied rather than dissecting it for publication.

Chen closed her laptop, checking her watch. 4:47 PM. Time to head home, prepare for the weekend, review the monitoring data before Tuesday's guardian meeting.

Her life had become smaller in some ways—smaller office, smaller salary, smaller sphere of influence. But it had also become larger in the way that mattered most: she knew, with absolute certainty, that her work had meaning beyond herself.

She locked the office door, pulling her jacket tight against the cold wind, and headed for her car. On the seat, a folder labeled "Marine Biology Curriculum - Spring Semester" waited. Inside were lesson plans about ecosystems, about protection, about the ethics of discovery.

About learning to listen before speaking, to observe before interfering, to consider whether some knowledge was worth keeping private.

Chen had become a teacher in more ways than one.

MARCUS CHEN STOOD IN his dorm room at Scripps Institution of Oceanography, packing the last of his belongings into boxes. The walls were bare now, the desk cleared of papers, the bed stripped down to the mattress. In two days, he'd drive back to Texas for winter break before the spring semester started.

His laptop pinged with a video call request. He accepted, and Chen's face appeared on screen, slightly pixelated from the distance.

"Dr. Chen. How's the conservancy?"

"Surviving. How's Scripps?"

"Intense. Amazing. Overwhelming." Marcus gestured to the boxes around him. "But I'm heading home for a few weeks. Thought I might swing by Rockport, check in with everyone."

Chen's expression softened. "They'd like that. Tod mentioned you haven't been down since you left."

"I know. I've been..." Marcus paused, searching for words. "It's hard, being here, studying marine biology, surrounded by researchers who would give anything to discover what we're protecting. Feels like lying by omission every day."

"It is lying by omission. That's the job." Chen leaned back in her chair. "But it gets easier. You learn which conversations to have and which to avoid. You learn how to be a scientist while keeping the most important discovery to yourself."

"Does it ever feel wrong? Keeping it secret?"

Chen was quiet for a long moment. "Every day. And every day I remember what would happen if we didn't—the research vessels, the media circus, the governments claiming ownership, the Light Speakers reduced to specimens and curiosities." She met his eyes through the screen. "The secret feels wrong. But revelation would be worse."

Marcus nodded slowly. "Yeah. I know you're right. It's just hard."

"Of course it's hard. If it were easy, it wouldn't be worth doing." Chen softened her tone. "When you get to Rockport, Tod's planning the monthly check-in. You should come."

"The two-seven-two signal?"

"Yeah. They always ask about you. I think they wonder if the young human is okay."

Marcus felt warmth spread through his chest. "Tell them I'm fine. Tell them I'm studying hard so I can help protect them better."

"Tell them yourself when you visit."

After the call ended, Marcus sat at his empty desk, looking out the window at the Pacific Ocean stretching to the horizon. Somewhere in that vast expanse, other intelligent beings probably existed—maybe not bioluminescent, maybe not even aquatic, but out there, unknown and waiting.

And if humanity ever made contact with them, Marcus hoped the first people to discover them would have learned the lesson he'd been taught: that some wonders deserved protection more than publication, that guardianship trumped glory, that silence could be more scientific than speech.

He pulled out his phone, setting a reminder: *Rockport visit - Tod's check-in - Saturday midnight.*

Some appointments you didn't miss.

THAT SATURDAY AT 11:55 PM, four figures stood on Tod's dock under a sky so clear the Milky Way painted a river of light overhead. Tod, Claire, Chen, and Marcus—bundled against the unusual cold, their breath visible in the still air.

"Water temperature's dropped," Tod observed, checking his phone. "Fifty-three degrees. They'll feel that."

"Will it bother them?" Marcus asked.

"No. They're from deep water originally—this is warm compared to what they're used to." Tod pulled out his flashlight. "But it might make them more active. Cold water holds more oxygen."

The bay was empty, the marina quiet, Rockport sleeping. Perfect conditions for secret conversations.

Tod knelt at the dock's edge, the familiar ritual steadying him. He raised the flashlight and tapped out the code: two-seven-two.

They waited.

From the deep channel, exactly where Tod expected, a faint glow began to rise. Not the whole colony—they never came en masse anymore, understanding the need for discretion. Just one or two messengers, rising to communicate.

The light pulsed in its seven-second rhythm, and then the response came:

"H-E-L-L-O-G-U-A-R-D-I-A-N-S"

Tod smiled. They'd learned to pluralize, to acknowledge all four humans. "HELLO FRIENDS. ALL WELL?"

"Y-E-S - C-O-L-D-W-A-T-E-R-G-O-O-D - F-O-O-D-P-L-E-N-T-Y"

"YOUNG HELPER IS HERE." Tod gestured to Marcus. "MARCUS VISITS."

The light pulsed brighter, excited. "W-E-L-C-O-M-E-M-A-R-C-U-S"

Marcus knelt beside Tod, his hands shaking slightly as he raised his own flashlight. Chen had taught him basic Morse code, but he kept it simple.

"HELLO. I STUDY OCEAN. I WILL PROTECT YOU."

"G-O-O-D - L-E-A-R-N-W-E-L-L - T-E-A-C-H-O-T-H-E-R-S-T-O-L-I-S-T-E-N"

The message hit Marcus hard. Teach others to listen. Not to discover, not to exploit, but to *listen*. That was the mission, encoded in five words of light.

"I WILL," he signaled back.

The Light Speakers pulsed once, acknowledging, and then sent a message to all four humans:

"T-H-A-N-K-Y-O-U-F-O-R-Q-U-I-E-T"

Thank you for quiet. For silence. For keeping the secret that kept them safe.

"YOU ARE WORTH IT," Tod signaled.

A pause, and then one final message, different from any they'd sent before:

"W-E-T-E-L-L-S-T-O-R-I-E-S-O-F-Y-O-U"

Stories. They were creating mythology, legends, oral history passed through bioluminescent pulses. Tales of the humans who protected them, who sacrificed for them, who kept them hidden.

Someday, if humanity and the Light Speakers ever met openly, those stories would exist. Proof that the first contact had been built on trust, on sacrifice, on choosing protection over glory.

"WE TELL STORIES OF YOU TOO," Claire signaled, her flashlight adding to the conversation.

The Light Speakers swirled in what Tod had come to recognize as pleasure, their light brightening briefly. Then they descended, fading back into the depths, leaving only the memory of their presence.

The four guardians stood in silence for a long moment, watching the dark water.

"They're happy," Chen said quietly. "I could feel it. They're not just surviving—they're thriving."

"Good." Tod lowered his flashlight, the ritual complete. "That's all we needed to know."

They walked back to the workshop together, boots clomping on the wooden dock, four people bound by a secret that no one else would believe and that they'd never try to prove.

Inside, Tod poured coffee while Claire pulled out a map to discuss next month's monitoring schedule. Chen opened her laptop to review recent Coast Guard patrol patterns. Marcus asked questions about the Light Speakers' biology, his scientific mind hungry for understanding even as he accepted that some questions would never be published.

It was work—constant, careful, crucial work. The kind of work that no one would ever thank them for, that would never appear in textbooks or earn awards. Work done in darkness for beings of light.

And it was enough.

LATER, AFTER CHEN AND Marcus had left, Tod and Claire stood on the dock one last time, sharing the comfortable silence of two people who didn't need to fill every moment with words.

The bay stretched before them, dark and still, holding its secrets close. Somewhere beneath that surface, fish dreamed whatever dreams fish had. Crabs scuttled across the bottom. And eighteen miles offshore, in a limestone cave that would never appear on tourist maps, beings of light pulsed in a seven-second rhythm that meant home.

"Do you ever regret it?" Claire asked. "Losing the storm-sense?"

Tod thought about the question, really considered it. "I regret not having that tool anymore. It was useful, powerful. But do I regret sacrificing it to save them?" He shook his head. "Not for a second."

"Because they're worth it."

"Because they're worth it," Tod confirmed. "And because that's what love looks like sometimes. Giving up something precious to protect something more precious."

Claire turned to face him, her expression serious in the moonlight. "Is that what this is? Love?"

"For them? Yeah. Not romantic love, but... I don't know. Kinship? Family?" Tod struggled for the right word. "I love them the way you love something you've chosen to protect, that you've suffered for, that you'd suffer for again."

"And me?" Claire asked softly. "What kind of love is that?"

Tod pulled her close, his arms wrapping around her against the cold. "The kind that chooses to stay. The kind that shares the burden. The kind that makes coffee at dawn and stands on cold docks at midnight because it matters to me." He kissed the top of her head. "The kind I want for the rest of my life."

Claire was quiet for a moment. "Is that a proposal, Tod Blackstone?"

"Not yet. But it's a promise that one's coming." He felt her smile against his chest. "When the time's right. When we're ready."

"I'm ready now."

"I know. But I want to do it right. Not on a dock at one in the morning when we're both exhausted." Tod stepped back, holding her at arm's length. "I want sunrise. And kolaches. And that moment when the light's just right and I can see exactly how lucky I am."

Claire laughed, the sound bright in the cold air. "You romantic fool."

"Guilty."

They walked back to the workshop together, hands linked, footsteps synchronized. Behind them, the bay whispered against the pilings, keeping its secrets safe.

Inside the warm workshop, Tod's equipment hummed with familiar electrical signatures. His sunrise tracker stood ready for tomorrow's dawn. His charts and tools and projects waited in organized chaos, the accumulated work of a life spent on these waters.

But it was Claire's presence that made it feel like home—her camera bag hanging on the hook beside his jacket, her coffee mug in the sink, her photographs tacked to the wall alongside his nautical charts.

Two different ways of seeing the world, learning to speak the same language.

Tod checked the weather forecast on his phone—not with abilities anymore, just with regular human technology—and saw clear skies predicted for the week ahead. Good charter weather. Good working weather.

Good living weather.

"Come to bed," Claire said from the doorway. "The guardians need sleep too."

Tod took one last look around the workshop, making sure everything was secure, everything in its place. Tomorrow would bring new work, new challenges, new moments requiring vigilance and care.

But tonight, the Light Speakers were safe. The secret held. The covenant remained unbroken.

And that was enough to let him sleep peacefully.

ONE WEEK LATER — DAWN

Tod stood on his dock, the morning ritual as familiar now as breathing. The kolache was warm in his hand, the coffee steaming in the cold air, the sunrise tracker rotating toward a sky painted in shades of pink and gold.

The bay stretched before him, calm and clear, holding its mysteries beneath a surface that reflected the heavens. A perfect mirror, showing both what was above and hiding what lay below.

Tod raised his flashlight—unnecessary in the growing light, but the ritual mattered more than efficiency. He tapped out the code one more time: two-seven-two.

He waited, watching the water.

Seven seconds passed.

From the deep channel, almost imperceptible, a single pulse of light answered. Brief as a heartbeat, subtle as a whisper, unmistakable to anyone who knew how to look.

The Light Speakers were out there. They remembered. They responded.

The bond held.

Tod lowered the flashlight, a smile crossing his face. Behind him, he heard Claire's footsteps on the dock, felt her presence before she spoke.

"They answered?"

"They always answer."

She handed him a fresh coffee, taking the cold one he'd forgotten about. They stood together, watching the sunrise complete its transformation of night to day, ordinary people witnessing an ordinary dawn that held within it the weight of extraordinary secrets.

"What are you thinking?" Claire asked.

Tod considered the question. He was thinking about the journey that had brought him here—from a man drowning in darkness to a guardian of light. He was thinking about the price he'd paid and the rewards he'd gained. He was thinking about the future that waited, uncertain but purposeful.

But what he said was simpler:

"I'm thinking some conversations are worth keeping quiet."

Claire nodded, understanding the layers beneath the words. "And some lights are worth protecting."

"Yeah. That too."

The sun cleared the horizon fully, flooding the bay with golden light. Tod's sunrise tracker locked onto the signal, clicks confirming function, technology and nature synchronizing in their daily dance.

Somewhere out there, eighteen miles offshore, beings of light were beginning their own day in a sanctuary that had become home. They would hunt, they would communicate, they would create their stories and pass them through generations.

And four humans would keep watch, would maintain the silence, would protect the secret that protected them.

Not forever—secrets never lasted forever. But for now. For as long as possible. For as long as it took.

Tod finished his kolache, drained his coffee, and turned back toward the workshop. He had charters scheduled, equipment to maintain, the ordinary work of an ordinary life waiting.

But he walked lighter now, carrying something more important than abilities or power: purpose, and the knowledge that some things were worth more than proof.

Behind him, the bay whispered its agreement.

And deep in the limestone cave, living light pulsed in a seven-second rhythm that meant safety, and home, and trust.

A covenant unbroken.

A secret kept.

A story just beginning.

About the Author

Wallace Berry was born in Little Rock, Arkansas, as World War II began, and his upbringing took place on a farm in the Arkansas countryside. His childhood was steeped in the rustic simplicity of farm life, absent of modern conveniences such as electricity, indoor plumbing, relying on wood stoves for warmth, and lanterns for light. This immersion in a world where nature and necessity dictated daily life deeply rooted in him a love for the wilderness. His adventures in the surrounding forests and the hands-on experiences of early rural living profoundly shaped his appreciation for nature and a life outdoors. As he grew older, Wallace chose the Texas Gulf Coast as his place of residence, carrying with him the values and passions developed during his formative years.